Caro kissed him. Not a mere feathering of flesh against flesh, but a hard, hungry embrace that she let go on for far, far longer than any proper young lady should dare.

"There, I have no doubt shocked you."

The tip of his tongue traced along the swell of his lower lip.

"I imagine you think me a wanton hellion, and I suppose I am. It must be my eccentric upbringing. I don't care very much for rules."

Caro knew she was babbling but she couldn't seem to stop. "You may consign me to the Devil. But at least I shall dance a merry jig on my way to perdition."

Was that finally a hint of smile? She finally dared pause to take a breath. Now was the time to flee, before she made an even bigger fool of herself. But Alec suddenly shifted again, blocking her way.

"I, too, shall probably regret this," he said as he slowly circled his arms around her and pulled her close.

She opened her mouth. *To protest?*

Before she could make any sense of what she had set in motion, their lips met again, setting off a fierce jolt of fire...

Acclaim for the Hellions of High Street Series

Passionately Yours

"A classic example of romance, adventure, and fun! Only Cara Elliott could balance all these elements and keep them equally as interesting...Carolina Sloane is such a fantastic character!"

—RamblingsfromthisChick.blogspot.com

"Entertaining...She writes with a very engaging and funny style."

—SweptAwaybyRomance.com

"Engaging characters and an intriguing storyline will keep you up all night turning pages...a very enjoyable read!"

—MyBookAddictionReviews.com

Sinfully Yours

"Sinfully fantastic!...I enjoyed this story immensely, would recommend and re-read!"

—RamblingsfromthisChick.blogspot.com

"Fun and well-written."

—RedHotBooks.com

"A pleasant and enjoyable read."

—HarlequinJunkie.com

"What a fun, little guilty pleasure read this turned out to be. I ate this book up like a fine dessert...A romance that should be on everyone's keeper shelf."

—GraceBooksofLove.com

Too Tempting to Resist

"Elliott provides readers with a treat to savor in this fun, sexy, delicious tale. With smart, sassy characters, a charming plot and an erotic bad boy/good girl duo, this fast-paced story will keep readers' attention."

—*RT Book Reviews*

"Nothing is more sensuous than a delicious meal, and Cara Elliott's food-inspired sex scenes are, quite literally, *Too Tempting to Resist*...likable characters, a fast-moving plot, and unique, engaging sex scenes that are deliciously tempting."

—HeroesandHeartbreakers.com

"Haddan and Eliza's charming wit and banter will absolutely capture the reader from their first meeting...[It] can easily be read as a stand-alone, though most readers will want to rush out and find a copy of the first book to get more of Cara Elliott's Hellhounds. A real page-turner, readers will not be able to put this book down."

—RomRevToday.com

Too Wicked to Wed

"Elliott packs the first Lords of Midnight Regency romance with plenty of steamy sex and sly innuendo...As Alexa and Connor flee London to escape vengeful criminals, their mutual attraction sizzles beneath delightful banter. Regency fans will especially appreciate the authentic feel of the historical setting."

—*Publishers Weekly*

"A surprisingly resourceful heroine and a sinfully sexy hero, a compelling and danger-spiced plot, lushly sensual love scenes, and lively writing work together perfectly to get Elliott's new Regency-set Lords of Midnight series off to a delightfully entertaining start."

—*Booklist*

"The romance, adventure, and sensuality readers expect from Elliott are here, along with an unforgettable hoyden heroine and an enigmatic hero. She takes them on a marvelous ride from gambling hells to ballrooms, country estates, and London's underworld."

—*RT Book Reviews*

Praise for the
Circle of Sin Trilogy

To Tempt a Rake

"From the first page of this sequel...Elliott sweeps her readers up in a scintillating and sexy romance."

—*Publishers Weekly*

"Has everything a reader could desire: adventure, humor, mystery, romance, and a very naughty rake. I was absorbed from the first page and entertained throughout the story. A warning to readers: If you have anything on your schedule for the day, clear it. You won't be able to put *To Sin with a Scoundrel* down once you start reading."

—SingleTitles.com

"Steamy . . . intriguing."

—*Publishers Weekly*

Passionately Yours

CARA ELLIOTT

FOREVER

NEW YORK   BOSTON

Forever
Hachette Book Group
1290 Avenue of the Americas
New York, NY 10104
forever-romance.com

Printed in the United States of America

Originally published as an ebook by Forever in March 2014
First mass market edition: May 2015
10 9 8 7 6 5 4 3 2 1

OPM

Forever is an imprint of Grand Central Publishing.
The Forever name and logo are trademarks of Hachette Book Group, Inc.

The Hachette Speakers Bureau provides a wide range of authors for speaking events. To find out more, go to www.hachettespeakersbureau.com or call (866) 376-6591.

The publisher is not responsible for websites (or their content) that are not owned by the publisher.

Passionately Yours

For Ammanda McCabe
who is always there to share laughter,
tears, and a glass of chardonnay
(or maybe two!)
Thanks for being such a wonderful
sister-in-spirit.

Chapter One

A slip sent stones skittering down the slope of the narrow country road.

"Watch your step," cautioned Carolina Sloane, as the rough-edged echo faded into the shadows. "The way turns steeper here, and the ground is very uneven."

She paused to glance up at the ominous gray clouds and then looked back at her companion, who was struggling to keep pace with her. "We can rest for a few minutes if you like, but we ought not linger longer than that."

Thunder rumbled off in the distance.

"The light seems to be dying awfully fast," she added.

"No, no, I—I shall manage," answered Isobel Urquehart in between gasps for breath. "I'm so sorry to be lagging—"

"Oh, please, don't apologize," said Caro quickly. "It's my fault—I should have paid more attention to the time." She squinted into the gloom up ahead, hoping to see some flicker of light from the outskirts of town. But if anything the shadows seemed to deepen and darken as the road wended its way into a copse of trees.

A gust of wind, its bite already sharp with the chill of evening, suddenly rustled through the overhanging branches, stirring a prickling of unease at the back of her neck.

"We haven't much farther to go." Repressing an oath, Caro forced herself to sound more cheerful than she felt. "It can't be more than a mile or so until we reach town."

"Yes, yes, it must be close, given how long we've been walking." Isobel hitched her shawl a little tighter around her shoulders. Her cheeks looked unnaturally pale in the fading flickers of sunlight, but she managed a smile. "And if night falls before we get there, we shall just pretend we are having a marvelous adventure."

Caro was relieved that her companion had such pluck and a sense of humor, for she hadn't realized that Isobel's health was so fragile.

That was because the two young ladies had only just met the previous afternoon. On discovering a shared interest in antiquities—as well as literature—they had made spur-of-the-moment plans for a walk out to see one of the Roman ruins that dotted the countryside around the spa town of Bath.

The day had dawned warm and sunny, so they had set out after nuncheon, thinking to be gone no more than several hours. But the setting had proved wildly romantic, and the two of them had lost track of the time as they chatted about books and history over a picnic of pastries among the weathered limestone columns.

But now, with dusk cloaking them in a swirl of shadows and stormclouds threatening rain, the decision did not seem so wise.

Impetuous. Caro gave an inward wince, knowing she did have a tendency to go off half-cocked—

"Why, just listen to the wind keening through the trees," went on Isobel, interrupting Caro's brooding. "If you use your imagination, you can almost picture yourself in the wild mountains of Sicily, evading a band of cutthroat brigands on your way to a midnight rendezvous with a swashbuckling count at the ancient ruins of Taormina."

Caro picked her way over a patch of loose stones. "Yes, I can see what you mean." A pause, and then she laughed. "So, you've read *Escape from the Barbary Pirates* as well as *The Prince's Evil Intentions*?"

"I confess, I've read *all* of Sir Sharpe Quill's novels." Isobel gave a shy grin. "Although I daresay I shouldn't admit it, I find them scathingly funny. Not to speak of intriguingly interesting when, um, Count Alessandro starts removing Emmalina's clothing."

"Oh, your secret is safe with me," replied Caro.

"You've read them, too?" asked Isobel.

"Every word," she assured her new friend.

And in truth, the statement was no exaggeration. That was because the reclusive author, considered by the *ton* to be the most intriguing gentleman in all of London, was not actually a *he*, but a she—more specifically, Caro's older sister Anna.

But that was a secret she was not at liberty to share.

And at the moment, there were far more pressing concerns than clever *noms de plumes* or dangerous pen-and-paper plots. Perhaps it was merely the rising whoosh and crackle of the leaves overhead, but it seemed that Isobel's breathing was becoming more labored.

Damn, damn, damn.

Caro bit her lip, wishing she dared quicken the pace. The prickling sensation at the back of her neck had turned sharper, like daggerpoints digging into her flesh. It was foolish, she knew, to let talk of ruthless villains and exotic dangers spook her. This dark stretch of road was a quiet country lane in England, and the black silhouettes were placid oak trees, not gnarled claws of doom stretching out to grab...

"And then, of course, the scene where Emmalina slithers down a cliff..." Behind her, Isobel had begun to recount the plot of the latest Sir Sharpe Quill novel. "...and pounces on the pirate leader, who is about to skewer Count Alessandro, is very exciting."

"Indeed," murmured Caro, trying not to be distracted by the jumpy black shadows flitting in and out of the surrounding trees.

"Of course, it's not very realistic to expect that a young lady would know how to fight tooth and nail against a muscled villain..."

Ha! thought Caro wryly. Her late father, a noted explorer specializing in exotic tribal cultures, had taken his three young daughters on several expeditions to primitive places. Being a very practical man as well as a serious scholar, he had made sure that they knew how to defend themselves with some *very* unladylike tricks.

"But of course, fiction allows—"

A loud *snap* startled Isobel into silence.

Caro whirled around, trying to spot any movement within the glade, but the softly swaying tendrils of mist seemed to mock her fears.

"Wh-what was that?" whispered Isobel.

"It's probably just a fox setting off on a hunt," answered Caro quickly, her gaze still probing among the muddled trees.

Her friend let out a nervous laugh. "Then it is a good thing we are not mice."

Or helpless little pigeons—the perfect prey for any hungry predator stalking through the shadows.

Shaking off such disturbing thoughts, she freed the ribbons of her bonnet from the folds of her shawl. "We had best keep moving."

Isobel sucked in a lungful of air. "Yes, of course."

They walked on in silence, which seemed to amplify the night sounds. *The screech of an owl, the crack of a twig, the rustle of—*

Another snap, this one even louder.

The echo reverberated through the woods like a gunshot.

Hurry, hurry.

As the road narrowed and turned sharply past a thicket of brambles, Caro slapped aside a twist of thorns, and in her haste to put the grove behind them, nearly slid into a puddle of brackish water. Before she could call out a warning, Isobel stumbled on the wet ground too and lost her footing.

"Oooh!"

Caro caught her just as she was about to take a nasty tumble. "Steady now," she murmured, keeping hold of her friend's trembling hand.

"Sorry to be such a ninnyhammer."

"Nonsense. You are a far more intrepid adventurer than any storybook heroine."

"J-just as long as I don't step on any c-cobras." Though she appeared on the verge of tears, Isobel managed an exhausted smile.

"Oh, there aren't any snakes in this part of Somerset." That might be stretching the truth a bit, but as reptiles did not come out in the chill of night, it didn't matter.

"Let's rest for a moment."

They slowed to a halt. And yet, Isobel's breathing only seemed to grow more ragged.

If only a cart would come by, thought Caro. But given the hour, that hope was unrealistic. There was no option save to forge ahead on their own.

Tightening her grip, she started forward again, hoping that the next bend would bring them free of the trees. There was something oppressive about the heaviness of the air and the canopy of leafy branches that nearly blocked out the twilight sky.

Rain—only a soaking shower could make matters worse.

She angled a look up at the scudding clouds, just as a sudden movement in the bushes caught her eye.

A scream caught in her throat as branches snapped and a man dressed all in black burst out from between two ancient oaks.

Seizing Isobel from behind, he tried to drag her back into the tangle of leaves.

But Caro reacted in the same instant and held on to her friend's hand for dear life. "Let go of her, you fiend!" she cried, then raised her voice to an even higher pitch. "Help! Help!"

Isobel struggled to fend him off. She was putting up a game fight, though in size and weight she was no match for her assailant.

He gave another wrenching yank, then swore a vicious oath as Isobel's flailing elbow caught him flush on the windpipe.

"Help, help—let me go!" She, too, had started screaming at the top of her lungs.

"Bloody Hell, shut your gobs," he snarled, clapping

a beefy hand over Isobel's mouth. "And you, you hell-bitch..."

The epithet was directed at Caro.

"Back off or I'll break every last bone in your body." The brute—for brute he was, with muscled arms and legs thick as tree trunks—punctuated the threat with a lashing kick aimed at Caro's knees.

She caught his boot and jerked upward with all her might.

Yanked off balance, the man fell heavily to the ground, his skull hitting the hard-packed earth with a thud.

The force of his fall took Isobel down, too. But she managed to roll free and scramble to her feet.

"Run!" urged Caro. "Run!"

However slight the chances were of outracing him, flight was their only option. Trying to outfight him was madness. Still, she snatched up a rock as she turned to follow her friend.

All too quickly, the man was up and after them, cursing with rage. His heavy footfalls were coming closer and closer...

Caro whirled and flung her missile at his forehead. *Thank God for the games of hunting skill she had played with the tribal children in Crete.* Hours of practice had honed her aim to a lethal accuracy.

Whomp.

The rock smashed into his right eye, drawing a pained howl. Half stunned, half blinded, he staggered on, fists flailing wildly.

As she dipped and dodged the blows, Caro decided that the only hope in escape lay in trying one last, desperate measure. Ducking low, she darted straight at him and brought her knee up hard between his legs.

Very hard.

The brute dropped like a sack of stones, his curses turning to a mewling whimper.

"Run!" she called again, seeing that Isobel had stopped and was staring in open-mouthed shock. The trick had bought them more time, but when he recovered, he would be out for her blood.

"How—" began her friend.

"Never mind that now," she said, shoving Isobel into action. "We must fly like the wind."

But they hadn't gone more than several strides when two more figures appeared from the shadows up ahead.

"Bull!" shouted the one in the lead. "Wot's wrong? Why ain't ye grabbed 'em?"

A pack of abductors?

The thought sent a spike of fear through her.

Things looked rather hopeless, but Caro wasn't yet willing to go down meekly.

Think! Think!

A quick glance around showed one last chance. Grabbing Isobel's arm, she pushed her off the road and toward the woods. The tangle of brush and trees might slow down their pursuers.

"Try to lose yourself in the darkness," she hissed. "I'll see if I can distract them for another few moments."

"But—"

"GO!"

To her relief, Isobel had the good sense not to waste precious seconds in further argument.

Scooping up a handful of rocks, Caro peltered the new assailants with a quick barrage, then turned to seek safety in the shadows.

With luck...

But luck chose that moment to desert her. Her shoe caught in a rut and she tripped, entangled in her skirts.

Cursing the constraints of female dress, she twisted free of the fabric, scrambled to her feet, and was moving again within the space of several rapid-fire heartbeats.

Quick, but not quick enough.

The first trees were only a stride away when one of the men snagged her trailing sash and whirled her around.

"Poxy slut," he snapped.

Caro blocked the first slap and countered with a punch that bloodied his lip. The second blow caught her on the side of the head with a force that set her ears to ringing. She tried to pull away but he yanked her back, and then his fist drove the air from her lungs.

The ground began to spin and blur.

Dizzy with pain, Caro felt herself slipping into a daze. Squeezing her eyes shut, she fought down a rising nausea. But things seemed to be spinning out of control. The voices around her were suddenly sounding strangely agitated, and the ringing was turning into an odd pounding.

Like the beat of galloping hooves?

Wishful thinking, she mused as she slumped to her knees. And yet, her captor seemed to have released her...

Forcing her lids open, she saw a jumble of dark shapes. *A horse. A rider flinging himself from the saddle. Flying fists. Her assailant knocked arse over teakettle.*

"Shoot the devil, Bull!" he croaked.

As her gaze slowly refocused, Caro saw their first attacker rise and run off, still clutching his groin, into trees on the opposite side of the road.

"Your lily-livered friend doesn't seem inclined to come to

your rescue," came a deep baritone shout. "That leaves two of you—whose neck shall I break first?"

Her wits must be so addled that she was hallucinating. How else to explain why the voice sounded oddly familiar?

The man who had hit her scuttled like a crab across the road. "Billy!" he cried in a high-pitched squeal.

The only answer was a scrabbling in the bushes that quickly faded to silence.

"Vermin," muttered her rescuer as he watched the man join his cohorts in beating a hasty retreat. Turning, he then gently lifted her to her feet. "Are you hurt, Miss?"

"I..."

I never swoon, she wanted to reply, if only her tongue would obey her brain. *Only peagoose heroines in horrid novels swoon.*

However, on catching sight of the chiseled lips, the too-long nose, and the shock of red-gold hair now looming just inches above her face, Caro promptly did just that.

Chapter Two

here, that should revive her."

The splash of chill water brought Caro none too gently back to consciousness.

"B-but are you sure she's not badly injured?" Isobel leaned in a little closer. "She looks pale as a ghost."

"It appears to be nothing more than an attack of maidenly nerves," answered Alec McClellan—or, more formally, Lord Strathcona, though as a radical republican he wasn't overly fond of using his hereditary title.

"Maidenly nerves!" sputtered Caro, as Alec cupped another handful of water and dumped it over her cheeks. "I'll have you know that I've never had an attack of maidenly nerves in my life."

"Apparently, there is a first time for everything," he said dryly.

"Alec, don't be so beastly. This is no time for teasing," chided Isobel. "If not for my new friend's heroics, those horrible men would have easily dragged us off to heaven knows where." To Caro she added, "Please forgive my brother. At times, he has a very peculiar sense of humor."

Caro slowly sat up. Folding back the broken brim of her bonnet she met his all-too-familiar sapphire gaze.

His eyes widened ever so slightly—whether in dismay or some other emotion was impossible to gauge. "*You*," he murmured, just loud enough for her to hear.

Yes, me.

The previous autumn, she and the baron had been among the guests at a Scottish castle. Sparks had flown between them, little flares of fire that had ignited a number of conflicting, confusing emotions.

What Alec had felt was impossible to tell. He kept his personal thoughts hidden behind a wall of reserve that was flintier and harder than Highland stone.

"Brother?" Caro repeated, breaking off eye contact. "But Isobel, I thought you told me your surname is Urquehart."

"Half brother," explained Alec tersely. He was no longer sounding quite so amused now that he had recognized her. "My mother remarried after my father perished in a hunting accident."

"Ah." Caro winced as she started to undo the muddied ribbons of her bonnet. The chipstraw was squashed beyond repair and, though it was barely heavier than a feather, the weight was making her head ache. However, the knot seemed hopelessly snagged...

Alec brushed aside her fingers and with surprising gentleness quickly removed the offending headgear. "I take it you don't mind if I feed this to the neighboring sheep?" Without waiting for an answer he flung it over the hedgerow that marked the end of the woods.

"Thank you," she murmured.

Strangely enough, his hand lingered on the curls just above her ear. "You've a lump forming here."

"Yes, well, that tends to happen when one gets punched by a miscreant with knuckles like granite."

His hand stiffened. "The fellow punched you?"

"I hit him first," replied Caro, allowing a smile of grim satisfaction. "And bloodied his lip."

"That was a damnably foolish thing to do," growled Alec. "Brave, but foolish."

"Alec!" huffed Isobel in reproach.

Caro made a face. "You would rather I had meekly submitted to letting those men kidnap your sister and me?"

His mouth thinned, but his only reply was a noncommittal grunt.

A typical male reaction when defeat was inevitable in a battle of words, thought Caro.

"Speaking of kidnapping," she began. "I cannot believe such a gang of men would try such a desperate act so close to Bath. Surely it was obvious we had no valuables worth stealing."

"They must have thought you the daughters of well-to-do families," replied Alec, "who would pay handsomely for your return—and for the matter to be hushed up."

"But who—"

"There are many soldiers returning from the war who can find no work," he said quickly. "They are desperate men."

Caro knew that was true, and yet something did not feel right about the explanation. No matter how desperate, the men had to know they would be signing their own death warrants. The local gentry would quickly be up in arms and clamoring for blood if their daughters started being snatched off the roads.

"But surely—"

Alec speared her to silence with a sharp look and a tiny nod at his sister. "Time enough for talk later," he growled. "Right now I would rather get you two young ladies back to town without delay. You both must be hungry and exhausted."

Caro bit her lip. A sidelong glance at Isobel showed her last reserves of strength were fast ebbing away.

His gaze came back to her. "I imagine your mother will be beside herself with worry."

"Actually she won't. The plan was for me to take supper with your sister and your aunt."

He exhaled a measured breath. "Then it seems we have an excellent chance of keeping this little incident a secret." It was said as a half question. "That would be best for a number of reasons," he went on. "Including the effect it might have on your reputation were it known the pair of you were out wandering alone after dark."

"You may think my tongue ungovernable, but I think when it comes to keeping secrets, I have proved my discretion can be counted on, Lord Strathcona," replied Caro a little tartly.

Despite her obvious fatigue, Isobel had been following the exchange with great interest. "I say, are the two of you acquainted?"

"Yes," replied Caro.

"How—"

"As I said, let us leave long-winded explanations for another time, Bella." Alec tucked her shawl a little tighter around her shoulders. "You're chilled and exhausted. I wish to get you home without delay."

"There's no need to fuss like a mother hen, Alec. I'm not

quite so fragile as I look." But the tremor in Isobel's voice belied her words.

"How did you come to rescue us, sir?" asked Caro, as he hurriedly fetched his horse and lifted his sister into the saddle. Bath was not a large town, and she was surprised that she had heard no mention of his being there. Gentlemen— especially unmarried, titled gentlemen under the age of sixty—did not go unnoticed. "I was under the impression that you are loath to spend any time in England."

"I am occasionally obliged to travel to the south," he replied, but offered no further explanation. "My plans on this trip include a stay in Bath while my sister is here taking the waters. I arrived this afternoon, and naturally went straight to the townhouse that my aunt has rented. She was becoming concerned about Isobel, and since she knew your intended plans, I decided to ride out and make sure there had been no sprained ankle or other mishap."

"How very lowering to find that you all think me helpless as a kitten." Isobel managed a smile, but pain pinched at the corners of her mouth.

"Do you mind walking, Miss Caro?" said Alec softly. "The truth is, my sister has been ill—in fact, that's why she's here in Bath. I am concerned that she doesn't suffer a relapse from this little adventure."

"Of course not," she answered. "I should never have suggested the excursion had I known—"

"How could you?" he interrupted curtly. "Besides, it is not your responsibility to have a care for my sister's welfare, it is mine."

Caro knew that fear and worry had him on edge. Still, she felt a little hurt by his tone. "Then let us be off without further delay, sir."

A small frown momentarily creased his brow, but he merely gave a gruff nod, gathered the reins, and started walking.

Without, noted Caro, so much as offering his arm or a backward glance.

"So much for dreaming of dashing heroes," she muttered under her breath, then shook out her skirts and hurried to catch up.

They weren't much more than a mile from town, and as none of them seemed to be much in the mood for chatting, the short trip was passed in silence, save for the steady clip-clop of the stallion's hooves. Alec chose a roundabout route through the side streets of Bath, arriving in the mews of his family's rented townhouse without encountering anyone.

"Thank God we are here," murmured Alec as he lifted Isobel from the saddle. "It seems the chances are good that we have given no grist for the gossip mills."

"All's well that ends well," quipped his sister. "And you may put me down," she added quickly when he turned with her still in his arms. "I am perfectly capable of walking from here to the door."

He hesitated, which earned him another gentle rebuke. "Truly, Alec. I do not wish to be treated like an invalid."

"Very well." He relented and set her on her feet. "Still, you must promise me you will not overexert yourself."

"On the contrary, exercise is very beneficial in building my stamina," she countered.

As long as future walks don't include attacks by a pack of ruffians, thought Caro, watching her friend prove her point by walking briskly across the small courtyard.

Which once again raised the question...

Her gaze slid to Alec. During the walk she had decided

the desperate soldier story did not fadge. And it was highly doubtful that Isobel had any enemies who might be moved to violence. But as for her brother, Caro was aware that he was involved in some very dangerous activities in Scotland.

Alec seemed to sense what she was thinking, for instead of following his sister, he shifted his stance and cleared his throat with a brusque cough. "I suppose that look means you aren't going to be satisfied with the earlier explanation for this evening's incident," he muttered.

"Should I be?" she countered.

He let out a sigh. Or maybe it was more of a snort.

"Soldiers may be desperate. But not *that* desperate," continued Caro. "So considering that I have—however unwittingly and unwillingly—been drawn into this intrigue, I do think I have a right to know what dangers I may be facing."

"None," he said quickly. "That is, there won't be any as soon as I take care of a few matters."

She noted that he avoided meeting her gaze. "I can't say that's entirely reassuring." A pause. "You forget that I saw some of your radical friends stealing an arsenal of weapons from Dunbar Castle. I'm well aware of what dangerous circles you move in, Lord Strathcona."

"As you eavesdropped on our meeting, Miss Caro, you should know that they are *not* my friends," he retorted.

"Let's not quibble over words," she huffed. "The fact is, you are involved in a secret political society seeking independence for Scotland. And your fellow members, be they friends or otherwise, are not afraid to use violence to achieve their ends."

He didn't argue.

"So whether you like it or not, I feel I have a right to know what is going on." She drew a deep breath. "Especially if you wish me to keep silent on the matter."

"That," he growled, "is blackmail."

"I prefer to think of it as persuasion. I am merely pointing out a sensible course of action."

His jaw tightened.

"Alec!" Isobel's call interrupted their exchange. "Don't be so rag-mannered as to keep Caro standing in the chill. She, too, is tired and hungry."

"We are coming," he called to her. Offering his arm to Caro—rather ungallantly, she thought—he added, "I would rather not upset my sister's delicate sensibilities with talk of this. I must leave town at first light for a few days on a matter that cannot be put off—"

Caro opened her mouth to protest.

"However," he went on, "as soon as I return, I shall meet with you and explain the situation more fully."

It was Caro's opinion that Isobel was not as delicate in spirit as Alec seemed to think. But as the friendship was so new, she did not feel it was her place to say so.

Instead she merely asked, "Is that a promise?"

"Ye gods, would you like me to write it down in blood?"

Her lips quirked up at the corners.

"Yes," he snapped before she could reply. "You need not resort to knives or razors—it's a promise. Though I daresay I'll regret it."

She bit back a retort, suddenly feeling too tired to argue. But as he paused to relock the gate to the mews, another thought occurred to her. "You may not wish to worry Isobel, but surely you will have to give her a more convincing explanation than rogue soldiers run amuck."

"I'll think of something," he muttered.

"Yes, well, I've reason to know your imagination is more active than you wish to let on to the people around you," murmured Caro. When they hadn't been arguing at the house party in Scotland, she and Alec had actually engaged in some very interesting discussions on poetry and novels. Much as he wished to hide it, there was a softer, more whimsical spirit lurking behind the mask of stone-faced reserve.

"But whether prevarication will do any good," she went on slowly, "remains to be seen."

"By the bones of St. Andrew." Exhaling a sigh along with the grumbled oath, Alec took up the decanter from the sideboard and poured himself a glass of Scottish whisky.

Thankfully his aunt hadn't questioned his story of Isobel taking a nasty tumble on one of the road's slippery hills and her new friend coming to grief in trying to rescue her from a ditch. In short order, his sister had been taken up to her bedchamber for cosseting, while Caro—well fortified with hot tea and her disheveled garments brushed free of mud—had been escorted home by the footman.

So one potential bombshell had been defused.

But the current situation was still threatening to blow up in his face.

"Damnation," he added under his breath. The one thing he didn't need was the distraction of a spitfire hellion setting off dangerous sparks.

Dangerous. He took a long swallow of the amber-dark spirits and felt it burn a trail down his throat.

Miss Carolina Sloane was the last person he had expected to encounter in Bath. By all accounts in the London newspapers, she had been one of the leading belles of the just-ended Season, with a bevy of suitors seeking to win her hand. *Not* that he deliberately read the gossip columns recounting the parties and soirees, but one couldn't help skimming over the pages while turning to the section of political news.

By all rights, she ought to be enjoying the gilded pleasures of some fancy country house party rather than be found rusticating in the staid quietness of a provincial spa town.

But then again, Caro was unpredictable.

Inquisitive. Adventurous. Stubborn. Passionate.

Oh, yes—most of all, passionate.

And that was the trouble. Alec stared morosely into his empty glass. He couldn't decide whether he found her frightening or fascinating.

"Do you plan to drown yourself in a sea of spirits?" Clicking the door of the library shut, Isobel moved to one of the armchairs by the hearth and nestled in a cat-like curl on the soft leather.

"Perhaps." Alec swirled his whisky, setting off a flickering of amber flashes as the candlelight reflected off the cut crystal.

"Is there a reason you are seeking oblivion?" she pressed.

"Aside from the fact that my beloved little sister was nearly ravaged by a pack of rabid curs?"

"I don't think they intended to hurt us," mused Isobel. "Just take us captive."

"Somehow that does not make me feel like dancing a jig of celebration." Alec exhaled, trying to ease the constriction in his chest. "You should be sleeping," he added abruptly.

"So should you. You look bloody awful."

His mouth quirked up in a reluctant smile. "While it appears that Bath and its medicinal mineral waters agree with you. It seems you are making great progress in regaining your health."

Isobel make a rude sound. "I would have recovered just as quickly in Scotland. You are worse than a nervous mother hen when it comes to worrying about me."

With good reason, thought Alec as he took another long swallow of his drink.

"Yes, I caught a chill," she went on. "But honestly, I'm not quite as delicate as you seem to think."

"You were at death's door," he said tightly. *All because of me.* Thank God she did not know the contents of the note she had carried on to his friend in the neighboring town.

"An exaggeration." She drew her knees up to her chest. "You must stop blaming yourself for that night. I'm not a child any longer, Alec. I am capable of making decisions for myself."

"If I had been there—"

"Well, you weren't. So I chose to carry the message on to Angus. Mr. Multoon seemed to think it was very important that it be delivered as soon as possible. And as I knew a shorter way over the moors than the road, it seemed the best decision."

He grimaced. "In a raging storm?"

She had the grace to color slightly. "If the rocks hadn't been loosened by the rain and given way, I would not have lost my footing.

"You are bloody lucky you didn't lose your life."

"Auch, we Scots are far too sturdy to succumb to a wee bit of fever."

Her attempt at a jest only sunk him deeper into a brooding mood. Ignoring her frown, Alec reached for the decanter.

"You really ought to be resting, to ensure that overexertion and overexcitement brought on by Miss Caro Sloane's little adventure doesn't bring on a relapse."

"*Miss Caro's* adventure?" Isobel's expression tightened. "What is *that* supposed to mean?"

Alec wordlessly lifted the glass to his lips.

"Surely you aren't suggesting that what happened was in any way her fault?" pressed his sister.

She was right, of course. It was absurdly unfair and illogical. But at the moment, his brain was not functioning very rationally.

"Wherever she goes, trouble seems to be only a step or two behind," he growled.

"While I, on the other hand, walk carefully enough so as not to ever kick up a dust?" asked Isobel.

"For the most part, yes." The heat of the liquid tingled against his tongue. "Thank God."

Alec heard her inhale sharply. "Why, that is quite the most bloody, *bloody* awful insult you have ever made to me."

He nearly choked on the mouthful of whisky.

"I would have hoped you had a better opinion of my character," she went on. "But clearly you think me a spineless ninny."

"That is the last thing I think," he replied, once he had managed to swallow the fiery malt as well as his initial shock. "The truth is, you have too much steel in your spine."

"I don't have nearly as much as Caro Sloane does."

How had the conversation strayed down such a slippery slope? Unwilling to slide any deeper into brooding about the fiery English beauty, Alec muttered, "Count your blessings. Steel sharpened to a razored edge can cut both ways. She is..."

Isobel tilted her head, waiting for him to go on.

"She...she is hardly someone you ought to use as a patterncard of propriety," he finished lamely, knowing he sounded like a pompous prig.

"Perhaps not," replied his sister thoughtfully. "But her unorthodox courage and fighting skills saved us from being abducted by those men."

"Miss Caro Sloane may rival Boadicca, England's mythical Warrior Queen, for bravery in battle," responded Alec. "But that is not to say that other mortal women ought to aspire to such bellicose spirit."

"And why is that?" she challenged. "Because men find a strong woman threatening?"

Damnation. There was an old Scottish adage about being caught between a rock and a stone.

"Kindly sheath your sarcasm, Bella. If you don't mind, I'm in no mood for verbal fencing," he muttered. "I've fought enough opponents for one evening without having you, too, cut up at me."

Isobel fixed him with a speculative stare, which lasted for an interlude of awkward silence. He would have poured himself another drink, but the decanter was now empty.

"By the by," she finally said. "Since Caro confirmed that the two of you are not strangers, I can't help but be curious as to how you met, given your reclusive habits and your dislike...that is..." Her words trailed off.

"My dislike for the English," he finished for her. "Given my history, I don't consider that an unreasonable sentiment. Do you?"

When Isobel didn't reply, he chuffed a sigh. "If you must

know, it was at Dunbar Castle last autumn, during Cousin Miriam's hunting party."

"Good heavens, the one where the French jewel thieves made off with her diamond necklace?"

"Yes," he answered tersely. That was the official explanation given out for the skullduggery that had led to a wild chase through the castle's dungeons and subterranean tunnels. The truth was far more…complicated. Intrigue and deception had swirled around the invited guests, heavy as the Scottish mists rising from the moors. Caro's older sister and the gentleman who was now her husband had been involved in the thick of the action.

As for Caro…

There was no denying that she had helped pull his cods out of the fire. And he still wasn't sure how he felt about that.

"My goodness, how very exciting," murmured Isobel.

"You've been reading too many novels," said Alec, hoping to discourage any further questions. "Like most gatherings of rich, overfed aristocrats, it was for the most part a tedious, boring affair."

The comment caused her lips to twitch. "I daresay you shocked most of them with your outspoken political opinions on virtues of hereditary monarchy versus democracy."

"As a courtesy to Cousin Miriam, I refrained from expressing my views." With a few notable exceptions. To his surprise, Caro Sloane had proved to be unexpectedly radical in her own ideas. On a number of subjects.

"That must have cost you dear," quipped Isobel.

"She is a very generous benefactor of my efforts to see that the Highland crofters have schools for their children. So muzzling my radical ideas was a paltry price to pay."

She nodded thoughtfully. "Speaking of radical ideas..."

Alec silently cursed himself for mentioning the subject, hoping she would not pursue the matter of his involvement in the clandestine political movement that sought independence for Scotland. The less she knew, the better.

"Caro has some very interesting thoughts on Lord Byron and his epic poetry."

He exhaled in relief—a fraction too soon.

"She wonders whether passion and sex—"

"*Sex!*" sputtered Alec.

Isobel raised her brows. "Good heavens, shall I fetch Aunt Adelaide's bottle of vinaigrette? You look on the verge of swooning."

"And with good reason," he retorted. "My baby sister ought not...ought not be exposed to..." He paused for a fraction, wondering how he had managed to lose control of the conversation.

"Why is it that men assume we ladies are completely ignorant of the ways of the world?"

"Because," he said through gritted teeth, "Gently reared ladies of delicate sensibilities should be protected from the grim realities—"

"Sex is grim?" Isobel's brows rose a notch higher. "Strange, that's not the impression I get from the books and poetry I read."

"You are," he snapped, "banned from the library as of this moment."

"Ha!" she answered. "That's a bit like closing the barn door after the horses—or rather, the stallions—have bolted free."

Alec was sorely tempted to make a run for the Scottish border.

"Oh, don't look so queasy," she added. "Having some knowledge of the world is not a bad thing for a lady. Ignorance can make one vulnerable."

He couldn't argue with that.

"That's another reason I like Caro Sloane. She has such interesting knowledge about a wide variety of subjects. I wish I knew half the things she does."

"Be careful what you wish for," replied Alec. "In London, the three Sloane sisters are known as the Hellions of High Street. The mean-spirited gossip died down once the eldest married the very rich and very proper Earl of Wrexham. But the family is still considered a trifle odd."

"Why?"

"Because their late father was an eccentric scholar and adventurer, and believed his daughters should have the same education as any son would receive."

"He sounds like he was a very wise man," murmured Isobel. "You've always encouraged me to be inquisitive and to learn new things."

"I may revise my thinking," shot back Alec.

She regarded him thoughtfully. "Interesting."

Ignoring the comment, he spent several moments rearranging the empty decanter and glasses on the silver tray.

Looking up to find her gaze still focused on him, he gave an exasperated sigh. "*What?*"

"I've never seen a lady make you so agitated," mused his sister. "It must mean something."

"Yes—it means that she is too..."

Dangerous.

"Different," he finished.

"I'm not sure that is such a bad thing." Isobel tapped at her chin. "Lady Fiona Sunderland remarked last year that the wall around your heart is thicker and harder than Highland granite."

"She should know," he growled. "She tried using a hammer and chisel to chip away at my refusal to make her an offer of marriage."

"Oh, I agree that the two of you would never have suited, but my point is, you've never shown the least emotion over any of the many ladies who have set their cap at you, since..."

Since he had been a callow, youthful fool.

Isobel looked apologetic.

"Forgive me, but if that is your point, I fail to see its meaning." The whisky, which he had downed to bring a pleasantly mellow fuzziness to his thoughts, was now beginning to make his head ache.

"It means you've never let a lady pique your interest since...a long time ago."

"Bella," he warned in a low growl.

She ignored him and went on, "But admit it—you find Caro Sloane intriguing."

"A more accurate adjective is 'infuriating,'" replied Alec.

"Even better," countered Isobel. "Heated feelings bode well for a passionate relationship."

Deciding not to ask how she had come to that conclusion, he merely responded, "As I said, we are too different."

"There is an old adage that says opposites attract."

"And there is an even older one that says oil and water don't mix," scoffed Alec.

Isobel's eyes lit with mirth. "Actually they do. Just ask any woman who's spent time in a kitchen. You just have to put them together and shake or stir *very* vigorously."

Chapter Three

... Nothing exciting ever happens in Bath.

"Ha!" Exhaling a wry sigh, Caro looked up from her sister Anna's letter. "For the most part that is true," she murmured to the potted geraniums who shared the Pump House alcove with her. "Quite likely the next few weeks will bring only the usual boring activities that make this town such an uninspiring place for anyone seeking to pen passionate poetry."

Especially as Lord Strathcona had not yet shown his face since playing the hero five nights ago.

"Wretch," she added under her breath, before returning her attention to the letter.

Oh, but never fret, went on Anna. *The time will likely pass more quickly than you imagine. And who knows, you may end up being pleasantly surprised. After all, the spa waters do occasionally attract interesting gentlemen...*

Ha, that was easy for her sister to say. Anna had recently married the dark and dangerously dashing "Devil" Davenport, and the new couple were spending their wedding trip in faraway Russia, visiting St. Petersburg, a city known for its opulent splendors and extravagant parties.

Sparkling ballrooms, exotic men, exciting flirtations, thought Caro glumly. *While I pine for—*

"Miss Caro?"

A familiar voice interrupted her brooding.

"I say, is that really you skulking among the flowerpots?"

"Lord Andover." Edging out from between the marble display pedestals, she smiled at Anna's former beau. "Yes, it's me."

"Thank God," he said in a conspiratorial whisper. "I was beginning to fear there was no one in town under the age of eighty."

"I fear we are few and far between," replied Caro.

"Then how fortunate that I spotted you among those exquisite roses," replied Andover. "Your bloom, of course, puts them to the blush."

"They are geraniums, Andy," pointed out Caro.

He grinned. "Didn't Shakespeare say something about a rose by any name would look as lovely?"

She rolled her eyes, drawing a chuckle. "You are mangling his magnificent poetry."

"No doubt. I am not nearly as well read as you and your sisters." He offered his arm. "Regardless, come take a walk with me around the fountain, so that I may bask in your reflected beauty."

"You need not waste your flatteries on me," said Caro, falling in step with him. "I know you've never really forgiven me for the frog incident." It was not for nothing that the Sloane sisters were known as the Hellions of High Street. And she, as the youngest, was the most devilish of the three.

"Having a small, green croaking creature hop out of my

pocket and into Lady Tilden's soup tureen was not overly amusing at the time," he conceded with a smile. Thinking it a deliberate prank, the imperious dowager countess, one of the highest sticklers in Society, had threatened to have Andover banned from Mayfair's ballrooms for the rest of the Season. "But in retrospect, I do see the humor in it. And the fact that I've never been invited back to one of her boring dinner parties is a blessing in disguise."

"I was only sixteen and still a silly schoolgirl. And if truth be told, I was chafing at the fact that I was still a child in the eyes of Society, while my two older sisters were part of the glittering, glamorous adult world of parties and balls and dancing until dawn."

"Which really isn't quite so exciting as it sounds, is it?" replied Andover dryly. "One limps home on aching feet, feeling utterly exhausted. Being gay and charming requires an awful lot of effort."

Caro smiled. Of all Anna's erstwhile admirers, Andover was her favorite. His quick wit and self-deprecating sense of humor complemented his sunny good cheer and faultless manners.

"Not for you, it doesn't," she pointed out. "Everyone adores you because you are so thoroughly nice."

"Nice." He made a wry face. "That smacks of being damned with faint praise."

"You need no flowery compliments from me," she said. "You hear more than enough from the rest of the *ton*."

Andover inclined a polite nod to a trio of passing dowagers before answering, "As do you. The silly schoolgirl has grown into a lovely young lady and quickly made up for lost time." He turned his head, and their gazes met. "Was your first Season all that you hoped it would be?"

How to answer?

Caro felt a flush steal to her cheeks. The endless parties, the elegant entertainments, the glittering ballrooms aswirl in sumptuous silks and satins—it had all been an exciting experience, as heady and effervescent as the champagne bubbling in the cut crystal glasses. But she was also aware that at times, the blazing lights had seemed overbright, the laughter overloud, the ladies overdressed.

"I am not sure," she admitted. "There was much that was wonderful. And yet..." She gave herself a little shake. "I know this may sound silly, but I sometimes felt a little lonely because I was not able to share the experiences with my sisters."

Olivia and Anna had both been traveling with their husbands, so the townhouse on High Street had been empty, save for herself and her mother, whose health was taking a turn for the worse. It felt strange and a little unsettling. She missed her sisters dearly—the laughter, the words of wisdom. She even missed the teasing.

"I don't think it's silly at all," murmured Andover. "My two brothers joined Wellington's staff and marched off to the Peninsula last year. I miss their camaraderie."

They walked on in silence for several moments, then Andover turned their steps to the table selling the sulfurous mineral water for which the town was famous.

"A toast," he said, handing her a glass. "For despite any personal reservations you may have, I assure you that your debut into Society was a smashing success."

"As to that, my sisters and their husbands have done much to smooth the way—"

He cut her off with a quick exclamation. "Fustian! You have earned the admiration all on your own."

Her color deepened. She was sure her face must be a vivid shade of scarlet. _So much for being worldly and sophisticated when a simple compliment from a friend had her near speechless in confusion._

"Indeed, I must congratulate you on attracting a bevy of ardent admirers. I vow, it was often impossible to see you through the throng of surrounding gentlemen."

"Oh, you are teasing me."

Andover grinned. "Just a little."

She sipped her water, hoping it might help cool her flaming cheeks.

"I imagine you will have a number of offers to consider when you return to London," he went on. "I suspect that Russell and Noyes are the ones who have the best hope of capturing your heart."

They were both interesting and engaging gentlemen. But somehow—she wasn't sure she could explain quite why—they did not light any excitement in her soul.

No spark, no fire.

And surely a poet should feel more than a mild warmth for any gentleman who was seeking to win her hand.

Her fingers tightened around her glass. "N-n-not necessarily," she stammered.

"Oh, you can confide in me. Since your sisters aren't around, consider me your brother." There was a glint of amusement in his eyes. "So come now, which one will you accept?"

Caro looked away for a moment. Strangely enough, the only image that came to mind was of a gentleman with red-gold hair and austere features that might have been carved out of Highland granite—

_No, no, no._

She quickly blotted out the mental image. It was absurd to think of the fleeting moments all those months ago when they had set aside their differences to talk of art and literature. Most assuredly *he* didn't.

As Andover pointed out, there were any number of far more amiable men. Polite, adoring men.

So why didn't that lift her spirits?

Forcing a smile, Caro made herself match his playful tone. Time enough in the solitude after midnight to try to sort out her tangled emotions. "Surely you don't expect me to tell you before my intended?"

The twinkle in Andover's eye became more pronounced. "I suppose that's fair enough."

"Assuming there is an offer I mean to accept," Caro added hastily, hoping her cheeks weren't on fire.

"Ah, is that why you are rusticating in Bath, rather than enjoying the attentions in London?" he inquired. "Because you are trying to make up your mind?"

She gave him what she hoped was an enigmatic smile.

"I vote for Noyes. Russell is a nice fellow, but I'm not sure he has enough backbone for you."

The comment caused an odd pinch in her chest. "Am I that much of a headstrong hellion?"

Andover's chuckle died away. "It was meant as compliment, Miss Caro. You have a rare spirit."

For an instant, she wondered whether his flirtations were more than brotherly. She hoped not. There was no denying his charm, his good looks, or the fact that his company was delightfully companionable. He was the best of friends, but as for being more than that—

"And in case you are thinking that I mean to work my wiles on you, perhaps we ought to, um, make sure there are no misunderstandings between us." He cleared his throat with a cough before adding, "We have a wonderful friendship, which—"

"Yes, yes, I couldn't agree more," she interrupted in a rush of relief. "Nothing could be more perfect."

"Right-ho. Absolutely nothing!" He, too, blew out his breath. "Well, now that we understand each other perfectly, I trust I will be the second to know when you decide who the lucky fellow will be."

"You are forgetting one thing, Andy. The decision is not entirely up to me. The lucky fellow does have some say in the matter." She was careful to keep her mind's eye firmly shut. "Despite what you think about me being a hellion, I'm not about to club him over the head—assuming there *is* a him—and drag him to the altar."

He grinned. "Oh, I don't know. If you really felt strongly enough about the fellow, I suspect you might be willing to resort to extreme measures."

"Well, there *is* no fellow, so let us not waste our breath in arguing the point," said Caro.

"Very well." They strolled on, making several leisurely circuits of the Pump Room promenade while chatting about the just-finished London Season. Most of the other patrons that afternoon were elderly, and Andover left off his teasing to nod politely to many of the ladies.

"A number of them are bosom bows with my grandmother," he murmured out of the corner of his mouth. "And she will ring a peal over my head if my manners aren't up to her exacting standards."

"I wouldn't think that the prospect of a grandmotherly lecture would strike terror into such a stalwart heart as yours," remarked Caro dryly.

"Oh, but it does!" he replied. "You see, she has a very pointy cane and knows how to wield it."

As they rounded the next turn, Andover was obliged to stop and converse about the upcoming races at Newmarket with the Marquess of Webster, allowing Caro a chance to survey the surroundings.

Craning her neck, she hoped to spot Isobel among the crowd. A cough had kept her new friend confined to her bed for the last two days, but a note she had sent this morning had indicated that the physician might allow her out for a short stroll to fortify herself with the healthful waters.

Growing up, friendships with girls her own age had not come easy to Caro. Between the travel to exotic locales while her father was still alive and the family's reputation for eccentricity, Polite Society was not overly willing to have their children mingle with the Hellions of High Street. It hadn't really mattered while her sisters were still at home.

But now, with the house feeling forlornly empty, the chance to talk about literature and art with another young lady who shared her interests was something she sorely missed.

She had a feeling that Isobel Urquehart might be a kindred spirit. Despite the fact that Alec McClellan was her brother.

As if summoned by some perverse Celtic imp of mischief, a shock of all-too-familiar red-gold hair suddenly appeared among the more muted shades of silver.

Caro felt her heart thud against her ribs as Alec skirted around a group of matrons and paused by the archway to glance around the room.

In the play of shadows, his chiseled profile looked even more austere and forbidding than usual, but something about his face—a beguiling hint of both light and dark—sent a frisson of awareness down her spine. In contrast to his stiff expression, his big, broad-shouldered body moved with a panther-like grace, the muscles rippling beneath his dark coat and trousers.

He turned, and their eyes met.

And suddenly her breath seemed to catch in her throat.

She tried to look away but her rebellious body refused to obey the simplest command.

It was Alec who broke the connection. Squeezing through the throng by the pump, he was at her side a moment later.

"Miss Caro," he said stiffly.

Andover looked around and raised an inquiring brow at the sight of Alec's unsmiling face.

"Sir," she murmured in reply to the greeting. To Andover she explained, "Lord Strathcona and I are acquainted, Andy. We met last autumn, while attending the hunting party at Dunbar Castle."

"Ah." Her friend inclined a friendly nod.

To which Alec responded with a stony stare. "If you will excuse us," he said, before Caro could make any formal introductions, "I should like to have a private word with the lady."

"Yes, of course," replied Caro quickly, hoping to forestall any further rudeness. Ye gods, the man had the manners of a Highland goat. "Andy was just taking his leave."

Too polite to ignore her hint, Andover retreated gracefully.

"No wonder the people all look ill in here," muttered Alec. "The sulfurous fumes are strong enough to choke the Devil himself."

"It is said to be healthful," pointed out Caro, but secretly she agreed with him. The water had left a bilious taste in her mouth.

"Shall we take a walk in Queen Square?" He offered his arm, adding gruffly, "It will afford a bit more privacy."

Impatient to hear what he had to say, she didn't object to his loping, long-legged stride as they hurried down the street, though she had to lift her skirts to keep pace.

"Well?" she demanded, as soon as they passed through the iron gates and turned down one of the graveled paths. The ominous rainclouds hovering low on the horizon had scared off all but a few hardy souls, so they had the walkway to themselves.

He slowed his steps all of a sudden, appearing in no hurry to get down to business. His hat required adjustment, his coat buttons needed to be undone and refastened.

Caro made herself count silently to ten.

"Forgive me," he finally said. "I trust I did not interrupt an important conversation."

The baron acknowledging social convention? It was amusing enough to bring a wry smile to her lips.

"It is a little late to worry about that," she replied. "But no, there is no cause for concern. Lord Andover will be in town for a month, so we will have ample time to talk."

"Hmmph." Alec's grunt gave nothing away. "I take it," he said after another drawn-out pause to smooth the wrinkles from his gloves, "that the gentleman is one of your London admirers?"

Perhaps it was merely the breeze ruffling through the sharp-edged holly leaves, but his tone seemed shaded by doubt.

"You think it impossible that I might have any?"

Alec looked taken aback by her question. But rather than

snap back with one of his usual gruff responses, he took his time in responding. "I meant to imply no such thing. I have no doubt that you are surrounded by a bevy of men seeking to make themselves agreeable to you."

For a moment, Caro thought he was being sarcastic, but the momentary flicker in his eyes just before he lowered his lashes said otherwise.

Lud, he had very intriguing eyes.

"A compliment from you, sir? Good Heavens, I should have brought my smelling salts."

The corners of his mouth tugged upward. "Consider it an observation, not a compliment. So no need to swoon."

"Thank God," she murmured. "The stones look awfully sharp and uncomfortable."

"You don't think that I would catch you?"

"I wouldn't want to wager my quarterly allowance on it. Besides, you already rescued me once in recent days. I daresay you don't want to make a habit of it."

His face wreathed in a grudging smile.

"Actually," she hurried on, forcing herself to ignore the sinuous curl of his lower lip. "I am far more interested in your observations about the recent attack on your sister and me, and the reasons that lie behind it. Did you discover any new information while you were away?"

"Yes." A pause. "But I can't say it's overly helpful."

She frowned.

"It turns out that in fact there *has* been a gang of ruffians roaming the area and committing violent crimes. A carriage outside of Bristol was accosted a week ago and the occupants robbed. An estate house was broken into and ransacked. Several of the men were apprehended the other night and are awaiting trial. The rest escaped capture."

"So you are saying that it truly was a random attack?"

He took a long moment to form an answer. "I have no evidence to the contrary." .

To Caro, who considered herself attuned to the nuances of language, the words seemed very carefully chosen.

"And yet," she pressed, "the night it happened, it was clear to me that you suspected it might have something to do with your involvement with the radicals in Scotland."

"I am, on rare occasions, wrong," he quipped. "But to answer your question, yes, I considered it a possibility. But I have uncovered nothing that would suggest it is the case."

"You are quite sure?"

Another hint of hesitation. "Not entirely. I shall, of course, keep looking into the matter. But for now, it seems there is no reason to fear any further threats."

"Thank you for the reassurance, Lord Strathcona." *Crunch, crunch*—the pebbles crackled under the tread of her shoes. "Now, kindly dispense with the platitudes and tell me what you *really* think." .

Alec could almost hear the tiny flashes of fire crackle and spark beneath the dark fringe of her lashes. Her eyes, an unusual gold-flecked hazel color, were intriguing enough to begin with. But when her passions were aroused, they lit with a mesmerizing mix of heated hues that seemed to swirl down, down to some secret depth.

A man could drown in such treacherous currents.

He angled his gaze to a twist of ivy behind her right ear. "I have told you all that I know, Miss Caro."

"Indeed?" Her eyes narrowed. "So why do I feel you are not being entirely forthright with me, sir?"

Alec raised a brow and waggled it up and down. "You are

asking me to explain the complex workings of the feminine mind? That, I fear, is beyond the power of my feeble intellect."

She made a rude sound and stepped closer to confront him. "Ye gods, you are an impossibly provoking man."

Ye gods, you are an impossibly alluring lady.

He could feel the heat of her aroused ire pulsing against his skin, bringing with it the beguiling scent of verbena, edged with a more exotic spice that he couldn't put a name to.

He inhaled and, for a flickering instant, felt a little dizzy.

"Hmmph. I am quite certain there is more to this matter than you are telling me, sir."

Exhaling sharply, Alec managed to break the strange spell that held him in thrall. "Believe what you wish, but the truth is, you know as much as I do about the reasons for the incident."

"Have I your word on that?"

"Yes." Honor allowed him to reply without batting an eye. She did now possess all the facts. As for his conjectures, those he wasn't about to share with anyone.

Especially a headstrong hellion.

During the trouble in Scotland, Caro Sloane had proved she was more than ready to charge in where angels should fear to tread. Courage, passion, fire that blazed bright as a mountain sunset.

Such fire could lead a lady into serious trouble.

"I suppose I shall have to be satisfied with that," grumbled Caro, as the first leaden drops of rain splashed on the brim of her bonnet.

Taking her arm again, Alec quickly turned them back in the direction of the Pump House. "Indeed you should be. As far as I'm concerned, the matter is resolved."

"I'm not quite as convinced as you are," she protested. "I think the matter requires further investigation."

God forbid.

"You need not concern yourself with that," he growled. "Leave it to me. If there is anything you should know, I shall pass it on."

He pretended not to hear her muttered "Ha!" over the rumble of distant thunder.

Chapter Four

*T*he musicians struck up the notes of a country gavotte, the lively tempo of violins matched by the steps of the couples capering across the dance floor as the weekly Assembly festivities turned even more exuberant.

Caro watched the festivities from the archway of one of the side salons, the flicking of her fan stirring a welcome breeze. The humid air, still redolent with the recent rain, hung heavy with mingled scents—the floral sweetness of the lush tuber roses, the cloying richness of the French perfumes, the earthy exertion of the heated bodies—and she was uncomfortably aware of a trickle of moisture tickling down between her breasts.

"Hot as Hades, isn't it?"

Andover's voice made her jump.

"Sorry, did I startle you?"

"I—I was just thinking," she replied.

"Of what?"

Of chiseled cheekbones, sharp as Scottish flint. Of blue-gray eyes, changeable as a stormblown loch.

"Oh, just woolgathering," murmured Caro.

"Would you care to leave off chasing sheep long enough to dance with me?" he inquired.

"That would be lovely." Perhaps twirling across the polished parquet would help dispel her brooding mood.

They joined the set forming on the floor, and moving through the figures of the country jig did indeed make it hard to stay blue-deviled. The merriment was infectious, and Andover's pithy comments when the steps brought them together had her laughing aloud.

Her cheeks were flushed with a pleasant heat by the time the tune came to an end. "La, dancing works up a thirst," she said, as Andover led her to a spot by the cluster of potted palms, where the nearby open window was letting in a gentle breeze.

"Wait here and I shall fetch us some punch." Ever the gentleman, Andover immediately hurried off, sparing her the discomfort of squeezing through the crowd around the refreshment table.

"Caro!"

She turned to catch the last little flutter of a pale, peach-colored glove before it was swallowed in the sea of swirling silks. A moment later, Isobel appeared near the entrance to the card room and slowly began making her way along the perimeter of the room.

Her friend waved again as she approached, a smile illuminating her whole face. "This is marvelous! Our local assemblies in Scotland are not nearly so dashing."

Her escort did not appear nearly as enthusiastic.

"Wait until your toes are crushed beneath some oaf's foot for the fourth or fifth time," groused Alec. "Or an elbow pokes you in the ribs." He shot a glowering glance at the crowd. "You really ought not be here, Bella. I fear the crush and the heat will be too taxing on your strength."

"Oh, pish. Doctor Bailey said a little exercise would do me good," she chided.

Her brother scowled but refrained from replying.

Taking his silence as a sign of surrender, Isobel turned back to Caro. "What a beautiful gown!" she exclaimed. "The design is so elegant, and the color is absolutely divine. I've never seen such a rich hue of green. Why, it looks like melted emeralds."

Caro was aware of a new warmth spreading over her flesh. The gown was new and a bit daring, with a low-cut bodice and artful arrangement of folds that made her feel very sleek and sophisticated. She had received gushing compliments from the gentlemen in London...

A surreptitious glance at Alec showed him to be studying the fronds of the nearest palm tree.

"I am very fortunate," she replied, trying not to feel a twinge of disappointment. "My eldest sister has arranged for me to have access to one of the leading modistes in London. Madame Mathilde is a true artist with silk and thread."

A wistful sigh slipped from Isobel's lips. "How I would love to visit London."

That got Alec's attention. He expelled a dismissive grunt. "It's a dirty, noisy city."

"There are some saving graces," pointed out Caro. "The shops, the museums, the lectures at the Royal Institute, the sights like Westminster Cathedral, the Tower, and Astley's Amphitheater."

"Are we singing London's praises?" asked Andover, returning with two drinks in hand. "Lord Elgin's marbles are not to be missed, the concerts are sublime, and the current exhibition of watercolors at the Royal Academy is quite good."

"No," growled Alec.

"Yes," responded Isobel at the same time.

"Lord Strathcona is not fond of anything English," explained Caro.

Including me.

Andover smiled politely at Isobel. "I do hope you haven't taken the same aversion to our country and its people, Miss..."

"Oh, forgive me," said Caro, and quickly performed the requisite introductions.

"As to your question, Lord Andover, so far I have had a very pleasant stay here in Bath," said Isobel.

"Excellent, excellent. We must see that your experience remains a favorable one."

Caro saw Isobel cast a longing glance at the dance floor. Giving Andover a discreet nudge, she waggled a brow. "Oh, look, Andy—a new set is forming already."

Taking his cue, Andover dutifully set aside his punch glass. "Miss Urquehart, might I ask for your hand in this dance?"

Two spots of color appeared on Isobel's cheeks. "Me? B-b-but surely you ought to ask Caro."

"No, no, poor Andy has been very kind in keeping me company..." Caro lowered her voice. "He is far too gentlemanly to admit it, but I'm sure he'll be greatly relieved not to have to worry about frogs or snakes appearing in his pockets."

"You don't, I trust, have any reptiles hidden in your reticule, Miss Urquehart?" murmured Andover.

Isobel stifled a giggle. "No, milord. There were none the last time I looked."

"Excellent." He offered his arm. "Shall we?"

"Th-thank you." Her face pink with pleasure, Isobel placed her hand on his sleeve.

"Frogs?" murmured Alec, as they moved away to join the other couples on the dance floor.

"It's a long story," replied Caro. "I was still in the schoolroom."

"Ah."

It was hard to tell in the shifting shadows of the leaves, but she thought she detected a slight twitch in his solemn expression.

"It's fortuitous that Andy is very good natured," she explained. "Lady Tilden threatened to have him banned from the ballrooms of Mayfair for the remainder of the Season when her French chef's special soup started croaking in the middle of a fancy supper party."

He made an odd little sound in his throat. If it hadn't been Alec, she might have taken it for a chuckle.

"Now, if it had been turtle soup," he drawled, "His Lordship might have been able to talk his way out of trouble."

Caro drew in a deep breath. And let it out in a low laugh. "I'm shocked, sir. You actually have a very sly sense of humor."

"I do?" He sounded rather bemused by the idea.

"Yes." Caro wished she could see his eyes through his lowered lashes. "Definitely."

Alec reached up to brush one of the swaying fronds off his shoulder. "I shall try to nip it in the bud."

"Don't," she blurted out. "It's rather nice."

He finally allowed his gaze to meet hers. The connection sent a frisson of fire—or was it ice—down her spine.

"That is," she stammered, "it's nicer than constantly being at daggers drawn with you."

"Contrary to what you might think, I am not always deliberately sharp, Miss Caro," he replied.

An oblique apology?

She wasn't certain.

"I don't..." Alec began, then paused for a brief moment as his gaze drifted down a notch and then up again. "I don't think that I have yet commented on your gown."

"No, you have not," agreed Caro. "I would remember."

That earned another twitch of his lips. "You look... well."

Well, well, well, thought Caro wryly. It was not the most scintillating of compliments. However she wasn't going to quibble.

"Why, thank you, sir," she murmured.

"The color is unusual. It suits you... well."

Good Heavens, the man was becoming positively chatty.

Clasping his hands behind his back, Alec shifted his stance and returned to his silent contemplation of the room.

Tapping her foot lightly in time with the music, Caro shifted her own attention to the capering couples. The steps of the cotillion soon brought Isobel and Andover close, and she couldn't help but notice that Alec's sister moved her lips and waggled a discreet hand signal at her brother.

He expelled a martyred sigh.

"I take it she is telling you something," said Caro. "My sisters and I have the same sort of private communication."

Alec gave a gruff nod. Whatever the message, he didn't seem too happy about it.

"I hope she is not finding the event too taxing on her strength. The noise and the heat might be a little overwhelming."

"No, she seems to be enjoying herself immensely."

"It's clear you are a solicitous brother, so I would think

that would bring a smile rather than a frown to your face."

Another spasm of surprise. "I didn't realize I was frowning."

"You frown quite often. It is very intimidating."

That provoked a smile. "Not to you."

Yes, to me, she thought.

He hesitated, then added, "It was kind of you to have Lord Andover ask my sister to dance." Another pause. "However, I hope you are not regretting being separated from your suitor for such an interminable duration. The cotillion is a *very* long dance."

"Oh, Good Heavens, Andy is not *my* suitor," exclaimed Caro. "He was one of Anna's." She repressed a sigh as she recalled the pressure Anna had felt to marry well in order to keep the family from sinking into genteel poverty. "In fact, Mama had high hopes that he would offer for her."

"Why didn't he?"

"Oh, actually he did, though Mama has no knowledge of that private event. Anna turned him down, gently, but firmly."

"For what reason?" asked Alec, watching the other man lead his laughing sister through a skipping turn. "He seems a solid enough fellow."

"Oh, he is. More than solid, in fact," she replied. "As to the reason, Anna did not say it herself, but Davenport..." Beneath his devil-may-care manner, the gentleman her sister did marry was an astute observer of human nature. "Davenport is of the opinion that he is *too* nice to stand up to a lady of Anna's strong-willed temperament. He would have put her on a pedestal, and she would not have liked it one whit."

Alec looked thoughtful.

Caro allowed a tiny smile. "In truth, Anna thinks Andy was secretly relieved, and I agree. I am of the opinion that he will be happier with someone else."

"The two of you seem very comfortable with each other," remarked Alec. "To my eye, he seems very attentive."

"No, no! Andy isn't interested in *that* sort of way." She made a wry face. "As you have noticed, I am even worse than Anna when it comes to being a headstrong hellion. I would drive him to distraction, and he's far too nice to suffer such a fate. So I assure you, we are simply friends."

A low "*Hmm*" was his only response.

The music quickened, and the dancing couples reformed into the last circling steps that would bring the cotillion to an end.

"I've been ordered by Isobel to ask you for the next dance," said Alec, abruptly changing the subject.

"It sounds like you would rather walk to your execution," said Caro. "So consider yourself relieved of obeying such an onerous command. Dancing is supposed to be enjoyable."

He shifted his weight from foot to foot. "I shall endeavor not to crush your toes."

"Lord Strathcona, you need not suffer through—"

"It would please Isobel," he said gruffly.

"It ought to please you," she pointed out. "Which does not seem the case. So please don't feel obligated."

"If I seem reluctant, it is not because I find it onerous, but rather because I fear it is *you* who would find the experience a sore trial."

"I have very sturdy toes," she said softly.

"Sturdy enough to withstand the clomping of a Highland ox?"

"Having seen you in action, sir, I have reason to know

you are far more nimble than that. I am willing to take the risk if you are."

A few tentative trills sounded as the musicians retuned their violins for the next dance.

"In that case..." He smoothed the wrinkles from his sleeve, as if considering the challenge. His wrist twitched, then he offered his arm. "Let us give it a try."

The parquet floor was a simple, sensible pattern of dark wood, made from the sort of solid English oak that could withstand centuries of stomping.

So why was it that the room seemed suddenly to tremor beneath his feet as he turned to face her?

It was a waltz. Alec had recognized the first notes and dutifully taken her hand and drawn her closer. Only to feel a jolt of electricity thrum through his entire body.

Leaving his brain feeling a little singed.

Somehow he managed to go through the proper motions—his other hand set on the small of her back, his feet slid into the first figures of the dance, no matter that the floor seemed to be tilting at a very odd angle.

Breathe, he told himself. And slowly, as his lungs began to function again, his mind began to clear.

She, too, seemed aware of the current coursing through the layers of wool and silk. Her cheeks were a trifle flushed, and the rise and fall of her bosom had suddenly quickened.

Her bosom. Alec realized his eyes were glued on the creamy expanse of flesh revealed by the low-cut bodice of her gown.

"Sorry," he intoned, as his shoe grazed her slipper.

"N-no harm done," responded Caro. That her voice was a little unsteady made him feel less like an idiot.

They danced on for several minutes in silence.

"You surprise me, Lord Strathcona," she said after a series of spins. "Not only are you familiar with the waltz, but you dance it very well."

"As do you, Miss Caro." She moved with a liquid grace, and with her raven-colored hair and sea-green gown, she reminded him of a Scottish loch on the cusp of a storm.

Dark and slightly dangerous. Quixotic and infinitely intriguing.

A challenge.

Test the waters and experience exhilaration—but risk being dashed to flinders on the jagged rocks.

"Oh, I suppose that's because I've had a lot of practice lately," she replied airily, after they had spun through a breathless turn.

Was she deliberately trying to provoke him?

Narrowing his gaze, Alec searched her expression for any hint of mockery in her expression. But Caro kept her face at precisely the right angle to hide her eyes. A clever, sophisticated ploy, no doubt, learned in the fancy Mayfair ballrooms.

As for her lovely mouth, and the delectable little curl playing at its left corner...

He masked the sudden urge to touch his tongue to the spot with a brusque cough. "With all your elegant footwork, I imagine you've twirled out a number of marriage offers, if not from Andover, then from a host of other besotted swains." His own steps seemed to turn more leaden, though why was not something he could explain. "Is that why you are rusticating in Bath? To mull over which tulip of the *ton* to accept?"

Her mouth thinned, and he could almost feel the prickles

sprouting from her smooth skin. "I am here in Bath because my mother has been feeling poorly and she wished to take the waters." Her spin through the next turn was not quite so smooth as before. "As for my gaggle of offers—or lack of them—I cannot imagine that is of any interest to you, Lord Strathcona."

Alec gave himself a mental kick for spoiling the moment of harmony between them. "I am sorry," he said stiffly. "I do hope your mother will fully recover her health."

"You are acquainted with my mother," she replied, a hint of humor returning to her voice. "She would be quite unhappy if she had nothing to grouse about."

Alec noted that Caro tactfully omitted the fact that Lady Trumbull was not overly fond of him. She preferred gentlemen with polished manners and prestigious titles. A lowly Scottish baron was not the sort of suitor she wanted sniffing around her daughters.

Not that he had been sniffing—it had been more snorts. And growls. Lady Trumbull had misjudged the dangers swirling around Dunbar Castle. The threats to her daughters had not come from him.

"But that said," went on Caro, "we are hoping the thermal hot springs will help ease the creaking in her knees."

Another sliver of silence, this one sharp with regret for having ruined the interlude. But it was best, he reminded himself, to keep a distance, keep a detachment.

Danger lurked all around him and in far more sinister shapes than a spitfire beauty. Shadows and secrets were swirling like a poisonous mist, and the thought of the nameless, faceless threat sent fear slithering down his spine. Isobel was so very vulnerable, as was . . .

It took him a moment to realize the music had ended

and the sensation was half-caused by Caro surreptitiously squeezing his shoulder.

"We can stop now," she whispered. "You need not keep counting the seconds until the ordeal is over."

He blinked, trying to clear the last fugue of brooding from his head. "I'm sorry."

"For what?" she countered.

"For asking you to dance," he replied without thinking—then realized he had just put his foot in his mouth.

"Oh, I haven't had such fun in ages," said Caro. "Though clearly the same can't be said for you." In contrast to the coolness of her voice, the intensity of her gaze nearly scorched his skin. "In the future, you need not feel compelled to heed your sister's commands."

He drew in a deep breath, but to his relief, Isobel and Andover chose that moment to reappear.

"Oh, the waltz looks like such fun," gushed his sister. "But Lord Andover warned me that a young lady may not dance it in Bath without having been approved by the Assembly's Master of Ceremonies. Otherwise she runs the risk of being considered 'fast' by Polite Society." A sigh punctuated the explanation. "So we had to sit out and watch."

"Silly strictures, I know," murmured Andover, shooting him an apologetic look. "But it seemed prudent to err on the side of caution and not stir needless gossip." Caro's friend then looked back at Isobel and smiled. "By next week's Assembly, Miss Urquehart, you will certainly have permission through the proper procedures."

"My thanks to you, Andover," said Alec, saved from the ticklish task of having to respond to Caro. "I'm grateful for your good sense. Gossip is always dangerous." He glanced at Isobel, noting a sparkle in her eyes that had been missing for weeks. Perhaps the evening's festivities had not been such a bad idea after all, despite his own errant stumbles. "And for keeping my sister company. I trust she didn't chatter your ear off."

"Alec!" she squeaked, looking mortified.

"Not at all, sir," replied Andover quickly. "We had a very interesting discussion."

"On Mozart's sonatas," interjected Isobel.

Alec repressed a grin. His sister was passionate about music and played the pianoforte and harpsichord with great skill. "You are being exceedingly kind to call such a talk interesting. Having been subjected to her lengthy lectures on the subject, I daresay you could use a glass of brandy." He paused. "Or maybe several."

"Alec!"

"Actually, Andy plays the pianoforte," volunteered Caro. "Quite well in fact."

Andover looked a little embarrassed. "Oh, no, not really. I dabble, that is all."

"Men," huffed Caro, fixing her friend with a quizzical look. "Why are all of you so reluctant to admit to an interest in anything that doesn't involve firearms, horses, or hounds?"

"In many circles, it isn't considered very manly to be enthusiastic about the arts," admitted Andover.

"Then perhaps you are spending time with the wrong people," replied Caro.

He smiled. "Miss Caro is passionate about literature, especially poetry, Lord Strathcona, so—"

"I am aware of that fact," said Alec dryly.

"Lord Strathcona is also passionate about prose and

verse." Her flash of teeth was quite likely not meant as a smile. "Though he takes great pains to keep it a secret."

"It's true," said his sister. "Beneath his stony scowls, he has a very sensitive soul."

"I suppose I deserved that for the chatty comment," he growled.

"Yes," shot back Isobel. "You did."

Andover's mouth twitched, but he was sensible enough to remain silent. As for Caro's reaction, it was impossible to gauge, for she had turned away to watch the dancing.

"Perhaps it's time for us to return home," he drawled. "Before you make any more embarrassing revelations."

His sister's eyes flared in alarm. "Oh, I was just teasing."

"As was I."

Isobel let out a sigh of relief.

"However, I think it wise that you don't overexert yourself," he added softly.

Andover cleared his throat. "As to that sir, I have asked your sister if she would like to see the organ at Bath Abbey on the morrow. That is, if she's not feeling too fatigued. It was built in 1708 and has twenty stops spread over three manuals. One and a half octaves of pedals were added during the renovation in 1802, and..."

A rueful grimace squeezed his words to a stop. "Sorry— I tend to get carried away. But it is considered a very magnificent instrument. And the Abbey itself is a historic cathedral."

"I have a feeling wild horses could not keep my sister from the outing," replied Alec.

"Excellent! Then with your permission, I will call at your townhouse at two."

He nodded.

"Oh, you must join us, Caro," exclaimed Isobel.

"Thank you," she replied. "It sounds like a lovely afternoon."

The invitation, noted Alec, was not extended to include him.

Just as well. From now on, he meant to stay far away from Caro Sloane. He couldn't afford the distraction.

Or the temptation.

Chapter Five

Sunlight filtered in through the stained glass windows, dappling the high arches in flickering patterns of pastel colors. Caro watched for a moment longer, her own thoughts mirroring the erratic play of the hues dipping and dancing over the carved limestone. Then, lowering her gaze, she retreated into the shadows of the nave.

The notes of the organ reverberated through the soaring transept of the Abbey, the magnificent sound mellowed by space and stone. It was beautiful, and yet the *thrum, thrum* was making her head ache.

Leaving Isobel and Andover to enjoy the practice session, she slipped out one of the side doors and wandered into the adjoining churchyard.

Her spirits, often criticized as too exuberantly high, were feeling depressingly low, and as she took a seat on a small stone bench shaded by the outstretched wings of a massive sculpted angel, Caro made herself start a list of all the reasons she should be happy.

First and foremost...

Her mind remained stubbornly blank.

"Oh, come," she muttered to herself. "To begin with, I danced every night of the Season with a bevy of handsome men."

None of whom set my heart to fluttering.

"Fluttering hearts are vastly overrated," she snapped back at the voice of the Devil's Advocate, who had apparently taken up residence in the back of her skull. Shifting on the stone slab, she moved on to the next reason.

"Now that we're no longer poor as churchmice, I need not rush into making a match for pragmatic reasons, but may look for a kindred soul." She smiled and offered up silent thanks to Olivia and her husband. Wrexham, who was known as the Perfect Hero, had proved to be just that. Indeed, both of her sisters had found just the right match.

She sighed and added, "Yes, I may look for someone who will be a friend as well as a husband."

A man who likes verse and novels, can laugh at himself, and is not averse to long walks through the scenic countryside to admire the beauty of nature is rarer than hen's teeth, responded the Devil's Advocate.

The imp of Satan was really becoming very annoying.

Caro gave an inward grimace. Surely in Africa or Cathay there were species of barnyard fowls with fangs.

Determined to quiet the voice, she thought very hard. "I've more freedom than ever to write poetry."

For a moment there was no answer. But the silence was short-lived.

Exceptional poetry, pointed out the Devil's Advocate, *requires exceptional experience in life*.

Damnation, the dratted voice was right. A few months of

swirling through the ballrooms of Mayfair had done little to inspire dramatic verse.

Caro fingered her shawl, slowly unraveling one of the knotted fringes. What she needed was a challenging adventure, like the ones her sisters Olivia and Anna had gone through.

Danger, dashing heroes, the triumph of Good over Evil.

"Yes, and why don't I slay a few dragons while I am at it," she added under her breath.

The whisper echoed off the surrounding stone, growing oddly louder rather than fading away. Perhaps it was the breeze, amplified by her own unsettled mood. Closing her eyes, she slumped back into the shelter of the stone wings and drew a deep breath, trying to still her agitated thoughts.

"I tell you, things are becoming too dangerous."

Caro nearly jumped out of her skin at the sound of a man's voice, kept deliberately low.

"I'll deal with it." A second voice, and it was fast approaching. "But it will cost you."

The crunch of steps halted close by.

"Are you sure we are alone?" demanded the first speaker. "I thought I heard something just now."

"Keep a grip on your nerves," ordered his companion. "The place is deserted at this hour. No one will spot us."

Something about the second man's voice kept her from standing up and announcing her presence. She held herself still as the statue, praying to go unnoticed.

More muttering, then an oath. "Bloody hell, you would squeeze blood from a stone if you could."

"I am a pragmatic fellow..." Though the answering voice was barely above a raspy whisper, she thought she detected a hint of a Scottish burr to it. "And know my worth."

Caro heard the muted chink of a purse changing hands.

"How do you mean to manage it?" asked the man who had passed over the money.

"Since when have you cared about my methods?" countered his companion. "Suffice it to say, you have no need to worry. As you know, it's in my interest to have the threat eliminated, leaving no trail that can be traced back to us."

There it was again—a hint of the Highlands.

Caro darted a quick look through the carved stone, trying to catch a glimpse of the men. But all she could see was part of one polished boot and the tail of a dark coat.

She shrank back, not daring a second try.

"You want the problem to disappear and so it shall," added the man with the Scottish accent.

There was another short exchange, too low for her to make out the words, and then the steps retreated.

The silence deepened the chill within the shadows, stirring a pebbling of gooseflesh up and down her bare arms.

Repressing a shiver, Caro stayed very still in her hiding place, unwilling to move, unwilling to think...

She had reason to know that Alec McClellan had been involved in some very radical political activities in Scotland— some of which were considered treasonous by the British government. And while he had denied being part of the faction that favored violence as a means to achieve their goals, she had only his word to go on.

True, he had helped her sister and Lord Davenport thwart a sinister French plot at Dunbar Castle, but she was under no illusion that he had shared all his secrets with them.

The dratted man was more tight-lipped than the Sphinx.

"Caro?" Isobel's call interrupted her musings.

Rising quickly, she hurried down a narrow pathway, a lingering sense of unease impelling her to appear as if she had been sitting in a different part of the churchyard.

"Yes, I'm here." Stepping out from behind a granite obelisk, Caro flashed a quick wave.

"We thought perhaps you had been abducted by an evil demon," teased Andover, pointing up at one of the stone gargoyles decorating the flying buttresses.

The innocent remark squeezed the air from Caro's lungs. But she quickly recovered and managed a weak laugh. "What a wild imagination you have, Andy. As if there are devilish creatures lurking in Bath, waiting to swoop down on unsuspecting young ladies."

"I know, I know." He grinned. "It's absurd."

Isobel was staring at her with some concern but said nothing.

Andover's expression slowly pinched to a quizzical frown. "I say, you look awfully pale. Are you feeling unwell?"

"The air was awfully musty inside the nave," she answered. "It was making it hard to breathe."

"Ah, well, then perhaps a little fresh air and a bit of walking will help clear your head." He offered her his arm before belatedly recalling that his other companion was not in the pink of health. "That is, unless you are too fatigued, Miss Urquehart."

"Some tea would be reviving," suggested Caro. "There are several shops on York Street."

"Tea would be lovely," agreed Isobel.

"Splendid!" Andover escorted them through the gate and past the classical façade of the Pump House, his cheerful commentary on the musical practice session relieving Caro of the need to speak.

Her thoughts were still elsewhere, and playing out in a decidedly minor key.

"Was the organ as impressive as promised?" called a voice from the archway of the ancient Roman baths.

Out of the corner of her eye, Caro saw Alec step out from the shadows.

"Oh, it was even more so! The sound was magnificent," answered Isobel, turning to fix her brother with a winsome smile. "We are going to take tea at one of the shops. Would you care to join us?"

As Alec quickened his pace to join them, Caro shot an involuntary look at his boots. *Dark and well polished.* But that described the footwear of most gentlemen.

As for the flutter of his coattails—

She looked away quickly, pretending a sudden interest in the architectural details of the elegant Georgian townhouses, which had been designed by John Wood the Elder and his son John Wood the Younger at the end of the previous century. In the bright afternoon sun, the golden-hued local limestone—known as Bath stone—glowed with a mellow warmth, as if it had been drizzled with melted honey.

And yet, it did nothing to lighten her spirits. A sea squall, dark and blustery, with the rumble of distant thunder deepening the first spitting drops of rain, would have been a more fitting reflection of her mood.

"Did you enjoy the playing, too, Miss Caro?" For some inexplicable reason Alec chose to fall in step beside her instead of his sister. She couldn't help but notice that his gait had the muscular grace of a prowling predator. Deceptively relaxed, but ready to spring for the kill at an instant's notice.

A lordly wolf. With sharp, chiseled nose and ice-blue eyes that seemed lit by an inner fire.

"I have an indifferent ear for music," she replied.

"Indeed?" He cocked an appraising look. "I would have thought a poet would appreciate the nuances of sound."

"Then I must be a bad poet," said Caro a little tartly. "Or your assumptions are mistaken."

"Or perhaps there is some other answer that is not quite so obvious," he said slowly. "The world can rarely be depicted in such stark shades of black and white."

His gaze didn't waver, and Caro could feel it burning like phosphorous against her skin.

"Ah, a lecture on painting, as well as poetry and music?" It was, she knew, a shrewish reply, but she couldn't help herself. The exchange she had heard in the churchyard had left her very unsettled. "It seems we shall cover all of the arts before we reach York Street."

"You seem bent on deliberately misunderstanding me," replied Alec softly. "Is there a specific reason? Aside from the fact that, in general, you find me an odious oaf?"

"I don't..."

When she didn't go on, he murmured an encouraging "Yes?"

"As you say, sir, it's not so black and white."

His mouth quirked, softening the forbidding lines of his face. At that moment he no longer looked like a wild arctic wolf. But nor did he look like a housebroken lap dog.

"Your skill with language seems as sharp as ever," observed Alec. "Which is no surprise. I would imagine that the author of a poem as lyrical as 'Mist-Shrouded Moors' would never be at a loss for words."

"H-how did you know I wrote that?" Shocked, Caro released his arm and came to an abrupt halt on the walkway. "I swear, I shall throttle Anna when she returns from Russia. She promised she wouldn't tell a soul."

"Anna didn't tell me."

"Then how—"

"It was simply an educated guess," he replied. "You said it was by McAdam, and I happen to own a copy of his complete works." He fixed her with a speculative stare. "There seemed little reason for the subterfuge unless you had written it yourself."

"Hmmph, I see that I shall have to work on becoming a better liar," grumbled Caro.

He didn't smile. "Concentrate your talents on learning to become an even better poet. There are enough accomplished liars in the world."

She wasn't sure how to answer. *He thought her a good poet?* Her stomach gave a queer little lurch.

"Come, we had better catch up with the others." Taking her arm, Alec lengthened his stride.

"McAdam is very good," she said in a small voice, as they crossed to the other side of the street. "It is poetic justice that I was caught trying to fob off my own verse as his."

"You are better," said Alec brusquely.

Her foot slipped on one of the smooth paving stones, pitching her up against him.

Wrapping an arm around her waist, he steadied her stumble.

Caro was instantly aware of myriad sensations—the lithe strength of his muscles, the solid breadth of his shoulders, the subtle scent of bay rum pervading the crisp linen of his cravat.

"Don't tell me the intrepid Miss Caro Sloane is going to swoon again?" he murmured dryly.

She realized that her legs had gone all soft and floppy like those of a rag doll, and she was clinging to his coat like a helpless peagoose. It would have been utterly mortifying if it hadn't been so utterly silly.

Stifling a laugh in the soft folds of merino wool, she managed to say, "Oh, dear, I seem to be making a complete cake of myself. You must think me an idiot."

Or worse.

A flash of amusement accentuated the sapphire highlights in his slate-blue eyes, giving hint that there was sunlight behind the stormclouds. "You are," he drawled, "far too interesting to be an idiot."

"I dare not try to think of what other words you might consider more appropriate."

"Even with your impressive vocabulary, I doubt you would come close to guessing," he agreed.

Oh, but it was a very tantalizing game to play. As well as a little frightening.

"That sounds like a warning," she said.

Rather than reply, he handed her off with an exaggerated bow to Andover, who was waiting at the tea shop entrance.

"You aren't going to join us, Alec?" asked his sister. She sounded disappointed.

"Not today. I have some matters to attend to."

Caro watched him march away with a purposeful stride, leaving a swirl of dust in his wake. A poet, she mused wryly, might describe it as kicking up sparks and smoke—Alec McClellan attacked everything he did with an intensity that scorched anything in his path.

Including me.

She wished she could shake off the unwilling attraction. Like a moth, she seemed inexorably drawn to fire. And had been forever since she could remember. Her father had often counseled her on the danger, and all of a sudden she could hear the whisper of his long-ago words.

Flames have a sinuous, seductive beauty, poppet. But they must be treated with caution. If you aren't careful and try to snatch them up and hold them close, you risk being badly burned.

"Miss Caro?" Andover's tentative query pulled her back to the present moment.

"Sorry," she replied, turning her gaze back to him. "I was simply trying to discern whether I recognized the gentleman who just hailed Lord Strathcona. Do you know him?"

Andover squinted into the bright sunlight, but the two men had already disappeared around the corner. "I didn't catch his face. But you know how small Bath is. Whoever the fellow is, I am sure that we shall meet up with him very soon."

"McClellan."

Alec looked around abruptly. Only his radical Scottish friends called him by his surname rather than his title.

"Thayer," he murmured, as the man fell in step with him and inclined a polite nod. "I wouldn't have expected to encounter you here."

"I might say the same." A smile, showing a flash of perfectly aligned pearly teeth.

Which Alec was sorely tempted to ram down the fellow's gullet.

"So, what does bring you to the favorite retreat of England's upper classes?" went on Thayer. Dropping his voice a notch, he added, "Have you shrugged off your so-called moral principles as well as your support of our cause?"

"You are one to speak of moral principles," growled Alec. Thayer had once been a close friend and comrade, but rumors concerning the seduction of an innocent young lady and the demand of money to hush up the affair had caused the initial rift between them.

"Still gnawing on that old bone?" Thayer's smile remained in place. "Your old friends think your betrayal of our goal is far more serious than any of the vague accusations that have been hurled at me."

"Betrayal is a serious charge indeed," replied Alec. "If I were you, I'd be careful how you use it."

Recent rumors about Thayer's activities had stirred even more serious concerns. If there was even a grain of truth to them . . .

But surely his former friend could not have sunk to such depths of depravity.

"Don't you ever tire of parsing words and their nuances, McClellan? Or is that how to justify your fear of putting those fancy phrases you mouth into action?"

"Since I take responsibility for my actions, I consider what I say very carefully," he countered. "People suffer and people die if one is too selfish to consider the consequences."

"A very pretty speech," murmured Thayer, his voice rich with mockery. "But then, you were always exceedingly good at appearing eloquent and high minded."

"And you were always exceedingly good at appearing charming and sincere."

A low laugh. "Dear me, are we going to continue trading insults indefinitely?"

"No," answered Alec. "Because we are going to part company here." He turned at the corner, hoping to put an end to the meeting. But like a cocklebur, Thayer clung to his coattails.

"Anxious to be rid of me?"

Alec kept his head down and quickened his pace. Perhaps if he didn't answer, Thayer would grow tired of baiting him and go away.

"Do me a single favor, for old time's sake, that's all I ask," said Thayer after several more silent strides. "And then I'll take myself off."

He remained silent.

"Our group has a traitor in its midst," went on his former comrade. "I was hoping you would tell me the name of your private contact in Edinburgh. He may prove helpful in unmasking the guilty party."

"What makes you think I'd share such sensitive information with you? One errant whisper and the fellow would be dancing the hangman's jig on an English gallows."

"Because, despite our differences on the means of achieving the end, we do have a common goal."

Alec hesitated, but only for an instant. Violence only kindled violence, and despite his silvery tongue, Thayer had proven in the past that he didn't care who was hurt as long as he got what he wanted.

"Go to the Devil," he muttered. "We have chosen different paths, and whatever we once shared has been left in the dust."

"What a pity you feel that way." If anything, Thayer pressed closer until their shoulders were nearly touching. "By the by, was that your sister you were walking with? I had heard she had grown from a pretty little child into an even prettier young lady."

A clench of fear squeezed the air from Alec's lungs.

"I see the compliments were not misplaced. You must introduce us, next time we are all together."

Recovering his breath, Alec put a hand on the other man's sleeve. To the casual onlooker it might have appeared a friendly gesture, but his vise-like grip was almost tight enough to crack bone.

"I suggest you leave my sister alone, else the misplaced thing will be your liver. Because I shall tear it out of your body with my bare hands and feed it to the crows."

Chapter Six

Caro added a dash of sugar to her morning coffee, wishing there were some magical powder to slip into the teapot to sweeten her mother's grumblings. That they were already in fine fettle at breakfast did not bode well for the rest of the day.

"And what a pity," went on Lady Trumbull, "that of all the eligible bachelors who might appear in Bath, Fate would have to bring us that *dreadful* man from the north."

"Lord Strathcona?" responded Caro. "*Dreadful* seems a rather harsh word, Mama. If you recall, he did play a key role in rescuing Anna."

"Hmmph." Lady Trumbull gave another aggrieved sniff. "Please do not mention that horrid house party. I would rather *not* be reminded of our stay in Scotland."

"Anna did end up marrying a marquess," pointed out Caro.

"True." Another disgruntled sigh from the baroness. "But I was *so* hoping for a prince."

Caro bit back a laugh. "Anna and Prince Gunther would not have suited each other. Not at all."

"Nonsense! You girls have been reading too many silly novels about love and romance. Princes do not grow on trees..."

Thank God for that, thought Caro. Otherwise her mother would have her making a tedious tour of every garden in England.

A scowl pinched at her mother's mouth, then suddenly gave way to wistful smile. "But they do, on occasion, visit Bath to take the spa waters. Perhaps one—"

"If one does arrive in town, he would likely be advanced in years, Mama," interjected Caro, determined to nip this particular matchmaking idea in the bud. Thank goodness she had been able to cut off any hints that Andover might be brought up to scratch. Even her mother had to admit that if the fellow hadn't succumbed to Anna's winsome charms, the youngest Sloane was unlikely to fare any better.

"Maturity is an excellent quality in a husband," countered Lady Trumbull after a moment of thought.

"You are quite right, Mama." She flashed a winning smile. "Why, perhaps *you* should think of setting your cap at him, if such a paragon of perfection appears."

Lady Trumbull's eyes lit with a speculative gleam. "My figure is still rather pleasing..."

Exhaling a sigh of relief, Caro quickly excused herself to make a visit to the local bookshop and run some other errands, leaving the baroness murmuring to herself about the latest styles in ballgowns and bonnets.

Caro couldn't blame her mother for wanting to see all her daughters well settled. Life had been hard for the family after their father's death. Money—or rather, the lack of it—had been a constant threat shadowing their every move, like a lurking wolf with snapping jaws. Society was not kind to young ladies without dowries, and the thought of being swallowed up into genteel poverty had been terrifying for the baroness.

Now, of course, with Olivia married to the exceedingly wealthy Earl of Wrexham, such fears had disappeared.

But old habits were hard to change. And not only for her mother. The unsmiling face of Alec McClellan came to mind...

Determined to push such musings aside for the moment, Caro entered the bookshop and made her way past the display tables to the nook-and-cranny comfort of the back rooms.

Squeezing between two towering cabinets of architectural prints and a chipped Argand lamp, she pulled a book down from the crammed shelves, setting a cloud of dust motes to dancing through the blade of sunlight cutting in through the diamond-paned window. Apparently poetry was not nearly as popular as guidebooks to the area or the latest novels from Minerva Press, for the small alcove was deserted, save for herself.

She was not unhappy to have a bit of solitude, for even though she understood her mother's concerns, the none-too-subtle hints about marriage always left her feeling unsettled. But the chance to spend a quiet hour perusing the bookshop's excellent selection of verse was already proving to be a balm for the spirit.

Setting the hard-to-find edition of McAdam's complete works on the window ledge, Caro then added a slender volume of odes by another Scottish poet whose work was unknown to her.

Was Alec familiar with his work? she wondered as she reached for a third book.

No doubt he would *not* approve of her current find. The odes of William Wordsworth and his fellow Lake Poets were so quintessentially English in their celebration of Nature and all its many splendors.

Opening to a random page, she began to read aloud, "It is a beauteous evening, calm and free—"

"What a singular bookshop," murmured a voice behind her. "Why, even the very walls resonate with lyric verse. And in a wonderfully beguiling voice, I might add."

Flustered, Caro spun around so quickly the little volume slipped from her grasp.

The gentleman moved and deftly caught it before it hit the floor. "Fie be it that such lovely words would suffer any knocks or bruises." He buffed the spine with his sleeve before holding it out to her. "Forgive me for startling you."

"Th-thank you, sir," she replied, trying hard not to gape like a mooncalf schoolgirl. With the angled light feathering his face in a soft caress, he looked like a Greek god. The smoothly sculpted features—straight nose, high cheekbones, tapered chin, framed by ringlets of hair the color of burnished bronze—radiated a classical beauty, saved from being too effeminate by the strong shape of his full, firm mouth.

Wrenching her gaze away from his lips, Caro hugged the book tight to her chest. "That was very quick thinking and kind of you to keep it from suffering any harm."

"It was the least I could do, seeing as I was the cause of the trouble," he replied, quirking that marvelous mouth into a smile. "Please assure me that you won't hold it against me."

"I..." A quick breath helped still her fluttery nerves. "I shall consider it," she answered, hoping to appear more composed than she felt.

"Is there nothing I can do to win back your good graces?" Spotting the two books she had placed on a rather precarious perch by the window, he tucked them under his arm. "Perhaps I can start by holding these until you are ready to proceed to the sales counter, Miss..."

"Caro Sloane," she replied.

"I am delighted to make your acquaintance, Miss Caro Sloane. I am Edward Thayer. Though I apologize again for the circumstances."

"No apologies necessary, Mr. Thayer. All's well that ends well," replied Caro.

"Ah, a young lady who can quote Shakespeare as well as poetry? How very lovely." A pause as he slanted her a meaningful look through his gold-tipped lashes. "Very lovely, indeed."

It was a handsome compliment—perhaps just a touch too handsome. His clever hands weren't the only fast things about Mr. Edward Thayer, she decided. His tongue was moving a little too quickly as well.

"You are from Scotland?" she asked, steering the conversation to a more proper subject. His voice had a northern accent, though the burr was much softer than Alec's flinty tones.

"Yes, but I spent several years at Oxford studying philosophy."

"You are a scholar?" asked Caro.

The smile now showed a peek of perfectly white teeth. "Among other things."

Including a practiced charmer, skilled at casting flirtations at the opposite sex.

She decided not to rise to the bait.

After taking a long look within the book of Wordsworth

Odes, she snapped the covers shut. "I think I am finished with my shopping," she announced, moving for the archway of the alcove.

"So soon?" asked Thayer, following along.

"I have some errands to run for my mother."

"Perhaps you would have time for a cup of tea before you do so, Miss Sloane," he pressed.

"The proper form of address is Miss Caro, as I am the youngest of three sisters," she pointed out. "As for tea, that would not be proper, sir, seeing as we have not been formally introduced."

"Quite right. Again I must apologize," he said contritely. "I confess to being a bit rusty on English protocol."

Caro softened somewhat in her resolve to remain aloof. "The strictures can be confining," she said. "But you must understand that a lady cannot be too careful."

"Of course. It's just that I saw you at the teashop yesterday with Lord Strathcona, did I not? So I assumed..." The pause seemed deliberately drawn out. "Well, never mind. It isn't important."

His intention had clearly been to hook her curiosity, and this time she couldn't resist rising to take the lure. "You are acquainted with Lord Strathcona, sir?"

"Yes." He blew out his cheeks with a mournful sigh. "We were close in the past, but alas, a recent falling-out has severed the friendship."

That was not overly hard to imagine, thought Caro. Alec was not an easy man to get along with under the best of circumstances. And yet, despite his faults, she had always found him to be scrupulously fair in his assessment of both others and himself. So she couldn't believe he was mean-spirited or petty in his dealings with others.

Which raised the question of what had caused the quarrel.

"It seems that you, too, know His Lordship," went on Thayer.

Caro nodded. "We met at a hunting party given by his cousin, Lady Dunbar."

"How very fortunate for you to be included in one of her gatherings," murmured Thayer. "The countess is known as a superb hostess who sets a sumptuous table."

"It was a memorable experience," said Caro absently, her thoughts still dwelling on what might have caused the rift between the two men.

"Oh?" He seemed hopeful of eliciting greater detail.

"Yes," she said flatly, as they strolled back to the main room. Perhaps it was something about the Scottish burr, however soft, that was scraping against her skin, but at that moment Caro found herself unwilling to satisfy his curiosity.

"Did you enjoy Scotland?" To his credit, Thayer didn't press, but turned the talk to general pleasantries while Caro completed her purchases and directed that the package be delivered to her residence.

He opened the shop door with a gentlemanly flourish as she turned to leave and accompanied her outside. "I hope I shall be permitted the pleasure of continuing our acquaintance, Miss Caro."

"Does that mean you will be staying in Bath long, Mr. Thayer?" she inquired.

"Certainly long enough to ask for you to save me a dance at next week's Assemblies."

"Very well, sir, I shall." The thought of twirling across the ballroom floor in the arms of a handsome stranger ought to ignite something other than than a flutter of wariness. And yet, despite his striking looks and smooth charm, she found herself feeling a little guarded. "And now, if you will excuse me, I need to pay a visit to the millinery shop and pick up a few sundries for my mother."

Thayer took the dismissal with good grace. Bowing politely, he murmured, "Until later, then."

Caro paused to adjust her shawl, using the gesture to watch him in the window until he disappeared around the corner of the next street. The reflection seemed to mirror her own reactions—the image was just blurry enough to make the details impossible to discern.

For some reason, one of the aphorisms her father was fond of repeating popped to mind. *Beware of Greeks bearing gifts.*

For all his scholarly detachment from the real world, the baron had been surprisingly astute in judging people and had impressed upon his daughters the importance of being careful about whom to trust.

The phrase meant that one should be exceedingly careful when dealing with those who might be the enemy. Perhaps it was the hint of the Highland accent stirring her misgivings, but until she knew more about Mr. Edward Thayer, Caro intended to keep her guard up.

Alec shifted in the shadows of the arched entryway, watching his former friend take his leave from Caro. A graceful bow, a winsome smile—oh, yes, the smooth-as-silk Edward Thayer certainly knew how to make himself appealing to the fairer sex.

It was, he supposed, no surprise that such practiced flirtations should please her. Even from a distance, Caro's smile was evident.

Pinching back a scowl, he edged deeper into the recess between the marble columns, unwilling to be spotted. What young lady wouldn't respond to flattery? And yet, he would have hoped...

Hoped for what?

That she might be different and see the true serpent beneath the superficial glitter of its golden scales?

That a high-spirited, vivacious beauty might find a gruff, gravel-mannered introvert more pleasing company than a gentleman who possessed all the social graces?

Alec pulled a face, cursing himself in several different dialects of Gaelic for being such a buffle-headed fool. Yes, he had been a bloody fool.

But only a complete lackwit made the same mistake twice.

He lingered in the shade, allowing ample time for Caro to be gone, before emerging from his hiding spot and continuing on his round of errands. A length of lace from the mantua-maker for his aunt, medicinal draughts from the apothecary for his sister, a volume of American poetry from the bookshop for himself... a half hour later, duty done and the parcels deposited in the entrance foyer of their townhouse, Alec tucked the book in his pocket and slipped out again, preferring an interlude of solitude to joining his family for the midday meal.

Making his way to the end of Great Pulteney Street, Alec skirted around the Sydney Tavern and entered the famous gardens to its rear. A sprawling, picturesque parkland of formal plantings and wild, natural beauty, the grounds were dotted with stone pavilions, scenic grottos, and refreshment boxes for dining during the various evening entertainments. He cut away from the main walkway and chose a path that brought him to a more isolated spot overlooking the Kennet and Avon Canal.

The soothing sound of the breeze ruffling through the water and the leafy trees made it a perfect place for a quiet hour of reading.

Unfortunately, someone else seemed to have had the same idea, for as he rounded the rock outcropping at the crest of the hill, he caught a glimpse of muslin skirts stretched out on the grass.

Swearing under his breath, Alec was about to retreat when the lady looked around.

"Oh!" Caro hastily snapped shut the book in her lap.

"My apologies," he said. "I did not mean to intrude. I had no idea you were here."

"No, of course you didn't. How could you?" She seemed a little flustered, and as she looked down to fiddle with her skirts, the flare of emotion in her eyes wasn't at all what he expected.

Annoyance would be understandable, given their past history. As would defiance. Or sarcasm. This reaction was very different, though he couldn't explain why.

"But I suppose you can't be blamed for thinking I was going to hurl sharp words at you," added Caro, still fingering the fabric.

"The words don't worry me. It's when you start looking around for pointy objects that I start to become a trifle nervous."

"Am I that bad?" Her smile was a little tentative, which only made her look more endearing. "You have to admit, I never resorted to swinging one of those ancient Scottish broadswords on display at Dunbar Castle at your head."

"That's only because they were bolted to the wall."

"True. And besides, they looked awfully heavy. How

very embarrassing it would have been to slice off my own toes, instead of your ears."

His earlier mordant brooding was forgotten in the enjoyment of their verbal dueling. The thrusts and parries had brought a bloom of color to her cheeks and a martial spark to her gaze. She looked like...

Poetry in motion.

"Rather my ears than my..." Clearing his throat with a cough, Alec quickly looked around for a distraction. He spotted the corner of the book peeking out from between the folds of muslin. "What are you reading?"

"Oh, er, nothing."

He angled his head. It was definitely something.

Caro shifted just a fraction, causing a pencil to fall from her lap.

Ah, a notebook—it was a notebook.

"Are you working on a poem?"

"Just scribbling some rough ideas," she mumbled, making a show of searching through the wispy grass.

"Might I see them?"

"What?" Her head jerked up. "No!"

His jaw tightened. The rebuff stung, more than he cared to admit. The playful banter had led him to think that maybe...

"Quite right," said Alec through clenched teeth. "Why share your creative efforts with me?" He retreated a step and pushed back an overhanging branch from his path. "Forgive me for interrupting your writing. I shall leave you and your Muse in peace."

"Wait!" cried Caro impulsively.

He hesitated, his face half in shadow from the leaves.

Had she merely imagined the wounded look in his eyes? The idea that Alec McClellan could be hurt by anything she said was a little absurd, and yet, in the instant he had turned away, a spasm had swirled their slate-blue color to the strangest hue.

"That is," she faltered, "you need not feel compelled to leave, sir. There is room here for all three of us." A rueful grimace tugged at the corners of her mouth. "And as the Muse never seems to stay for long, it will likely be just the two of us."

"An intruder is likely to make Her even more skittish," replied Alec. But he made no further move to leave.

"Yes, well, you know females—we are all such flighty creatures, aren't we?" she murmured. It made no sense, but she couldn't resist bantering with him, despite his solemn expression.

His mouth twitched ever so slightly. "Not all. There are a few of the fairer sex who don't take wing at the first sign of adversity." He paused. "And writing certainly tests the mettle of anyone—man or woman—who is brave enough to try it."

She fingered the point of the pencil, leaving a smudge of graphite on her thumb. "Do you compose verses, Lord Strathcona?"

"Just scribbles," he said, echoing her earlier assertion.

"I—" Caro caught herself.

Alec dropped his arm and stepped free of the shadows. "You what?"

"I shouldn't say it."

"I've rarely known you to be rendered speechless."

She blew out a gusty sigh. "What you really mean is that you've rarely known me to show any restraint in voicing what I think, no matter how outrageous."

"Don't put words in my mouth," he chided, but gently. There was no sting to the reproof.

"I was going to say that I should like to see your scribbles. However, I don't suppose you'll let me."

He moved away from the bushes bordering the footpath and seated himself on the grass near her. "I could reply that what's good for the goose is good for the gander."

"You could," agreed Caro. "That would be only fair."

Leaning back on his elbows, Alec looked up and appeared to be more interested in contemplating the scudding clouds than in responding.

After a prolonged pause, she spoke again. "To be honest..."

Still no discernible reaction from him.

Caro wondered whether to go on. Peeling off a protective layer might not be a wise move. The last thing she wished was to make herself vulnerable to Alec McClellan.

A skittering of sunshine broke through the clouds, and for a moment the play of light over his profile seemed to bring out softer nuances in the chiseled planes.

Or maybe it was just wishful thinking.

He turned his head slightly and, on catching her staring, raised an inquiring brow.

"To be honest, I refused your request because I feared... well, I feared you might laugh at my efforts."

The brow remained hovering in an elegant golden arch. "But you know I never laugh."

So why was it that the twinkle of mirth showing through his lashes caused her breath to catch in her throat?

"Th-that's not entirely accurate," she managed to croak. "You laughed in Scotland." A pause. "Once, if I recall correctly."

"It was more of an ironic snort," he murmured. "Your

brother-in-law had just accused me of being a spy and an assassin."

"With good reason, I might add," pointed out Caro. "You have to admit that the circumstances looked awfully incriminating."

She didn't add that it was on account of her clandestine surveillance that he was exonerated. They both were aware of the fact, and while some men might have been grateful, she secretly suspected that with Alec, it wasn't a point in her favor.

"Never mind that." His brusque retort seemed to confirm the surmise. "We were talking about your poetry, a far more interesting subject."

"Not really," she replied quickly. "I meant it when I said I had only jotted down a few scribbles. They really aren't worth sharing. Aside from the opening stanza, there are mostly just rough ideas and a few descriptive words I'd like to work in."

He held his hand out for the notebook.

"Must I?" she questioned.

His fingers waggled a come-hither command.

"Really, sir, it is like asking me to strip off my bath towel," she protested. "I shall feel embarrassingly naked."

Alec's gaze sharpened and as it flicked up and then down, she suddenly had the unnerving sensation that he could see right through the layers of cotton and lace, could penetrate right through the depth of flesh and bones, could delve right down to her very essence.

Her body began to feel hot all over, as if a glowing coal had rubbed over every inch of skin.

"You are suggesting," drawled Alec, "that if I were a gentleman, I would not demand to see the verse-in-progress?"

She nodded.

His lips curled up at the corners. "Most people would assure you that I am no gentleman."

"Well, are you or aren't you?"

Alec plucked the book from her skirts and started thumbing through the first few blank pages. "I leave that for you to decide."

Drat the man. She wanted to feel annoyed with him, but the only emotion churning within her chest was a sense of nervous anticipation. She found herself watching his face very intently.

His fingers stilled as he reached her penciled notes. Dropping his head, he studied the first page for what felt like forever.

Damnation. Caro wished she could see his eyes. Even then, she suspected that she would see nothing he didn't want her to see.

He flicked to the second page. And then the third.

When finally she could stand it no longer, she made a small sound in the back of her throat.

Alec responded with a grunt. After a sliver of silence, he asked, "May I borrow your pencil for a moment?"

A hundred—nay, a thousand—questions hovered on her lips, but she handed it over without comment.

For a moment, the only sound between them was the *scratch, scratch* of the point on the paper.

Snapping the covers shut, Alec placed the book on the ground beside him, carefully aligning the spine with the bent blades of grass.

"I must be going," he announced as he rose and dusted the seat of his trousers. "If I spot the Muse eating a strawberry tart at one of the teashops on Milsom Street, I shall tell her to return to keep you company."

Caro wasn't quite sure she liked his newfound sense of humor.

With that, he gave a small salute and sauntered off.

Dignity demanded that she wait until he was well out of sight before snatching up the notebook. Paging furiously through the blank sheets, Caro quickly skimmed over her notes.

Alec had added a few entries to the list entitled "Intriguingly Poetical Words." She couldn't argue with any of them—though the last did make her cheeks flame.

As he had no doubt intended.

Muttering under her breath, Caro was about to tuck the book back in her reticule when she noticed that a string of words had been penciled in at the very end of the section, so lightly as to be nearly illegible. Angling the paper to catch the light, she leaned in for a closer look.

You are very good.

And with experience you may even become great.

She traced a finger over the faint lettering, unsure whether to laugh or gnash her teeth.

"Impossible man," she huffed. "It's not so easy for a young lady to experience the sort of Meaningful Things that she needs to know in order to write powerful poetry."

A smile slowly smoothed away her grimace. "But then again, I've never been daunted by a difficult challenge."

Chapter Seven

The weekly Assembly was even more crowded than the previous gathering. The dowager Duchess of Ainsley had arrived in town to take the waters, accompanied by an assortment of young relatives to keep her amused. Their party had added a welcome number of enthusiastic dancers to the festivities, and for the last hour, Caro had been spinning through every one of the lively reels.

As the Master of Ceremonies signaled the musicians to strike up the next set of dances, she slipped into the shelter of the potted palms, wanting a quiet moment to compose her wayward thoughts.

She shouldn't be darting glances at the entrance every few moments, wondering if a certain figure with a dark-as-a-stormcloud scowl would make an appearance.

Not that Alec McClellan wasn't capable of a sly-as-a-devil smile when he so chose.

Caro felt a flutter in her chest on recalling the surprising flashes of humor that had lit up his face yesterday afternoon. Like flashes of lightning, they had left her a bit shaken by their blinding brilliance. Blinking back images of those sinfully attractive lips, she rubbed her palms over her bare arms, hoping the soft kidskin would dispel the sudden prickling of gooseflesh.

Stop mooning over a man who is too difficult, Caro chided to herself.

And perhaps too dangerous.

The meeting with him in Sydney Gardens and the mention of the events that had taken place at Dunbar Castle had compelled her to give serious thought to the disturbing exchange she had overheard in the Abbey churchyard. The Scottish accent had been unmistakable—that, and the reminder of Alec's past involvement in dangerous political activities, sent a slight shiver down her spine.

Could a man who appreciated the passions of poetry also be a man willing to do whatever it took to accomplish his objectives—even if it called for committing violence?

Caro swallowed hard, her throat suddenly feeling dry as dust. She might be inexperienced in many ways, but she knew enough of the world from her family's unconventional travels to understand that passion was a powerful force for both light and dark.

"What dark thoughts are bringing such shadows to your lovely face?"

She looked up to meet Thayer's inquiring gaze.

"This is supposed to be an evening of merriment." He held out a glass of champagne. "Come, you look as though you need a dash of effervescence added to your spirits."

She accepted the wine and took a small sip. The coolness did feel good on her lips.

"You ought not be hiding your charms under a bush, as it were," he went on, brushing a frond from his evening coat.

"I wished to take a respite from the heat and crowd of the dancing," she replied.

Thayer offered his arm. "Then I daresay a stroll out on the terrace would offer a more pleasant interlude than huddling in the greenery."

Though she would have preferred to remain alone with her thoughts, Caro reluctantly accepted his invitation. There was really nothing offensive about his manner, which was perfectly pleasant and polite, despite being a trifle overdone. So it seemed only fair to give him a second chance at changing her first impression.

Whatever thorn was pricking at her consciousness was likely the fault of her own straying into a mental briar patch.

"It is a very mild night, is it not?" remarked Thayer as he guided her through the French doors. "With such a clear sky, I daresay the chances are good that tomorrow will dawn bright and sunny."

"I daresay you are right," she replied, hoping the conversation wouldn't stay mired in boring platitudes. Debating the likelihood of rain was even more tedious than discussing which type of sleeve was the most *au courant* choice for a ballgown. "Though I warn you, English weather can be changeable. Though not as violently so as in Scotland."

"We can be a country of extremes," commented Thayer. "In both our climate and our temperament."

Her ears perked up. An interesting assessment. Perhaps he was more astute than she had imagined.

"Indeed?" she murmured, casting him a sidelong smile in further invitation to go on.

"Alas, yes. Sudden storms can blow in with little warning, and their fierceness can cause great harm, especially for those who are not used to them." He blew out a long sigh.

"I fear the same can be said for our people. The harsh conditions have made the Scots very tough, unyielding and independent—sometimes to a fault."

"You paint a brutally honest portrait," said Caro, deciding to test his candor. "Does the brush also capture your own likeness?"

He grinned. "I am, of course, the exception. Perhaps the several years I spent at Oxford helped rub off the rough edges. In any case, I would describe myself as a man of moderation in all ways."

They were passing a pair of arched windows and something appeared to catch his eye within the glitter and gaiety of the Assembly room. "Unlike," he added softly, "my esteemed countryman."

Caro spotted Alec hovering in the shadows of the side saloon. "You mean Lord Strathcona?"

Thayer hesitated. "I do not wish to speak ill of a former friend, but he has a history of instability." A cough. "Some might call it worse."

"Worse?" she repeated.

"Suffice it to say, a young, gently bred lady would be prudent to be on guard in his presence."

"Are you saying that a lady would have fears for her virtue?" she demanded.

The answer was more than eloquent. Lifting his shoulders, Thayer made a pained face.

It took great restraint for Caro to hold back a snort. Whatever Alec's faults, he would never—*never*—act dishonorably toward the opposite sex. The certainty of that resonated right to the very depth of her heart.

"I think," she said, once her emotions were under control, "that you must be mistaken."

"I assure you, I wish I were," replied Thayer mournfully. "You don't believe me?"

Not for an instant, she thought. But aloud, she gave a more tempered response. "No. Having some acquaintance with His Lordship, I find it hard to accept such an unrelentingly black portrait of the man."

"That you should find a dark-as-the-devil heart impossible to imagine is not surprising, Miss Caro. No young lady should have any concept of what evil may lurk inside a man."

Caro was tempted to tell him that he had been reading too many horrid novels. But something in his eyes made her bite her tongue. It was just a fleeting spark, and it might only have been a quirk of candlelight refracted through the windowglass. However, in that instant, the red-gold flare seemed tinged with malice.

"I—I defer to your greater knowledge of such things," she murmured softly.

His expression immediately softened, and his winsome smile made her question again whether she was overreacting.

As her sisters were wont to point out, a penchant for drama was one of her shortcomings.

"I am glad to think I have been able to offer a helpful warning," responded Thayer. He said no more.

She nodded, glad to let the subject drop. Thayer might only be misguided, not malicious, but there was something about him that stirred the hairs at the nape of her neck to stand on end.

What motive would he have to blacken Alec's name?

She walked on in silence, only half hearing Thayer's description of his visit to the ancient Roman baths beneath the

Pump House as she pondered the question, as well as an equally compelling one.

How many Scotsmen were currently visiting Bath?

As an aspiring poet, she considered herself attuned to the nuances of language, both written and spoken. And the more she heard his voice, the more it stirred misgivings. The man she had overheard had spoken too softly for her to be sure. But...

Thayer slowed his steps. "I fear I am boring you," he said contritely.

"No, no, not at all." Caro forced a laugh. "I was simply trying to recall the history lesson from my father about the Roman ruins here in town. I believe the baths were dedicated to the goddess Minerva." That the ancient deity represented wisdom was, hoped Caro, a good omen.

"Correct," replied Thayer. "But forgive me, you have come here to enjoy an evening of dancing, not to listen to me prose on about history. Shall we go back inside?"

"I suppose we ought to. I am promised to the dowager's grandson for the cotillion," she answered. As they passed through the open doors, she looked around and waved to the young man, who quickly left his friends to come claim her hand.

"Enjoy your dancing," said Thayer with a polite bow. "I must take my leave from tonight's festivities, but I look forward to continuing our interesting conversations, Miss Caro."

"As do I, sir." She batted her lashes. But not for the reasons he might think.

An attempted abduction, a suspicious meeting, a handsome stranger whispering dire warnings—there was something havey-cavey afoot in Bath, and all at once the questions needling at the back of her head sharpened to a sudden realization.

What better way to pursue both the adventure and the worldly experience she craved than to take on the challenge of discovering what was going on?

Alec tore his gaze away from the sight of Caro clearly enjoying Thayer's company. Her face was flushed, her eyes were sparkling. *With pleasure, no doubt.* The man was a manipulative spider and knew just how to how to ensnare impressionable young ladies in a web of seductive charm.

He had thought that perhaps Caro was different. That she, of all people, would be perceptive enough to see through the superficial glitter to the heart of darkness...

His mouth quirked in a quick grimace.

And why was that?

Because she could pen poetry that seemed to understand the nuances of human emotion?

"Stop scowling, Alec." Gliding into the recessed alcove, Isobel set a hand on his sleeve, and gave him a playful pinch. "You are supposed to be enjoying yourself."

He responded with a wordless grunt.

"Is there a reason you are in a foul mood?"

"You know I do not care for these frivolous gatherings."

"You are far too serious," she chided. "You need to loosen your cravat and have..." Her gaze suddenly locked on a figure moving along the perimeter of the dance floor. "Is that Mr. Edward Thayer? How odd. I wonder what brings him to Bath?"

So do I, thought Alec.

Isobel hesitated, following Thayer's progress until he exited the room. "You've never explained to me why the two of you ceased to be friends," she finally said.

"That's none of your concern," Alec answered, a little more sharply than he intended.

She slanted a quizzical look at him, but didn't press the matter. "You may dislike dancing, but I know you are not averse to enjoying the romantic and picturesque splendors of Nature. Lord Andover has proposed having a picnic in Spring Gardens tomorrow, which is reached by taking a boat across the River Avon—"

"I can't," interrupted Alec.

"Oh, you are not allowed to say no," announced Isobel airily. "It will be a lovely outing, and Andover is already asking Caro as we speak. We need you to make up the correct numbers."

"We aren't sitting down to a formal supper," he said softly. "Besides, my absence won't be a disappointment to her."

"But it will be to me," she said. "I've seen so little of you since you arrived here. Please say you will come."

He was about to refuse again when the recollection of rough hands reaching out to seize her suddenly leapt to mind.

His heart skipped a beat, as if a steel fist had caught hold of it for an instant and given a warning squeeze.

"Very well," he muttered.

"Thank you." Fluffing her skirts, Isobel made to take her leave. "Don't look so glum. Chances are you might actually enjoy the outing."

As she shifted the picnic hamper on the slatted seat, a sudden gust caught Caro's bonnet strings and swirled them into a flapping tangle of azure-colored silk.

"Mmmph!" A laugh cleared the tail end of ribbon from

her mouth. "Andy, this outing was an absolutely splendid idea," she announced, tilting her cheeks up to the sun. "Crossing the river feels like an adventure."

The ferryman's boat bobbed through the rippling currents. Gold-flecked sparks skimmed over the water, their flashes warming the Pulteney Bridge to the color of melted butter.

"What a lovely view," exclaimed Isobel, clamping a hand on her hat to keep it from blowing off. "Why, it looks even more charming from this perspective."

"It was modeled after the famous Ponte Vecchio in Florence," explained Alec.

"I should like to travel some day," mused Caro. "To Florence, to Rome, to Venice, and beyond." Her sigh was quickly swallowed by the breeze. "Such historic places are so rich in history and fascinating sights that they can't help but be inspiring."

"Many a great sonnet has been penned about those fabled cities," said Alec softly.

Was he teasing her? A sidelong glance told her nothing. All she could see was the dark silhouette of his profile backlit by the bright blue sky.

"I can well imagine that," she responded, deciding to answer from the heart. "How could a poet not be moved by thinking of all the experiences the city's stones have witnessed?"

"Oh, I daresay there are poems written about Bath," said Andover cheerfully. "Though I can't seem to recall any."

Isobel giggled.

"Obviously they weren't very memorable," murmured Caro.

"No matter. This outing is something I shall not soon

forget," said Isobel. "A glorious day, good friends, and the company of my dear brother, whom I see so rarely when I am at home."

"You forgot to mention the fresh strawberry tart and clotted cream," pointed out Andover.

"That's because if our cook keeps feeding me such rich treats, I shall soon be plump as a Strasbourg goose."

"You're still naught but skin and bones," growled Alec.

His sister shot him a reproving look. "There is no need to dwell on my illness, Alec. The danger has passed."

His expression might be unreadable, but now that she had decided to have a closer look at the recent havey-cavey events, Caro had every intention of quizzing him on what more he had learned about the attack as soon as she could get him alone.

Isobel turned back to Andover and huffed a sigh. "Pay no heed to my brother. He fusses like a mother hen, but the truth is, I am usually hearty as a horse."

"You look nothing like a hen or a horse, Miss Urquehart." He winked. "Or a Strasbourg goose."

"As you see, Andy is always the perfect gentleman," said Caro.

The casual comment, though clearly said in fun, seemed to make Alec flinch. Looking away with an inward sigh, she wondered whether she would ever understand his odd quirks and moods.

Not that it mattered. There were any number of jests about the incomprehensible workings of the female mind. But as far as she was concerned, the male thought processes were just as inscrutable.

The boat nudged up against the landing dock, putting an end for the moment to further speculation.

The hampers and blankets were gathered up, the ferry-man was paid, and the little party set off along the main footpath leading past a parterre of colorful flowers.

"The heroine of Smollett's novel *The Expedition of Humphry Clinker* called Bath an earthly paradise," said Isobel as she paused to catch her breath and admire the lush profusion of plantings. "I can see why. Everything about it has such a tasteful elegance to it, even the natural beauty of its gardens. It is very unlike Scotland, don't you think, Alec?"

"Scotland is a harder, wilder place," he answered. "But to my eye, there is great beauty in its rough-cut austerity."

"I agree," offered Caro. "There is a softness, a gentleness that is pleasing about our present surroundings. But for me, the Scottish moors have a more transcendent power."

Alec looked as if he was going to say something, but after a moment or two of hesitation, he simply turned away to continue up the winding path that led to the crest of the knoll.

As she watched him go, Caro could swear the intensity of his gaze was still tingling against her skin. Her cheeks felt oddly warm despite the shade of the trees.

"It's not much farther, Miss Urquehart," assured Andover. "And the view of the city is quite spectacular." Shifting the hamper from one hand to the other, he offered her his arm. "Allow me to assist you." He cast Caro an apologetic look as he added, "The path is a little uneven up ahead."

"B-but…" Isobel stammered.

"I'll go on ahead," said Caro quickly, "and help Lord Strathcona choose a spot to set out the picnic."

Alec had already chosen a spot in the sun to spread out the blanket. His expression, however, remained just as unreadable in the bright light. He was a cipher—no, a Sphinx! A stone face whose carved features gave absolutely nothing away.

His mood seemed even more reticent than usual, and they unpacked his hamper in near silence. The other two soon joined them, and as they both were in high spirits, the meal passed in pleasant conversation, despite the fact that Alec seemed to withdraw even further into himself. His aunt's cook had indeed packed a generous repast—roasted fowl, rich cheeses, fresh bread, and the luscious-looking strawberry tart.

Andover let out a blissful sigh as he forked up the last bite of flaky pastry and clotted cream on his plate. "I don't think I can move a muscle for at least an hour."

"Mmmm." Isobel leaned back on her elbows. "I may need a sedan chair to carry me back down to the boat, for I'm now definitely heavier than an overfed goose."

"Nonsense—you're light as a feather," assured Andover. "I can simply tuck you in the hamper, next to the remains of the cheddar."

She gave a groan at the mention of food.

"Well, I for one, feel the need for a brisk walk," announced Alec, who had barely touched a morsel of the food on his plate. "There is said to be a very interesting Roman ruin just beyond the glade of oak trees. I think I shall take a closer look."

Andover waved him on. He had brought a guidebook of the city with him, and he and Isobel were engrossed in trying to identify the buildings across the river.

Too restless to sit still for such amusements, Caro rose a few minutes later and after excusing herself began to wander down one of the side paths. High rhododendron bushes screened her view, and it wasn't until she came to the top of a wooded hill that she realized the twisting turns had brought her to the remains of the ancient observation tower.

Alec turned from his study of the stonework.

"Sorry," she said, not wanting him to think she had deliberately followed him. "I did not know the other path also led to this spot. I didn't mean to intrude on your solitude."

He shrugged. "You are welcome to have a look. The details of the carving are quite nice. Perhaps not nice enough to inspire an ode, but enjoyable, nonetheless."

"You," she muttered, accepting the invitation to approach, "are in a very strange mood."

"Am I?"

"Yes. Very." They were now standing side by side, their shoulders almost touching. "One would almost think you were going out of your way to avoid speaking to me."

"We're speaking now," he pointed out.

"I would call it verbal sparring." Caro edged around impatiently, forcing him to look her in the face. "But now that I have you alone, I'd rather not keep trading thrusts and parries. I would rather discuss far more important matters—such as whether you have learned anything new about the attack on your sister?"

Pursing his lips, Alec shifted his stance just enough to allow him to return to his perusal of the lettering on the column. "Not really."

"Ye gods." She restrained the urge to take hold of his arm and give him a hard shake. "What sort of answer is *that*?"

"The only one I intend to give," he replied calmly.

"Fine." Caro watched the breeze ruffle his long hair, causing a tangle of red-gold strands to curl around his ear and dance down the freshly shaven line of his jaw. The faint scent of bay rum tickled at her nostrils.

"Fine," she repeated, after forcing herself to exhale. "Then I'll just have to do a little poking around on my own."

That got his attention. He looked around abruptly, his gaze narrowing to a slitted stare. The movement was quick, but not quick enough to hide the sudden darkening of his eyes.

"That wouldn't be wise," he growled. "The only thing I will add for now is that you should stay well away from Edward Thayer."

"Why?"

"Because…" He let out an exasperated grunt. "Must you always plague me with questions?"

"I wouldn't have to if you would stop treating me like a feather-headed wigeon."

Alec's scowl became more pronounced.

"Haven't I proved myself trustworthy and capable?"

A small muscle on his jaw twitched. "I am not at liberty to give you any more details right now. All I can say is that…" As he drew in a breath, he seemed to change his mind about what to say. "Thayer is a charming fellow. No doubt his smooth words are more to your liking."

Deciding Alec deserved a bit of teasing, Caro pretended not to notice the roughness edging his voice. "Yes, he's *exceedingly* charming."

If his storm-blue stare squeezed any tighter, it would be sharper than a razor's edge.

"And scrupulously polite," she added.

Alec was becoming more flustered. Small sounds were beginning to rumble in his throat, like the growling of a bear. "I do not have Thayer's knack for making myself agreeable.

He has a honeyed tongue, which seems to appeal to all the ladies."

"Honey is, after all, a great deal more palatable than vinegar," Caro pointed out.

He now looked utterly nonplussed.

Caro let him stew for a moment longer before huffing an exasperated sigh. "Oh, for heaven's sake, give me some credit for having a brain, Lord Strathcona! Of course I don't find Thayer appealing. When honey drips that freely, it ought to catch naught but flies."

The growls ceased.

Caro waited for him to speak.

Ever so slowly, Alec shifted his feet, stirring tiny puffs of pale dust beneath his boots.

The flicker of dark leather caused a momentary spasm of doubt as she recalled her chilling encounter in the churchyard.

Alec as evil? She couldn't explain how, but she knew with a certainty that resonated right down to her very heartbeat that it couldn't be true.

"Are you saying you would trust my word over his?"

"Yes, you big lummox! I don't know why I should, but I prefer your snaps and growls."

A dappling of sunlight seemed to catch on the curl of his lashes, gilding them to a gleaming gold.

"You are forthright, you are honorable in your own maddening way," she went on. *Oh, no man ought to have such beautiful eyes.*

She found herself staring, and at that moment, all rational thought seemed to dance away in the breeze. His face was utterly intriguing—a mix of chiseled planes and well-defined features that hinted at hidden secrets.

"And...well, you are quite the most interesting man I have ever met." Her legs suddenly seemed a little unsteady, so Caro reached out and caught hold of his lapels.

Looking up, she found his mouth was only inches from hers.

"Oh, bosh—I shall probably regret this..." Standing on tiptoes, Caro kissed him. Not a mere feathering of flesh against flesh, but a hard, hungry embrace that she let go on for far, far longer than any proper young lady should dare.

"There, I have no doubt shocked you."

The tip of his tongue traced along the swell of his lower lip.

"I imagine you think me a wanton hellion, and I suppose I am. It must be my eccentric upbringing. I don't care very much for rules."

Caro knew she was babbling but she couldn't seem to stop. "You may consign me to the Devil. But at least I shall dance a merry jig on my way to perdition."

Was that finally a hint of smile?

She finally dared pause to take a breath. A long, shuddering breath. Now was the time to flee, before she made an even bigger fool of herself.

But Alec suddenly shifted again, blocking her way.

"I, too, shall probably regret this," he said as he slowly circled his arms around her and pulled her close.

She opened her mouth. *To protest?*

Before she could make any sense of what she had set in motion, their lips met again, setting off a fierce jolt of fire.

Chapter Eight

Ye gods.

Her mouth was more tantalizingly sweet than Alec had allowed himself to imagine. Soft and yielding—in contrast to the stubborn strength of her words and ideas. Strangely enough, he found both equally alluring.

Equally arousing.

Framing her face with his hands, he slid his fingers up the delicate line of her jaw to tangle in her raven-dark hair. It was like spun silk against his calloused flesh. Beauty and the beast—he was so big, so awkward, so rough-hewn, while she was ethereally slender and graceful, like a Celtic faerie.

And yet, her perfect mouth parted willingly, and the taste of her flooded his senses.

Sweet beyond words.

Her tongue flicked against his, and that was the last conscious thought he had before all rational powers escaped on the rasp of a deep groan.

Madness—this was madness.

Alec was dimly aware that a part of his brain was warning of the danger. But the message went unheeded by the rest of his body.

It was reacting on instinct rather than reason.

Another groan rumbled as he deepened his kiss. Need, desire, pure primal lust—emotions he had thought were locked safely away in the darkest recesses of his heart suddenly slithered free. And he was, at that moment, helpless to hold them back.

Caro hitched her body closer, and heat pulsated against his chest and his thighs, bringing him to instant arousal.

It was frightening—no, it was exhilarating—to be so out of control. Pulling one hand free, he traced the line of her spine. She moaned, and bringing her hands up to the slope of his shoulders, she slid them back and forth, the friction of the fabric setting his skin on fire.

Breaking free of the embrace, he feathered a trail of kisses across her cheek, wanting to savor the sensations of her smooth skin and beguiling scent. Neroli and roses?

Alec inhaled, only to feel a little light-headed.

"You are," he rasped, "sweeter than sin."

Was this sin?

Caro closed her eyes for an instant, overwhelmed by the feel of liquid fire bubbling through her blood.

She had, of course, read about kisses. And her sister Anna described them very well in her novels. But the actual experience defied words. Textures—a man was a mix of intriguing textures. Soft lips, skin stubbled with a faint hint of whiskers, jawline sculpted of smooth steel.

Pressing closer, she felt the roundness of her breasts yield to the hard planes of his chest. Through the layers of muslin and linen, the subtle slabs of his shape seemed to imprint on her body. Her palms stroked over and over the ridge of his broad shoulders, exploring the contours of muscle.

He was so very big and very solid, like a chunk of Highland granite. And yet, beneath the surface she could sense heat coursing through him. Above the starched points of his shirtcollar, his skin was a little damp, and each throb of his pulsepoint stirred a mix of very masculine scents. Tobacco, leather, bay rum, and an earthier essence that she couldn't put a name to.

Desire?

His mouth found hers again, hot and demanding. Responding with equal ardor, she opened herself. Eagerly, eagerly. That he was not impervious to passion sent a fresh frisson of fire through her.

If this was sin, then she was damned for all eternity.

I am bad—very bad, she thought hazily as she touched and twined her tongue with his. And cheerfully unrepentant. This irresistible attraction to Alec simply felt...

Right, not wrong. Good, not evil.

Everything about his long, lean body—his sculpted shoulders, his tapered waist, his corded thighs—radiated an essence of honorable strength.

A shiver sizzled through her, and with a soft sigh, she touched a tentative caress along the line of his jaw.

A ragged groan whispered against her lips.

"Alec." His name slipped free from her lips.

He eased back, looking...well, she wasn't sure how to describe his look.

Longing? Lustful?

Quite possibly, it was an expression of utter shock.

"Good God, I'm sorry—"

"Oh, please!" Her hand stilled. "If you apologize, I swear I shall strangle you."

His mouth went through an odd set of contortions. Was he whispering a prayer of penance? Or trying not to laugh?

"Caro? Alec?" The calls were coming from close by.

"Damnation." Stumbling back a step, Alec tugged at his coat and cravat, trying to restore some semblance of order.

Echoing his oath, Caro shook out her skirts and straightened her bodice. A few hasty jabs refastened her hairpins, but with a fleeting touch to her mouth, she realized there was nothing she could do about the kissed-ravaged swell of her lips.

Thankfully, Andover was far too much a gentleman to comment on her appearance.

And hopefully Alec's sister was too innocent to notice.

"Ah, there you are!" Isobel started across the clearing, then stopped short. "Sorry, am I interrupting?"

"No, no, nothing important," said Caro, hoping her voice didn't sound as brittle as glass to her friend. "We were just discussing..." Her mind went utterly blank.

"Roman ruins," finished Alec.

"A fascinating topic," said Andover, who had followed a few steps behind Isobel. He darted an amused glance at Alec and then at the ruins. "Clever chaps, those Romans. Very adept with their hands."

Alec gave a strangled cough. "Yes, weren't they? The lettering on the column is quite interesting."

"Oh, really?" Andover raised a brow. "What does it say?"

The rather lengthy reply, uttered in classical Latin, then translated into English, quickly wiped the look of amusement off his face. "Er, right-ho. Well, we just came to say that it's getting late and the ferryman will soon be arriving to collect us. Why don't I hurry back and start packing up the hampers so we are not tardy."

"An excellent suggestion," said Alec.

"I'll come along and help," volunteered Caro. Not waiting for an answer, she hurried to take Andover's arm. A little shove started her feet moving. "We shall meet you and Isobel at the fork in the main footpath," she called over her shoulder to Alec.

"You can stop pulling at my sleeve," murmured Andover, once they were out of earshot. "My valet will swoon if he finds the fabric stretched. He is very fond of this coat."

Caro released her grip.

"Might I ask—"

"No!" she said. "In fact, if you say a word on the subject, I shall...I shall see to it that you don't get the last slice of strawberry tart."

"Oh, dear." He stifled a chuckle. "In that case, my lips are sealed."

"Good." She marched on in awkward silence, hoping her cheeks weren't as flaming as they felt.

He let several more moments pass before asking, "And what happens when the tart is gone?"

"I shall think of something else," answered Caro sharply. "And as you know, I have a *very* vivid imagination, so unless you want something slimy and slithery appearing at an inopportune moment, you'll not mention the matter again."

"I didn't know you had developed such an interest in Roman antiquities," remarked Isobel as she and Alec started down the lower footpath.

"Don't be impertinent," he said, summoning his most imperious scowl to accentuate his words.

The warning silenced her. But only for a few steps.

"Caro is exceedingly nice, as well as exceedingly interesting, don't you think?"

"Don't be impertinent," he repeated.

She lifted her chin and waggled a brow. "Since when is it impertinent to speak the truth?"

He pursed his lips, wondering how to extract himself with any dignity from a very deep hole. No doubt it served him right for being a bloody fool.

"Since I have invoked the privileges of an older—and wiser—brother to say it is so," he answered, deciding humor was the only option.

As he had intended, she laughed. However, the sound quickly floated away on the breeze—along with his hope that she would drop the subject.

"Caro is very knowledgeable about poetry." Isobel picked up where she had left off. "Apparently she writes it as well, though she hasn't yet shown me her work."

"I am well aware of Miss Caro's interests," snapped Alec. "*And?*"

"And that is the end of this conversation."

His sister fixed him with a searching look. "Because you intend to live in the past for the rest of your days?"

"Damnation!" Alec bit back another oath. "Stop plaguing me with your ridiculous questions."

"It's not *my* questions you need to answer," she replied stiffly. "But rather your own."

"What is that supposed to mean?" he said through gritted teeth.

Isobel looked away with a sniff. "I would hope that my big brother is wise enough to figure it out on his own."

Damn, Damn, Damn. The crunch of gravel echoed his

testy mood. They walked the rest of the way to the meeting place without speaking, Isobel wrapped in a fugue of injured pique, while he...

He wasn't quite sure how to order his emotions.

Having his innermost private wounds probed was horribly painful. Though old, they were still raw and unhealed, and even the gentlest touch hurt more than he cared to admit. But the first searing stab had quickly died down to a dull ache. Isobel meant well, and a part of him knew she was quite right. He *should* face the past.

But at heart, he was a coward.

Hiding deep within himself was far easier than facing the chance of being hurt again.

"I'm sorry," he muttered.

"Don't be," murmured Isobel. "I have no right to intrude, but I only do so because I wish to see you happy, Alec."

"That may be beyond the power of any mortal man to make happen." Or woman.

"You don't know that until you try."

He didn't argue. Youth was a time for fairy-tale dreams. The odds were that she would be disillusioned soon enough.

"Only look at Caro. She has the courage to pursue what she wants."

Alec jerked his head around, hoping his cheeks weren't as scarlet as they felt.

"She wishes to write poetry," went on Isobel, "and she isn't daunted by the challenges."

His shoulders relaxed. "I wish her well in achieving her goals. But it won't be easy."

"Things that are worth having rarely are."

A reluctant smile softened his scowl. "How did my baby sister become so sage?"

She answered with a smug grin. "By listening to my oh-so-wise older brother."

"It seems I am skewered with my own petard," quipped Alec. Spotting Caro and Andover waiting with the hampers, he added, "Thank God our friends are up ahead. Let us cry pax, if you don't mind. I've been cut up enough for one afternoon."

"Very well. But please think on what I said."

Too restless to sleep, Caro threw back the bedcovers and, after tugging on her wrapper, went to stand by the window. Mist floated over the garden, ghostly swirls of vapor silvered by the pale moonlight. Somewhere in the bushes a lone nightingale sang a plaintive song. There was, perhaps, a poem hidden somewhere within the magic of the midnight hour.

But her musings—those maddeningly rebellious little meanderings of the mind—weren't focused on the beauties of Nature. Instead they insisted on wrapping themselves around a tall, broad-shouldered Scot with a scowl that would put Satan to the blush.

The thought of "Satan" naturally stirred the thought of "sin."

Ye gods, had she really thrown herself at Alec and done everything in her power to kiss him—and herself—witless?

A sigh fogged the windowpane, which was just as well, for surely if the glass were clear she would see the word "Jezebel" lettered in scarlet script across her forehead.

In indelible ink.

Though to be fair, Alec had actively participated in the embrace. Quite enthusiastically.

Caro blushed on recalling where his mouth and his hands

had wandered. She had been just as wicked, intimately exploring every bulge of masculine muscle and...

That she could arouse primal passions in Alec was heartening to know. She sometimes feared that he was made of inanimate rock and stonedust rather than flesh and blood. But no, liquid fire could pump through his veins when he let his emotions do more than just simmer inside him.

Moving from the window to the escritoire in the corner of the bedchamber, Caro struck a flame to the candle and picked up the latest letter from her sister Anna.

Poor lamb—I know that things must be awfully boring in Bath. There are likely no men under the age of eighty, so I feel a little guilty regaling you with descriptions of the handsome Russian princes (sorry for the smudge— I had to slap Davenport's hand away. He wanted to add a very rude word) and the sumptuous palaces here in St. Petersburg where we dance until dawn...

Taking out a fresh sheet of paper, Caro dipped her pen in the inkwell to write a reply.

How to start?

Things are not quite so boring—I've experienced my first real kiss, and while your descriptions in your novels are good, they don't quite capture the experience.

Drumming her fingers on the blotter, she thought about how to go on.

That first touch is not exactly like lightning striking, true there is an electric current but it's more of a...

No, that wasn't quite right. Crumpling the paper, she tossed it in the fire and took out a fresh sheet.

After several more tries were consigned to the coals, Caro leaned back in consternation. Staring down at the blank page, she exhaled a frustrated sigh. Drat, she couldn't seem to quite capture in words what she wanted to say. But as it was Anna who was the master of prose, why should it be any great surprise that she couldn't wax as eloquent as her sister on the subject?

"Oh, bosh. Perhaps I should just try writing a poem instead," she muttered under her breath.

The words were said half in jest. And yet, as she tapped the tip of the feathered quill against her chin, the first line of an ode seemed to compose itself in her head.

Ha! The Muse must be feeling a little guilty for her recent quixotic moods.

Whatever the reason, an aspiring poet could never afford to ignore inspiration, no matter when it chose to strike.

Putting pen to ink yet again, Caro began to write...

*Lips, their flesh afire with longing that chased doubt
    from the sliver of space between them...*

For the next little while the only sound in the room was the scratch-scratch of the nib and the whispered hiss of the candleflame as it danced in the draft curling in through the cracks in the casement.

When the last stanza was done, Caro pinched at the bridge of her nose, wondering if she dared to read what she had just written. She had just allowed the words to flow.

So perhaps it was drivel.

"A poet cannot be a coward," she scolded. "If it's bloody awful, I can toss it away with the rest of the failures."

She took a reluctant peek.

Not bad.

Emboldened, she continued on. When she came to the end, she quickly reread it again and then blew out her cheeks with a mingled sense of surprise and a touch of pride.

Now *that* was a poem.

There was a passion that crackled through the paper, leaving her fingertips feeling a little singed. An inner fire of sinuous, swaying flames. Indeed, Anna might fear that her impetuous younger sister had sacrificed her virtue on the altar of... artistic inspiration.

Would I? wondered Caro.

Would I?

Her father's eccentric views on what women should know about sex meant that the three Sloane sisters had some ideas on the rules of maidenly behavior that were shockingly different from those of most young ladies of the *ton*. Caro suspected her two older sisters hadn't been virgins at the time of their marriage, but though the three of them shared most confidences, on this particular subject they deemed her still an innocent schoolgirl and hadn't included her in their whispered exchanges on men.

And listening at the keyhole had proved fruitless. Olivia and Anna had very soft whispers.

"Drat," she muttered. There was much she would have liked to ask them, especially after The Kiss.

Perhaps it was wicked and wanton to have so thoroughly enjoyed everything about Alec's body—the muscled contours, the masculine textures, the taste of his mouth, the fiery surge of desire its touch sent spiraling straight to her very core.

"I would probably surrender my virginity to Strathcona in a heartbeat," she murmured. "Which no doubt makes me the Devil's own harlot."

But as there wasn't a snowball's chance in Hell that Alec would ever ask her to, she seemed safe enough from eternal damnation.

The Kiss was . . . just a kiss.

She had taken him by surprise, that was all. He hadn't had time to think. He had reacted purely on instinct. How was it that men seemed to know those things by second nature? It was as if they came into the world with a manual on seduction tattooed on their primitive little brains.

So, what about women?

It was all a bit confusing to know what women were and were not supposed to feel. Society's rules said one thing, and yet the heart seemed to say something quite different. Somehow it didn't seem fair.

Shouldn't great artists, be they men or women, be they painters or poets, understand the fine points of human emotion?

Questions, questions.

Which tangled into conundrums.

Quickly folding the poem before she could change her mind, Caro sealed it with a wafer of scarlet wax.

Chapter Nine

"Ugh," said Isobel over the rim of her glass. "I shall be heartily glad when this regime of drinking the Bath mineral waters is at an end." Crinkling her nose, she let out a gusty sigh. "The taste is quite vile."

"The physician does say it is healthful," replied Caro helpfully. The odor wasn't very pleasant either, but as her friend's frail looks and stamina appeared much improved over the last ten days, it was hard to argue with the water's medicinal qualities.

Heaving another sigh, Isobel forced herself to swallow the remaining liquid. "Arrrgh."

Caro had offered to accompany her friend to her daily cure, though after her first few sips, she had abandoned the idea of her own daily dose. The onerous task done, they completed their circuit of the Pump House promenade and paused by the main doors to hand the glass back to the elderly attendant who dispensed the daily doses.

"Have you visited the Hedge Maze yet?" asked Caro. She had been perusing the guidebook on Bath over breakfast, seeking some amusement with which to brighten Isobel's spirits. Her friend's mood had seemed downcast during the boat ride back from Spring Gardens yesterday, and she couldn't help wonder whether it had to do with Andover.

Andy was a very charming, good-hearted fellow, but in London the mamas with daughters of a marriageable age despaired of him settling down anytime soon.

Would a discreet word of caution help head off any heartbreak? She hadn't yet decided whether it was wise to interfere. A walk together, just the two of them, might help her make up her mind.

"No," answered Isobel, her voice perking up. "But I have heard it is quite a diverting challenge."

"Shall we try it?" suggested Caro. "It's still early in the afternoon, so we should have plenty of time to finish before suppertime. I believe there is a spotter stationed on a platform high above the greenery to help those who become impossibly lost."

"Oh, yes, let us test our skills! I daresay you are too clever to lose your way."

Caro wished she were half so certain of that. Of late, the needle of her inner compass had been spinning in all directions.

If only I had a lodestone, an inner North Star to help me navigate my way through my emotions.

But she quickly put aside such musings on mental journeys, and turned her attention to enjoying the upcoming stroll.

It was just a short walk to the entrance of the maze, which was located in a stretch of parkland off one of the hilly side streets. Caro paid the fee for both of them and returned with the tickets and a brochure listing some of the basic facts about the design.

"It says here that the layout is copied from the famous maze at Hampton Court, which was built in the late 1600s for William III," she read. "The original has a half mile of pathways, while this one is considerably longer, as it has nearly three quarters."

Isobel looked suitably impressed as she eyed the towering hedges. "It sounds a bit daunting."

"We'll be fine." For a moment, the memory of their assailants bursting out of the bushes made her pause, but she quickly shook off any trepidation. It was midday, and they were in a civilized town, not wandering down a dark, deserted country lane.

"Ready?" Leading the way, Caro stepped into the leafy puzzle.

Thayer seemed in no particular hurry, noted Alec. His former friend was sauntering slowly up the street, pausing here and there to peruse the shop windows. Swearing under his breath, he ducked into a shadowed recess so as not to be spotted.

Following the man was likely a fool's errand, conceded Alec, but he was curious as to what he was doing here in town, and whether he was meeting anyone.

Thayer took another turn, this one into a side street.

Alec waited a few moments and then stealthily followed. As the way rounded a bend, he saw it led up to the hedge maze, a popular attraction with the visitors in Bath. There were several people buying tickets to enter through the arched opening...

A flutter of sprigged muslin caught his eye.

Including his sister and Caro.

Damnation. His heart suddenly jumped and thumped against his ribs as he saw Thayer purchase a ticket and disappear through the opening in the high yew hedges.

There was no danger, he told himself. The maze was a popular public spot. What trouble could possibly happen within its playful paths? But even as he said it, he was already imagining the diabolically twisting turns, designed to trap the unwary.

Alec hesitated. He wasn't anxious to encounter Caro again, not with the memory of their recent kiss still burning on his lips. She had ignited all sorts of wild desires that he had meant to keep locked safely away.

Danger, danger, danger.

The warning echoed against his skull. But alas, at the present moment, danger took many guises, and he couldn't afford to guess at which one was most threatening.

Quickening his steps, he paid his fee and hurried through the needle-wreathed opening.

Once inside, Alec forced himself to slow down and allow reason to reassert control over impulse. He seemed to recall reading that the key to moving correctly within a maze was to always keep touching the right-hand wall of the hedge.

But that, he realized wryly, was of little import. His sister and Caro might already be lost within the wrong turns.

With Thayer close on their heels.

He drew several deep breaths to quash the twinge of fear twisting in his gut. No harm was going to come to Isobel. She wasn't alone...

But the memory of Caro knocked unconscious by the blow of a brute caused another sharp clench.

Resisting the urge to shout out their names, Alec plunged

ahead, determined to find the two young ladies if he had to strip off every cursed needle from the devil-damned bushes.

Faster, faster. It felt like an eternity before he spotted a flicker of feminine skirts just before it was swallowed in the shadows of a turn. Breaking into a half-run, Alec skidded around the sharply angled corner.

Caro whirled around, a look of alarm spasming across her face.

Damnation—she was alone.

"Where is Isobel?" he demanded in a near-breathless voice.

"She is with Andover and Lord Tilden. We encountered them just as we entered, and as they have been here before, they offered to show us the secrets of navigating the pathways."

Relief flooded through him, but quickly gave way to another fear. Given her fiercely adventurous spirit and utter disregard for danger, Caro Sloane was all too likely to stray into trouble. "Then what the devil are you doing, wandering around all on your own?"

Caro's brows pinched together in a frown. "I wished to explore how the dead ends are designed." Her mouth thinned as well. "Not, I might add, that it should be any concern of yours."

She turned away, making a show of studying the tightly twined yew branches. "Really sir, I don't understand why you always feel compelled to snap and snarl at me. Granted, I have many faults, but taking a simple stroll in a maze ought not elicit your ire."

He shuffled his feet, shifting his position just a fraction. *Dear God—was that a glint of tears flickering through her downcast lashes?*

"My apologies," he said gruffly. "I did not mean to snap. Or snarl. I saw the two of you enter alone and I was... concerned."

She lifted her head, and the shadow of her bonnet brim made it impossible to see her eyes. "To my knowledge, there are no lurking dragons hidden in the shrubbery, waiting to devour unwary patrons." A dappling of sunlight caught the curl of a wry smile. "The management would likely charge extra for experiencing the thrill of such a danger."

The sight of her lovely mouth caused a clench of longing in his belly... well, to be honest, it was a little lower than his belly, but Alec tried to ignore his baser instincts.

"Let us not jest about dangers," he replied. "I am sorry if I am, as Isobel terms it, acting like a mother hen. But I suppose recent events have made me feel overprotective."

"Such sentiment does you credit, sir," said Caro softly. "She may tease you, but be assured that any sister would be happy to have such a thoughtful brother take on the role of her knight in shining armor."

Alec moved a step closer. "I, um..." How ridiculous to be standing there stammering like a puling schoolboy. He pulled himself together. "That is, I am of course concerned for your safety as well."

"That is very kind of you." Caro withdrew a little farther into the shadows. "However, that's really not necessary." She exaggerated a flex of her fists. "I can take care of myself."

Without thinking, he covered the distance between them. "You shouldn't have to."

"I'm not your responsibility, Lord Strathcona."

"No, but you are my friend."

At that her head jerked up, a look of surprise deepened by an undertone of something else.

Blast—he wished he could fathom what it was.

"*Are* we friends?" she asked tentatively. "At times, it certainly doesn't feel like it."

Alec reached out to tuck an errant curl behind her ear.

Don't. The warning voice in his head was in fine fettle this afternoon—clear, loud, insistent. He ought to listen.

But he didn't.

His fingers grazed the delicate shell-pink curve, the merest gossamer touch of flesh against flesh. Yet it sent a jolt of awareness thrumming through his entire body.

She must have sensed it too, for her muscles tensed and the tiny pulsepoint just above the ruffle of her neckline began to quicken.

"Unlike many men, I don't have the gift of making myself pleasing to ladies." His voice sounded a little rough, which only proved his point. "My tongue is unable to put a silvery shine on my words. But that said, Miss Caro, yes, I *do* consider us friends."

Their gazes locked, and for a long, drawn-out moment, she seemed to be searching to see something.

God only knew what. Whatever the mysterious quality was, it must be lacking, or else...

No, he had vowed not to think of the past.

"Your words don't need artificial glitter and gleam, sir," said Caro softly. "Not every lady wishes to hear conversation so highly polished that all hint of individuality has been rubbed off it."

Alec hardly dared breathe. The breeze had stirred her scent and its softly sweet spice was making him feel a little woozy.

"Well, if you are looking for roughness," he rasped, "you have certainly found it."

She touched a fingertip to his jaw and traced a line to the

tip of his chin. "Rough and smooth," she murmured. "You are a man of very interesting textures, Lord Strathcona."

Interesting?

At that, he flashed a rueful smile. "I would have thought you would choose a very different sort of adjective. 'Prickly' or 'bristly' are the first that come to mind."

Her laugh—a sound that defied description—was almost lost in the ruffling of the emerald green needles.

"You forgot 'thorny.' Anyone who tries to touch you risks getting badly scratched." Her hand, however, remained hovering in the air, keeping them physically joined.

By some strange alchemy, the current between them suddenly seemed to draw him closer.

Closer.

Her lips parted ever so slightly and he was lost.

Caro met his kiss eagerly. Wantonly. Wickedly.

Was it wicked to feel such an elemental connection to Alec?

She should care, but she didn't. All that mattered was the jolt of fiery awareness sparked by the first touch of his mouth. His touch, his taste—somehow she was sure it was right, not wrong.

Her palms slid urgently over his shoulders, longing to imprint every nuanced contour of his shape to memory. They had maybe a moment or two, no more, before reason must reassert itself.

And Caro intended to savor every sweet second. She hugged him closer, feeling the starched folds of his cravat yield with a whispery crush to the pressure of her ardor. Through the layers of fabric—linen tangling with wool, muslin, and lacy petticoats—his heart was beating so hard that its thud was loud as cannonfire in her ears.

She shifted, sure the sparks were scorching her skin.

A fresh wave of pleasure shot through her as Alec's kiss became hotter, hungrier. The deep, masculine sound rumbling in his throat—a growl or a groan, it didn't matter—was reassurance that his tightly wound self-control had given way to passion.

Passion. Oh, yes, he was capable of passion, though it seemed to frighten the devil out of him.

His hands framed her face. Big, strong capable hands, with calloused palms that felt gentle as velvet against her skin.

He shifted, and the scrape of his boots on the gravel seemed to break the madness of the moment.

The fire, so quick to ignite, seemed to die away just as fast.

"What are you afraid of?"

"You. Me. Everything."

"Oh, is that all?" quipped Caro with a tentative smile. "That shouldn't be very hard to overcome."

His lips gave a reluctant twitch. "Are you always such an optimist?"

"But of course! As you no doubt recall from the interlude at Dunbar Castle, my sister writes romance novels, and they always have a happily ever after."

His expression hardened. "Well, real life rarely has the hero and heroine riding off in perfect bliss to a castle in the clouds. If you think otherwise, you are doomed to be disappointed."

"Does that mean one shouldn't dare to dream?"

He didn't answer.

"What a bleak existence that would be," she went on. "Of course there are disappointments in life. But if you are too frightened to pick yourself up off your arse when they knock you down and try again, why, then you deserve to be miserable."

"I'm not miserable," he protested.

"Yes," she countered, "you are. You just refuse to admit it."

He seemed to be searching for some reply when the crunch of steps on the graveled path announced that someone was approaching.

"Forgive me." Thayer stopped short. "Am I interrupting a private tête-à-tête?"

"Not at all," said Alec brusquely. "We were just leaving. This particular path is a dead end."

"Ah." Thayer remained where he was, blocking the way out. "A wrong turn is hardly surprising."

It was said lightly and with a smile, but Alec's already dark expression turned even blacker. Suppressed rage pulsed from every pore.

Caro had never seen him look so...dangerous. She wondered once again what had caused such bad blood between the men.

Thayer flashed an apologetic smile at her. "It seems my presence is unwelcome, so I shall take myself off."

It was a gracefully done apology, and he did sound contrite. Perhaps Alec was exaggerating the man's faults.

Thayer started to turn and then hesitated. "If you are attending the Assembly tonight, Miss Caro, might I ask for the honor of a dance?"

The request took her by surprise. Unable to think of an excuse, she allowed good manners to dictate her response. "Yes. Of course."

"Excellent," he said. "I shall look forward to making up for my misstep here."

Again, a handsome apology. After adding a polite tip of his hat, he strolled away.

Alec's jaw was clenched so tightly that she expected to hear molars crack at any moment. He stared straight ahead at the dense wall of yew needles, and she counted to ten before he finally relaxed enough to speak.

"Why the devil did you agree to dance with him? I thought you said you weren't blinded by his false charm."

"I'm not," she said, a little stung by his sharp tone. "But good manners dictated that I do so." That and the fact the she didn't wish to alienate Thayer quite yet.

"Allow me to repeat my earlier warning, Miss Caro. You should stay away from Thayer."

"It would help if you explained why you dislike him so," she replied.

"I am not at liberty to say," he answered.

Huffing an exasperated sigh, Caro said, "That's not an answer, that's an evasion. Surely you can trust me with more than that."

The molars began to grind again.

"Stop that. You'll break your jaw."

"I'd rather break Thayer's," he muttered through gritted teeth. "And then pound it into a thousand little shards of bone."

"That's clear," she replied. "But the reason isn't."

"You don't need to know it."

Hot and cold—his mercurial moods had her body thrumming with confusion. "Fine. Keep me in the dark." Caro's patience, already dangerously frayed, suddenly snapped. "I'll just have to decide for myself whether he is as evil as you imply."

Fisting her skirts, she turned away.

"Wait. I'll escort you to the entrance."

"There's no need. I can find my own way," she said testily.

"Wait." He had moved so swiftly and silently that Caro wasn't aware he was right behind her until his arm hooked around her waist and yanked her to a halt.

Furious, she wrenched free, only to have her cry of outrage swallowed in a kiss that took her breath away.

Drat the man for making her insides turn as soft and sloshy as boiled oats!

"Please. I ask that you trust me for now," he said softly, after pulling back from the all-too-short embrace.

"Wh-why should I?" she stammered.

"Because I am your friend and he is the enemy." His eyes were dark as a stormblown Scottish loch, the swirl of slate-blue hues impenetrable.

Trust? It was a lot to ask when God only knew what secrets were hidden beneath the churning surface.

Alec didn't wait for a reply. Taking her hand, he placed it on the interwoven yew branches' leaves. "Keep touching the left side of the hedge and it will lead you out of the maze."

With that, he turned and disappeared into the shadows.

Chapter Ten

The candleflames swayed in the soft, jasmine-scented breeze wafting in from the open windows of the Assembly Room. Music serenaded the trilling laughter and the clinking cups of claret punch, adding an extra note of gaiety to the cheerful chatter of the crowd.

Caro stood alone in one of the alcoves, trying to lift her spirits to match the mood of the evening. The afternoon had left her unsettled.

A poet must suffer doubts and uncertainty for the sake of art, she told herself.

So maybe I should consign art to Satan, since the cloven-hoofed demon seems bent on bedeviling me with emotions and desires that defy description.

Ha! A fine poet she was if she couldn't find words to express her feelings.

"Such beauty shouldn't be hiding under a bush." Thayer pushed aside a handful of palm fronds. "So I've come to lead you out to the center of the dance floor, where I shall bask in your reflected brilliance under the glittering lights of the chandeliers. Though in truth, the candles will look dim in comparison."

She pinched a polite smile, though the effusive comment rubbed a little raw. It wasn't his fault. Men were expected to mouth such flatteries, and women were expected to appreciate them. That way, Society sailed along smoothly on unrippled waters.

God forbid that unconventionality stirred up any waves.

"You look a little pensive," he murmured, coming to stand beside her. "Would you rather forgo capering across the dance floor?"

That he sensed her mood chased away her irritation. Not many men, she mused, would have noticed. "I confess that I would," she replied quietly. "That is, if you don't mind."

"Not at all." He blew out a sigh. "If you must know, I find it a trifle fatiguing to constantly be dancing through all the proper steps of social convention."

The fluttering blur of leaves and shadows seemed to mirror her own uncertainties. Perhaps she had misjudged him after all. As Alec had said himself, things were rarely black or white.

"So I am quite happy to just stay here and talk." He made a wry face. "That is, if you don't mind."

This time, her answering smile was unforced. "I should like that very much," she answered sincerely.

"Do you find the quiet pace of Bath a welcome change from the gaiety of London?" he asked after a fraction of a pause.

It was a solid, sensible question, and for the next little while they compared the differences between a large, bustling city and a quiet spa town.

"Good heavens, it sounds as if you danced until dawn

every night of the week," said Thayer, in response to her description of the past Season in London. "No wonder you welcome a respite from the social whirl."

"Surely Glasgow has its own glittering array of parties and balls," replied Caro.

"It does," he said softly. "But I..." Thayer cleared his throat. "To be honest, I avoid attending many of them. It is a world aswirl in falsehoods and flatteries that can lead to trouble if one is not very careful. I find that a little danger-ous."

How true.

"Yes," agreed Caro. "I know what you mean. One must be on guard against those whose intentions are not always honorable."

"Speaking of being on guard..." He hesitated, tactfully waiting for her permission to go on.

She gave a small nod.

"I can't help but notice that you are spending time with Lord Strathcona," he said.

"Yes," answered Caro warily, keeping in mind the words she had just uttered.

"Might I ask how well you know him?"

Her mouth gave an involuntary quirk. "A good question." She thought for a moment before adding, "Strathcona is a very private man. He does not share a great deal about him-self."

"No, he does not."

She waited. Clearly he wished to make some revelation, but she decided to make him do so on his own.

"He was married, you know," confided Thayer in a low voice. "Though it's all kept rather hush-hush."

Married? Alec was married?

"It wasn't for long. His wife died in a carriage accident fleeing a dreadfully unhappy situation—or at least that is the story," he went on. "There are rumors that the truth is even more ugly."

A slow, painful swallow loosened her throat just enough to allow a shallow whisper. "Indeed?" she said, unable to summon any other response. Her mind was still reeling.

He nodded. "It was a scandal, though his title and his family connections allowed him to cover up the sordid details. The poor girl was English, and had few friends in Scotland to defend her from his cruelty."

The implied accusation speared Caro into finding her voice. "I—I can't believe Lord Strathcona is such a monster as that."

"Which of course does you credit, Miss Caro." Thayer blew out a mournful sigh. "Alec McClellan is a man well versed in disguising his true persona with a multitude of ... layers."

Left unspoken, but resonating in the still air loud and clear, was the word "lies."

"I wouldn't say anything, save for the fact that I have noticed him paying attention to you," continued Thayer. "So I feel beholden to offer a warning to be on your guard. He has secret vices."

Which include devouring innocent young ladies for breakfast, along with a plate of kippered herrings?

Despite the sardonic quip that jumped to mind, Caro felt as if a huge lead weight had settled in her stomach. Much as she found it nigh on impossible to imagine Alec as a conniving dastard, Thayer's earlier question echoed uncomfortably inside her head.

How well did she really know him?

Thayer was right about one thing—Alec kept himself shrouded in many layers. And for the most part, much of his portrait had been painted by the brush of her own imagination.

A sound of dismay must have leaked from her lips, for he gave her a sympathetic look. "I am sorry to upset you," he responded softly. "It's shocking, I know." A pause. "And to be truthful, that's not the worst of it."

She stared at him blankly, still stunned by the initial revelation.

"There is a reason I am here in Bath. It is feared that McClellan—that is, Strathcona—may be up to no good here in England, and I have been asked to keep an eye on the situation." He darted a quick look around. "I cannot say any more than that on the situation, save to stress that you would be wise to keep your distance from the baron."

Truth and lies.

Caro suddenly felt a little light-headed. Her thoughts were spinning in dizzying circles, tangling light and shadows into a whirling dervish blur of light and dark.

"I can see that you would prefer to forgo our upcoming dance." Thayer gave a swift, solicitous squeeze to her hand. "You look a little shaken. May I fetch you a glass of punch?"

"N-no, thank you," she replied. "If you don't mind, I would simply prefer a few moments alone."

"Of course." He stepped back with an apologetic shrug. "I truly regret causing you such distress. But gentlemanly scruples demanded that I warn you, before it was too late."

She managed a curt nod, which thankfully he took as a signal to withdraw without further ado.

Alec had been married, and his wife was now dead.

Caro stared unseeing at the fluttering palm fronds. A

small voice in her head said there was no earthly reason why he would have told her such intimate details of his life. Why would he? And yet, a louder shout—a chorus of bruised feelings—piped up in protest.

Damnation! He had spoken of trust, of friendship. And he had kissed her, with a passion that seemed to promise that the connection between them was very real.

Caro clasped her hands together in a fist and forced herself to breathe. Her lungs seemed to be having trouble moving in and out on their own.

He should have shared such a fact...

Shifting within the shadows, Caro searched the crowd, hoping to spot Isobel. If anyone could confirm the veracity of Thayer's story, it was Alec's sister.

To her relief, Caro spotted her dancing with Andover in the group near the doors to the terrace. Skirting slowly around the perimeter of the room, she waited for the music to end.

"Isobel," she called, as the laughing couple headed toward the refreshment table.

"Oh, there you are!" Isobel's flushed face wreathed in an even brighter smile. "We were looking for you on the dance floor—I thought you were engaged for the set."

"I was." She forced back the hurt welling up in her throat. "But Mr. Thayer and I ended up talking instead. Which was just as well. It seems overly warm in here tonight and I find myself a little fatigued."

Isobel fanned herself. "Oh, as do I."

Seizing the opportunity, Caro indicated a stone bench by the terrace railing just outside the open doors. "Why don't we sit and catch a breath of fresh air while Andy fetches us some punch."

Andover grinned. "Which is feminine code for 'go away for a bit while we ladies enjoy a bit of gossip.'"

"I take it you have sisters, sir," teased Isobel.

"Two," he answered. "Like Miss Caro, I too am contemplating writing a book. Not, I hasten to add, one composed of lyric verses, but rather a compendium of all the diabolical wiles that ladies use to twist us men around their little fingers."

"How very ungentlemanly of you to think of exposing our secrets," murmured Caro. "You gentlemen have enough of an unfair advantage over us as it is."

"Ha!" he retorted, though he seemed to sense something in her tone that made his brows tweak up in query.

She turned away and took Isobel's arm before he could ask any questions. Andover's affable manner and self-deprecating sense of humor fooled many people into thinking he was a pleasantly slow-witted fellow. But in truth, he was sharp as a tack.

"Take your time," said Isobel over her shoulder. "We shall not perish of thirst if you choose to linger over a glass of champagne with Lord Tilden and his friends before bringing us our punch."

"You seem to be enjoying Andy's company," observed Caro as she seated herself. In contrast, the coolness of the smooth stone seeping through her skirts was an uncomfortable reminder of how hard and impenetrable Alec seemed at this moment.

Isobel's flush immediately deepened to a vivid scarlet. "I—I am. He is very...nice."

"He is thoroughly nice," she agreed. "In every way that matters."

A small silence intervened as Isobel twisted the fringe

of her shawl between her fingers. Without looking up, she hesitantly said, "You seem to be enjoying Mr. Thayer's company."

"I wouldn't call it that. I confess, there are things that disturb me about him."

"Alec has warned me that he is a dirty dish," answered Isobel in a small voice.

"Yes, he has said much the same thing to me as well, but would not explain why."

Isobel lifted her shoulders in a baffled shrug. "Other than that pronouncement, he is very close-mouthed about his former friend. I am not sure why."

Caro drew in an unsteady breath. "Well, Mr. Thayer is more forthcoming about your brother. He told me that Lord Strathcona has been married. And that his wife was killed in an unfortunate accident."

The color drained from Isobel's face, leaving her as pale as the cream-white sash beneath her breasts.

"Is that true?"

"Yes, it's true," Isobel whispered. The opening notes of a lively gavotte drifted out from the dance floor, painfully at odds with the moments of strained silence that followed. "But please, I beg of you not to ask me to say more. I—I cannot bear to talk about it."

Caro felt a numbness grip her chest and slowly spread outward, like fingers of ice.

"Besides," added Isobel, "it is not me but rather Alec who should rightfully tell you about the circumstances."

"Lord Strathcona owes me no explanation," replied Caro flatly. "I merely wanted to know whether it was true in order to judge whether Mr. Thayer is a reliable source of information."

"But..." Isobel bit her lip.

But what? There really wasn't much else to say.

However, despite her obvious agitation, Isobel felt compelled to go on. "But...but things are not always as they seem from the simple facts. As we both know from our fondness for novels, a story may be told in many different ways, in many different slants, depending on what the narrator wants the reader to see and feel."

"I am not sure I understand what you are trying to say," replied Caro, in no frame of mind to puzzle out whatever oblique message was being conveyed. "Fact and fiction are not the same."

"I wish I could say more." Isobel's response was barely audible over the rustling of the ivy vines twined around the balusters.

Caro didn't feel she could press her friend any further. And really, for what purpose? Details seemed pointless, for the worst seemed confirmed. Looking down, she carefully smoothed her skirts into precise pleats in order to hide her dismay.

She was bitterly disappointed, and not just in Alec.

Apparently I am not a very good judge of character.

And yet, much as Caro told herself that Alec had been revealed as a cad, doubt still nibbled at the corners of her consciousness. What Thayer had hinted at was dastardly behavior, and she didn't think she could be *that* wrong about someone.

"Have I given you ladies enough time for a comfortable coze?"

Andover's cheerful greeting pulled her out of her brooding.

"I've brought you champagne instead of ratafia punch, since it adds such a festive sparkle to an evening of dancing."

The torchlight suddenly flared brighter in a swirl of the breeze, causing him to stop and clear his throat with a tentative cough.

"Er, has something serious occurred?" He asked it lightly, but a glimmer of concern flickered in his eyes as they met Caro's gaze. "A torn flounce? A lost hairpin?"

She managed a wry smile. "Nothing so devastating as that. We were simply discussing the plot of a novel we didn't care for."

"Yes," agreed Isobel. "A most unsatisfactory story so far, but I have hopes that everything will turn out for the best."

"Oh, those books *always* have happy endings," he exclaimed jovially as he handed them their glasses of wine. "Let us drink a toast to love conquering all adversity."

Caro lifted the glass to her lips. She adored champagne, but never had it tasted so flat.

"If you will excuse me, I had better go back inside." She set the barely touched drink on the railing. Firelight sparked through the bubbling effervescence, accentuating the myriad tiny explosions. "I just recalled that I am promised to Lord Stiles for the upcoming set."

To her dismay, she was claimed for the following dance, and then the one after that. It was an hour before she could slip away, intent on finding her mother in the card room and suggesting an end to the evening.

Making her way around to the side saloons, Caro was just passing through a narrow corridor when she spotted Thayer in the entrance hall, taking his overcoat from the porter and draping it over his shoulders. As he moved beneath the crystal chandelier, the bright reflections flickered over the folds of dark fabric, and a flash of decorative black braid along the hem caught for an instant in a wink of candlelight.

She froze, suddenly seeing in her mind's eye the same fleeting flutter.

Thayer took another step, and it was gone.

Caro tried to shake off the sensation of having seen the coat before, telling herself it was mere illusion.

Mere delusion.

Truth and Lies. Good and Evil. She wasn't sure anymore about what was real and what was a figment of her imagination.

Alec swore in frustration as he flung off his mud-spattered oilskin cape and went to pour himself a brandy. It had been a long ride through spitting rain, and all for naught.

His contact in Bristol, a Scottish sympathizer with the independence movement, had not been able to ferret any further information concerning the attack on Isobel and Caro. Nor had he received any news from north of the border on why Edward Thayer was spending time in Bath.

"Blast," he muttered, jabbing a poker at the glowing coals in the hearth and stirring a fire to life. "Perhaps he has gout and is seeking a cure." Another jab. "Or the Plague." More likely, given the man's predatory habits with women, that if he was ill with any malady, it would be the clap.

"That log is long since deceased, Alec. There is no need to render a coup de grâce."

He turned to find Isobel standing in the doorway, observing him with a look of grave concern.

"Sorry. It was a rotten night for a ride. I'm wet, cold, and in a foul temper." He gave the coals another raking. "So it's probably best that you leave me to my own company."

Heedless of the warning, she entered and perched a hip on the arm of the chair facing the hearth. "Well, I fear you are going to be in an even fouler temper when I tell you about my evening."

"Good God, you weren't attacked—"

"No, no, not me."

He jerked around, the poker banging against the brass fender.

"Not Caro, either," she added hastily. "Rather it was *your* character being hit upon. With innuendo and suggestion, not outright blows. But nonetheless, it did damage." Her lips compressed in concern. "Mr. Thayer is a very nasty gentleman."

Alec let out a grunt. "Let him say whatever he wants. Why the devil should I care?"

"Because I have the feeling he is poisoning Caro's mind with twisted tales of the truth."

He had worked hard at making himself impervious to pain, but in that instant, a small stab somehow slipped under his guard. Thrusting aside the blade, he repeated, "Why should I care?"

His sister flinched at the roughness of his tone. "Oh, Alec," she whispered. "Elizabeth hurt you more than enough in her lifetime. Must you keep letting her wield such power from the grave?"

"Don't," he warned. "Don't speak of my late wife. There are private places where not even you are allowed to trespass."

Her chin took on a defiant tilt. "Because you wish to cower in the shadows all alone?"

Good God, Isobel was all sweetness and light—what did she know of shadows?

A dull throbbing began to pound at his temples. If he couldn't do a better job of protecting her from darkness that lurked inside the hearts of some men, she would learn all too quickly. There were crevasses and corners where the sun never stirred a flicker of illumination.

"Yes, all alone," he snapped. "Indeed, I can't think of a place I would rather be than a solitary sanctuary, be it a damp, dark hole in the ground, where I won't be bedeviled by plaguey women."

Hooking the poker back in place, Alec took up his glass and the brandy bottle. "So I shall leave the bright blaze of the fire to you and retire to my black-as-Hades bedchamber."

He stalked out, too angry to care about her stricken expression. It wasn't until he had slammed the door to his room shut that the flare of emotion died down to remorse.

"Bloody, *bloody* Hell." Expelling a harried sigh, he tilted the bottle and eyed the brandy, knowing there wasn't near enough to submerge him in blissful oblivion. Instead of pouring another measure, he sunk down on his bed and took his head in his hands.

Coward.

Isobel's accusation cut right to the quick. He had never thought of himself as lacking in backbone. But perhaps that was simply another mistake.

Another delusion.

Her challenge compelled him to admit that he had been afraid to confront the failure of his marriage. Like demons, the reasons teased and tormented him with their whispers of his faults.

Perhaps it was time to fight back. If he was to have any hope of...

Alec suddenly found himself repeating the lines of Caro's poem on the Scottish moors. She seemed capable of seeing strength and beauty in the harsh ruggedness of the mist-gray stone and storm-colored heather. So hers was the sort of serious sensibility that might overlook his lack of practiced charm and social polish.

She might see their shared interests, their intellectual engagement of more substance than fine manners and flowery compliments.

"Ha," he breathed, after contemplating the thought for a brief moment. "And pigs might fly."

Caro was, he reminded himself, a lovely, lively spirited heiress, with legions of London aristocrats seeking to win her hand. Given such circumstances and such choices what lady in her right mind would prefer a rough-cut Scottish savage?

The answer was too depressing to contemplate.

And yet, she had kissed him.

Practicing her flirtations? A spur-of-the-moment whim?

Alec fell back against the pillows, uncertain of anything—save for his simmering attraction to Miss Carolina Sloane.

If he wasn't to go stark raving mad from desperate desire, he was going to have to decide what to do about it.

Chapter Eleven

Staring absently into the looking glass, Caro was only half aware of her maid sliding in a pair of hairpins and giving the ribbon threaded through her topknot a last little tweak.

"There, Miss, you look the picture of loveliness if I say so myself," said Alice with a measure of satisfaction as she stepped back and admired her handiwork.

"You are truly an artist with brush and comb," said Caro, though in truth her hair could be painted purple and lit afire for all the attention she was paying to her toilette. Her thoughts were elsewhere.

"You'll be the belle of the Venetian breakfast," went on Alice. She pursed her lips. "Though why the *ton* calls a party that starts in the late afternoon a 'breakfast' is beyond me."

"Most likely because many of the fancy ladies of Society don't rise until well after noon."

Her maid shook her head in disbelief. "Revelries night and day. I'm sure it must be exciting, what with all the beautiful clothes and sumptuous food, but I'm not sure I could ever get used to such a life."

Nor am I.

"It's not as exciting as it might seem," said Caro, recalling Andover's description of the Season. "Frivolities quickly become..."

Alice cocked her head, waiting for Caro to go on.

"Frivolous," she finished. "And rather boring. No one talks about anything interesting or original for fear of being thought too different."

Her maid looked thoughtful as she assembled the matching accessories to go with Caro's gown.

"I think I'd rather take the blue reticule," murmured Caro. "It's big enough to fit my book of Byron's poetry. So if things become truly dull, I can sneak away behind the bushes and read."

"What with all the reading you do, you always have so many interesting things to say," mused Alice. "It must be hard to have to keep them bottled up inside." She made a face. "Begging your pardon, Miss, but I have to say, I'm glad I'm not a fine lady and can just be myself."

"There are a few people with whom I can share my thoughts," replied Caro. "Miss Urquehart is a kindred spirit."

And her brother?

Determined to push the maddening Alec McClellan out of her head, she quickly rose from the dressing table and turned to find the volume of Byron's poems among the books on her desk. Whatever bond had formed between them felt strained—or perhaps broken.

Truth and lies. Caro stared at the leatherbound book in her hands. It wasn't as if Alec had lied to her, she told herself. But the omission seemed perilously close to an untruth.

Trust was an integral part of friendship, and Alec had not

trusted her enough to tell her about an integral part of his life.

That hurt. More than she cared to admit.

"Still, it must be rather grand to attend a party given by a dowager duchess," remarked Alice.

"What?" Caro looked up from her brooding. "Oh, er, yes. Her country estate is said to be quite lovely, and no doubt there will be a crush of guests, so I am sure it will be a very lively gathering."

Her voice must have sounded a trifle brittle, for Alice glanced at her in concern. "Is there anything else I can do for you, Miss Caro?"

"No, no. You've seen to everything. There's no need for me to keep you any longer."

Alice bobbed her head as she set a pair of kidskin gloves on the dressing table and turned for the door. "Have a lovely time."

"Thank you," she replied, unable to muster any enthusiasm. Despite the cloudless skies and shimmering sunshine, her own dark thoughts would likely shadow the festivities.

The door clicked shut.

Glancing down once again at the gilt-stamped "Byron" on the book cover, she bit back a sigh. Passionate emotions were all very well for romantic poetry, but they wreaked havoc with the mundane workings of real life.

It would be easier to be a silly, simpering featherhead, Caro decided as she jammed the book into her reticule.

An active imagination could be a curse as well as a blessing.

Heaving an inward sigh, Caro looped the strings over her wrist and went downstairs to meet her mother for the carriage ride out to the party.

* * *

A plateful of creamed lobster patties and a goblet of sparkling champagne punch did little to brighten Caro's spirits, despite the festive mood of the party.

It was a lovely late summer afternoon, with the first blush of evening hovering on the horizon. All around her, the other guests strolled within the high-hedged swath of garden, enjoying the rich assortment of delicacies and wines. A mild breeze swirled through the lush plantings, perfuming the air with the sweet scent of roses and lilac as it ruffled the stylish gowns of silk and satin worn by the ladies. The jeweltone flutters were nearly as colorful as the blooms, their sun-dappled hues accentuated by the darker hues of the gentlemen's dress coats.

Caro forced a smile as she listened to Andover and Isobel's cheerful chatter about the previous evening's dancing. But as they turned to fetch a selection of cream tarts from one of the refreshment tables, she drifted over to the far hedge and ducked through the opening to escape from the sounds of laughter and the serenading violins.

Following the winding gravel path, she passed by several walled garden nooks before finding herself at the crest of a wide, sloping lawn, where a massive fountain of ornately carved marble marked the end of the formal walkway.

Struck by the sheer scale of it, she stopped short to stare up at the cavorting dolphins and mermaids.

Is every creature under the sun—including those sculptured from stone—in a merry mood save for me?

After watching the gold-flecked sunlight play across the glistening white figures, Caro felt a little ashamed of her maudlin mood.

"Oh, don't be so cynical," she muttered to herself.

"*Arrgh.*" A sudden watery whisper of breeze-ruffled droplets seemed to gurgle in agreement.

A reluctant smile tugged at her mouth. Whether she liked it or not, imagination was part of her—

"*Arrgh.*" The gurgle came again, louder and more distinct. It sounded...human.

Mystified, Caro looked upward, for it seemed to be coming from the very top of the fountain. Craning her neck, she edged a step sideways, trying to peer into the huge half-open clamshell balanced atop the noses of the highest leaping dolphins.

"Help, help!" A bedraggled little girl peeked out from the slivered space, a tangle of wet ribbons and dripping curls framing her face.

Caro quickly climbed atop the circular bench carved into the fountain's base. "Don't move, sweetheart," she called, fearing the child might tumble from the precarious perch.

"I can't—I'm stuck!" came back the reply.

"Oh, dear—are you hurt?" she asked. "I'll run and fetch help—"

"NO!" cried the little girl. "Please don't. I'll be in terrible trouble if I'm discovered. I'm not supposed to be here."

Caro repressed a wry laugh. *That* had a very familiar ring, she thought, recalling all the times she had trailed after her older sisters, determined to share their adventures.

"I could climb down myself, but the back of my dress is snagged on a bit of stone." The face disappeared, muffling the rest of her words. "And. I. Can't. Reach. It!"

"Sit still," ordered Caro as she eyed the intricate carvings. There were plenty of juts and crevices—climbing up would be easy, despite the smooth, slippery surface. But there was no getting around the fact that the shower of cascading water would leave her wet to the bone.

Ah, well. I shall think of some excuse—

"Perhaps I can be of help to the damsel in distress."

Caro whirled around at the sound of Alec's drawl.

"My clothing will suffer far less from a soaking than yours will," he pointed out.

"But what of your dignity, sir?" she countered.

"You think me so stiff-rumped?" He was already removing his boots and stockings.

"I think that I can easily make up some fanciful excuse for why I fell into the fountain, while you . . ." Caro's voice faltered as she watched him peel off his coat and cravat. The light shone through the light linen of his shirt, silhouetting the slabbed contours of his shoulders.

"While I have no sense of whimsy?"

Don't stare at his muscles. Don't stare at the intriguing glint of golden curls peeking out from his open collar.

"Th-that's not exactly what I meant." She made herself look away, knowing it was foolish beyond words to still harbor a *tendre* for him. "I know you have an impish side, sir, but you seem so very loath to show it."

"I do?" He arched a brow. "Perhaps you are only imagining it."

Was he teasing her? A small smile seemed to be playing at the corners of his mouth.

"Me?" she muttered, trying not to think of how much she would miss their verbal sparring. "Surely not. You know very well that a young lady is not supposed to have any imagination."

The smile gave way to a chuckle as Alec stepped up onto the bench. "Well then, we had better keep this little interlude a secret." He glanced upward. "To ensure that all three of our reputations don't suffer irreparable damage."

A silvery spray misted his red-gold hair, and with the late afternoon sun setting behind his head, he looked like some glorious ancient sea god rising to life out of the polished stone.

"Hold this," he said, breaking the spell by thrusting his coat into her hands. "I'll just be a moment."

With that, he grabbed hold of a mermaid's curled fin and started to climb. The cascading water quickly soaked his shirt and trousers, causing the fabric to cling to his body.

A proper lady ought to look away, thought Caro.

Thank God I have no pretensions to being a proper lady. The view was really too delicious to miss.

Alec hauled himself up to the crowning clamshell and peered inside. "Halloo, what have we here?"

Caro heard a burble of laughter echo within the carved marble.

"Hmmm. Let us see how we are going to extract you from your shell." Alec's head and shoulders ducked through the opening.

He reappeared a moment later with the very wet and very beaming little girl in his arms. "Look what a lovely little pearl I found inside the oyster," he called down to Caro.

"It's not an oyster, silly—it's a clam!" trilled the child.

Alec gave a look of mock surprise. "By Jove, you're right. But if you're not a pearl, shall I put you back?"

She shook her head, spraying his face with a fresh shower of drops. "No, I wish to go down." Her arms wound tighter around his neck. "Now, if you please, sir."

"Very well." He picked his way carefully down through the frolicking sea creatures and dropped lightly onto the bench, his bare feet making a watery slap on the stone.

"Thank you," said the little girl.

"You are most welcome, Pearl."

She giggled. "My name is Catherine."

"Which is a very pretty name." He bowed. "Mine is Alec."

Watching Alec's unguarded expression as he bantered with the little girl, Caro knew her intuition was correct—beneath the shell of steely reserve, he was a very different man. *Hard, yet soft. Strong, yet sensitive.*

Her heart gave a little lurch as he curled a smile and winked at the little girl.

Catherine responded with a ladylike curtsey.

"Now, where does the Pearl live, if not in the clamshell?" he asked.

The little girl pointed to the manor house.

"A much more comfortable dwelling," he murmured. "Shells can be cold and wet."

"Yes, but I shall be in very hot water when I return to my room," replied Catherine. She bit her lip, her gaze turning wistful as she darted a look behind her. "I am forbidden to play in the fountain, but it looked so pretty in the sunlight, and the fish and their friends seemed to be having such fun."

"So they do," agreed Alec. "But as you have learned, it can be dangerous to play alone around water and such towering heights."

"Accidents can happen, no matter how careful you are," added Caro.

For an instant she shut her eyes, recalling a long ago day when she, too, had disobeyed the rules and run off on an irresistible adventure. To this day, she was still terrified of...

She quickly shook off the grim memory. Thankfully, Catherine had suffered no more than a tiny tear to her dress, which was easily mended. A small price to pay for a valuable lesson.

Lifting her lashes, Caro found Alec eyeing her quizzically. He then crouched down and put his hands on Catherine's slim shoulders. "Miss Caro is quite right. So please promise me you won't do it again."

The little girl sighed, then gave a solemn nod. "Very well." A pause. "I was a little frightened when I couldn't get down," she admitted.

"No harm done." He smoothed a scraggly curl from her brow. "As for being in hot water, I am sure that Miss Caro and I can come up with a plan to keep you out of trouble."

"You *can*?"

"Oh, indeed." Alec shot her an amused look. "Miss Caro has a very clever imagination. And she's very experienced at creating stories."

"We need not get too imaginative," murmured Caro. "We'll simply say I asked you to show me the fountain, and you were kind enough agree. I was too curious and stood on the bench for a closer look and slipped. You tried to help me, but I knocked you into the pool."

"And then of course, I happened along," interjected Alec. "And rescued both of you."

Catherine stared at them in open-mouthed admiration. "That's a corking good bouncer! You think it will work?"

"*Not* that we are encouraging you to tell Banbury tales," said Caro hastily. "But as this is a special day of festivities, we shall make an exception."

Alec covered a chuckle with a cough. "So yes, Pearl, I daresay it will work." Swinging the little girl into his arms, he set off for the back of the house. Caro gathered up his coat and boots, then hurried to catch up.

A quick explanation to one of the maids who answered the knock on the kitchen doors resulted in a flurry of activity. The nanny was called, Catherine was much fussed over, and effusive thanks were offered to Alec, along with a vigorous toweling of his boots and an insistence that he stand by the stove until his trousers were dry.

As Catherine was carried away to be given a warm bath and a posset of honeyed milk, the little girl managed a last little wave. And a wink.

"You are very good with children," observed Caro, once she and Alec had made their way back to the gravel walkway.

"I like bantlings," he replied. "My cousins have a great brood of them, so I often have them underfoot at my estate in Scotland."

"And obviously children like you. They have an unerring knack for knowing when someone is insincere in their attentions."

"They are not yet tainted by the sly subterfuges and false flatteries of the adult world."

The hard-edged Alec was suddenly back, she noted with a pang of longing, the impish smile shuttered behind a sarcastic scowl.

They walked on, the *crunch, crunch* of the small stones the only sounds between them.

Caro shot a furtive look at his profile, watching the slanting shadows sharpen his features. Only the fringe of his lashes, which caught a few flickering sparks of light, softened the somber shades.

"You are looking at me rather strangely," said Alec

abruptly. "Have I done something wrong, or—" He cut off with a wry grimace. "No, allow me to rephrase that. I know that you hold me in low regard, but have I done something *recently* to increase your displeasure?"

Caro looked away, embarrassed that he had caught her staring. "I—I can't imagine that my opinion concerning your behavior, low or otherwise, matters to you, sir."

"On the contrary, Miss Caro," he responded gruffly. The breeze ruffled through his damp hair as he came to a halt and turned to face her. "It does matter to me."

She opened her mouth to reply, but as the flutter of his open shirtfront accentuated the "V" of sun-bronzed flesh, her mind was suddenly blank. All she could muster was a faint "Oh."

"Speaking of which..." His boots stirred another scrape of stone as he shifted his weight from foot to foot. "I have reason to believe that certain recent revelations made to you by Mr. Thayer have lowered that opinion considerably," he went on haltingly.

That Alec was as ill at ease as she was made Caro feel a trifle less awkward.

"No doubt you are wondering why I never mentioned the fact that I was"—he paused, as if needing an extra breath of air to expel the next word—"married."

"It did seem a subject that should have come up," she replied softly. "Given the fact that we are supposedly friends."

"I don't find it easy to speak of personal things with anyone, Miss Caro," said Alec slowly. "A character flaw, no doubt. Of which I have many."

Clasping his hands behind his back, he stared out at some point in the distant trees for a long moment before speaking again. "Be that as it may, I should like to make one thing clear. I have heard of the version that Thayer tells of my marriage, and suffice it to say, he has twisted the truth."

It didn't suffice at all, thought Caro. Indeed, there were myriad questions she wished to ask. But on seeing Alec's stony expression, she guessed that even with a chisel and hammer she wouldn't have much luck in prying any answers out of him.

Still, she decided to venture a try. "Thayer said your cruelty drove your wife to flee."

A mirthless laugh. "And most people believe him."

"I don't," said Caro. "But I should like to hear from your lips that it is a lie."

"It is a lie," he replied in a near whisper. "A damnable one."

The vise-like force squeezing around her chest relaxed ever so slightly. Breathing was all at once a little easier. "Thank you."

Their eyes met, but he looked away too quickly for her to discern what was causing the rippling beneath the storm-blue surface.

"The accident—" she began.

"No, I ask that you don't press me for the details," he interrupted brusquely.

Had he loved his wife so much that it still caused him great pain to think about the accident?

"I do not intend to talk about them," continued Alec. "Or of any specifics concerning the relationship. All I will say is that Thayer's account of my actions is not accurate, and I wished for you to know that."

Once again, he was retreating, holding her at arm's length.

For a fleeting moment she wondered whether it was hopeless to think they might ever be close.

"I—I am very sorry for your loss," Caro said after several heartbeats had thumped against her ribcage. "You must feel her absence very deeply."

His face tightened, the skin drawing so taut over his cheekbones that they looked sharp as knifeblades. Expelling a ragged breath, he muttered something under his breath.

An oath?

"Real life is rarely like a storybook romance," he muttered.

"Despite what you seem to think, I'm not a silly schoolgirl," she responded. "I know that love is complicated—"

"Love?" Alec shook his head. "Ye gods, there is so much you don't understand."

"Then tell me," she challenged.

He said nothing in reply.

His silence seemed to freeze away all the warmth from their earlier laughter. Feeling hurt and confused, Caro stepped back. "I—I should return to the festivities before Andover and your sister begin to wonder what has happened to me."

Alec nodded grimly. Pinching a wrinkle from his disheveled trousers, he glanced at the path leading off to the stables. "Given my appearance, I think it best if I avoid the crowd and take my leave from here." He tugged on his coat. "Good evening."

She watched him walk away.

You are right—there is much I don't understand.

And perhaps she was merely beating her head against a wall of Highland granite in trying to make any sense of Alec McClellan.

But sense had nothing to do with love. There was no rhyme or reason to its teasing, taunting grip.

Caro stood still in the fading light, listening to the splashing sounds of the fountain and the rustle of leaves as the *thump, thump* of her own disappointment echoed in her ears.

Love. No wonder poets spoke so passionately about pain as well as pleasure.

Blinking back a tear, she finally turned away from her musings and set off to rejoin her friends.

"Damn. Damn. Damn." The phaeton bounced dangerously over the rutted road as Alec urged his matched pair of bays to a faster pace. He was risking a broken wheel, but in his current frame of mind, the danger didn't matter.

"Damnation," he swore again. His tongue seemed to tie in knots when he tried to speak of personal feelings to Caro. Baring his heart was hellishly hard. The idea of standing naked...

Naked. A sudden vision of her lithe body lying on rumpled sheets sent a jolt through his body that had nothing to do with the careening phaeton.

It should be simple. Caro was nothing—nothing!—like his late wife. She was so fiercely honest in all her passions.

So what am I afraid of?

Alec wrestled with the question yet again. Physical dangers, cerebral challenges—fear had no hold on him.

Save for my heart.

Isobel had called him a coward for fearing to believe he could be happy again.

The echo of Caro's laughter and Catherine's giggles suddenly drowned out the rattle of rocks and metal.

Gripping the reins tighter, Alec straightened on the seat, recalling a line from one of Lord Byron's poems...

Love will find a way through paths where wolves fear to prey.

Thayer was a skulking predator, and it was time to turn the bite of fear on him.

Chapter Twelve

Caro slipped the package of ribbons into her handbasket and then signaled to her maid that she was ready to leave the shop.

"I think we have purchased everything that Mama requested," she said, after consulting the long list one last time. Though she was feeling a little blue-deviled this morning, she tried to muster a cheerful face. "Except for the jet buttons, but Mrs. Bertram promised that she will be receiving a shipment from London on Thursday."

"Aye, Miss Caro," replied Alice. "Now there are just the two new bonnets that your mother ordered to be picked up from Madame La Florette's establishment."

"We will soon have enough feathers in the house to fly to the moon," sighed Caro. The baroness was very fond of ostrich plumes, and despite having brought a trunk full of bird-bedecked turbans, shakos, and chipstraw fripperies from London, she hadn't been able to resist purchasing several more.

Alice stifled a giggle.

"These latest designs are particularly hideous," added Caro. "I am tempted to nest them in the garden's linden tree rather than Mama's armoire. Perhaps a hawk will think them a tasty morsel and carry them away."

The comment earned another choked laugh.

As they reached the street corner, Caro hesitated and came to a halt, even though the way was clear for crossing. "Would you mind terribly if I asked you to fetch them and bring them home by yourself, Alice?"

Hitching in a breath, she went on in a rush. "I—I am accompanying Isobel and her aunt on a visit to friends from Scotland who are spending the summer on an estate near Bristol. The drive is a long one, and as we will be returning tonight, I don't wish to delay them. But if I return to the house, there's a good chance that Mama will ask my assistance on some other errand—and you know what a fuss she can make if she's feeling fretful."

It was a lie—an innocent one, but a lie nonetheless, and she felt a spasm of guilt as Alice gave a sympathetic huff and waved her away.

"Oh, but of course, Miss Caro! Your mother has been running you a bit ragged these last few days, so I'm happy to have you get a bit of a holiday for yourself. Never you worry—I shall see that Her Ladyship has no reason to complain."

"Thank you." Relief nudged aside any lingering remorse. Her emotions were still in a bit of a turmoil over the recent revelations concerning Alec and his marriage. And despite their encounter yesterday—or perhaps because of it—she was desperately in need of some peace and solitude in which to sort them out.

The dratted man was an enigma tied up in a riddle!

Alec's halting hints had implied that, contrary to Thayer's nasty whispers, it had been *his* heart that had been badly bruised, not that of his wife.

Alec hurt by love? A part of her was angry that the lady had failed to treasure such a gift. A part of her felt hope flare. Perhaps with the right spark, the fire could be rekindled.

Oh, yes, there was much to mull over. And so, on impulse, she had made up the Banbury tale of having been invited to accompany her friend on a visit to the country. Isobel and her aunt were in fact making the day trip, so it was unlikely that she would be caught in the falsehood.

"Thank you," she repeated, shaking off her musings for the moment.

"You just leave behind any troubles, Miss, and simply enjoy the day," said Alice cheerily as she took the handbasket from Caro.

"I'm certain that I will." With freedom beckoning, she shifted her reticule, which was stuffed with books, pencils, and a packet of pastries, anxious to be off. The prospect of escaping to some secluded spot in Sydney Gardens until dusk seemed heavenly. And the fact that Alec was accompanying his sister to the country meant she didn't have to worry about another unexpected encounter.

"Please remind Mama that I shall not be returning until late this evening," she added.

Being out alone after dusk was risking her reputation. But Caro was tired of Society's rules, tired of the polished manners, the sharp-eyed tabbies waiting to claw a lady's reputation to shreds, the silky innuendos that slithered like a serpent through the world of aristocratic privilege.

She was feeling a little dangerous.

"Don't fret—I'll soothe any ruffled feathers." Her maid

smiled. "You deserve a bit of carefree fun. I daresay you must miss the company of your sisters."

Caro swallowed hard, trying to loosen the sudden constriction that took hold of her throat. "Yes, I do miss them." *I miss their wisdom, their humor, their guidance.* "I shall be very glad when they return home to England from their travels."

But for now, I must rely on my own judgment.

Parting ways with Alice, Caro chose a route through the more out-of-the-way side streets, avoiding the Pulteney Bridge in favor of a less-traveled footbridge over the canal.

For today, she was determined to seize the moment and break free of convention. She desperately needed time and space to sort out her conflicting emotions.

Black and white. Light and dark—the two had somehow blurred and become terribly tangled.

If only she could unravel all the protective layers that Alec McClellan kept wound so tightly around him.

Though she knew Thayer's hints at his erstwhile friend's nefarious actions were likely lies, there was a grain of truth to the fact that Alec was keeping some secrets from her.

As to what they were...

Well, speak of the Devil.

Cutting through a narrow passageway between two buildings, she was about to step out from the shadows when she spotted Thayer at the top of the street.

She paused where she was, held in check by a sudden feeling that there was something oddly furtive about his movements. It was a matter of subtle little things—the angle of his body, the tilt of his hat, the way he seemed to hug close to the buildings. But all at once they stirred a prickling sensation at the back of her neck.

Why the stealth if he wasn't up to no good?

Flattening herself against the dark brick wall, she waited and watched, growing more and more certain with every step that something havey-cavey was afoot.

Sure enough, he turned up a narrow lane that only led to one enclave of residences higher on the hill.

Abandoning her original plan, Caro made the split-second decision to follow him. Perhaps her imagination was running wild, but having given herself permission to break the rules for the day, she might as well throw caution to the wind.

She counted to ten, then slipped from her hiding place and quickly crossed to the lane. Up ahead, Thayer had picked up his pace and after a quick look around he darted into an alleyway that ran along the back garden walls of the elegant townhouses lining the adjoining street.

"I knew it," whispered Caro as she gathered her skirts and hurried as fast as she dared to catch up.

Thankfully, the area was a quiet residential part of town, and aside from a maid walking two frisky spaniels there was nobody else around. Hoping her luck would hold, she ducked through the narrow opening and took cover among the heavy twines of ivy.

Her heartbeat kicked up a notch as she saw Thayer stop halfway down the alley and begin to fiddle with the lock on the gate.

Which, as she had good reason to know, gave access to the residence rented by Isobel's aunt.

Ha—she had suspected that this might be Thayer's destination, and now she was sure of it!

But what was he up to?

Caro thought for a moment. Yes, Isobel had mentioned

the trip during a break between dances at last night's Assembly, so Thayer was aware that the house was empty, save for several servants. With a modicum of caution he could avoid them, assuming his intention was to enter the house.

The gate creaked open, and Thayer shouldered his way through the slivered opening.

Her heart was now hammering against her ribs, each thud a warning that from this point on, the chances of getting caught rose dramatically if she dared to follow him.

"And yet drama is the essence of poetry," she murmured to herself.

To retreat now would be prudent.

But it wouldn't be me.

She took a moment to hide her reticule, bonnet, and shawl among the leafy vines, and then crept forward in a low crouch.

In for a penny, in for a pound. She could only hope that there wouldn't be hell to pay.

"Damnation." The thump of wet leather hitting stone punctuated the oath as Alec tugged off his muddy boots and dropped them on the scullery floor. His sodden coat followed.

"Damnation," he repeated, staring balefully at his filthy shirt and breeches. "If I had any brains in my cockloft, I would be lounging in one of the comfortable armchairs of Lord Merton's study, enjoying a glass of his excellent port."

Instead, he had sent two burly footmen in his place to accompany his sister and aunt on their visit to the viscount's country house. His own journey had involved a meeting with his Scottish contact, who had sent urgent word that he had information to pass along.

A remote spot along the River Avon had been designated, one that demanded wading through waist-deep water because the rickety footbridge had given way at first step.

He was still undecided on whether the plunge—and the ruin of his favorite footwear—had been worth it. The news from Scotland had helped cross several names off his list of possible traitors, but as for providing any clue as to why Isobel had been attacked . . .

He was still in the dark.

Frowning, Alec leaned back against the large copper washtub and spent a moment longer pondering the conundrum as he watched the ooze of mud seep out from his stockings.

A bath, he decided, might help stir his thoughts to greater clarity.

And at least he wouldn't smell like a swamp.

Alec was about to head up to his rooms when he recalled that the maids had been given a half-day holiday and the footmen were traveling with Isobel and his aunt.

"Hmmph." A glance back at the copper laundry tub and massive cistern of water made up his mind. It was far easier to bathe here—and it would avoid the sticky problem of how not to track mud over the freshly swept carpets and polished parquet.

The water was unheated, but as he was used to swimming in the frigid Scottish lochs, it felt positively mild as he quickly filled the tub with one of the nearby buckets.

Rummaging around in the large storage cabinet produced a towel, a sponge, and a cake of pine-scented soap. Stripping off his filthy garments, Alec let out a contented sigh as he sunk up to his chin in a swirl of suds. It was rather relaxing to float in such a spacious tub, and he found himself closing his eyes and letting his mind drift off to puzzle over the problem at hand.

He wasn't sure how long he had been submerged in thought when a soft scuff roused him from his reveries.

His sense now on full alert, Alec held himself still and cocked an ear to listen.

For a long moment there was nothing.

And then the faint rustle of fabric caught his attention.

Lifting his head ever so slightly, Alec peered over the edge of the tub. The scullery was awash in hide-and-seek shadows, the only light coming from a pair of windows on the far wall. But as he squinted into the gloom, he suddenly could make out a flicker of movement. It was only a vague shape at first, a blur of gray on gray hugging low to the ground as it wove its way past the mops and clothes mangles.

Alec frowned as it came closer and slowly materialized into a the form of a young lady...

What in the name of Hades was Miss Caro Sloane doing, crawling across the scullery floor?

Whatever the answer, he had a feeling he wasn't going to like it.

Waiting until another slither brought her abreast of his bath, Alec shot out an arm and snagged her by the scruff of her collar.

"Mmmph!" She bit back a strangled yelp.

"Bloody Hell—" he began, only to have her twist free and clamp a hand over his mouth.

"Shhh!" she hissed.

Feeling the tension radiating from her palm, Alec made no further effort to speak but merely raised his brows in silent question.

Caro leaned close—close enough for him to see in her face that this was no silly schoolgirl prank. "Thayer has just entered the house by the back door," she whispered. "Clearly he is up to no good, but I need to keep moving, and quickly, so I can spy on what is he doing."

Thayer? Alec grabbed hold of her wrist and lifted her hand from his lips. "How—"

"There's no time for explanations," she exclaimed in a rushed whisper, trying to wriggle free of his grasp. "Let me go! We need to know what's he's up to."

"Not *we*. Me." Without thinking, Alec shot up out of the water...

Then just as quickly, he dropped to a crouch.

"Damnation. Find me some clothes."

"There's no time!" Caro repeated. She picked up the towel and tossed it at his chest. "For God's sake, don't be missus. I've seen a penis before. Lots of them, in fact."

For an instant, gentlemanly scruples warred with practicality. But she was right—they couldn't afford to waste a moment if they wanted to learn what mischief Thayer was intent on wreaking.

Out of the tub he stepped—naked as a newborn. He was taking her at her word that the sight of his pump handle wouldn't frighten her into a faint.

"Avert your eyes," Alec muttered as he quickly blotted the dripping water from his limbs and wrapped the towel around his waist.

There was an old adage about girding one's loins for battle...

A glance showed she was still upright.

"Now, let us go see what game Thayer is playing. Which way was he headed?"

* * *

Caro had started to turn away, but at the sight of his lean body emerging from the tub, the chiseled planes and wet muscles glistening wet in the flickering light, she went very still.

It was wicked, it was wanton to let her gaze linger. A proper young lady should be shocked into a swoon.

But swooning would mean missing such a magnificent, masculine sight. Alec was like one of the breathtakingly beautiful marble statues she had seen in Greece of the classical gods—

No, he was better than a sculpted god of perfectly polished stone, for he thrummed with flesh-and-blood life.

An impatient flick of his hand brushing the tangle of damp hair back from his brow broke the momentary spell that held her in thrall. Forcing her eyes away, Caro suddenly realized she hadn't responded to his question.

"He was creeping down the corridor leading to the main stairs," she answered.

Alec was already in motion, his bare feet skimming noiselessly over the dark stone tiles. "My guess is that he'll be looking for my bedchamber or the study."

Fisting her skirts to keep them as quiet as possible, Caro hurried to catch up. "That makes sense," she said softly, as he paused to check that the corridor was clear. Spotting a narrow door set discreetly into the dark wood paneling, she asked, "Wouldn't it be better if we take the servant stairs?"

He shook his head. "The risk of an unwanted encounter is greater than if we chance the main stairs."

Taking her hand, he darted across the foyer and started up the carpeted treads. "The maids have been given the day off, but if we're spotted by the housekeeper, we'll just have to brazen it out."

Brazen. A behavior that seemed to come naturally to her.

Caro kept her eyes averted from his bare chest and the intriguing golden curls glinting against his sun-bronzed skin. "As you know well, sir, that won't present any problem for me."

A hint of a smile quirked at the left corner of his mouth, softening the hard-edged planes of his face.

Her heart, which was still thumping hard against her ribs, ratcheted up another notch.

"For which I am profoundly grateful," he replied. "We don't want to kick up a dust that might alert Thayer to our presence."

As they came to the top of the landing, Alec pressed a finger to his lips indicating no more talking. Crouching low, he peered through the balusters, and after studying the three arched entryways for a long moment, he indicated the one on the left.

Caro knew from earlier visits with Isobel that through it lay his set of rooms.

A stillness hung heavy in the corridor. She felt a shiver skate down her spine as she tiptoed through the shadows. Alec was moving slowly, slowly... and then suddenly came to a stop.

Peeking over his shoulder, she saw it too—a small sliver of light on the Oriental runner indicating that one of the doors was slightly ajar.

A warning touch reminded her of the need for absolute silence.

She held her breath, hoping it might help control her pounding heart. Each beat seemed to be echoing loud as cannonfire off the walls.

Alec inched forward.

Caro followed.

Through the gap between the molding and the door, she caught sight of Thayer hunched over the desk in the sitting room. He had the bottom drawer open, and after rummaging through the contents, he took a small sack from his coat pocket and stashed it inside.

Whatever he did next was lost in a blur as Alec quickly retreated, pulling her along with him. Easing open the door of the adjoining suite, he hustled her inside and drew it shut.

A few moments later, she heard a latch click and hurried footsteps rush past their hiding place.

"What do you think that was all about?" she whispered, once the sounds had faded away.

"We shall soon see," replied Alec. He waited a few more moments before leading the way back to his own rooms and kneeling down by the desk.

The sack had been shoved to the back of the drawer and covered with several ledgers. After fishing it free, he untied the cords and shook out the contents onto the blotter.

"Ye gods." Caro's eyes widened at the flashes of gold glittering against the dark leather.

"Ye gods, indeed," said Alec through his teeth. He picked up the object and subjected it to a careful examination.

"Have you any idea—" she began.

"Yes," he said curtly. "Having just yesterday accompanied Isobel and my aunt to the Antiquities Museum, I recognize it as the Hadrian Eagle, a very rare and very valuable ancient artifact from the days of the Roman occupation of Britain. It is—or rather, it was—the most important item they had on display there."

"But why?" she mused.

"Oh, come, Miss Caro. Surely you've read enough novels to follow the plot."

"Yes, yes, it's clear he wants to frame you for its theft." She frowned. "But again I ask why?"

"Pure malice is one reason," responded Alec. "Thayer is a thoroughly dirty dish. As for the other reason, I have not yet put together all the pieces of the puzzle."

"But you think it has something to do with the attack on Isobel and me," she asked.

He nodded. "I suspect so, but have not yet discovered his motive. There is trouble in Scotland, however—"

A loud metallic *rap* on the front door reverberated through the whole house, followed in rapid-fire succession by several more.

"The dastard didn't waste any time," growled Alec. "I assume that will be the magistrate."

"Well, don't just stand there!" Caro snatched the eagle from his hands and thrust it back in the sack. "We have to hide it!"

"And you." He glanced at the door. "There's no time to reach the back stairs."

Rap, rap.

"Damnation." Alec grabbed her arm. "Come with me."

Chapter Thirteen

Scandal. Ruin.

Alec felt the sharp taste of bile rise in his throat. It was all because of him that Caro had been drawn into danger.

She had taken a terrible risk in following Thayer. He could not—would not—let her be destroyed because of her own intrepid sense of courage and loyalty.

Though why she had felt beholden to come to his aid was a mystery. He had been nothing but rude and snarly...

"A-are you sure this is a good idea?" asked Caro, as he pulled her into his bedchamber.

"It's a bloody awful idea, but I can't see that we have any other alternative," he replied, marching her past the ornately carved four-poster bed and into the small adjoining dressing room. "It's the only chance we have of dodging disaster."

She edged around a rack of boot brushes and bottles of polish. "You don't think it will occur to the authorities to search in here? It seems an obvious hiding place."

"Of course they will look in here." Alec set to shifting a stack of trunks and bandboxes. "But with luck, they won't find you."

"Lord Strathcona..."

A last heave cleared a space near the right corner of the back wall, revealing the faint outline of a small door, only three feet high, set in the wainscoting. "It's a storage nook," he explained. "It's lined in cedarwood, so it must have been used to keep woolens."

He saw her stiffen.

"It's dark in there."

"So take a nap," he replied. "You'll find a blanket. Granted, it's a bit cramped—"

"It's *dark*," repeated Caro a little shrilly, shuffling back a step. "As in 'black as Hades.'"

Alec heard voices in the corridor.

"Your name will be even blacker," he shot back, "if you don't get inside there *now*."

She didn't move.

Which left him no choice but to seize her shoulders and give her a shake. "Trust me. Please."

"All right." Squeezing her eyes shut, Caro allowed him to push and prod her into the small space.

Her reaction seemed strangely at odds with her usual bravado, but Alec didn't have time to ponder why. Already he could hear a clatter of steps in the corridor. He swung the door shut, scrabbled the trunks back in place, then stripped off his towel and bolted for the bedchamber.

"Here now, you can't barge into His Lordship's quarters without permission." The housekeeper's aggrieved protest rose above the grumbling of male voices.

"Oh yes, we can," came a gruff reply. "Stand aside. I'm

the head magistrate of Bath and I need to have a word with the baron."

Alec managed to slide under the bedcovers just as the main door to the suite banged open.

Darkness.

Caro clasped her knees to her chest and choked back a burble of panic. Her whole body was trembling uncontrollably, and every inch of her skin was suddenly clammy with sweat.

Steady, steady, she told herself. Surely it was time to put childish terrors behind her.

She had been six years old, a precocious child, stubborn enough to disobey her nanny and sneak away to follow her older sisters into the caves around their campsite in Crete. It had seemed a great lark until a rock had shifted, trapping her in the confines of the cold stone and utter darkness.

Hour upon hour had passed before her father was able to find her, and even though she had been unharmed, the memory of the ordeal still stirred the occasional nightmare.

"Coward," she whispered. "How can I hope to be a real adventurer if I am afraid of the dark?"

The only sound that rose in answer was the ragged rasp of her own breathing.

"Strathcona must think me an idiot." Caro said it aloud, thinking perhaps the words would spark a show of spirit. But they seemed to have the opposite effect.

All the fight seemed to leak out of her in a stifled sob. No matter how hard she tried, she seemed to make a mull of every attempt to win his regard.

I am too headstrong. Too outspoken. Too passionate.

His last exasperated snaps seemed to take on a louder

echo in her ears. *Your name will be blacker...* Clearly he thought her an impossible hellion—and with good reason.

Ye gods, she had stood staring in shameless interest at his naked muscles, his naked manhood.

Wicked. Of course that had been wicked. So it served her right to be buried in a black hole.

Tears beaded on her lashes as she curled herself like a hedgehog into a tight little ball on the dusty blanket and tried to will herself into the sweet oblivion of sleep.

"Who the devil is making such a racket out there?" bellowed Alec from over the folds of the coverlet. "There had better be a damnably good reason for rousing me from sleep. I have a cursedly sore head from last night and am in no mood for levity."

"Lord Strathcona?" The magistrate was no longer sounding quite so sure of himself.

"Who else do you expect to find sleeping in my bed—the Marquess of Carabas?"

Silence.

Clearly the man had not read Perrault's famous fairy tales.

"Er, might I have a word with you, Lord Strathcona?" the magistrate finally asked.

"Come in if you must. I'm in no shape to rise." Alec raised his head from the pillow and scowled at the magistrate as he entered.

Seeing his expression, the two men accompanying the fellow remained lingering in the doorway.

"I beg your pardon, milord, but a very serious charge has been lodged against you," intoned the magistrate. "And I have no choice but to investigate the matter."

Narrowing his eyes, Alec demanded, "What is the accusation?"

"Theft, milord." The fellow shifted his weight from foot to foot. "Of an exceedingly valuable antiquity."

He responded with an oath in Gaelic that needed no translation.

"Er, I understand your ire, sir. Nevertheless, I must ask that we be allowed to search your quarters. The information we received included a specific description of where we might find the object."

Alec made a show of massaging his temples. "And where, pray tell, might that be?"

"Your desk, milord."

"If I were so idiotic as to put a purloined treasure in my desk, I would deserve to be hung," he snapped.

The magistrate swallowed hard.

"Well, don't just stand there." He shoved the covers down to his waist. "Kindly step into the sitting room while I don my dressing gown—I've no intention of flashing the family jewels to strangers, if you don't mind. Then we shall have a look."

The man flushed and began to back away.

"And prove you to be the most bumbling magistrate in all of Christendom," added Alec.

The last words hastened the retreat of all three men.

Smiling grimly, he waited several moments to let them stew in their embarrassment before throwing on his wrapper and joining them in the sitting room.

"Well, what are you waiting for?" Perching a hip on the sideboard, he crossed his arms. "Go ahead and perform your duty—and do it quickly, so that I may return to my slumber."

"Yes, milord!" The magistrate signaled his companions to approach the desk.

"Careful," snarled Alec, as they gingerly opened the top drawer. "I shall hold all three of you responsible should anything be damaged." A deliberate pause. "Aside from the valuable antiquity, of course. That I don't give a fig about."

Handling all the papers and sundries as if they were made of the most delicate porcelain, the two men slowly worked their way through each of the drawers, searching methodically to ensure no corner or cranny was left unexamined.

"Nothing," announced the taller of the two, gently sliding the last drawer back in place.

"Hmmph." Alec let out a low snort.

The magistrate was now looking even more uncomfortable. "Lord Strathcona..."

He had already decided that the best way to quash any ugly rumors was to remain aggressive. "I suppose you are now going to ask to search the rest of my quarters."

"I had not—"

"Well, I demand that you do so!" he barked. "I'll not have my name dragged through the mud because of these false accusations and whispered innuendos."

"That isn't necessary, sir."

"Indeed it is!" shot back Alec.

"Very well." Heaving a reluctant sigh, the magistrate ordered his men to check around the sitting room, and after a moment of indecision he joined in as well.

The task was performed quickly, whereupon Alec marched them into the bedchamber.

From there it was on to the dressing room.

By now, the magistrate was looking thoroughly mortified,

and despite the array of boxes and clothing crowding the space, he hurried his men through a cursory search.

Breathing a silent sigh of relief, Alec followed them back into the sitting room.

"My apologies, milord." Blotting the sheen of sweat from his brow, the man inclined a small bow. "I hope you understand that duty demanded I pursue the accusation. The truth is, the antiquity *has* been stolen and the town officials are very anxious to recover it."

"I wish you luck in doing so," growled Alec. "But I trust you are satisfied that the culprit is not me."

"Yes. Absolutely."

"You are, of course, welcome to search the rest of the house," he offered. "Though I daresay my aunt would not be pleased to have your men ruffling through her unmentionables."

The magistrate's face turned beet red. "No, no, that really won't be necessary." His two assistants started toward the corridor. "I can see that our informant was mistaken."

"Of course he was," growled Alec. Raising his voice, he called to the housekeeper, who had remained hovering in the corridor throughout the search, muttering darkly about impudent country officials who dared to disturb their betters.

"Mrs. Battell, please see these men out. And please ensure that I'm not disturbed again. A fellow really ought to be able to sleep in peace in his own quarters."

"Yes, milord!" Keys jangling, the housekeeper escorted the interlopers toward the stairs.

Alec waited for the sound of the front door slamming shut before moving quickly into the dressing room. Privacy here was now assured—the next challenge was spiriting Caro out of the house.

"But first, I had better make myself decent," he murmured, turning to fetch a shirt and trousers.

A muffled moan froze him in midstep.

It came again, louder and more agitated.

"The devil take it!" Bolting to the back wall, Alec hurriedly shoved aside the trunks and yanked the storage door open. "Caro?"

No response.

"Caro!" Fear lanced through his chest as he dropped to his knees.

Dear God in heaven, had there not been enough air in the space?

What if she were—

A low cry shattered the silence. "Help, Help!"

Alec ducked through the low opening, arms outstretched, a myriad of horrible possibilities swirling in his head.

He touched her hand—it was trembling and cold to the touch. Twining his fingers with hers, he drew closer.

"I'm frightened." Her voice was fuzzed, as if she were tangled in some bad dream. "So frightened."

"You're safe, sweeting," he murmured, drawing her close.

"Mmmm. Warm." She snuggled closer, her hand sliding beneath the silk of his dressing gown.

The friction of her palm ignited a fiery prickling on his chest, and as she slowly traced a tentative circle over his skin, her touch left a trail of exquisite sparks.

"Caro," he whispered, trying to hold back the heat plummeting to his groin. Only the worst sort of knave would give way to baser instincts at a time like this. "Come, wake up."

His voice finally seemed to draw her back from whatever netherworld fears had held her captive. He felt her body jump, then go limp as she slumped against his shoulder.

"Oh." Her breath, soft and slightly ragged, tickled his ear. "Oh, I'm so, so sorry."

"Don't be," replied Alec, feathering a caress to her hair. The pins had come loose in her tossings and turnings, and a knot of curls had fallen across her cheek. He gently brushed it back, feeling the tension still tremoring beneath his fingertips. "You should have told me you were terrified of the dark."

"It's too absurd," said Caro unsteadily. "I wish to think of myself as brave and adventurous, and I'm..." Her breath caught for a moment in her throat. "And I'm not. I'm a craven coward."

"You're incredibly brave," said Alec. That she was so very vulnerable at this moment clutched at his core. "Incredibly resourceful."

"N-not really," she answered. "My sisters are both far more clever and admirable—Olivia is brilliant and wise, Anna is imaginative and steady. While I seem to be ruled by uncontrollable passions."

"Don't," he chided. "Don't compare yourself to your sisters. You have your own special strengths that make you unique."

Uniquely wonderful.

"Your passions do you proud."

His words drew a small sound—something between a laugh and a sob. "But my passions always seem to arouse naught but trouble."

Trouble.

"Ah, but life would be awfully boring without passions, sweeting," soothed Alec. "Safe, but sadly flat."

He smoothed at the tangle of her tresses. The darkness suddenly sharpened all of his senses. *Touch*—her hair was the texture of finespun silk. *Smell*—her scent was a beguiling mix of verbena and spice. *Taste*—her tears were salty as the storm-tossed Scottish seas.

Caro flinched ever so slightly as his lips brushed her cheek. She shifted, releasing a shaky sigh. Her chin lifted, and their mouths met.

Trouble, trouble, trouble.

Alec felt her pull loose the sash of his dressing gown, her hands clutching at silk and skin. A groan mingled with a growl as her fingers grazed over the coarse curls on his chest.

He felt his resolve slipping away.

Her palms were now on his shoulders, tracing the dips and curves of his muscles. "You are so very solid and strong," she whispered, drawing back from the kiss.

No, I am so very brittle and weak.

In another instant he feared his willpower would crack into a myriad of tiny crystalline shards.

"And so very warm." She shivered and snuggled closer, teasing her tongue along the line of his jaw.

He wasn't sure whether he was in agony or ecstasy.

Caro rocked against his body, molding her sweetly yielding shape to his. Entranced by the sensations shooting through his limbs, Alec needed several moments to realize she had untied the tabs of her gown and wriggled the sleeves and bodice down to her waist.

"Please hold me close, Alec." Need resonated in her plea. She was still achingly vulnerable. And afraid. "The darkness is so very cold—I'm chilled to the bone."

While Alec felt as if every pore of his flesh was on fire. "I have you, sweeting," he replied, wanting to protect her from whatever nightmare was clawing at her consciousness. "You're safe in my arms, and I won't let go until you tell me to."

Chapter Fourteen

*S*till half in a daze, Caro was aware of an encircling warmth, and suddenly her spirits brightened even though the surroundings were still blacker than the Devil's lair.

Alec.

Through the thin layer of silk, she could feel the steady thud of his heartbeat, a calming counterpoint to her own racing pulse. Without thinking, she pushed the folds away, drawing comfort from the chiseled contours of his unclothed body.

"I like your textures," she murmured, wishing she could feel him with more than the scant few square inches of her palm.

Flesh to flesh, limb to limb.

Heart to heart.

For one aching moment, she longed to make his pulse race, his blood heat, his steely reserve melt into a need as fierce as her own.

I want, in this instant, to be the only woman who matters.

Something deep within urged that it was now or never.

And maybe it was the muzziness still gripping her mind that allowed her to listen.

Finding her corset strings, Caro hurriedly unlaced them. She heard his harsh intake of breath but kept going, dizzily aware that she was only a hair's breadth away from losing her nerve.

"Caro..."

Her chemise was next, then her drawers. Garters...stockings...his hand seemed to be fluttering over her flesh, whether trying to help or to hinder she couldn't quite tell.

His warmth was now meltingly wonderful, like sunlight caressing her skin. With a wriggling stretch, she pressed closer.

A groan, low and deeply masculine, rumbled in his throat as her hips touched his.

"Oh!" Momentary shock gave way to a more complex swirl of emotions. Alec was aroused by her? The thought was both frightening and exciting. Screwing up her courage, Caro pressed her palms to his chest and slowly circled them outward, reveling in the feel of his coarse curls, his flat nipples, his slabbed muscles.

"You are...wonderful," she whispered, coiling her arms around his neck and breathing in his scent. A wisp of pine, a hint of leather, and some earthier essence that was all his own.

"And you," he rasped in reply, "are..."

The Devil's own harlot?

And yet, against all reason and rules, this felt so desperately right, not wrong. Or perhaps she was still half-trapped in a dark dreamworld of need and longing.

"You are like wild Highland heather," Alec finished, his voice so soft she almost missed his words. "Beautiful, resilient, strong, and fiercely independent." His breath blew through the loose strands of her hair. "It will grow even in the most inhospitable ground."

"Prickly—you forgot prickly." She sighed. "I know you don't really want my attentions—"

"Don't want you?" Alec shifted, and suddenly his big muscled body was atop her. "Ye gods, I have been trying like the devil to hold my wanting in check from the first moment I met you."

His hands found and framed her face—he was pulsing with heat and some raw emotion that seemed to be shooting sparks out from every pore.

Caro closed her eyes for an instant as his lips touched hers, perfectly willing to burn to a crisp.

"I should be roasted in Hell for this," he whispered, pressing a kiss to her mouth. "Seducing an innocent—"

A tiny laugh cut him off. "Oh, Alec, I think there's a question of who seduced whom." She reached up, tangling her hands in his silkspun hair. "So I'll gladly join you in the flames."

"Will you, sweeting? For once you make the plunge, there is no going back."

Caro didn't hesitate for a moment. "Yes, I am sure."

Right and wrong. Was it the darkness or his own fierce desire that was blurring the distinction?

Alec knew what reason demanded. But all of a sudden he was tired of listening to reason, tired of keeping an iron-willed rein on his feelings, tired of pretending that his heart had truly turned to stone.

There was still a thudding of flesh-and-blood feeling deep inside, though he did his best to deny it in the harsh light of day.

Here, beneath the black velvet cover of the moment, could he give way to his wildest desires?

Caro feathered a kiss to his cheek, a sweetly tentative touch, and all restraint was lost.

Lost in a swirling vortex of need, want, and a longing so fierce that he thought every bone in his body might crack from the force of it.

"Then sweeting, I am sure, too." *Come what may.*

No more thoughts. Just elemental emotion—raging, rolling, thundering with the force of a Scottish gale sweeping over the rugged lochs.

But despite the turmoil inside him, he traced his hands ever so gently over the swell of her hips and down the curve of her thighs, the gloom heightening his awareness of her softness and her strength.

"You are exquisite," he whispered. "Exquisitely perfect."

Her arms tightened around him. "Oh, Alec, I'm not—perfection is impossible, but that does not matter. It is the chips and flaws that make us interesting."

"How perfectly true. You are far wiser than I am." He pressed his lips to the corner of her mouth, savoring the softness of her skin, the tiny twitch of her lips.

A smile, unfailingly brave and bold.

He adored her smile, and suddenly wished to see it as well as taste it. With his foot, he felt for the small door and nudged it open a crack, allowing a wisp of light to penetrate the storage nook.

It was only a weak flutter, but suddenly her face looked luminous in the faint dappling.

"I'm not wise." Caro slid her palms along his shoulderblades. "Merely stubborn."

He inhaled, filling his lungs with the scent of her, and let it out in a soft laugh. "Wisdom sometimes requires persistence, so perhaps the two are entangled."

"Entangled." Caro's breath tickled, soft as satin against his cheek. "Like us."

"Like us," agreed Alec. And then suddenly words were no longer important. Only the feel of their bodies so intimately entwined. She seemed to mold to his shape, as if made out of moonlight mist by some magical Highland faerie.

Gently spreading her legs, he eased himself closer, closer. *Wanting, wanting.*

His fingers stroked lightly through her damp curls and delved within her feminine folds.

A gasp. Then a whisper, rich with questioning surprise. "Alec?"

"Yes, yes, sweeting." He found her hidden pearl and began a slow, circling caress.

Caro let out a gossamer-soft cry and pressed her mouth to his shoulder. Her breath pulsed hot and ragged against his skin.

That her body responded to his touch sent a surge of satisfaction thrumming through him. Quickening his tempo, Alec felt the coil of tension within her core tighten.

"Oh, oh, oh." Her wordless wonder urged him on.

This was madness—he knew it.

Mad and reckless, when he had sworn that he would never give way to dangerous emotions again. But Caro had stripped away his defenses, had slipped through the cracks of his stony resolve.

Dangerous, and yet, somehow nothing mattered but Her.

Caro—fearless, exuberant, adventurous. She made him feel so elementally alive.

She arched up against his hand, her own need growing as

urgent as his. Alec shifted, and all at once he was inside her, enveloped in a honeyed warmth that nearly made him come undone.

He kissed her—madly, hungrily, thinking of nothing but her, and how right they felt together.

Us. Entwined.

And then all thought gave way to passion.

Caro clutched tighter at Alec's broad shoulders, feeling the flex of his taut muscles and heat-pulsed skin. She drew in a ragged breath and held still for a moment, but the pinch of their joining gave way to sublime warmth.

"Shall I withdraw?" he asked in a concerned whisper.

"No, please—don't stop," she replied. "It's wonderful." *You're wonderful.* "I want..." *I want this to go on forever.* "I want you to teach me about...about..."

Was it too wicked to say pleasure and passion?

He started moving inside her, an elemental ebb and flow that sent a lick of heat spiraling through her. And suddenly words like "wicked" and "wanton" dissolved in waves of liquid fire.

All that mattered was Alec.

Matching his rhythm, she rose and fell, her body somehow sensing how to move in perfect harmony with his.

I was wrong—perfection is possible.

He groaned—or perhaps it was she who had made the sound. Her insides were thrumming with such pleasure that surely its joyful echo was making the air rumble.

Alec quickened his tempo and as he pressed kisses to her cheeks, to her lips, her senses were enveloped in his earthy scent and salty taste. The powerful, primal essence of aroused male.

Caro shuddered with the pleasure.

Heat was cresting within her, a wild force that seemed to twist and spiral as it sought release. She must have given voice to her need, for Alec kissed her again, murmuring hoarsely, "Yes, yes, sweeting. I know what you want, and I want it too."

Faster, faster.

The heat was unbearable. Surely in another instant they were both going to burst into flames.

With a cry, Caro arched into his thrust and cried out. For what, she wasn't sure. But then, a blaze of light seemed to fill the tiny space and then shatter apart in a crackling of diamond-bright shards.

Her crystalline cry was echoed by his low growl as Alec thrust deep and then withdrew from her in a rush, rolling to one side, just as his sweat-slickened body convulsed.

The sensation lasted an instant...or was it an eternity?

Time seemed to hang suspended, as she floated on a cloud of golden sparks, mesmerized by the dying glitter of their fire. When at last her heartbeat came back down to earth, Caro shifted her spent body and found herself enfolded in Alec's arms.

He turned her and pulled her close, tucking the curve of her spine up against his chest.

She nestled closer, feeling their bodies come together as if made for each other. The searing heat had mellowed to a softly pulsing warmth, like honey drizzling over her flesh.

With a wordless sigh, Alec stirred and settled his palms just beneath her breasts.

Her heartbeat thudded gently against his skin. Through half-closed eyes, she was vaguely aware that the door to the little storage space had shifted again, shading the space with an inky gloom. But the darkness no longer seemed so frightening.

She felt safe within his steadying hold, taking strength she didn't know she had from his closeness.

Two as one.

We fit together, like pieces of a puzzle, thought Caro, before sinking into a hazy sleep.

Chapter Fifteen

Alec drifted out from a silverspun fog, and slowly opened his eyes.

Only to see a muddled darkness.

How strange. Surely the gossamer sensations of spun-sugar warmth suffusing his body could only have come from the firebright sun. Momentarily disoriented, he blinked and shifted ever so slightly.

And suddenly realized that the languor in his limbs was not because of a sweet, sweet dream.

Remorse squeezed the smile from his lips. Not that he regretted his feelings, but his actions had been unforgivable.

Caro shifted in his arms, snuggling, closer.

Ye gods—I am a beast—worse than a beast, for I should possess some sense of right and wrong.

He had taken ruthless advantage of Caro's trust, her vulnerability, her innermost fears.

And now he had ruined any chance she had of finding the happiness she so richly deserved.

She was trapped...

Caro stirred again and slid her arm around his waist. "It's nice to feel you close when I wake up," she said, her voice still muzzy with sleep. "Mmmm, I could lie here for hours..." Her fingertips crept down the curve of his bum. "And memorize every little dip and curve of your body."

The mention of time speared away his other dark musings. They didn't have hours to linger here. They must be leaving, and quickly.

But first...

"Caro, we can't stay here any longer."

"Mmmm, I suppose you are right." She brushed her lips to the tip of his chin—a fleeting touch that made his heart thump against his ribs—before starting to sit up.

"A moment," he responded, catching hold of her wrist. "There's something I have to say first."

She went very still.

Alec drew a breath, trying to loosen the terrible tightness in his chest. He felt like the worst sort of bounder, forcing her hand. But there was no time for wrapping the stark truth in silk ribbons.

"This should be done with flowery words and sparkling champagne," he went on awkwardly. "But I'm afraid you will have to settle for my plain, rough-cut words at this moment."

"What are you trying to say?" she asked, her tone turning wary.

For an instant, his voice seemed stuck in his throat. "However unpolished, a proposal of marriage."

He heard her inhale a long, measured breath. "You are asking me to *marry* you?"

Alec wished he could see her face. Her voice, normally so expressive, was toneless and impossible to read.

"Actually, it's not really a request," he said softly. An unseen fist seemed to squeeze all the warmth from the air. "We both know we have no choice, considering what has just occurred between us."

A sliver of ice skated down her spine, and all at once Caro felt cold all over. "Of course we have a choice," she replied.

"There are consequences for giving way to passion, and we must accept them." Alec shifted on the rumpled blanket. "But think on it. We have much in common."

Was he trying to convince her or himself?

"We can be comfortable in a marriage," Alec went on. "We share mutual interests, mutual sensibilities." A pause. "I believe that we can learn to rub along without setting off sparks."

Fire—oh, but she wanted the fire!

She wanted the flames that had burned within him as he had joined his body with hers.

"You speak of comfort and common interests," replied Caro slowly. "But what about love?"

His hold on her wrist twisted and then tightened. For several long moments there was silence. To Caro they seemed to stretch on for an eternity.

"I—I made a grave mistake before," he said haltingly.

"And you fear you are making another one?"

He didn't answer right away, which told her all she needed to know. "Well, I want to be more than someone's mistake." *I want to be loved.* "I want sparks in my marriage," she added hotly. "I want poetry, I want passion."

He flinched.

"I know I am asking too much of you, sir," said Caro in

a near whisper. It hurt to admit it. "But I don't want to settle for less. So I shall not accept your proposal."

"Honor—" began Alec.

"Honor be damned," she exclaimed. "Among the many eccentric ideas my father taught me was that each individual must form his—or her—own sense of honor, no matter what Society dictates." Pain lanced through her chest. "I shall follow my own heart, not some silly strictures that will only make us both miserable."

She felt Alec look away, even though she couldn't see his face. "You deserve to be happy," was all he said.

But I won't be—not without you.

"Then we have an understanding?" she asked.

"I will, of course, defer to your wishes for now." An oblique answer if ever there was one. "But if on further reflection, you change your mind..."

"I won't," Caro assured him.

"You must think on it very carefully," pressed Alec. "It's never wise to make serious decisions in the heat of the moment."

"I told you, I'm not wise," she shot back. "I'm impetuous, and willful, and stubborn...and all the other annoying things that drive you to distraction. You are right—marriage would be a horrible mistake."

"Caro..."

She edged away and began to scrabble around in the dark to find her clothing. "As you said, we really need to be dressed and gone from here before your aunt and Isobel return."

A stocking, a chemise, a garter—how had her cursed corset strings become so entangled? Huffing a low oath, Caro wriggled out of the low opening with what she had gathered. She took cover behind a stack of bandboxes and, turning toward the wall, hurriedly set to pulling on her garments. A moment later she heard Alec emerge, and the sounds of rustling fabric indicated that he, too, was rushing to make himself ready to leave.

Blinking back tears, she managed to unravel the knotted laces and do up her fastenings. No doubt she looked like something the cat dragged in, but she would think of some excuse—a sudden squall, a carriage mishap...a herd of wild unicorns running roughshod over her.

After all, legend had it that unicorns could only be calmed by the touch of a virgin.

Shaking off such cynicism, Caro tried to just concentrate on the practical task of getting home without setting off a public scandal. With her emotions in such turmoil, there was no point in trying to sort through them. That could wait until the midnight hours, when darkness would once again wrap around her and remind her of fire and ice and—

"The antiquity." Caro spun around. "Good heavens, we can't leave it here in your quarters."

"It's safe in the storage nook." Alec stuffed his shirttails into his trousers. "I don't think the magistrate is keen on returning."

"His superiors may order a more thorough search, especially if Thayer plants another poisonous seed in their minds," she insisted. "I'll take it. No one will ever suspect me of having it."

"No!" he said flatly. "I'll not put you in danger."

"You aren't," Caro protested. "But Thayer has proved he's diabolically clever, and determined to wreak evil on you. As long as it's here, it's *you* who is in danger. And that may also threaten Isobel."

Seeing that her argument had given him pause for thought, Caro hastened to add, "I'll just keep it for tonight. Tomorrow we can decide on a neutral place to stash it until it can be safely returned to its rightful owners."

Alec darted a look out into the bedchamber. "Damnation, the light is fast fading."

"You know I'm right—on this at least," she urged.

"Just for tonight," he growled.

"Agreed," she said quickly.

He pulled a cloak from its peg and tossed it her way. "Put this on. There's a route through the back alleyways that leads to the bottom of Milsom Street. If we are careful—and lucky—we should be able to make our way there without attracting any notice. From there, we'll have just a short walk to your townhouse."

"The alleyways make sense," she agreed as he quickly retrieved the antiquity. "But we can't take a chance on you being seen with me."

"I—"

"Oh, stop being so noble," she said. "And be your usual practical, pragmatic self, Alec."

He looked up from refolding the wrapping around the ancient Roman eagle. The muted light accentuated the chiseled planes and angles of his face, making him seem very forbidding and far away.

Caro ached to bridge the distance that had suddenly come between them but she wasn't sure how.

"Sorry," she mumbled, embarrassed for having let the intimacy of his name slip out. It was a mistake she mustn't make again. "What I meant was, it's best that I walk home from the alleyway alone."

Alec said nothing in answer. Threading a hand through

his tangled hair, he brushed it off his brow, setting off tiny glints of gold.

Fool's gold, she told herself.

And yet the silky softness of the strands still felt imprinted on her fingers. Fisting her hands, she shoved them in the pockets of the cloak.

"Ready?" he asked, after selecting a wide-brimmed hat and pulling it low on his head.

She nodded.

"Then let's be off. Stay close."

Intent on following his lead, Caro gave little heed to the crumpled paper brushing against her knuckles. It wasn't until it gave off a soft *crunch, crunch* as she darted into the back stairwell that she quickly pulled it out and stuffed it down her bodice to silence the sound.

God forbid that she be the cause of tripping up their plan of escape. She had caused enough trouble for one afternoon.

Thankfully, they made it safely out of the house and into the shadowed alleyway without being spotted. From there, it proved a quick journey to the Milsom Street egress, their only encounter being with a tiger-striped tomcat who had just caught a mouse.

"Here we are," whispered Alec. He ventured a look up and down the street as she shrugged off the concealing cloak and handed it over. "There's no one around."

"Then I had best be going."

"Be careful." He turned, and after a tiny hesitation reached out to catch an errant curl and tuck it behind her ear. "You are sure that the eagle is well hidden—"

"Yes, yes." His touch sent a shiver skating across her skin. "It's safely stowed at the bottom of my reticule, under my books and pastries." They had retrieved her things from their hiding place, and she was grateful for the brim of her bonnet, which afforded some shelter from his probing gaze. "And I've a good hiding place within my armoire. Rest easy—no one will find it."

"As I said, it mustn't remain in your room after tonight," he growled. "Tomorrow, we must contrive to hide it elsewhere."

"As to that, I thought of an idea while we were walking." Caro edged closer to the opening. "First thing in the morning, I shall send a note to Andy suggesting that he drive Isobel and me to the Abbey ruins outside of town for a picnic. You could ride by, as if by chance, and we can take a walk and find some suitable place to stash it."

"Abbey ruins, purloined treasures, hidden secrets." He, too, was shadowed by his hat, but Caro thought she detected a quirk of a smile. "You are stealing a page from your sister's novels."

"Actually, I'm writing my own adventure," she murmured. "Anna's heroines are far more clever and..."

And capable.

They never made egregiously awful mistakes, they never turned into watering pots, they never felt like bumbleheaded fools.

"Suffice it to say, they always triumph in the end. The ending of this story remains to be seen." Caro squeezed back a tear. "I had better be going, before we are spotted."

"Be careful," he cautioned again as he checked the street once more time. "I shall see you tomorrow."

She started to ease by him, but Alec gripped her arm. "Think over what I said, Caro. We shall talk more about it soon."

"There is no need," she whispered.

"Be assured, the discussion is far from over."

Leaning back against the bedpillows, Caro slipped her bare feet beneath the coverlet and drew her knees to her chest. A hot bath had helped warm the chill from her bones, but feathering a sponge over her naked body had been an all too visceral reminder of Alec's caresses. She had shocked her poor maid by bursting into tears as a soft trickle of lavender-scented soapsuds had slid between her breasts.

Claiming fatigue, she had immediately retreated to her bedchamber after drying off. Though she had been forced to invent several bouncers to explain her appearance, that statement hadn't been a lie. She had never felt so utterly exhausted.

But then, it wasn't every day that one became entangled in a dangerous adventure *and* lost one's virginity.

Not even Anna's intrepid storybook heroine, Emmalina Smythe, had managed *that* feat.

Chuffing a sigh, Caro wasn't sure whether she wanted to giggle or sob at the absurdity of it.

Oh, how she wished her sisters were here to counsel her and offer advice on the mysteries of men.

And sex.

She suspected that Anna had... well, the Devil Davenport had a *very* roguish reputation. And as for Olivia, the Earl of Wrexham was said to be a paragon of propriety, but he had a certain gleam in his eye that hinted he wasn't quite as proper as people thought.

But it wasn't their handsome faces that haunted her mind's eye. It was the lean, chiseled visage of her very own Highland hero.

Alec, with his storm-blue eyes and red-gold hair. His fire-bright smile and brandy-warm kisses, both of which he kept so well hidden behind a mask of flinty reserve.

Men.

She huffed a frustrated sigh. The jumble of conflicting emotions they set off was all so confusing. Did it ever get any easier to understand the mysteries of the heart?

Despite her fatigue, Caro felt too unsettled for sleep to come. Kicking back the coverlet, she decided to seek solace in paper and pen. Writing a letter to Anna would be comforting just for the sense of connecting with her sister rather than seeking any specific advice. Though Anna was sharp enough that she would likely read between the lines and guess that Cupid's arrow had struck the youngest Hellion of High Street.

Love.

Caro paused for a moment to look out the window at the sliver of moon hovering just above the dark silhouette of the trees. It looked so fragile, a tiny glimmering of pale, pearlescent light winking against such a vast stretch of midnight black.

Did it ever feel lost and lonely as it made its arc through the faraway stars? Did the diamond-bright pinpoints...

Ah, but that was a subject for a poem.

For now, however, she would content herself with writing a simple missive describing the stay in Bath.

As she took a seat at her desk and reached for her inkwell, Caro spotted the crumpled piece of paper she had fished out from the bosom of her gown. It was probably just an old bill from Alec's bootmaker or a list for his wine merchant. Still, it bore the faint trace of his scent—that beguiling whiff of bay rum and earthy spice that made her heart give a tiny lurch.

She inhaled a gulp of air and held the breath in her lungs for a moment before going on.

"I am a hopeless romantic," she murmured wryly as she smoothed out the crinkles, imagining Alec's fingers touching the same small stretch of foolscap. Drawing it closer, she peered down at the faint script.

Caro recognized his handwriting, but the penciled lines were smudged and hard to read. To make out the words, she shifted the paper nearer to the branch of candles.

Light flickered over the paper as she slowly deciphered the scribbles. It was ... a poem?

She leaned in, nose now nearly touching the paper, and skimmed over the stanzas.

Yes, a poem.

Caro read it again, and then again. Not just a poem, but a wonderful poem. Lyrical. Imaginative. Provocative.

And most of all, passionate.

Pressing her palms to the page, she drew a long, measured breath. He had such an artistic nature and mischievous spirit to go along with his chiseled strength and steely principles.

It was achingly sad to see him keep so much of his true self bottled up inside.

Why did he do so?

When she had first learned of his marriage, Caro had feared that it was because his heart still belonged to his late wife. However, she was beginning to suspect that the answer was not so simple. Though it might be unfair, she decided that she would quiz Isobel more on his marriage, in order to understand what demons were holding him hostage.

Slowly, slowly, she folded the creased paper and slipped it into her notebook.

Despite the fact that the distance was back between them, that his heart was not hers, Caro refused to give up on Alec quite yet. Whatever else had come between them, they were still friends, and she was determined to make him acknowledge the better side of himself.

Yes, I will make him see that strength and steel aren't diminished by laughter and love.

Love.

Caro knew he didn't love her. But perhaps in freeing himself from the shackles of his unhappy past he would find someone to love—truly love—in the future.

Alec deserves no less.

And so do I.

She wouldn't settle for embers, she vowed. Not when she wanted the blaze of fire-bright flames.

"I will find passion," she promised herself in a low whisper. "I will find love."

After all, poetry was all about believing that light was stronger than darkness.

Chapter Sixteen

Dragging himself out of bed, Alec padded toward the washstand, careful to keep his eyes averted from the cheval glass. He didn't need a glance at his own reflection to know that he looked like Hell.

No doubt the sight would show that a pair of scarlet horns had sprouted up to crown his head during the long, sleepless night.

Shame sluiced over his skin as he splashed a handful of cold water over his face. *The Devil's Disciple*—the warning ought to be tattooed on his forehead in matching red letters to frighten off innocents.

Caro hadn't been frightened, whispered one of the dreadful demons who had taken up residence in his head.

She had been willing.

Even more reason to have exercised gentlemanly restraint, he shot back. But instead, he had behaved like a snabbering, selfish beast, letting lust get the better of him.

He hadn't been just a beast, he had been a fool.

Seating himself at his dressing table, he raked a comb

through his hair, trying not to dwell on how damnably disappointed he was in himself. What made it worse was that she seemed to see a much more admirable Alec McClellan dwelling inside him than he did, one who was capable of laughter and love and passion.

That man didn't exist anymore.

Alec finally forced his gaze to confront the looking glass. *Or did he?*

Uncertain of how to answer, he dressed for a day of riding and went down to breakfast.

Isobel looked up, but tactfully refrained from commenting on his haggard looks. "Cook has fixed a platter of your favorite Yorkshire ham, and there are eggs in the chafing dish, made just the way you like them." Her eyes lingered on his face. "Would you prefer coffee instead of tea?"

"A potful, please," he muttered. "Scalding hot and dark as Beelzebub's heart."

"My, my, aren't you in a cheerful mood." Arching her brows, she buttered a sultana muffin. "Caro has just sent around a note saying that she and Andy—that is, Lord Andover—are planning to take a picnic to the Abbey ruins this afternoon, and I am invited to join them. I was going to ask you to accompany us..." Another probing look as she took a nibble of her pastry. "But I think I shall reconsider."

"Just as well," Alec answered brusquely. "I have business to attend to in Weston." Without looking her way, he slouched into his seat and began toying with his empty cup.

"Is there a reason that you are acting like a bear with a thorn stuck in his arse?"

"Aside from the fact that my sister was recently attacked by unknown assailants who may still be at large?"

"Alec, your concern and protective instinct is most admirable—"

He gave an inward wince at the word "admirable."

"But firstly, we have agreed the attack was a random one and that the danger has passed," went on Isobel. "Secondly, I am tougher and more resilient than you seem to think, especially now that I am nearly recovered from my illness."

Alec had to admit that she looked in the first bloom of health. "That may be so. But until I am satisfied that the threat is truly over, I shall remain on guard." Given Edward Thayer's actions yesterday, it appeared that extra vigilance was in order. However, with Andover serving as her escort for the afternoon picnic, he felt she would be safe enough.

And Caro. Her courage and resourcefulness were undeniable, though he fervently hoped they would not be put to the test.

Pouring a cup of coffee from the steaming pot, he took a quick swallow, reminding himself that there was no need to worry. She would be alone with the antiquity only a scant hour or two before he contrived to join the excursion party. Then together they would find a hiding place for the stolen treasure until it could be returned to the Museum.

Which meant they would need to wander off on their own, for the others mustn't have a clue as to what they were doing.

"You had better have something to eat," counseled Isobel. "You are looking a little green around the gills."

Alec forked a helping of eggs onto his plate. Perhaps he ought to wash it down with a dram of whisky to fortify himself for the coming meeting. The purloined eagle wasn't the only serious issue they had to contend with. There was the matter of—

"Love," intoned Isobel.

His head snapped up. "*What?*"

"Love," she repeated softly.

He swallowed slowly. "What about it?"

"I can't help but wonder if in real life it happens the way it does in novels, with a flash of brilliant, blinding light." She crumbled a bit of muffin between her fingers before going on. "Or whether it creeps up on you slowly and softly, and, well, simply sneaks its way into your heart."

"You are asking *me*? I am hardly the right person to comment on the subject," he muttered.

A flush rose to her cheeks. "I'm so sorry—that was horribly tactless of me. I—I wasn't thinking."

He shrugged off the apology. "Don't look so stricken. The mistake is long in the past."

"Where it should stay," she replied under her breath.

"May I ask what prompted your question?" he inquired quickly, intent on keeping the state of his own heart from coming under scrutiny. "Is there something your older brother ought to know?"

"N-not really," she stammered, her color deepening to a telltale scarlet. "I was just curious, that's all."

"Andover seems like a pleasant fellow," he commented, just to tease her a little.

"Yes, very pleasant."

"I didn't say 'very.'"

"Oh, goodness, look at the time." After darting a desperate look at the clock, she rose so quickly that she nearly knocked over her chair in the process. "I—I had better go check with Cook on the preparation of the picnic basket," said Isobel, and then fled from the breakfast room.

A smile played over his lips, but only for a fleeting moment as his thoughts returned to his own predicament.

Love.

What Caro wanted in a marriage—poetry, fire, passion—was just an oblique way of phrasing it.

Love. He made himself say it again, and let the echoes reverberate inside his skull. Did he dare believe the sentiment could be rekindled in his heart? Or perhaps the more important question was whether he was brave enough to risk striking up a spark, lest he be burned again.

It was, of course, safer to stay at arm's length from fire. But safety suddenly felt awfully cold and dark.

Alec chewed thoughtfully on the last bites of his breakfast, then pushed aside his plate and headed out the back entrance for the mews, still lost in his musings.

Checking once more that the stolen antiquity was well wrapped in oilskin and well hidden within her reticule, Caro ducked her head into the morning room to take leave of her mother, then set off to meet Isobel and Andover in front of the Pump House.

It promised to be a very pleasant walk, for her friends were always good company. As for the coming meeting with Alec, the sunny mood would likely give way to stormclouds in a hurry.

"What a lovely afternoon for an outing," called Isobel, fluttering a cheery wave. "I am so glad you suggested it."

"Indeed." Andover flashed an amused grin as he nudged his boot against the hamper sitting on the pavement beside him. "Though Miss Urquehart's cook seems to think we intend to be gone for days."

"She's still trying to fatten me up," replied Isobel. "I vow, I am already plump as a Strasbourg goose."

"On the contrary, you look quite perfectly formed to me," said Andover gallantly.

Caro noted Isobel's answering blush with an inward smile. Things seemed to be taking an interesting turn between her two friends. They were, she decided, very well suited and had every chance of being happy together should the relationship progress to a proposal.

Though happiness did seem to be something that was deucedly difficult and daunting to define. Perhaps that was because Life felt so cursedly complicated at times, with no easy answers...

Caro quickly shook off such maudlin thoughts, determined to match her mood to the sunny skies and smiling faces of her friends.

Her feelings about Alec were best dealt with in...the velvet darkness of the midnight hours.

"Shall we be off?" Andover hefted the hamper and slanted a look at Isobel. "You are sure you don't mind walking? I could easily fetch my curricle. The three of us could squeeze in quite nicely on the driver's bench."

"Ha!" murmured Caro. "I shall refrain from asking who should be put in the middle."

Isobel's face now looked on fire.

"I am simply trying to be a gentleman," protested Andover, though a tiny twinkle did flash in his eyes.

"We'll walk, Andy," she replied. But then, on recalling the twilight attack and Thayer's ominous behavior, she decided to err on caution. "On second thought, the curricle might be a good idea. We may feel a bit fatigued after an afternoon of exploring and welcome a ride home."

"An excellent point," he agreed. "Why don't you ladies wait here with the hamper. I shall not be long."

"I hope you did not feel obliged on my account to forgo the walk," said Isobel softly, after he had hurried away. "I dislike being thought of as too delicate to carry my own weight." She paused. "Or too lily-livered to defend myself from peril."

"I think neither," assured Caro. She did not wish to alarm her friend. But nor did she wish to treat her like a helpless child. "The truth is, we still do not know whether we were attacked at random, or for a reason. So I believe it is wise to exercise caution."

"Alec said much the same thing this morning."

"He cares very much about you," she replied.

"He is the very best of brothers, even if he does tend to be overprotective. I only wish..." Her words trailed off in a sigh.

After a moment's hesitation, Caro seized the opening. "Forgive me if I am prying, but your brother has hinted to me that his marriage was not a happy one."

"Alec mentioned his marriage to you?"

"He did, but gave very few details." Caro paused to choose her words carefully. "He said only that it had been a mistake. I did not wish to press him on it, but..."

The rattle of carriages jostling over the paving stones filled the ensuing silence, and for a long moment it seemed that Isobel would not respond.

"I'm sorry, I shouldn't have—" began Caro, at the same time that her friend finally spoke up.

"He finds it very difficult to speak of it," said Isobel, her voice barely audible above the street sounds. "Men seem to think they aren't supposed to feel pain or hurt."

Caro sucked in her breath, wondering if she really wanted to hear the details. Perhaps her suspicions were wrong. Perhaps Alec *had* been madly in love with his wife, and his heart was still wedded to a ghost.

"I—I have decided that I would like you to know the real story, not the nasty hints that Mr. Thayer has told you, because..." Isobel looked up from plucking nervously at her skirts. "Because I feel you should know the truth, and I fear my buffle-headed brother is too stoic to do it himself."

"He can be vexingly stubborn about certain things," murmured Caro. "As can I."

That drew a fleeting smile from her friend before she cleared her throat with a cough. "Elizabeth Caldwell was...well, in short, she was selfish and manipulative," explained Isobel. "Alec had gone down to Oxford for his studies—at nineteen, he was hardly more than a boy! She was beautiful, charming, and vivacious..."

A tremor took hold of her voice. "And in dire need of money, for she and her secret lover had very extravagant tastes. Alec, it seems, presented a very appealing target. He was wealthy and titled, but being Scottish, he was far enough beneath the notice of the English aristocracy that any scandal that might swirl around his name would be ignored."

"I take it Elizabeth was English," said Caro.

"Yes. A baronet's daughter, though we later learned that her father had fled to the Continent to avoid debtor's prison."

The reason for Alec's aversion to all things English was suddenly becoming clearer.

"As you no doubt have guessed by now, she exerted herself to seduce my brother. I—I don't think it was a very hard task. You might not guess it, but beneath his steely, self-assured strength, Alec possesses a very sweet and sensitive soul."

"I..." Caro wasn't sure how to answer. But thankfully, Isobel didn't seem to need any encouragement to go on.

"She knew all the little tricks of making a man feel special, and Alec believed that she loved him. They were married, and for a short while all was well. But they returned to Scotland during the summer, and, well, Elizabeth's lover apparently made the trip north as well." Isobel's expression tightened in anger. "Her moods quickly turned surly, and she began to treat Alec abominably, taunting him with his youth and his lack of polish."

"How awful," whispered Caro.

"Oh, it gets worse." Isobel swallowed hard. "Elizabeth soon began to disappear for several days at a time. When Alec confronted her, she tearfully claimed to truly love him and begged for a chance to cast off her lover and reform. Honorable man that he is, he couldn't imagine that it was just another pack of lies."

The rumbling clatter of a passing barouche gave Isobel a moment to compose herself. "The following night, Elizabeth absconded with the jewels Alec had given her, along with several very valuable family heirlooms that would have brought a pretty penny when sold on the Continent. But a bad storm blew in from the sea, and the rains made the coast road treacherous. She and her lover perished when their carriage careened off a cliff on their way to the ship that was going to carry them across to Antwerp."

"I hardly know what to say," whispered Caro. "No wonder he is reluctant to let anyone close again."

"He keeps most people at arm's length," said Isobel. "You

are the only one who provokes a spark of interest in him. I
see how he watches you when he thinks none of us are looking."

"I fear that is because he is wary that I may do something
outrageous when he isn't looking," she replied wryly. "Your
brother thinks me a hellion, and with good reason. When
we first met at Lady Dunbar's castle, we had a number of
clashes."

"I'm not sure that is a bad thing," murmured Isobel. "For
far too long he has lingered in darkness, avoiding any spark
of light."

"Trust me, sparks flew between us. I think several singed
his bum. So as I said, he is wary of me."

"If he appears wary, it is not because of your spirit."
Isobel hesitated. "But enough said. I have perhaps already
trespassed on his privacy, but I thought it important that you
know the truth, and am certain that I can trust you with his
secret."

Caro was about to answer when the sight of an approaching gentleman caused the words to die on her lips.

"Good day, ladies." Thayer came to halt beside them and
tipped his hat politely.

Damnation. Caro pasted on a smile, hoping she wasn't
white as a sheet. It felt as if every drop of blood had drained
from her face.

"Good day," she answered.

Isobel, she noted, barely managed a murmur of greeting.

"Are you two planning an excursion?" he asked, eyeing
the picnic hamper. "I do hope you are not intending on trying
to carry such a heavy load by yourselves."

Loath to reveal any details about the planned outing, Caro
answered with a coy laugh. "I am far sturdier than I might

look, Mr. Thayer. My father was a noted explorer, and I accompanied him on several expeditions where we were required to lug our own supplies into the wilds."

"Well, if I ever plan on journeying to darkest Africa, I hope you will agree to accompany me," he said with a jesting smile.

Ha! And pigs might fly.

But aloud, she answered, "Actually, I have always wanted to experience the splendors of Cathay."

"That seems suitably wild and exotic," responded Thayer. "What about you, Miss Urquehart? Do you wish to join us?"

"I am not a world traveler like Miss Caro."

The bantering exchange was cut short by the arrival of Andover in his curricle.

"Ah, I see you have a gentlemanly escort after all," said Thayer, as Andover climbed down from his perch and stowed the picnic in the boot. "I would offer to come along and help, but it appears there isn't room."

"I fear not," said Caro.

"Perhaps another time." And yet, Thayer made no move to continue on. "Where are you planning to picnic?"

She thought quickly. "Oh, we are simply looking forward to viewing the countryside." A vague wave indicated a direction opposite that of the Abbey ruins. "We thought we might drive by the old Roman fortress by the river, or perhaps the thermal springs."

Andover looked up sharply, but remained silent.

"The thermal springs are said to be quite scenic," observed Thayer.

"Well, we ought not keep His Lordship's cattle waiting." Caro edged toward the curricle.

This time Thayer took the hint. Inclining a small bow to

the ladies, he took his leave and proceeded up the Pump House stairs to join the crowd in the Promenade.

"Have we a change of plans?" inquired Andover.

"No," replied Caro. "I cannot say why..." Which was the truth. "But there is something about Mr. Thayer that is unsettling. I'd rather he wasn't aware of our plans."

"Ooooh, a nefarious plot and a wicked villain. How very exciting," intoned Andover in a mock whisper. "You ladies are awfully good at imagining dark and dangerous adventures." He winked. "Perhaps you should consider writing a novel."

"Poetry is hard enough, Andy," she shot back. "Now help Isobel up to the seat and let us be off."

Chapter Seventeen

Reining his horse to a halt on the top of the wooded knoll, Alec stood up in the stirrups and surveyed the weathered bones of the sprawling old Abbey nestled in the meadows of the dell below. With the verdant ivy vines twined around the crumbled walls and arches of butter-colored limestone, it made a wildly romantic scene.

No doubt Caro's sister Anna could set a thrilling scene among the nooks and shadows of the sprawling ruins—a chase perhaps, with her intrepid heroine Emmalina Smythe evading the pursuit of the evil villain…

Alec checked such thoughts with a wry grimace, reminding himself that the last thing he wanted was any thrills or excitement. He was here simply to find a hiding place for the stolen antiquity—an easy task by the look of things—and be off.

But then again, nothing ever seemed to go along easily when Caro was involved.

The breeze blew through his hair, and for an instant, a ruffled strand tickled against his cheek.

Perhaps that wasn't such a bad thing.

He sat back in the saddle, and took a long moment to contemplate the clouds scudding across the sun, a peek-a-boo circle of shimmering light against the brilliant azure blue.

Everchanging shapes and hues—infinitely alive and unpredictable.

And that was, he conceded, what made the sky so infinitely interesting.

It could be inspiring, it could be frightening, it could be calming. But never, ever could it be boring.

A lone hawk floated into view, circling slowly on the currents of air. Reminded of his mission, Alec spurred his horse on and began the descent down the twisting path.

"Halloo!" From atop one of the low walls, Isobel greeted his approach with a vigorous wave. "What a nice surprise! I thought you were engaged for the afternoon."

"I finished early, so I thought I would stop by on my way back to town," he answered.

"There may be a few scraps of food to spare for you," called Andover, from the swath of grass inside the tumbled stones. A blanket had been spread on the ground, and he was busy unpacking the hamper.

"Knowing Cook, I am sure she packed enough to feed an army," said Alec as he dismounted and tethered his mount beside the curricle.

"At least a regiment," replied Andover with a grin.

"It appears the troop of ravens will not go hungry," he remarked, eyeing the numerous treats. He then looked around for Caro, a frisson of alarm stealing down his spine at the thought that she might have ventured off on her own with the stolen antiquity.

"Nor will we, I assure you," came a voice from within

one of the alcoves that still retained part of its roof. A moment later, Caro emerged from the arched opening, streaks of dirt smudging her cheeks.

"There are still the remains of a wooden storage cabinet in there." She held up a small copper coin. "Look—I found this lodged behind one of the broken shelves."

"Oh, how lovely!" exclaimed Isobel. "Finding a penny is supposed to bring good luck."

Let us hope so, thought Alec.

He watched her climb over a tumble of fallen stones and winced as one of them suddenly shifted beneath her feet. "Careful," he warned. "These ruins can be dangerous. You really ought not go into the covered spaces. The slightest jarring or jiggling could make the roofs collapse in an instant."

"Right-ho," agreed Andover. "You ladies really ought not wander off without one of us accompanying you."

"The slate tiles could just as easily fall on your heads," pointed out Isobel quickly.

"Yes, but we men have much thicker skulls."

"True," drawled Caro, drawing a giggle from Isobel.

"I'll not argue that," said Alec. "At least, not on an empty stomach. Shall we eat?"

Caro collected the empty plates, then passed around slices of the fresh-baked apple tart and wedges of the local cheddar cheese.

"Arrgh. I vow, I can't eat another bite." Closing his eyes, Andover lay back on a flat slab of stone and folded his hands atop his stomach. "I can't move either. I think I shall just nap for a bit."

Isobel gave a drowsy nod. "I'm going to rest as well." She reached for her reticule. "I brought a new book."

"What are you reading?" asked Andover, raising one eyelid.

"The latest Sir Sharpe Quill novel," replied Isobel with a grin. "It just came out last week."

"You couldn't have chosen a more perfect place in which to enjoy the hair-raising adventures of Emmalina Smythe—other than a dungeon with rattling chains and dripping water," he said jestingly. "But that wouldn't be nearly so comfortable as this."

"Why, Andover, you speak as if you are familiar with Quill's novels," teased Isobel.

"Oh, I've read every one of them. They are all the crack in London, and if a fellow wants to converse with the ladies, he has to be up to snuff on Count Alessandro's exploits."

Caro hid a smile as Alec caught her eye. She shook her head slightly in response to his raised brow. Andover was a very good friend and her sister's former beau, but still, he wasn't aware of Anna's secret identity. It was kept very closely guarded—Alec only knew because events at Dunbar Castle had forced them to admit him to their inner circle.

"I say, would you mind terribly reading it aloud?" asked Andover after blowing out a contented sigh.

Isobel readily agreed and opened to the first chapter.

With the two of them occupied, it was the perfect opportunity to wander off, decided Caro. The same thought had obviously occurred to Alec, for he was already on his feet.

"Would you care for a stroll?" he asked. "Or are you determined to vanquish that pie?"

"Good heavens, no!" she responded, quickly putting aside her untouched slice. "I surrendered all thought of that after fighting off the last bite of roasted capon."

"Then come along." Alec held out a hand. "Let us walk off our indulgences."

"Don't get into any trouble," murmured Andover.

Isobel left off her reading to remark, "My brother never gets into any trouble." A pause. "That, by the by, isn't a compliment."

He chuffed something unintelligible under his breath.

"Was that a grunt or a growl?" Caro couldn't resist teasing him. "As you see, Isobel, your brother gives a typical male response when stymied by a lady's wisdom."

Her friend laughed, as did Andover, who was always willing to poke fun at himself.

Alec turned and regarded her with a very solemn expression. "Ladies aren't always as wise as they think." His voice was serious as well, but then the corners of his mouth twitched ever so slightly.

"Nor," she replied swiftly, "are men."

A snort—this time there was no mistaking the gruff sound that slipped from his lips.

Isobel giggled.

"It appears we have dueled to a draw," added Alec.

"Consider yourself lucky, Strathcona," drawled Andover. "Now put your rapiers away before someone gets pricked. It's far too lovely a day to cross verbal swords."

"Agreed." Alec took hold of Caro's hand, and the warmth of his long, tapered fingers entwining with hers sent a tiny shiver running up her arm.

Oh, don't, she chided to herself. *Don't act like a flighty storybook heroine.* The poor man had been subjected to enough drama.

"If Miss Caro agrees to sheath her sarcasm, we may actually contrive to enjoy a walk without either of us suffering a grievous injury," he added, leading her away from the others.

As they rounded a row of stone pillars and crossed into the ancient transept, Caro murmured, "I wasn't being sarcastic."

Alec turned, and the fluttery shadows from the overhanging ivy deepened the blue of his eyes to the color of the ocean in winter.

Beautiful, but forbidding. Hinting at depths and hidden currents that could drown anyone who took the danger too lightly.

"Neither was I," he replied.

"Oh." Her insides gave an erratic little lurch, though she wasn't quite sure why. "I thought perhaps you were angry with me."

"Angry?" He sounded surprised. "Good God in heaven, why?"

"For... for..." She had been thinking of the story Isobel had confided, and a horrible thought had taken hold in her head. Perhaps Alec thought her no different from his late wife—a heartless seductress who took pleasure in toying with men.

"For throwing myself at you," she finally stammered. "For forcing you to hold me and comfort my hysterics."

Alec stopped, and before she quite knew what was happening, he placed his big hands on her shoulders and spun her up against one of the mortised walls. Trapped between cool, solid stone and a warm, thrumming mass of male, Caro felt her pulse begin to skitter.

"Let us clarify a few things between us," he said softly. "Firstly, you did not throw yourself at me." A pause. "It was more of a floppy little roll."

Was that a glint of amusement in his eyes? Or were the tiny sparks dancing on the tips of his golden lashes lit by some other emotion?

"Secondly, I am not in the habit of letting myself be forced into doing anything."

Her face must have betrayed her misgivings, for she felt a rippling of muscles as his shoulders tensed.

"Ah. I see that my sister has seen fit to tell you the story of my youthful folly in all its sordid detail."

She dropped her gaze, knowing he would hate to see any speck of sympathy in her eyes.

"Well, be advised that I am no longer a callow schoolboy."

"No one would ever mistake you for that." Caro knew the sensible thing was to say no more. However, being the least sensible of the Sloane sisters, she added, "But I think that sweet and sensitive schoolboy shouldn't be ashamed of believing in love."

She heard the harsh intake of Alec's breath, which only goaded her to go on.

"And I'll have you know that I didn't throw—or roll—myself at you for any Machiavellian reason. I did it because I think you are...nice."

The lungful of air came out as a strangled wheeze.

"I know, I know, 'nice' is a rather lame word," she muttered, "but I can't seem to think of another right now." His closeness—his scent, the curve of his collarbones showing through the sunwarmed linen of his shirt, the press of his broad palms—was making her mind a little lethargic right now.

"Nice will do very nicely," he said, leaning in close enough that she could see the stubbling of gold on his jaw. "I think you're rather..."

A cough.

Was that better than a wheeze? She was still uncertain of how to interpret his sounds.

"Nice, as well," he finished.

It was an awfully ordinary word, and yet it set her insides to doing a slow, spinning somersault.

"That's n-n-nice," said Caro.

He laughed, his breath tickling against her cheek.

"I—I told you, my mind's not feeling very poetic right now," said Caro. "Feel free to suggest a more inspired alternative."

"Actually, I'm not feeling much in the mood for musing over words either. Now that the subject of our feelings is *nicely* settled, we ought to proceed to the real task at hand."

And yet he made no move to release her.

"Right. The sooner it's done, the better." She shifted her gaze to look out over his shoulder, unwilling to look any longer at the sensuous curves of his mouth. "There look to be a number of possible hiding places around the old chancery."

"You have the ancient eagle?"

Feeling unsettled by his strangely whimsical mood, Caro responded a little sharply. "Yes, of course I do. I'm not so bird-witted that I forgot to bring it with me."

"Don't fly up in the boughs. You mistake my words. I wasn't implying any such thing, merely making sure you had it with you at this moment."

Drat. She had left it in the basket, hidden under the remains of the oilskin packet of cheese.

"Wait here. I'll be back in a moment."

"We all make mistakes," he murmured, as she wriggled free and stepped around him.

His mentioning the word "mistake" was...a mistake.

Reminded of his halting words after their lovemaking, Caro stopped and turned to face him. "Yes, we all make mistakes," she said hotly. "We all fall on our arses and make fools of ourselves. Ye gods, just look at me! I know I make more than my share of them."

A small voice in her head—the one she rarely listened to—warned her to stop. She was, however, feeling a little reckless.

After all, I've probably just made the biggest mistake in my life already by falling in love with a man who won't ever, ever let his heart feel light and laughter again.

"But you can't let mistakes squeeze the life out of you," she went on. "That makes for a pretty bleak existence."

"Caro," he began.

"So you, you big lummox, ought not let a past mistake make you keep your feelings, and your marvelous penchant for poetry bottled up inside you."

A lummox. Alec watched Caro stalk away, a wry smile pinching at the corners of his mouth. Skirts swirling, hips swaying, her glorious curls dancing in the breeze—she was always in motion, a fierce energy crackling from without and within.

Poetry in motion.

She wasn't afraid to take a risk. She wasn't afraid to dare to reach out and grab for her dreams.

Perhaps he *was* a lummox—a hulking, ham-witted brute, afraid of his own shadow and the dark little demons who lived in that blackness.

"Damnation," he muttered, more in bemusement than anger. Sunlight flickered over the weathered stone, dipping and darting over the cracks and crevices carved by the centuries of wind and rain. *A bleak existence, letting a small part of yourself be worn away each day by the hostile elements.*

Caro returned in a few minutes, a reticule swinging from the strings looped around her wrist.

"Ready?" she asked.

He stepped aside with exaggerated politeness. "Lead the way."

Swoosh, swoosh—she picked her way swiftly and surely over the fallen blocks of limestone, choosing to head for the jumbled remains of the small chapel attached to the rear of the ruins. Once through the low archway, she slipped through a small opening in the broken wall and started to climb the ancient circular stairs.

"Halfway up, there's a spot where we can shimmy down into an alcove that's impossible to see when you're strolling the grounds. I imagine we'll find some excellent hiding places there."

Alec found himself smiling at her spirit. "You are enjoying making an adventure of this, aren't you?" he murmured as he joined her on the stone perch. Staring down at the steep drop, he added, "Are you perchance plotting out a scene for your sister's next novel?"

"Life *should* be an adventure," she replied, hitching up her skirts. "Pulse-pounding excitement shouldn't exist only in books."

"Let me go first," he said.

"No need—"

Stripping off his coat, Alec lowered himself over the side. "If you slip, landing on a big lummox will be a trifle more comfortable than landing on a pile of rocks."

The gusting breeze tugged at the vines, so he wasn't quite sure if the ruffled whisper was an answering laugh.

His boots hit the ground with a thud. Steadying his stance, he looked up. "Have a care. The handholds are sharp, and there's a cluster of—"

Caro had already started her descent.

"Ouch," he murmured softly, seeing her fingers grab a patch of thorns.

"OUCH!" Her yelp, coming a split second later, was a good deal louder. For a moment, she hung suspended, balanced on one foot wedged in a crevice, but then...

He raised his arms just in time to catch her.

Whomp.

The force of her tumble staggered him, and he lost his footing on the slippery stones. Twisting hard, Alec managed to angle his body to take the brunt of the fall.

"Ouch," she repeated, slowly raising her head from his chest. "Are you hurt?"

"Not mortally," he rasped, trying to shake off the loud ringing in his ears. It couldn't be the church bells, for they had been gone for centuries.

"Don't move," she ordered. Untangling her hands from the folds of his shirt, she threaded her fingers through his hair. "I had better check for bumps."

"*OUCH!*"

"Or blood."

"Wishful thinking?" he asked.

"If I wanted to do you bodily injury, I'd take matters into my own hands, not leave it to chance."

In truth, her fingertips felt rather soothing as they caressed lightly over his temples.

A chuckle rumbled in his throat. "I don't doubt it."

"That's because you, of all people, know what an incorrigible hellion I am."

"You are..." *Unique. Intoxicating.* Her scent, a beguiling mix of verbena and some unnamable spice, was teasing at his nostrils. "You are that, and more," he finished.

"More what?" Caro shifted. She was lying atop him and the sensation of her glorious body sliding over his set off a jolt of longing, a spark of need. "More trouble?"

Trouble. Yes, definitely trouble.

"That's too easy a word," he answered.

She propped her elbows on his chest, a pensive look rippling through her gaze.

Alec thought for a long moment. "You challenge me."

"We should all feel challenged," responded Caro, her voice not quite steady. "It's not always comfortable, but it's by questioning ourselves that we learn and grow."

As she spoke, her mouth quirked into a rueful smile. He loved how expressive her face was—from the flash of her alluring eyes to the flush of her petal-soft skin, she was so exuberantly alive.

He tilted his head, angling his lips to within a hair's breadth of hers.

And then caught himself.

"Speaking of comfortable..." Much as the feel of her body against his was setting off all sorts of exquisitely delightful sensations, Alec forced his thoughts back to practicalities. His sister and Andover would soon be growing tired of reading.

"The shards sticking in my spine are awfully sharp, and besides, we ought to finish with our mission before the others get too curious as to what we are doing and come looking for us."

Caro scrambled to her feet and hastily tugged open her

reticule. "Right," she mumbled as she fished out the canvas-wrapped antiquity and held it out to him.

"You're more experienced in this sort of adventure than I am," said Alec. "I leave it to you to choose where to hide it."

"We'll do it together." Edging closer to the wall, she began poking around in the gaps between the stones.

Moving over to join her, Alec helped push aside the thick stalks of prickly thistles growing up from the weeds. "There looks to be a deep crevice here," he pointed out, after gingerly feeling around inside a slivered space half hidden by the greenery near the base of the stones.

"Yes, that should do." Kneeling down beside him, she handed over the antiquity and watched as he carefully pushed it into the hole and let the thistles spring back into place. "Once we smooth the ground a bit, it will look as if it hasn't been disturbed for centuries."

"Perhaps we had better draw a treasure map, so we can be sure to find it again," he jested, seeing she was clearly undaunted by the dangers. "Isn't that how it's done in the horrid novels?"

Caro grinned as she dusted her hands. "Come to think of it, Anna did have a map in one of her books."

"And?" he prompted.

"It was stolen by the evil pasha's monkey. Emmalina had to chase it through the souk, where it led her on a merry dance through the silk bazaar and the tents full of Bedouin weaponry..." She started to giggle. "It was actually very well written and madly exotic. I'm sure you can use your imagination to picture the scene."

"I'm not sure my imagination can rival that of the Sloane sisters, but yes, I can see where it would be highly diverting." He cleared his throat. "What happened?"

A teasing twinkle lit for a moment in her eyes. "Oh, you'll have to read the book."

She had the most mischievous sparkle to her eyes. He couldn't imagine ever growing tired of seeing it spark.

Forcing his gaze away, Alec rose and offered her a hand up. "I shall—once the chapters of this little adventure of ours are finished."

Caro's expression immediately turned deadly serious. "I was just going to ask you about Thayer, and what plans you have to bring an end to his evil scheming."

He frowned, but she ignored it.

"You've taken pains to keep your suspicions to yourself," she continued. "But after all that has taken place—the attempted abduction of Isobel, the plan to have you arrested for theft—I would guess that this all has something to do with your involvement in the clandestine group that is seeking independence for Scotland."

"Yes," he admitted grudgingly.

"Thayer is the leader of the more violent faction, I assume, and seeks to take control of the group by discrediting you?"

"It is not that simple," replied Alec. "But it's not necessary for you to know the sordid details." Hearing her inhale sharply, he held up a hand. "Don't fly up in the boughs. They involve secrets I am not at liberty to share. Suffice it to say, there are those in our group who believe Thayer has betrayed all of our goals and principles."

He paused, debating how much more to say, then decided she deserved as much of the truth as he could reveal. "The reason I journeyed to England was because I was asked to look into certain rumors about his activities. And it seems he has gotten wind of my purpose in being here."

"Which explains the acts against you and your family," she mused. "Have you found proof of his perfidy?"

"As to that, I received some interesting information this morning, but I need to make one more visit tomorrow before I am certain of the facts. If my surmise is correct, then I do have an idea on how to trap him."

"How?" she demanded.

"I know that you are slated to accompany Isobel and Andover to the fireworks display in Sydney Gardens tomorrow evening. I shall explain it to you then."

"But it's a masked fête, it will be dark, and there will be a large crowd. You'll never find me."

He let his gaze slowly sweep from the tips of her half boots to the errant curls tumbling over her brow. "I would know you anywhere, in any disguise, Caro."

Her eyes flared wider as a rush of red flooded her cheeks. "Lord Strathcona—"

"Alec," he corrected softly.

"It would be . . . a mistake to use such intimacies, sir." She turned away, the twisting tendrils of the climbing vines obscuring her face. "And it seems we've both made enough of them in the past without adding any new ones."

"Alec? Alec?" It was his sister's voice, rising above the sounds of approaching footsteps.

Caro looked up.

"Come, let me give you a hand," he muttered. "We had better hurry."

Before he made the colossal error of spinning her around and trying to kiss the quiver of hurt from her voice.

Setting his hands on her hips, he lifted her within reach of the sturdiest handhold.

As for his own grip on the way forward . . .

"Alec?" Isobel's call was getting closer.

Damnation. There seemed no clear path through the tangled shadows and looming obstacles up ahead. He could either take the coward's way out and retreat.

Or decide to forge ahead despite the dangers.

Chapter Eighteen

"Why is it," muttered Caro, "that men are the most impossibly confusing creatures on Earth?"

After adding a grimacing grumble, she admitted it was a rhetorical question. No doubt her sisters, with their infinitely greater wisdom and experience in such matters, would assure her that there was no rational answer for the workings of the male mind.

And yet, she couldn't help being terribly confused. Alec had seemed so...different yesterday.

Of course he's different, whispered a tiny voice in her head. *So are you—the two of you are lovers, which changes everything.*

And nothing.

Caro blew out a sigh as she sat down at her dressing table to finish arranging her hair for the evening outing to Sydney Gardens. The fact was, against all reason, against all rhyme, she loved him.

She loved his chiseled integrity, his impressive intellect,

his protective caring for his sister, his poetic soul and imp-ish humor—though he so rarely allowed either to peek through his stony reserve.

Ye gods, she even loved that enigmatic Sphinx-like expression he wore so often, the one that hinted at a myriad of mysteries swirling beneath the stone-faced mask.

"But it doesn't matter what I feel," she whispered into the looking glass. Despite the recent glimmer of whimsy in his mood, Alec was *not* going to fall in love with an English hellion. He was an intelligent man, and intelligent men did not make the same mistake twice.

That word again—mistake.

And I will not be merely a mistake, she vowed to her reflection.

After fastening the last few hairpins to hold her topknot—she had dismissed her maid, wishing to be alone—Caro glanced at the clock on the bookshelf. She need not rush. There was still time to linger in solitary thought before she had to don her mask and descend to the parlor to await Andover and Isobel.

Giving thanks that her mother had decided to attend a card party at Lady Greeley's home rather than endure the noise and jostling of the outdoor fete and fireworks, she rose and wandered to the window by her writing desk. Her nerves were already stretched taut enough by the prospect of seeing Alec, so it was a relief that she wouldn't also have to deal with a litany of the baroness's querulous complaints.

Staring out at the darkening sky and the first faint twinkling of stars, Caro found herself blinking back tears. Oh, it was times like these that she missed her sisters fiercely—their counsel, their camaraderie, but most of all their laughter. No matter how dire or daunting a problem seemed, humor always made it less frightening.

She looked down at her desk, where the latest letter from her middle sibling lay open on the blotter. Smoothing a hand over the travelworn paper, she couldn't help but quirk a smile.

Anna would likely cheer her up by making a jest of the current dilemma, weaving it into a wildly romantic adventure of...

Her fingers stilled.

Alec might not welcome her amorous feelings, but he was in danger—and Isobel was, too. So like it or not, he could use some help in fighting an enemy who had shown himself to be diabolically cunning.

She lapsed into thought, trying very hard to recall the snippet of conversation she had overheard in the churchyard. *Had it been Thayer?* The voice had been too low for her to be sure, but it seemed more than likely. And the realization was like a sliver of ice sliding down her spine. Whoever had spoken possessed a cold-blooded ruthlessness. He was a man who wouldn't bat an eye at committing violence.

Alec had said he was formulating his own plan to stop his nemesis. But having an alternative was always wise. He would use razor sharp logic, rather than emotion. So perhaps a more imaginative approach would be useful in stimulating ideas.

What would Anna's heroine, Emmalina Smythe, do? Granted, it was more an exercise in fantasy, as her sister was so far away, but still, merely writing would lighten her spirits, and she had a half hour to kill...

Taking up her pen and a fresh sheet of paper, Caro began to compose a missive to Anna.

*I have been musing over a possible idea for a novel,
and was wondering how would you would devise a
plot to thwart a dastardly cold-blooded villain who...*

Ducking under a string of brightly colored glass lanterns,
Alec entered Sydney Gardens and turned up the main walkway leading to the grounds overlooking the River Avon.
Music from the outdoor orchestra drifted down through the
trees, accompanied by the trilling laughter of the crowd.
Flickering lights, diamond-bright flashes winking through
the smoke-green leaves, punctuated the dusk. In another few
minutes the last lingering colors of sunset would give way to
the black velvet darkness of night.

He quickened his steps, not bothering to don the silly little mask that Isobel had insisted on putting in his pocket that
morning. The scrap of silk was hardly a disguise—it was
meant more as a merry diversion, as everyone would recognize their friends and acquaintances.

But even if it had been a hooded domino, designed to
hide all features, he hadn't been exaggerating when he had
said he would recognize Caro in any disguise. Nothing could
shroud her exuberant spirit, her willowy body, her lively
grace—like a lyrical rhyming couplet, she always seemed to
be in constant, playful motion.

Just watching the provocative sway of her hips was
enough to unman a saint...

Uttering an inward oath, Alec forced aside such thoughts.
Dealing with *that* challenge would have to wait until he
could eliminate the enemy that threatened not only him but
also the ones he loved.

Love.

The word had kept echoing in his head until he had finally admitted the truth.

Yes, he loved Caro.

And quite likely had from the very first moment at Dunbar Castle when she had fixed him with a defiant stare and dared to retort one of his cynical statements, despite the horrified hush-hush noises from her mother.

Spirit, courage, and beauty, complemented by a fierce loyalty and a kind heart.

She had been a wonderful friend to Isobel, who had no sisters, and he had no doubt that his sibling's dramatic improvement in health had much to do with Caro's cheerful camaraderie and encouragement.

That bond was easy to define. As for his current relationship with the young lady, that was far harder to articulate. He wasn't usually so clumsy with language, but he had made a complete hash of his proposal. His ill-chosen words had wounded her when she had been at her most vulnerable.

Caro had been brave enough to offer him her heart. And what had he done but hand it back to her with a muttered mumble about a "mistake."

She had misunderstood his meaning. How could she not, when he had been too proud to reveal the truth.

Could she—would she—ever forgive him?

As he threaded his way through the crowd gathered around the refreshment tables, Alec surveyed the laughing faces, trying to spot Caro. But there was no sign of her, nor could he see Andover and Isobel. Deciding that they must have chosen a spot closer to the river for viewing the fireworks, he shouldered his way to the nearest side path and headed off, his boots stirring a staccato *crunch, crunch* across the gravel.

* * *

The champagne prickled sharply against her tongue—whether it was a good or bad portent, Caro wasn't sure. Her pulse had unaccountably quickened, and for some reason, her nerves were on edge. Perhaps it was the masks everyone was wearing that added to the aura of devil-may-care mischief swirling through the dark shrubbery.

A branch snapped somewhere close by, startling her out of her thoughts. She looked around, surprised to find Isobel had disappeared from the circle of light under the hanging oil lanterns. Andover had gone to fetch more drinks after admonishing them not to wander off. It was odd that her friend would disregard his warning.

Unlike me, Isobel is very good about staying out of trouble.

Quelling a flutter of unease, Caro took a few steps down the darkened path and cocked an ear. The sound of voices rose from behind a cluster of nearby bushes, but she couldn't identify the low murmurings.

She hesitated, loath to interrupt an intimate assignation.

Then came a louder exclamation—definitely Isobel. "Sir, I must ask you to cease."

Caro quickly made her way around the leafy branches.

"Oh, here you are, Isobel," she said brightly, hoping to defuse any unpleasantness with a minimum of embarrassment. Gentlemen were prone to drink too much during fetes like these and take liberties they would later regret. The masks, at least, would allow everyone to escape an awkward moment with their dignity intact.

Her friend whirled around, a look of gratitude glittering through her unshed tears.

The gentleman then turned as well, forcing Caro to swallow a gasp of dismay.

Thayer. The very last man on earth she wished to encounter.

Think, think!

Whatever his motive for seeking a private conversation with Alec's sister, it could not be a good one. She had to extract Isobel, who knew nothing of his recent perfidy, and quickly.

Forcing a smile, Caro pretended not to notice that anything was amiss. "Ah, and Mr. Thayer, too."

He inclined a mock bow.

"Isn't it a lovely evening for pyrotechnics?" she went on. "Do you think this is the best spot for viewing the explosions? Or should we move closer to the crest of the ridge?"

"I think we're quite nicely situated here," replied Thayer. The dark silk masked his eyes, but his mouth quirked in a serpentine curl that sent a chill slithering down her spine.

"Yes, I daresay you're right," she agreed, after feigning a study of the surroundings. "This offers an excellent vantage point." Inching a little closer to shield Isobel from his shrouded stare, she added, "Andover will be returning with our drinks. Perhaps you ought to return to our meeting spot so he doesn't think that we've been abducted by cutthroat pirates who've sailed their rogue ship up the Avon."

"Pirates." Thayer let out a low laugh. "My, what a vivid imagination you have, Miss Caro. Evil villains, damsels in distress, and dashing heroes riding to their rescue—don't tell me you read those silly novels that set all the young ladies to swooning."

"But of course!" replied Caro lightly. "What young lady doesn't dream of a dashing hero carrying her off into the sunset?"

"No wonder such novels are thought to corrupt the female mind," he said, with a tinge of mockery. "The fairer sex suffers such a great disappointment when they discover that heroes are rarer than hen's teeth in real life."

While villains seem as plentiful as the stinging gnats that buzz around a barnyard.

"Why, Mr. Thayer, are you really so cynical?" asked Caro.

"I prefer to think of myself as pragmatic."

"As you say, I had better go find Andover before he becomes alarmed," said Isobel, inching back toward the pathway.

Leaves rustled, and the sound of her steps on the pathway quickly faded into the night.

"Miss Urquehart is a delicate little creature, isn't she?" he remarked. "No wonder her brother is so protective."

His words stirred another shiver.

"Isobel is actually much stronger than she looks," said Caro. "She is capable of taking care of herself."

"Indeed?" Thayer brushed a bit of leaf from his sleeve. "And what of you, Miss Caro? If I had to guess, I would say that you are the more adventurous of the two."

Was he flirting? The idea made her skin crawl, but Caro made herself flash a coy smile. "You think so?" she murmured, echoing his teasing tone.

Boom! The first explosion of the fireworks display shook the stillness of the night, filling the sky with a burst of brilliant sparks.

"Yes." He came closer, close enough that the cloying scent of his cologne clogged her nostrils. "Definitely."

Boom! Boom! The flashes of red-tinted light painted his face in a devilish glow.

His hand curled around her arm and it was all she could to keep from flinching. He must not guess her true sentiments.

"I..." Caro turned her head, suddenly aware of footfalls on the gravel. A figure took shape from out of the smoke-swirled gloom—*Boom!*—and as a fresh flare of gunpowder light fell across the path, she saw it was Alec, wearing nothing on his face but a black scowl.

A viper. Alec felt a cold rage cloud his eyes as he spotted Thayer slide a step closer to Caro and touch her. A cold-blooded, cold-hearted snake, who took pleasure in sinking his fangs into innocent flesh, seeking to poison all that was right and good in the world.

Fury quickened his steps.

"Strathcona," drawled Thayer, looking around from Caro's face. "You appear to have strayed into the wrong party. This gathering is a masquerade and you are not sporting a—"

Alec seized the man's fancy cravat, squeezing off the rest of his words. "It's not me who has made a mistake."

"Milord!" Caro clutched at his coat and tried to come between them. A flare of warning flashed amidst the fluttering silk of her mask. "Have you taken leave of your senses?"

Quite likely. Lifting Thayer off the ground, he shook him—hard enough to rattle teeth, he hoped.

"Milord!" cried Caro again, catching hold of his arm as he cocked back a fist. "No!"

Expelling a grunt, he reluctantly released his enemy. "I don't like seeing my sister or her friend accosted."

"It seems you've spent too long in the wild moors and mountains of our homeland, Strathcona, for your manners have become those of a savage." Thayer smiled as he smoothed at the folds of linen around his throat, but there was a malevolent glint in his eyes. "I was merely having a polite conversation with your sister and Miss Caro."

"Th-that's right, sir," she said softly. "Please calm yourself. There's no cause for anger."

Her voice held a veiled warning, and now that the first blaze of blind fury had died down, Alec belatedly cursed himself for giving too much away. Thayer had an uncanny knack for sensing a person's weakness and then striking hard and without mercy.

"Thank you for rushing to my defense, Miss Caro, before your Highland hero turned violent." A sneer. "But then, he has a history of that."

Innuendo and lies. Thayer could poison with his tongue as well as his fangs. Thank God Caro knew the truth.

Her cringe was convincing enough to give him a twinge of doubt, but as she backed away toward the path, she mouthed the word "later" before looking around to Thayer.

"I am sure it would not have come to that. A mere misunderstanding, that's all," she said. "And now, if you gentlemen will excuse me, I had better rejoin my escort, Lord Andover, and Miss Urquehart."

"But of course," replied Thayer. "My apologies that our conversation was cut short by such unpleasantness. I trust you will allow me to make up for it in the near future."

"I—I shall look forward to it." Caro dipped a quick nod and then hurried off.

"I do believe you have frightened the young lady with your temper," said Thayer, as he watched her go.

"Yes, well..." Alec swung around slowly and riveted his gaze on the black swath of fabric that hid the other man's eyes. "I can be a very frightening fellow when I so choose."

"Ooooo." Thayer exaggerated a mock shiver. "The thing is, McClellan," he added in a soft whisper, "I'm not afraid of you."

Alec bared his teeth—and not in a smile. "Oh, but you should be, Thayer. You should be."

"Might I ask, what was that all about?" inquired Andover as he offered Caro a glass of champagne. "Had I known there was a kerfuffle, I would have interceded."

"I am not sure," she fibbed. "It would seem there is bad blood between Lord Strathcona and Mr. Thayer. I simply was caught in the middle."

"My brother does not like Thayer," offered Isobel. "I don't know the reason, but Alec is not one to hold petty grudges, so I am assuming it is over something serious. He prefers that I have nothing to do with the man, but Thayer seems insistent on being friendly."

"The fellow ought to be gentlemanly enough to respect those wishes," murmured Andover. "He ought not impose his company on—"

"There was no harm done," interrupted Caro. "But you are right in suggesting that we should try to avoid fanning the flames of the feud. Isobel and I shall be more careful about finding ourselves in his company."

"Indeed," agreed Isobel. "And in truth I shall be happy to do so. There is something about him that makes me uncomfortable."

"Now that I am aware of that, I will be on guard as well," said Andover quietly.

Caro allowed an inward smile at his tone. It appeared that Andover's concern might be more than brotherly. But regardless of the reasons, that Isobel had acquired another protector was all for the good.

"I do hope Alec won't do anything rash." Isobel darted a look at her. "I've never seen such a murderous look blaze in his eyes."

"Lord Strathcona is not one to let his emotions get the better of him," said Caro.

Or so she hoped. Stirring the fires with Thayer had not been a wise strategy. But perhaps Alec's show of anger could be turned to good use in any plan to trap Thayer into revealing his perfidy.

An idea was beginning to take shape in her head...

"That may be, but I, for one, am not overly anxious to face him when he is flexing his fists in such a menacing manner," said Andover dryly as he watched Isobel's brother stalk toward them. "Do you ladies mind if I cower behind your skirts?"

"You should be safe enough, Andy," replied Caro, leaving off her own plotting for the moment. "You are far too nice for anyone to want to punch you in the nose."

"I'm not sure I would want to wager on that." Andover discreetly edged back a step.

Not that she blamed him. Alec's scowl was cold enough to freeze the fires of Hell.

"Bloody bastard," he muttered through his teeth.

Andover coughed.

"Sorry. Forgive me for using such language in front of you ladies," added Alec gruffly. "But Thayer is—"

"A bloody bastard," murmured Caro. "Yes, yes, but..."

She paused in frustration. Anxious as she was to hear what news he had learned earlier in the day, she thought it best for the moment that Thayer not see them conversing together. But saying so might stir suspicions with Isobel and Andover.

Thankfully Alec seemed to be thinking much the same thing, for he quickly finished her sentence. "Yes, but I ought not spoil the evening by bloodying his beak."

"It wouldn't be wise," she agreed.

Boom! Boom! The crowd by the refreshments burst into applause as a rainbow of sparks filled the sky.

"True." He watched the myriad points of light fizzle and dissolve into the darkness. "So I pray that you will excuse me if I take my leave from these festivities. I find I am in no mood to make merry."

Without a glance at her, Alec turned on his heel just as another explosion filled the air and walked off.

Caro heaved a sigh of relief—though a touch of annoyance shaded her breath. Any confidences would now have to wait until Alec could contrive to set up a private meeting.

And knowing his sentiments about sharing his thoughts with her, she might be waiting until Doomsday.

But perhaps there were other ways she could help to counter the threat against him and his sister.

Whether he wished her to do so or not.

Chapter Nineteen

$\mathcal{U}$pon waking the next morning, Caro was anxious to spring into action. The only trouble was, she hadn't quite formulated a plan. And as she knew it was dangerous to go running off half-cocked, she made herself dress unhurriedly and go down to the breakfast room.

Perhaps several cups of strong tea would stimulate some ideas.

"Mrs. Mifflin is hosting a card party this evening," announced her mother, on looking up from sorting through the morning's mail. "I do so love a good game of whist, though it is a pity that she serves a very watery punch instead of champagne."

"You are supposed to be taking the medicinal waters, not punch or wine, Mama."

"Oh, pffft! What fun is that?" exclaimed the baroness as she tore open another invitation. After a moment, a smile spread over her face. "Why, this is even better! Wrexham's elderly aunts—you remember Lady Hortense and Lady Alois from Olivia's wedding—are renting a manor house just outside of town for the coming month. They arrived yesterday."

Yes, unfortunately Caro did remember them. They were very sweet, hard-of-hearing old spinsters with a great fondness for cards and fine French claret. The earl's sister had remarked that her gracious townhouse in Mayfair felt as if it had been turned into a gaming hell for the duration of the visit.

"And I am invited to come keep them company for this first week!" The paper fluttered, mimicking the happy sigh. "Three friends have accompanied them from Yorkshire, so with me filling out the numbers, we shall make three pairs. But you—"

"Oh, you know I have no patience for card games," said Caro quickly. "I am sure Isobel and her aunt would be happy to have me stay with them while you enjoy a respite in the country."

"Well..." Her mother hesitated.

"It will be a lovely time for you," she assured. *And allow me a good deal more freedom to go about my own affairs.* "Especially as you feel the water regime is growing a little tiresome."

"A bit of wine and continental cuisine—the aunts have a very talented French chef in their employ—would not be too bad, would it?" mused her mother. "I have shed a great deal of weight—perhaps too much. Lady Henning remarked just the other day that I was naught but skin and bones."

Caro coughed on her sip of tea. "Er, yes, I daresay a few cream sauces and glasses of claret would be just the thing."

"Very well. I shall accept," said the baroness. "That is, as long as Isobel's aunt is agreeable to the arrangement."

Setting down her cup, Caro shot up out of her chair. "I shall go ask while you begin your packing."

"Well, this seems to leave little doubt," muttered Alec as he skimmed through a handful of documents.

"No doubt at all, milord," answered his contact. The man, a clerk at the military headquarters of the Royal Horse Guards, had journeyed from London to bring several military dispatches he had surreptitiously removed from the Scottish dossier. "Thayer is your man. And it seems that Dudley is also involved in the matter."

"My thanks, McDouglas." Alec stuffed the incriminating documents into his pocket.

"What will you do with the papers?" said the other man. "You could thank me by putting an end to their perfidy, because clearly the English are not going to mete out any punishment."

"I shall pass them on through the proper channels in Scotland. We may not be able to make the two of them pay for past crimes. However, Thayer will no longer be a threat to the independence movement," replied Alec. "Indeed, I would guess that he'll soon be taking up permanent residence in some faraway country. He'll have to know that his life isn't worth a spit of whisky once this becomes known to our friends in the north."

"Aye, that is for sure." McDouglas made a face. "Still, someone may choose to take justice into his own hands. And though I, like you, don't sanction violence to achieve our ends, it would not upset me overly to hear that the fork-tongued serpent has been sent to answer to his Maker."

Alec didn't reply. It went against all his principles to condone murder, yet in this case he couldn't help but secretly agree.

Turning for his horse, he unwrapped the reins from around a tree branch. "You should have no trouble walking back to town in time to catch the Royal Mail coach back to London." Setting his boot in the stirrup, he added, "I trust you'll suffer no consequences for this."

McDouglas gave a tight smile. "Nay. My copying skills are very finely honed. Even if anyone thinks to look carefully at the replacements I put in the file, they won't be able to tell that they are forgeries."

"Godspeed then."

"And you, milord." With that, his contact slipped away into the shadows of the trees.

Alec swung up into the saddle. A long ride loomed ahead. It would be dark by the time he arrived back in Bath. Too late to pay a visit to Caro, so it would have to wait until morning.

His mouth curled in a wry smile. At the moment, she was likely madder than a wet hen at his absence, thinking he was deliberately avoiding her. But the meeting with McDouglas had been a last-minute arrangement, and the discovery of military dispatches that detailed Thayer's misdeeds was too important to pass up.

Now there was no need to plan an elaborate—and perhaps dangerous—trap to ensnare the miscreant. With such tangible proof in hand, he could unmask Thayer as a traitor and make sure that his former friend would never dare show his face in Scotland again.

The threat to Isobel and Caro would be over. Thayer would be too busy trying to save his own skin to make trouble.

Urging his mount into an easy canter, Alec turned his thoughts to triumphing in an even more difficult challenge—winning the hand of the lady he loved.

Perhaps it was just as well that he had hours to go.

* * *

A short while later, all arrangements made with Isobel and her aunt, Caro stowed the last of the bandboxes atop the travel trunks and helped her mother into the hired carriage.

"Now, do not cause any mischief for Lady Urquehart," admonished the baroness as she leaned around her maid and waggled a warning finger. "She is not as used to having several lively spirited girls to watch over as I am, so please do not cause her any heart palpitations."

"I shall try not to, Mama," murmured Caro. "Bath is a very staid town, so you have no need to fret."

"Trouble can rear its head anywhere."

Her mother occasionally made an astute observation, but Caro refrained from making any reply. Instead she merely gave a cheery wave.

"Have a lovely visit—and try not to lose all your pin money to those two card sharps."

The baroness exhaled a startled huff while her maid managed to stifle a chortle.

Caro waved the driver on, then quickly turned and set off for Isobel's residence, leaving her own maid to supervise the packing and transporting of clothing for the short stay with her friend. Anxious to get Isobel alone for a lengthy chat, she had proposed a walk to Sydney Gardens. No brilliantly clever ploy for entrapping Thayer had yet formed in her head. However, she had made the decision that Isobel must be informed of what was going on.

Alec might howl with outrage, but in her opinion, it was far more dangerous for him to keep his sister in the dark.

"Now that the day has turned cloudy, it will likely be getting cooler." Isobel was waiting for her in the entrance hall. "You really ought to have a cloak for our walk."

"My maid won't be here for several hours with my trunk," replied Caro. "I'd rather not wait."

"Then here, take one of mine."

Caro regarded the softspun wool garment, which was trimmed with carved silver buttons and a stylish little shoulder cape made of tartan plaid. "But that is your favorite."

"Yes, but that shade of forest green looks horrid with the apricot stripes of my gown, so I would rather wear my biscuit-colored one," replied her friend. "And besides, it looks divine on you."

Refraining from further argument, Caro draped it over her shoulders and slanted a glance at the looking glass hung over the side table.

Yes, it did suit her rather well.

"Thank you." She fastened the carnelian and silver clasp. "Shall we be off?"

Isobel waited until they were out on the street before murmuring, "You seem in a hurry. Is there a reason?"

"Yes," answered Caro. "But I would prefer to wait until we have found a private spot in the gardens to explain."

"That sounds a little ominous."

She hesitated, letting the silence linger for several steps before replying, "That's because it is. Your brother will be angry with me, but I feel you should know what is going on."

"Ha! I *knew* Alec was hiding something from me." An uncharacteristic scowl darkened her friend's face. "I wish he wouldn't treat me as if I were a child."

"He wants to protect you," pointed out Caro. "Which is admirable, of course. But it is my opinion that for any lady with half a brain, knowledge is far better armor than ignorance."

"Oh, I couldn't agree more." An unladylike oath followed, which did not bode well for Alec's next encounter with his sister. "As to that…"

Caro shook her head in warning. "We ought not discuss it until we have found a secluded place where we can talk without fear of being overheard." She was determined not to give Alec any reason to accuse her of reckless behavior. "By the by, he had promised to tell me more about what is going on last night at the fireworks display, but Thayer's presence prevented it. I had hoped he would arrange to meet me this morning, but your aunt mentioned that he rode off at first light."

No doubt to avoid a tête-à-tête.

Isobel frowned. "He did leave a note for me saying an urgent matter required his attention, and that he planned on returning by supper." A pause. "Well, it seems he shall find more on his plate than roasted capon and creamed mushrooms."

Ha! Let us hope he will not stick a fork in my derrière.

The rest of the walk to Sydney Gardens passed in silence, each of them lost in her own thoughts. Passing quickly through the conservatory of the Sydney Hotel, they emerged onto the lawns, and from there Caro quickly chose one of the side paths, which wound around to one of the bridges that crossed the canal. She recalled from past visits that there were several wooded areas that were likely to afford some privacy.

As they came to a copse of trees near one of the marble follies that dotted the grounds, Caro took Isobel's arm and drew her into the leafy shadows. Spotting a small stone bench set in the shade of a spreading oak, she hurriedly took a seat and expelled a sigh.

"Well?" pressed Isobel as she sat down beside her. "And please, I want to hear the whole story, not some carefully edited version deemed fit for delicate ears."

"And so you shall." Caro took several moments to steady her breathing. "Once upon a time..."

"That's *not* funny," murmured her friend.

"Sometimes a bit of humor makes it easier to begin," she responded. "And I must say, at times my experiences with your brother do seem like something out of a horrid novel."

To put it mildly.

Caro pursed her lips. "I take it you know something of his activities in the movement for Scottish independence?"

"Yes, and probably more than he thinks I do."

"I thought that might be true," said Caro. "Perhaps you ought to hear the *real* story of the events that took place at Dunbar Castle, which will explain how your brother may have made enemies of a certain faction within the group."

With that, she quickly explained that the story of a jewelry theft had covered up a far more sinister plot, one in which both she and Alec—as well as her sister Anna and her soon-to-be husband—had been involved in a dangerous intrigue swirling around a visiting German prince.

"Does he truly think I don't know the full extent of his involvement in clandestine politics? Good heavens, I'm not a feather-brained goose. I knew exactly what message I was carrying to his associate on the night I was hurt on the moors." Isobel huffed in frustration. "It seems he and I shall have to sit down for a serious talk."

"I think that would be wise," replied Caro slowly. "But your brother won't like it."

Isobel's muttered response indicated that wasn't going to stop her. "Please go on. I take it that Alec is at odds with Thayer, and because of the recent events, he fears I am being used as a pawn in the struggle."

"Correct," said Caro. "Your brother has not confided all

the details, but my surmise is that Thayer is the leader of the faction that favors violence to achieve the group's goals, and he is trying to gain control of the movement..." She went on to explain what she knew.

"I see." Isobel sat back and stared up at the rustling leaves. "So, how are we going to stop Thayer?" she asked over the whispery sounds.

"Damnation."

Alec's stallion blew out an aggrieved answering whinny as he finished extracting a twisted shard of metal from the injured hoof and rose from his crouch.

"Yes, yes, I know—it hurts like the devil." He patted the big bay's lathered flank, cursing yet again the bad luck of galloping over an errant nail lodged among the pebbles of the dusty lane.

The nearest village lay several miles ahead. Fisting the reins, Alec set off at a slow walk, the lame stallion limping gamely beside him. He prayed that he would find a horse for hire. Now that he knew the full extent of Thayer's evil machinations, he was anxious to move quickly to protect his loved ones from any further threat.

Tomorrow he would head north with his aunt and sister, carrying the documents that would put an end to the other man's power.

As for Caro...

Tonight they must talk. *About a great many things.*

"I wish I were as clever as Sir Sharpe Quill in devising a plan to snare a cunning villain," said Caro wryly. "I have some thoughts, but as yet I cannot seem to come up with a workable plan."

"Perhaps if we put our heads together we can think of something," suggested her friend. "What if . . ."

For the next little while they batted around ideas like so many shuttlecocks, but none of them seemed to have enough feathers to fly.

"I have an even greater respect for Wellington and his staff," murmured Caro. "It is not easy drawing up a strategy of attack." She slanted a sidelong glance at Isobel and felt a frisson of concern. The clouds overhead had thickened, and the deepening shadows accentuated the paleness of her friend's face. Despite her much improved health, she still looked a little fragile.

"Indeed, plotting is awfully hard work," she added quickly. "I could do with a bit of sustenance, and I am sure you could as well. We passed a cart selling meat pasties that smelled delicious. I shall go fetch a pair for us."

"I can come along," volunteered Isobel.

"No, no, I'll just be a few minutes." Caro was already up and heading for the pathway.

The breeze was freshening, and she tugged up the hood of her borrowed cloak, glad she had worn the garment to ward off the damp chill. The feel of the thickly woven tartan trim, so very warm and solid against her fingers, was a reminder of Alec.

A comforting thought, as musing on Thayer's wickedness had left her feeling strangely unsettled.

"Miss, Miss." A piteous voice interrupted her musing. "Can ye spare a coin for a former soldier wots been blinded in the war."

Looking up she saw hunched figure wrapped in a thread-bare overcoat and muffler move awkwardly into her path. Eyes pressed closed, he rattled a cup holding several small coins.

"Yes, of course," she murmured, fumbling inside her reticule to find her money.

"Yer a kind soul." He shuffled closer.

She tried not to flinch at the scent of rancid mutton and stale onions. "Here is a shilling for you, sir."

"God bless ye." His boots scuffed against her skirts as he leaned into her.

Biting her lip, Caro tried to edge around him. But a steel point suddenly pricked against her chest.

"Not so fast," he whispered. "Come with me, and quiet like, or my friend will hurt yer companion."

She darted a look back at the grove and saw another shabby figure loitering among the trees.

"What—" she began.

"Shut yer mummer and do as yer told. Yer brother may be a titled toff, but right now it's me wot's giving the orders." The man shoved her forward, keeping one arm around her shoulders, and the knife pressed up against her ribcage. "March."

He thought she was Isobel?

Casting off all thoughts of screaming or struggling, she bowed her head and meekly followed orders, hoping her masquerade would hold up until they were well away from the Gardens.

Alec would be frantic with fear if Isobel were abducted.

And besides, whatever the ruffians had in mind, she had a better chance of escaping from them than Isobel did. An eccentric upbringing had given the Sloane sisters an arsenal of unladylike skills, including an expertise in lock-picking, knot-tying, and handling a pistol. Anna was the better shot, but Caro prided herself on foot speed and agility at climbing obstacles.

Thayer—for she was sure it was Thayer who had planned the abduction—was in for a rude awakening.

I have yearned for a swashbuckling adventure, and it appears that I have got it.

With Isobel free from Thayer's clutches, Alec would be...

No, she wouldn't think of Alec right now.

Up ahead, waiting just across the canal bridge was a nondescript carriage with dark draperies drawn closed behind the small glass-paned window. Despite her resolve, Caro felt a burble of panic well up in her throat as they approached and her captor reached out and yanked the door open.

It was awfully dark inside.

"In ye go."

After hesitating for just an instant, Caro steeled her nerve and climbed into the vehicle without protest. Her captor followed on her heels, the knifepoint now tickling against her spine.

A moment later, the springs rocked again, and a second man joined them. "Heh, heh, heh, that was easy as plucking a chick from a dovecote." He rapped on the trap and the vehicle lurched into motion.

"Aye, easy pickings," agreed his cohort with a nasty laugh. "The cove that hired us will pay us handsomely fer His Lordship's sister."

As Caro once again considered the confusion over her identity, an idea suddenly took shape in her head.

"He's going to hand over the money when we make the exchange, isn't he?"

"Ye think I'm daft—of course he is." She heard the sound of her captor tapping the blade against his calloused palm. "It's just a few miles to the inn on the north road, and then we shall be rich as lords."

"Lords! Heh, heh, heh. I shall drink to that with The Black Duck's finest ale."

Thankful for the hazy gloom, Caro pressed herself deeper into the corner and shifted the hood to muffle her face.

The carriage rattled on, the cobblestones of town giving way to hard-packed earth of the country roads. It seemed to take forever to travel the short distance, but at last she felt the wheels slow and cut a sharp turn before rolling to a halt.

She began to sob softly into the folds of wool.

A moment later the door wrenched open. "You have her?" growled a low voice.

Thayer. *The swine.*

"Have a look for yourself," answered her captor.

The dappling of low light barely reached the hem of her skirts. Still, a flicker lit the muted pattern of the plaid.

Thayer grunted, and she heard the chink of a coin-filled purse as he tossed it onto the stableyard ground.

"Get out," he ordered. "I'm in a hurry."

His two henchmen tripped over each other in their haste to scramble down the iron foot rungs.

The door slammed shut, cutting off their rough-cut laughter. At Thayer's signal, the carriage lumbered into motion again. A whip cracked, urging the horses into a shambling trot.

"Forgive me for not being hospitable and offering you some refreshments, Miss Urquehart," said Thayer with mock politeness. "But I prefer to put some miles between us and Bath before we make a more leisurely stop."

An unpleasant laugh reverberated against the paneling. "Your brother may be a dull-witted clod, but he's a crack shot."

Caro kept up her snuffling. The farther they traveled before he discovered his mistake the better.

"I do trust you will stop that caterwauling soon. We have a long journey ahead, and I assure you, it will not be an overly comfortable one for you if I am forced to tie a gag around your lovely face."

The seat creaked as he crossed one booted leg over the other. "However, if you behave yourself, there is no reason why we can't travel together in reasonable comfort."

And pigs might fly.

"Think about it," he counseled, when she didn't let up on her tears. "We have two hours until the next stop."

Two hours—time that Caro intended to put to good use in thinking and planning for the next move in this deadly game of cat and mouse.

Chapter Twenty

*C*ome, I am sure you would welcome a stroll to stretch your legs, Miss Urquehart." Thayer roused himself from his thoughts as the carriage pulled to halt. "But be advised that I have a pistol, and the inn is an out-of-the-way place whose proprietor has been paid to overlook any disturbances. So any attempt at escape would be futile."

He paused to peek out through the window draperies. "Not to speak of having unpleasant consequences for you."

Caro mumbled a muffled "No." Her unmasking was inevitable, but she had decided to try to put it off for as long as possible.

Thayer, however, had not meant the offer as an invitation, but rather as an order. He leaned over and grabbed hold of her arm. "Get out," he snarled. "I warn you, there will be precious few stops on the way to Scotland, so you'll take sustenance and use the conveniences when I tell you to."

Resistance was silly, so she allowed herself to be led out of the vehicle. Keeping her face averted, she made a quick survey of the place. It was, as Thayer implied, a ramshackle little establishment, surrounded by unpruned hedges and a rutted stableyard.

A none too clean rutted stableyard, she noted, looking down at the muck squished beneath her half boots.

Gritting her teeth, she started walking slowly, deciding to heed his warning and take advantage of the chance to gulp down a breath of fresh air. The faint scent of pine and meadowgrass felt cleansing.

The atmosphere within the carriage was thick with the noxious stench of evil.

Thayer kept close, the brush of his clothing sending shivers through her body.

"Miss Urquehart."

She didn't look around.

"Isobel." He said it softly, but the curl of menace in his tone squeezed the air from her lungs. Still, Caro kept her gaze on the faraway hills.

Quick as a cobra, Thayer shot out a hand and yanked back the hood of her cloak.

The wools snagged on her hairpins, allowing a tumble of dark curls to fall over her shoulders.

Thayer let out a string of oaths that no gentleman ought to say in the presence of a lady.

But then, he was not a gentleman—he was an odious serpent. *A twisted coiling of malice and evil.*

A shudder snaked through her, but masking her fear, Caro said coolly, "I assure you, sir, I am no more happy with your hired ruffian's mistake than you are."

"How the devil did this happen?" he snarled. His hand was still fisted in the tartan trim, and he gave the fabric a little shake.

"Isobel and I decided to take a walk to Sydney Gardens.

As the weather was turning chillier, she lent me a cloak. It must be that your men mistook me for her." Caro feigned a look of innocent uncertainty. "But I don't understand what is going on. Why would you wish to abduct Isobel?"

He didn't answer right away. Eyes narrowing in thought, he stared off into the distance.

Trying, no doubt, to come up with another way to sink his poisonous fangs into Alec.

Thank God he and his sister were out of harm's way. Thayer could not hurt them.

He seemed to think otherwise, for an ugly smirk slowly curled his lips. "Perhaps this mistake is actually a most fortuitous stroke of luck. You may be even more useful to me than the Urquehart chit."

"*Me?*"

"Oh, yes, I saw how Strathcona looked at you the other night in Sydney Gardens, and how he reacted to my being with you." His low laugh made the hairs at the back of her neck stand on end. "He cares for his sister. But I think he is besotted with you. To ensure your safe return, he'd be willing to do most anything."

"You are mistaken," she said, trying to keep the tremor from her voice. "His Lordship and I are merely friends."

"I think not." A speculative gleam lit in his eyes. "I would wager you are far more than that. He is a romantic fool and always has been."

The gleam then turned into a leer. "What about you, Miss Caro? Are you equally foolish? Have you given him your heart?" He leaned in closer. "And perhaps your virtue?"

She recoiled. "You disgust me."

"Do I?" His expression hardened.

Getting a grip on her emotions, Caro remained silent.

"A word of warning—you should have a care to keep a civil tongue in your head. Making an enemy of me would not be wise."

We shall see who turns out to be the most dangerous adversary, thought Caro. But in the meantime he was right— she would watch her words for now, and wait.

Thayer turned abruptly and pushed her back toward the carriage. "We have a long journey ahead of us. You will have plenty of time to think of ways to sweeten your words."

My thoughts will be on honey, but only because it is useful in trapping loathsome flies.

Swiping the sweat and dust from his brow, Alec slid from the saddle with a muttered oath of relief. The hired nag had been hell to ride, its jarring gait having left every bone in his body feeling bruised.

After lighting one of the stable lanterns, he quickly rubbed down the animal and then turned to make his way to the back entrance of the house. It was late and he was famished. A cold collation of beef and cheese, a glass of Highland malt to mellow—

"Alec!"

The narrow beam of light suddenly illuminated Isobel's pale face and red-rimmed eyes as she rushed through the doorway. "Thank God you have finally returned!"

His fatigue-fogged senses snapped to full alert. "What's happened?" he demanded.

"Caro..." she stammered. "The Gardens...a pair of horrible men...it happened so fast—"

"Take a deep breath and a moment to calm yourself," he counseled, though he was wild with worry. "If I am to be of any help, I need to know exactly what has occurred."

"Miss Caro has been abducted." Andover came up behind his sister. "By two men in Sydney Gardens, who forced her into a carriage just across the canal bridge and drove off."

"It was a nondescript vehicle, black with dark green wheels and no other distinguishing markings," added Isobel, who had quickly composed herself. "She had gone to fetch us some meat pasties from a costermonger. I—I should have gone with her."

"Then you both would be captives," said Alec, forcing himself to react reasonably. "And we would have no clue as to what occurred. Your observations will help me find her all the quicker."

Her look of remorse eased ever so slightly. "You will save her, won't you?" she asked in a small voice.

"Yes," said Alec grimly. "And then I shall pummel Edward Thayer to a bloody pulp."

"Isobel came straight to me," said Andover. "But much as I wished to rush off to the rescue, I had no notion of where her captors may be headed. Isobel told me that Thayer is the likely culprit, but whether he would head north or to some other hideaway was impossible for me to guess at." He gave a helpless shrug. "So I thought it best to wait for you to return."

"That was the right move," assured Alec. Already he was making a mental checklist of what he would need to set off. *Pistols, powder, foul weather cloak, bread and cheese so he could ride hard...*

"Hell and damnation." He smacked a fist against one of the stall doors. "My stallion went lame this afternoon. I'll need to find a decent mount, but at this hour—"

"Take my chestnut gelding," said Andover without hesitation. "He has both spirit and stamina. You may push him hard and he won't let you down."

"My thanks."

"I'll go fetch him now, and bring him around through the back gate of the mews, so as not to attract any undue attention." Andover cleared his throat with a cough. "The authorities have not yet been informed of what has happened. I thought it best to let you decide how to handle the matter. Your aunt and servants have been sworn to silence for the time being. And Miss Caro's mother is away visiting friends, so we need not deal with that complication just yet."

"I'm grateful for such quick thinking," murmured Alec, his regard for the other man rising another notch. Despite his easygoing manner, Andover appeared to be a very solid, sensible fellow in a crisis.

"While you gather your weapons and clothing, I'll make up an oilskin sack of essentials, along with a blanket roll in case you need to sleep rough," said Isobel, her fears giving way to steady resolve. "We haven't any time to lose. With each passing moment, Thayer is taking Caro farther and farther away from us." She swallowed hard. "To God knows where."

"As to that, I think I know exactly where he is headed." Alec waved Andover on his way and took his sister's arm. "And when I catch up with him, there will be hell to pay."

Once in the house, he left Isobel and his aunt to assemble supplies while he raced to his rooms for his pistols.

Oh, yes—he would cheerfully put a bullet through Thayer's brain without blinking an eye if the miscreant gave him half a chance. But his former friend had a coward's cunning and never dared face a fight unless he had found a way to cheat the odds.

Not this time, vowed Alec. The villain would be made to stand and account for his treachery.

As he slipped a packet of extra powder into his pocket, he heard the scuff of steps behind him.

"I've packed up all the essentials I could think of," said Isobel.

He turned around. "Thank you. I've gathered what I need here. As soon as Andover arrives I shall be off."

"Oh, Alec." She caught him in a fierce hug. "I'm terrified."

"As am I," he whispered. "But—"

"But what I mean to say is," she interrupted, "those terrors don't really matter. Your strength and courage are more solid than our Highland mountains—I know in my heart you will rescue her. It is *your* inner fears that worry me. Please, don't be afraid of your feelings. The past is the past. The future..."

Isobel hugged him tighter. "The future is whatever you dare to dream it to be."

Alec brushed a kiss to her brow. "You are wise beyond your years."

"That is because you still think of me as a toddler in leading strings," she replied with a wry smile. "Speaking of fears, you really need not fear so much for me. I'm far stronger than you think. I knew exactly what I was doing that night on the moor. You did not put me in danger—I chose to bear the message for the group knowing full well what it contained."

Isobel met his gaze. "In fact, I served as a courier on several other occasions for the group, but did not tell you because I knew you would worry about me."

He drew in a ragged breath. "Well, a night of surprises."

"I'm telling you this now, so you know that ladies are willing to take a risk when they feel the stakes are worth it," went on Isobel. "And so, my dearest brother, should you."

The truth was, he already knew that he was willing to risk everything, including his heart.

Alec squeezed her shoulders, then broke away. "I shall try not to disappoint you."

Or myself.

Hunger was beginning to gnaw at her stomach, and a damp chill was creeping up through the slatted floorboards and penetrating the thin fabric of her skirts. Shifting on the hard bench, Caro pulled her cloak a bit tighter around her shoulders and tried to get comfortable.

Thayer appeared to be dozing, but with the weak flame of the carriage lamp giving off only a ghostly flutter of light within the inky shadows, it was impossible to tell. His hand was curled firmly around the uncocked pistol. For a fleeting moment she thought about trying to wrest it away, but quickly realized the idea was foolhardy.

Even if she managed to get it—doubtful at best—the chances of stopping the carriage and then eluding both her captor and his driver on a deserted road were virtually nil.

That sort of swashbuckling scenario might work perfectly in novels, but for this all-too-real ordeal, she would have to devise a more circumspect plan of escape.

As if confirming such thoughts, the carriage hit a deep rut and careened sideways, the wheels bumping over the rocks and tufts of grass bordering the high hedgerows.

Swearing loudly as his shoulder slammed into the paneling, Thayer righted himself and reached up to thump on the trap. A curt exchange with the driver ended with the decision to stop at the next inn for a brief respite.

Hot tea and a crust of bread, thought Caro longingly. Or perhaps he meant to starve her into submission.

"Might I have a bit of sustenance when we stop?" she asked, keeping her tone meek.

He turned, the dim light playing along the smug curl of his mouth. "Since you asked nicely, I will see that you have something to eat and drink." The nasty smile stretched wider. "You see, if you make yourself agreeable, this can be a perfectly pleasant journey."

Caro swallowed a sarcastic retort and merely made a small noise in her throat.

It must have sounded suitably submissive, for he laughed softly. "I'm glad to see you are not one of those silly, simpering chits who clings to the notion of true love."

Love. The word made her heart flutter for a fleeting moment. A man as twisted as Thayer would never understand that love was far more powerful than hate.

"Like me, you are far more pragmatic."

I am nothing *like you*, thought Caro.

"Which will, of course, make things easier on you, once we reach Scotland," he continued.

"Just what do you intend to do with me there?" she asked. Knowing what she was facing would help her map out her own plans.

"That depends. I think Strathcona will gladly trade the incriminating evidence he has on my activities in order to get you back."

"You misjudge his sentiments," she murmured. "And even if he did have a *tendre* for me, I believe His Lordship cares more for principles than he does for any personal feelings."

"I think not. Alec McClellan is a weak-hearted fool when it comes to women. Just look at his history." His laugh took on a nastier edge. "Indeed, he's a buffle-brained idiot when it comes to many things. He's so besotted with the notion of gentlemanly honor that he'll actually believe I'll keep my end of the bargain."

Repressing a twinge of fear, Caro forced herself to remain dispassionate. She needed to keep her wits sharp and learn what he was thinking. "Once you have the evidence, why keep me hostage?" she asked. "My family and I will hardly want to make any accusations of abduction, so you need not fear that your misdeeds will be made public."

"Precisely!" A flash of teeth—like a prowling predator about to seize his helpless prey. "You see, I have been thinking, and in all modesty, I must say I possess a very clever mind."

"Y-yes, that's quite clear," Caro responded haltingly. He was not the only one capable of devious deceptions, though in truth it took little skill in playacting to sound confused. She couldn't quite follow where his twisted machinations were going.

"But I don't understand…" she added softly, hoping to coax him into revealing more.

"Of course you don't," said Thayer with savage satisfaction. "It takes a superior intellect to take a mistake and turn it into a stroke of genius." He smoothed the wrinkles from his sleeves, the predator now turning into a preening peacock, admiring his own iridescent beauty.

"As I said, I have been thinking these last few hours. And it has occurred to me that you are even more useful than I first thought. As a hostage, you will force Strathcona to hand over documents, making it impossible for him to prove certain accusations against me. But as a bride, you will serve as even more solid protection."

Caro jerked upright.

"Your sister's husband, the Earl of Wrexham, is a rich and powerful peer," Thayer went on. "He would never let scandal taint the family, so if I am his brother-in-law, he'll use all his considerable influence to see I am never accused of any wrongdoing. Should Strathcona ever try to make trouble for me, he will be squashed like a bug."

The man was mad. Even if Wrexham, who was known for his integrity and sense of honor, possessed such power, he would *never* use it for unsavory purposes.

However, she swallowed her outrage and instead simply mumbled, "How extraordinary of you to think of that."

The comment seemed to please him. "Consider yourself fortunate to have had me take you away from the oafish attentions of Strathcona." He shifted and his leg touched hers. "You're a pretty enough chit that it won't be a chore to bed you."

A shudder slithered over her skin.

"And I imagine Wrexham has provided you with a very handsome dowry as well," he mused. "So I shall be not only protected by an influential aristocrat but wealthy in the bargain."

Another flight of madness, thought Caro. As if the earl would hand over a farthing to a miscreant who was guilty of abduction, as well as a host of other foul deeds.

But for now it was prudent to play the meek mouse and bide her time until the moment was right to transform into the cat with claws.

Thank God for the full moon, thought Alec as he passed through the outskirts of town and urged the big gelding into a canter along the road leading north. He meant to ride hard, and Andover had not exaggerated the sterling qualities of his horse. Beneath the pounding hooves and sweat-lathered muscles, the miles were flying by.

Eight hours.

He calculated that Thayer had a headstart of at least eight hours. The carriage would travel more slowly and be required to stop more frequently to change the horses, so he would quickly begin to cut the distance between them. There was, of course, the question of what route Thayer was taking and where he was heading.

But Alec was confident that he was right in guessing his enemy's destination.

A hunting lodge just over the border—a place Thayer had bragged about to an erstwhile friend as a spot where he had debauched more than one young lady by seducing her with false promises of marriage.

A poisonous snake does not lose his venom, thought Alec, unless his fangs are pulled out by force.

Bending low, his own hair tangling with the flying mane, he spurred the bay to a faster pace.

Chapter Twenty-One

Stiff with fatigue, Caro stumbled on descending from the carriage and nearly pitched headlong onto the rutted ground.

"Be careful, you silly chit," growled Thayer, steadying her with a rough grab. "We don't want to call attention to ourselves."

Her only response was a small nod. He seemed to enjoy her silence, taking it as a sign that she was thoroughly cowed.

Let him think that, she mused, flexing her aching shoulders to loosen the knotted muscles. In the meantime, she was watching and waiting for her chance to escape.

Already she had managed to find the small penknife in her reticule and hide it in the sash of her gown. She had also dropped a few coins into the "V" of her corset.

Other than those paltry things, she had only her own imagination and resolve to rely on.

Her sisters would be proud of her, thought Caro with an inward smile. Rather than act on impulse, she had controlled the first blaze of anger and was being guided by pragmatism, not passion.

Perhaps I am getting older and wiser.

Reminded of the need to stay alert, she put aside such musings and took a careful look around her. It was important to learn where she was. They had traveled all night with only a few short stops for the driver to rest. It was now late afternoon, which meant they had been on the road for a little over twenty-four hours...

Caro gave thanks for the fact that Anna was a stickler for accuracy when it came to the details of her novels. Because of her sister's research, she knew that a carriage could cover roughly five miles in an hour.

One hundred and twenty miles. That meant they were almost halfway to the Scottish border. So, that left her another day and half to find a way to escape. Flight would be easier while still in England.

Quickening her pace, she hurried to get in as many steps as possible in the small area Thayer had allowed for stretching her legs. When the time came to bolt, she would need to move quickly.

As for rescue...

Caro tried not to think of Alec galloping in on a white charger, a knight in shining armor flashing a mighty sword and heroic smile.

For one thing, his horse was a dappled gray.

Expelling a rueful sigh, she reminded herself that even if he wished to be a hero, he had no idea of where to start looking for her. Yes, he would suspect that Thayer was behind the abduction, but there were a thousand—nay, a hundred thousand—places that her captor might be headed.

No, she must play the intrepid heroine and save herself.

That Anna would be over the moon at having first-hand inspiration for her next novel helped steady a sudden little flutter of nerves.

Surely she could be as brave as Emmalina, who had no more substance than ink and paper.

Flesh, blood, brains, heart—I will have to put them all to the test.

Turning on her heel, Caro walked through several more tight circles as she thought over her options.

Tonight—after weighing her options, she decided that she must try to make her move tonight.

A spattering of chill raindrops woke Alec from a fitful doze. He quickly rolled up his blanket and resaddled his horse.

"I owe you a bushel of apples," he murmured, patting the big chestnut's muscled flank.

The gelding snorted and kicked up clots of the damp earth, looking rested and eager to run from Hades to Xanadu if need be.

Running a hand over his bristly jaw, Alec wished he felt half so fresh. He had pushed himself hard, allowing only brief respites to rest his mount. Fatigue now wrapped around his limbs, along with a coating of dust and sweat. Perhaps at the next inn, he would stop long enough for a hot bath and a meal.

Both mind and body were getting muzzy, which wouldn't help in the coming confrontation with Thayer.

His nemesis was a lowly snake, but a clever one who could strike from any angle.

When it came, he must be ready.

A gust of wind rattled the window as the first drops of rain peltered against the paned glass. Caro craned her neck to peer up at the darkening sky. A squall was blowing in from the west, the gunmetal-gray clouds still swirling with the storm-lashed fury of the North Atlantic seas.

"Hell and damnation," swore Thayer, eyeing the blurred landscape. Already the carriage was slowing as the road turned muddy. He threw himself back against the squabs, muttering under his breath as he tugged his pocketwatch out from his waistcoat and flipped open the case.

Was there a rendezvous planned?

Caro felt a frisson of trepidation. But rather than be afraid, she must look at it as an opportunity.

Thayer swore again, and after a few more minutes of nervous fidgeting, he rose and rapped on the trap.

Though the wind garbled most of the driver's response, Caro caught mention of an inn, and the guess that it would be another half hour before the carriage reached it.

Wiping the rain from his face, Thayer fixed her with a dirty scowl. "We will be stopping for a while. You had best not make any trouble, if you know what's good for you," he warned.

Caro gave a mock shiver. "Perish the thought. All I can think of is a mug of hot tea and a chance to rest from all the jostling." Making her voice sound even fainter, she asked, "M-m-might I be permitted to lie down somewhere if we are to linger for more than the usual short interlude?"

His mouth pursed in thought, but he didn't answer.

For what felt like an age, the only sounds were the howl of the wind and the squelching *clop, clop, clop* of the wheels rattling though the mud and stones. Thayer had lit the carriage lamp, and the lurching shadows only added to the air of gloomy tension.

At last, they came to a shuddering stop, and Caro found

herself hustled out of the vehicle and into a ramshackle inn. Smoke hung heavy in the entrance corridor, hazing the weak flickers of oily light from the wall sconces.

Thayer muttered a few orders to the proprietor, and as the man shuffled off to fetch a key to one of the upstairs room, a figure stepped out of the shadows of the taproom.

"It's about time you arrived."

Caro tensed. His voice, though hardly more than a whisper, sparking a sudden flare of foreboding.

"I trust you have dealt with the problem?"

"We'll discuss it in a moment," snapped Thayer, flicking a look at Caro. "But yes, the fellow will no longer present a problem."

The churchyard, the exchange of money—Caro was now overwhelmingly certain that these were the two men she had overheard. Not that she needed any corroboration that her captor was thoroughly evil.

The proprietor returned and after a brief exchange, Thayer shoved her toward the stairs. "I won't be long," he said to his cohort, and then led her up to a dreary chamber set off the unswept landing. The guttering candle showed a small bedstead with a lumpy mattress and yellowed sheets. The lone window was barred with thick iron rods, no doubt to keep travelers from absconding without paying their bill.

Now if fleas could be charged a nightly rate, thought Caro, the innkeeper would be rich as Croesus.

A slat-back chair, a battered chest of drawers, and a washstand with a cracked pitcher and dusty basin were the only other furniture in the room. Trying not to let her spirits plummet, Caro turned at the sound of someone pushing open the door.

A skinny serving lass set plate of brown bread and a watery stew on the chest, along with a none-too-clean glass of water. "Yer supper," she mumbled, before skittering out.

"Make yourself comfortable, Miss Caro. And remember, don't try anything foolish. It would be pointless." Flashing an unsavory smile, Thayer brandished the key to highlight his warning. "And I warn you, there would be very unpleasant consequences."

Caro dropped her gaze to the tips of her half boots to hide the flash of anger his words provoked.

"I'll come fetch you in an hour or two."

Ha—by that time she hoped to be out of his clutches for good.

Darkness enveloped her as he left with the candle and drew the door shut behind him. The metallic *click* of the key turning in the lock followed.

Caro made herself choke down the unappetizing food as she waited for the tread of his steps to trail off into silence. It might be quite some time before she ate again. Satisfied that he wasn't going to return, she then quickly drew out her penknife and several hairpins from her tangled tresses.

Locks were child's play for a Hellion of High Street. In the wilds, her father had made a game of teaching his daughters survival skills, believing a lady ought to know how to fend for herself.

"Thank you, Papa," she whispered as she knelt down and pressed the knifeblade against the main lever, then slipped in a straightened pin and began to jiggle.

It was only a matter of moments before she heard a welcome *snick*.

Easing the latch open, Caro checked that the narrow corridor was deserted. Earlier, she had spotted a window at its far end, and as she hurried to check the casement, she found it was merely locked, not barred. Once again, her knife made quick work of the levers, and in a trice, the iron-framed leaded glass swung open.

Tucking up her skirts, she swung out and edged along the narrow ledge to the drainpipe at the corner of the building. Once again giving thanks for her unladylike upbringing, she shinnied down to the ground.

The rain had let up, giving way to a drifting fog. Only the faintest mizzle of moonlight peeked through the swirls of silvery mist making the dark silhouettes of the surrounding moors look even more forbidding. There was no flicker of light, no sign of life.

Caro steadied her thumping heart with several deep breaths. The lone road was too dangerous to try, she decided. It was the first place Thayer would look. Better to hide in the hills until morning, when she could get a better lay of the land.

A harsh laugh rang out from behind the shuttered window of the taproom. Spinning around, she darted past the stables and headed up a narrow path that wound its way into the looming darkness.

All senses on full alert, Alec tethered his horse in a copse of trees and stealthily approached the rear of the inn. At the last village, a barmaid had confirmed that a carriage matching the description of Thayer's vehicle had passed along the road just a few hours ago.

Caro was close. He could feel the certainty of it thrumming through his blood.

Cocking his pistols, he slipped in through the scullery door and moved noiselessly through the dimly lit corridor, heading for the sound of clinking tankards.

Flickering candles, two faces—one of them familiar. But Thayer was not there.

"Well, well, it seems I've stumbled into a nest of vipers." Taking dead aim at the pair, Alec stepped into the taproom. "Not a move, not a sound, unless you wish to meet your Maker."

The proprietor—a balding, pasty-faced man wearing a greasy apron—shrank back, fear slackening his heavy jaw.

"Sir," he whispered. "I—I am . . ."

"Quiet," growled Alec. His gaze remained locked on the other man. "Where are Thayer and Miss Caro, Dudley?"

"The chit fled into the hills. Thayer went after her." Dudley let out a nasty laugh, looking confident that he held the advantage. "We're willing to bargain with you." Another laugh. "But if you hope to get her back undamaged, I daresay you've come a bit too late."

"You had better pray not," responded Alec. He aimed one of his weapons at the proprietor. "I suggest you tell me exactly what has happened here. Unless you, too, wish to be thrown in the gaol along with this miserable cur."

The details quickly spilled out—the stableboy spotting Caro as she fled up a path into the moors, Thayer's rage and his saddling of Dudley's horse to go in pursuit.

"How long ago?" he demanded.

The man wet his trembling lips. "Twenty minutes . . . maybe a half hour."

Dudley laughed again.

Keeping a tight rein on his emotions, Alec tucked one of the pistols in his pocket and grabbed the proprietor's arm. "Show me the path."

"Yes, yes, of course. This way, sir!"

As the man turned, Alec caught a flicker of movement in

the corner of his eye. Spinning around, he lashed out a kick just as Dudley rose from his chair and squeezed off a shot from the pistol he had pulled from inside his coat.

The bullet smashed into the ceiling, sending an explosion of plaster and splinters raining down on them.

Snarling an oath, Dudley regained his balance and swung the butt of his spent pistol at Alec's head. "I trusted Thayer to finish you off, but I see I shall have to do it myself."

"You may try." Alec dodged the blow and countered with a hard punch that knocked his adversary back against the table. He followed it with another. And another.

Dudley tried to slide away, but Alec caught him by the collar. "Both you and Thayer have done enough evil. You're now going to pay for all your betrayals."

As Dudley tried to grab up a knife from the table, Alec punched him again, his knuckles hitting the other man's jaw with a savagely satisfying *thunk*.

Dudley's head snapped back, and with a grunt, he dropped to the floor like a sack of stones.

Alec stepped over his unconscious enemy. *That was for all his friends who had perished because of the pair's treachery.* He flexed a fist, every fiber of his being aroused with a primitive warrior bloodlust. The next blows would be for Caro—the lady he loved who was now alone on a desolate moor, fleeing a dangerous predator.

Thayer had better start praying to the Almighty for mercy, for the dastard will find none from me.

"Now show me the path, and quickly," Alec barked at the proprietor. "Then tie up this miscreant and lock him in the cellar. If he escapes, you'll take his place on the gallows."

"Th-this way, sir."

In a scant few moments Alec was remounted on the big

bay and riding along the narrow trail that led up through the wind-carved rocks to the ridge crowning the steep moor.

Caro paused to catch her breath.

Was it merely the wind, or did she hear the faint *clip clop* of a horse's hooves?

Telling herself it was naught but her agitated nerves, she tightened her cloak around her shoulders and started to climb again. The slippery rocks shifted beneath her boots, making the going slow and treacherous, but she forced herself to keep moving.

Thayer was desperate. And deluded. He would not allow her to escape easily.

The thought spurred her on.

Rounding an outcropping of granite, she slipped and fell, scraping her hands on the painfully sharp shards.

A clench of fear squeezed the breath from her lungs as Caro pressed her raw palms together, trying to warm the chill from her heart. She was exhausted, she was hurting, she was on her own against a ruthless adversary. But the wind's harsh echo off the stones warned that now was no time to allow courage to surrender to tears.

"I yearned for an exciting adventure, and now I have got it," she reminded herself. "In spades."

Though I hope my clever plan is not digging my own grave.

Thrusting aside such mordant thoughts, Caro regained her footing and began picking a path up through the steep tumble of rocks. As the clouds parted for a moment, allowing a shimmer of moonlight to brighten the blackness, she cast a look over her shoulder at the way she had come.

For just an instant, a spidery thread of silvery light outlined a figure dismounting from a horse and starting to scramble up through the rocks at a furious pace.

And then, in the blink of an eye, the scene was swallowed in a swirl of fog-blurred darkness.

A fresh burst of fear gave new force to her steps. *Faster, faster.* From the crest of the ridge just ahead, it was only a short traverse to where a forest of pines rose up to cover the hillside. If she could just reach its needled shadows, she had a good chance of losing herself in the trees.

Though her legs were feeling heavy as lead, Caro tried to hurry her pace. But the howling wind kept tugging at her skirts, and the demon stones seemed intent on tilting and twisting beneath her half boots.

Gaze glued on the narrowing ledge, she started to skirt around a jagged boulder when a sudden clap of thunder shook the night. Startled, she slipped in midstep. A gust tangled in the billowing folds of her cloak, spinning her around. The smooth leather soles skidded over weathered stone, the wet wool pulled her off-balance.

Caro felt herself begin to fall.

No, no!

Arms flailing, she fought to steady herself. But the wind kicked up, knocking her over the edge. For a heartbeat she hung suspended in the air...

And then everything went black.

Lightning lit the sky, the fiery flash illuminating the silhouette of a man standing on a ledge not far ahead. Wind whipping at his hair, Alec covered the distance with swift, sure-footed strides as rain started to fall.

Thayer turned, and a second booming blaze caught the look of surprise on his face. In an instant, the twist turned to a malevolent sneer. "You've lost yet another lady, McClellan," he snarled, as Alec slowed and stepped onto the ledge. "You're not very lucky in love, are you?"

Alec saw a crumpled form among the rocks and felt a roar rip free from his throat.

Thayer raised his pistol. "I was going to shoot the meddlesome chit, but she's saved me the trouble." The sound of the hammer cocking rose above the whoosh of the wind. "It will give me far greater pleasure to put a bullet through your oh-so-noble heart."

To the Devil with bullets. No earthly force was going to stop him, vowed Alec. This was the man who, through his traitorous machinations, had been the cause of Isobel nearly losing her life on the moors in a storm like this one. And now Caro...

Out of the corner of his eye, he saw Caro move.

Thank God—she was alive!

The knowledge made him even more grimly resolved that Thayer would never harm anyone again. As his nemesis squeezed the trigger, Alec lunged for the gun barrel.

The hammer hit the frizzen with a metallic snap, only to be followed by a deathly silence.

Thayer stood frozen in shock for a fraction of a second— just long enough for Alec knock the pistol from his outstretched hand. Swearing a vicious oath, he tried to smash a knee into Alec's groin.

Anticipating the foul blow, Alec turned and took it on his thigh. Oblivious to the pain shooting through his leg, he countered with a hard jab that broke the other man's nose.

Howling in agony, Thayer staggered back, blood streaming down his chin. He kicked out blindly, forcing Alec back a step, then slid sideways and yanked a knife from his boot.

"Wet powder may be useless," he said, "but wet steel cuts just as sharply."

"True. But your only skill lies in stabbing your friends in the back." Alec calmly dodged a lethal slash. "In a face-to-face fight, let us see who holds the edge."

Thayer tried an upward stab.

With a flick of his bare hand, Alec hit the flat of the knife, deflecting the blade. "My bet is that you're a dead man."

His taunt and his icy sangfroid goaded Thayer into lashing out with a flurry of wild strikes.

"The serpent seems a little sluggish," said Alec, as he kept dancing just out of reach, deliberately drawing his adversary away from where Caro lay and toward a patch of unstable stone.

"Coward," jeered Thayer, though his voice was sounding a little ragged. "You've always been lily-livered coward, though you hide it behind your babblings about honor."

"It's no wonder that any talk of honor sounds like gibberish to a greasy mawworm like you," replied Alec.

The knife suddenly sliced out in a downward arc, its blade cutting through his sleeve and scoring a bloody furrow across his forearm. Thayer let out a cry of triumph, but Alec merely smiled and slid back, impervious to the pain, to the wind, to the rumbling thunder—to anything but beating the other man at his own devil-benighted game.

Growling in frustration, Thayer slashed again and hit nothing but a swirl of wind.

Alec laughed.

The other man's breath was now coming in raspy gasps. Abandoning all caution, Thayer rushed forward and swung another arcing stab. But as his boots hit the loose rocks, his weight caused them to suddenly shift, causing him to lose his footing.

Crying out a curse, he twisted and threw out his arms, trying to break his fall just as the rocks lurched again and broke apart.

Too late. In a blur of thrashing limbs, he tumbled over the edge of the ledge.

A sickening thud, a groaning gasp—and then silence, save for the patter of the dying rain on Thayer's body as it rolled face up on the jagged stones fifteen feet below.

Alec looked down at the corpse for a fleeting moment, eyeing the knife protruding from the dead man's chest without a twinge of regret or remorse. It was, he decided, poetic justice that such a thoroughly bad man should die by his own evil hand.

But thoughts of a far more compelling poetry quickly pushed aside any musings on death and destruction. Whirling around, Alec raced to where Caro was trying to rise and gathered her in his arms.

Chapter Twenty-Two

I'm sorry." Caro forced her eyes open, hardly daring to believe that she wasn't imagining the murmuring voice, the muscular arms lifting her from the cold, hard ground. "I'm sorry, I'm—"

The press of lips stilled the rest of her words.

Alec. Alec. She reached up to feel the familiar shape of his jaw, the slant of his cheekbones, the texture of his hair, unsure whether the moisture streaming down her face was the rain, her tears...or his.

It didn't matter—he was here. Solid and warm, a safe haven from any storm.

He lifted his mouth to feather a kiss to her brow.

"Th-Thayer..." she whispered.

"Hush, Love," he murmured, when she tried to speak again.

Love?

The wind and wet wool muffled around her ears must be playing tricks with sound. She tried to shift.

"Don't tax your strength. You're safe. He won't hurt you or anyone ever again," said Alec. "I'll soon have you sheltered from the wind and cold."

Caro wanted to assure him she was fine, but she couldn't seem to make her body obey. Her head was still woozy from the fall, and her limbs felt too weak to move. Snuggling closer to his chest, she closed her eyes and let the steady *thump, thump* of his heartbeat lull her to sleep.

Alec took cover beneath a ledge of overhanging rock to survey the surroundings. He dared not try to carry Caro back down to the inn until he knew how badly she was injured. A broken rib could be dangerous.

As could a fever. The memory of how close Isobel had come to death from exposure to the elements sent a spike of fear through his chest. Caro felt cold as ice in her wet garments, and her face looked unnaturally pale.

Damnation—Thayer deserved to die a second time for all the harm he had caused.

Cradling Caro tighter in his arms, he edged along the high ledge looking for a niche in the granite big enough to protect them from the wind and rain. The cluster of pine trees on the nearby slope would provide wood for a fire, and the sack tied to his saddle contained a small cooking pot and provisions for tea and porridge.

Rounding an outcropping of tumbled stones, Alec spotted a large crevasse in the rock wall. Closer inspection of the wind-carved space showed it was more than deep and wide enough to be a comfortable shelter from the storm. He ducked inside and, after laying her down on the smooth stone, quickly stripped off his coat to wrap her in another layer of wool.

"Rest easy, sweeting," he murmured. "I shall not be gone long."

She stirred and her hand found his. Their fingers curled together.

For a long moment, Alec didn't move, letting the warmth suffuse their wind-lashed skin. *Two as one*, he thought, looking down at the dark-on-dark silhouette. Despite the dangers swirling around them he felt a surge of hope.

Gently untwining himself, he rose and hurried into the night.

After fetching his supplies and the oilskin-wrapped bedroll, he sheltered his horse within a cluster of trees close to the trail, then made his way to the pine glade. Grateful that the dead branches beneath the needled boughs were moderately dry, he quickly gathered an armload and returned to the rocky refuge.

Caro was sleeping fitfully. Alec touched her brow. *Was it only his own exertion, or did she feel too hot?* Unrolling the dry blankets, he peeled away his damp coat and tucked them around her.

Fear speared him to hurry in pulling out his flint and steel. A swift strike lit a spark in the tinder and the flames came to life.

Blowing out a sigh of thanks, he built up the fire to a cheery blaze and heated a potful of rainwater.

"Come sweeting, drink this down." He roused Caro and held a tin mug of sweetened tea to her lips.

Her eyes flew open as its warmth coursed down her throat. "That's ambrosial," she said, after several swallows. "I've had nothing but rancid gruel and bitter tea for the last day and a half. But perhaps it was just Thayer's presence that made everything taste so foul." She sat up before he could stop her. "Is he really gone?"

"Yes. He fell from the rocks and impaled himself on his own knife," answered Alec. He pressed a hand to her shoulder and tried to ease her back down. "You mustn't move. Broken bones can be hellishly dangerous. A punctured lung—"

"My lungs, as you well know, are far too tough to be punctured by anything short of sharpened steel," quipped Caro as she fended off his hand. "I've naught but a few bumps and bruises."

He started to protest, but she cut him off. "Truly. I would get up and caper through a jig to prove it." A smile. "But the ceiling is too low, and when I dance, I have tendency to tread on your feet."

Alec drew in a deep breath as Caro gave a vigorous wriggling to prove her point. And let it out in a soft laugh that took with it the worst of his fears. That she was sparring with him proved her spirit was unhurt.

"Only because I seem to turn into a clumsy lummox whenever I'm around you," he replied.

Her smile turned more luminous in the light of the shimmying flames. "You're quite agile when you want to be." She held his gaze, the flicker of emotion in her eyes far more warming than the blaze of the fire. "I caught only a blur of the action, but you were quite magnificent. He had a knife, and you—you had only your bare hands. And yet, you beat him."

"Right makes might," he quipped. "There wasn't a snowball's chance in Hell that I was going to let him escape to hurt anyone again."

"If anyone was a spawn of Satan, it was Thayer," she murmured.

"Indeed. I can't say that I feel a whit of pity or remorse for his demise. He was thoroughly evil."

Alec added a few branches to the fire. "I finally discovered the evidence that he was betraying our political group to the British military authorities in Scotland. Because of his actions, several meetings were raided and a number of people were shot or imprisoned."

"Was that the reason you came to England?"

He nodded. "I had a suspicion it might be Thayer, but there were several other possibilities. However, when he appeared in Bath just after you and Isobel were attacked, it seemed too much of a coincidence. I began to delve deeper into his recent activities."

"I wish you had confided your suspicions to me."

"I wasn't sure." About a lot of things. "I didn't want to frighten you."

"Lord Strathcona, you—"

"Alec," he corrected.

Caro hesitated, but only for a heartbeat. "Alec, you must resign yourself to the fact that some ladies—myself and your sister included—do not wish to be wrapped in cotton wool. We are not helpless wigeons and prefer to be treated as if we have a brain."

A rueful quirk pulled at his mouth. "So I am beginning to understand. As for accepting it, well, I shall try. But it will not be easy."

"You think I wasn't terribly worried about you? Give me some credit—I sensed right away Thayer was dangerous and that you were taking terrible risks facing off against him."

"Touché." A glimmer of amusement flashed between them, and once again he realized how much he enjoyed their verbal duels. "But speaking of risks, why the devil didn't you reveal that you weren't Isobel when Thayer's hired henchmen abducted you?"

"I...I feared that if Thayer had Isobel captive, you would be frantic with guilt and worry, allowing him to force you to do anything. With me as a hostage, you would have more freedom to fight him." She shrugged. "And besides, I figured I would find a way to escape. My unconventional upbringing and my experiences in the primitive places where my father did his research have made me adept at fending for myself."

Her unselfish sacrifice—her love—for him and his sister brought a lump to his throat. *You won't have to fend for yourself ever again*, vowed Alec to himself. *Assuming I can manage not to trip over my own tongue.*

Aloud he asked, "You thought I wouldn't be frantic with worry about you?"

Caro looked away. "Maybe a little. But I didn't think you would have any idea how to follow, so I assumed I'd be on my own."

"I made a calculated guess," replied Alec. "Thayer had a hideaway in Scotland which he had used in the past for his misdeeds. It seemed logical that he would do so again."

She tried to repress a shiver. "Luckily for me you were right."

He raised the dregs of the tea and deliberately spilled a few drops on the stone. "An offering of thanks to the Celtic spirits of Luck. To go along with a prayer of gratitude to the Almighty."

He set down the cup as Caro shivered again. "You're chilled to the bone. Take off your wet clothes while I go out to gather more wood. You can wrap yourself in the dry blanket while they dry by the fire."

"I—"

"Please humor me," interrupted Alec. "Isobel nearly perished from a fever caused by exposure to the cold and rain of a mountain storm." He forced a smile, trying to make light of his fear. "Given how noxious the Bath mineral water tastes, I am sure you do not wish to undergo the same cure."

"Well, since you put it like that..." She waved him away. "But hurry, the storm looks to be turning worse."

A clap of thunder reverberated within the cave. Caro pulled the blanket tighter around her bare shoulders, though the warmth suffusing her body was coming mostly from within.

Alec.

As a flash of lightning illuminated the hills, she searched for his silhouette within the wind-carved shapes of the rugged terrain. Like the surrounding stone, he possessed an immutable strength. And a sense of honor which gave that strength heart and soul.

Heart. Dared she think that the walls around his heart might have cracked just a little? A ripple within the depths of his storm-blue eyes seemed to hint that his defenses might be softening.

Yes, he cares for me, she mused. But that wasn't the same as love.

She stared at the glowing coals, letting her thoughts wander to some of the poetry she had memorized on the mysteries of the heart. *Of what is the spirit made? What is worth living for and what is worth dying for? The answer to each is the same. Only love.* Lord Byron, for all his cynicism, could be profoundly lyrical...

"A penny for your thoughts?"

Looking up with a start, Caro met Alec's pensive gaze. She hadn't heard him come in. "I'm not sure they are worth a farthing." Eyeing his windblown hair and rain-drenched clothing, she added, "Put down that wood and let me help build up a blaze, so you can warm yourself."

"No need," he replied, kneeling beside her and expertly coaxing the coals into new flames with the damp sticks. He added some small stones to the ring he had built around the fire, then set a fresh pot of water to come to a boil.

"You are very adept at taking care of yourself under primitive conditions," she observed. Not many aristocrats would know the first thing about surviving in the wilds.

"I'm not a fancy London lord who needs a valet's help to put on my coat," responded Alec. "I've spent a lot of time on the moors in Scotland, which taught me from an early age to be self-reliant." The coals crackled and sparked as another branch fed the flames. "I suppose I've always enjoyed challenging myself, both physically and mentally."

"My father was much the same way. He found exploration endlessly interesting for just those reasons." She paused to reflect, feeling a fond smile play over her lips. "Papa told us that seeing other lands, other cultures, made him look at himself in new ways. I think he passed on that curiosity and sense of adventure to me and my sisters."

"He sounds like an extraordinary man," said Alec. "Exotic travels with him must have been very exciting."

"Indeed they were. My first trip was to Crete..." Caro began to recount some of the memorable moments from her family's stay in the remote mountain village.

"Anna once nearly set our whole camp on fire when she decided to try cooking a wild boar stew." She looked up from her reveries, suddenly aware that steam rising from Alec's clothing. "Oh, here I am rattling on while you are sitting there suffering stoically in wet boots and breeches. You, too, must take off your wet garments and let them dry by the fire."

Turning away, she gathered up the second blanket and tossed it over her shoulder. "Put this on, Alec. I won't peek."

But as "wet" and "Alec" suddenly stirred the memory of seeing him rise naked as a newborn from the copper wash kettle, she couldn't hold back a mischievous laugh. *Talk about daring to experience new things!* And what a magnificent sight he had been, standing dripping wet in all his magnificent masculine glory.

"How very lowering to think that the idea of me out of my clothes is cause for naught but amusement," murmured Alec over the sounds of rumpling linen and buckskin.

"You were far more mesmerizing than Venus rising on her scallop shell," she said softly.

"Ah, well, that's a trifle reassuring." The thud of his soggy boots hitting the stone echoed off the walls. "You may turn around now. I am decent—or as decent as a man can be, wrapped in a blanket that smells suspiciously of horseflesh."

After smoothing out his damp garments, he took up the provisions sack. "Along with oats, there is half a loaf and some cheddar left. It's hardly a fancy repast, but it will keep our stomachs from growling like wolves."

They sat together by the blazing fire, bundled in scratchy wool and a comfortable camaraderie, eating stale bread and cheese as they shared stories of their lives, their experiences.

"And you, what caused you to become so passionate about politics?" she asked.

Alec made a rueful face. "At university, I was foolish

enough to believe that abstract ideals like freedom and justice could become reality if one were willing to fight for
them."

"That's not foolish," said Caro. "That's wonderfully
courageous and admirable. Only those who dare to try can
achieve their dreams."

"Your example has taught me much about that."

The glow in his eyes made her feel hot all over.

"As have some new political thinkers," added Alec. "I
have recently been reading some essays that inspire a shining hope in these grim times. They were penned by a man
who calls himself The Beacon."

Caro choked on a bite of her bread.

"You are familiar with his writings?"

"Yes, very familiar." She cleared her throat. "You haven't
yet met my oldest sister, Olivia. She is the most cerebral of
the three of us."

Alec raised a brow. "Are you saying..."

Caro nodded.

"Good Lord," murmured Alec, allowing a small chuckle.
"I am beginning to have more sympathy with your mother's
megrims."

"The two of you would have some *very* interesting conversations about law and government."

"So it would seem."

"You would like her," went on Caro. "And Wrexham. He,
too, is an idealist and believes that change can—and will—
happen through lawful, peaceful persuasion."

He looked thoughtful as he watched the undulating
flames. "I look forward to meeting them both."

That sounded like...

Caro slanted a sidelong look at the play of firelight gilding his features. Perhaps the end of this adventure wouldn't be the last time they would ever see each other.

Or perhaps I am reading too much between the lines.

Suddenly too tired to try to puzzle it out, Caro closed her eyes and let the warmth of the pine-scented fire and Alec's muscled closeness envelop her body. It took a moment to realize that she was now pressed against him, her head resting on his shoulder.

"Sorry," she said sleepily, and started to pull away.

He hugged her close. "Stay."

"Oh, but I've been such a sore trial to you," she protested. "Intruding on your privacy, wreaking havoc with your plans, knocking to flinders all your—"

His hands came up to frame her face, and suddenly the rest of her words seemed to lodge in her throat.

"Knocking to flinders all the fears I had allowed to wall up my heart."

A wild thudding seemed to come alive inside her chest. "I—I do have an unfortunate tendency to barge around and break things. It's the curse of a passionate nature, I suppose." An uncertain smile wavered on her lips. "My sisters have cautioned me that I should try to temper my emotions."

"Don't." Alec kissed her cheek. "Ever." His mouth moved to hers. "Change."

If only this moment could go on forever.

Caro curled her arms around him, heedless of the blanket slipping away. "I love you," she whispered. "I know a lady should never, ever say it first to a gentleman. But I'm a hopeless hoyden, so there you have it."

"I love your courage, I love your passions, I love your spirit." Alec's voice had turned a little rough, a little ragged as he whispered his reply. "I love you." Shrugging off his own blanket, he lay her back on the rumpled wool. Their bodies met, flesh on flesh. "More than my feeble words can possibly express."

Three short, simple words. That was all he had uttered, and yet they had tilted the world to a whole new axis.

"You've said all I've longed to hear," she whispered.

Chapter Twenty-Three

$\mathcal{A}$lec hitched in a breath, savoring how the soft curves of her body molded so perfectly to him. "I hope you will listen to yet another thing I wish to say," he said slowly. "I bumbled it badly last time, but perhaps you will give me a second chance."

Because we are made for each other.

The fringe of her dark lashes hid her eyes, but a spark of light peeked through as they fluttered. "We all need second chances. It's so awfully hard to get it right the first time around."

Caro touched her fingertips to his cheek. "So that is why we must keep trying, no matter if we feel bruised from the bumbles and stumbles."

He traced a whispery laugh around the shell-shaped curve of her ear, thinking of how her exuberant spirit made him want to shout to the heavens with joy.

"It's you who have taught me that elemental truth. And so I will try a second time. And a third, and a fourth, and *ad infinitum*—until you relent and agree to marry me." He inhaled, filling his lungs with her beguiling scent. "God knows, I have a legion of faults, which—"

"Which makes us perfectly matched."

Hope flared in his breast.

"Well, almost perfectly matched," she added with a shy smile. "I have *two* legions of faults, but I was hoping you wouldn't notice."

"All I see is the lady with whom I wish to spend the rest of my life."

"A lifetime with you?" Caro kissed the tip of his chin. "That sounds like it might be almost long enough."

"Only if we don't waste a moment more." He shifted, feeling her spark penetrate to the very depth of his being. Never again would he dwell in cold and darkness. "Say yes, Caro."

"Yes." She said it so sweetly, so simply.

Yes.

He hardly dared to believe his ears. "Thank goodness. Otherwise I might have had to resort to extreme measures."

She shifted beneath him. "I like your extremities."

Their laughter was muffled by a long and lush kiss.

"Don't tempt me," Alec murmured, lifting his lips from hers just enough to speak.

"I can't help it." Caro arched her body and rubbed against him. "I seem to stir up trouble wherever I go."

"Trouble, trouble, trouble," he rasped, sliding his hands down her hips to her thighs and easing them apart.

She gave a little gasp of pleasure as his rigid phallus delved between her legs, just at the crest of their joining.

Her honeyed warmth was like fire against his flesh. Exquisitely unbearable. Surely in the next instant he would burst into flames.

"At some point," he said tightly, "we really ought to be making love on a soft featherbed with silk-smooth sheets and down pillows."

"That would be nice," she whispered. A twinkle of the firelight reflected in her eye. "But not nearly so adventurous."

"Loving you will always be adventurous."

Because you challenge me. You excite me. You dare me to be more than I think I can be.

Caro held him close, letting her hands explore up and down the contours of his back. "In a good way, I hope."

"The very best way."

He rolled, turning so she was atop him. The red-gold light bathing her naked limbs in a rosy glow. Swaying in and out of the smoky shadows, she moved in time to some primitive tempo, her dark hair tumbling in silky waves over her shoulders.

An earthy, erotic vision of beauty.

"I love you." The words had once seemed impossible to say—now Alec couldn't seem to repeat them enough.

Caro's sweetly sensuous smile was far more luminous than the dancing flames. "And I you."

A fierce longing seized him. *Need. Want. Desire.* And yet, the realization that this was not a last desperate grasp for a fleeting moment of happiness left him a little giddy, as if he had drunk too much champagne.

He reached up, skimming his palms slowly, tenderly over the length and breadth of her creamy skin, committing to memory every dip and curve of her lithe body. The rounded shape of her bottom, the inward sweep of her waist, the swell of her breasts, the perfect dusky pink points of their nips, hardening beneath his palms.

Ye gods, she was so achingly lovely.

Their eyes met and a sound rumbled in his throat—a laugh, a groan, a cry of exultation?

What did it matter? All that counted was Caro.

She leaned down, taking his mouth in a hot, hungry kiss. Her fingers stroked over his chest, twining through the coarse curls, tracing over muscles, dipping down over his ribs.

His blood was pulsing through his veins, and as their tongues twined, deepening their play, he was no longer thinking of going slowly. Grasping her slender waist, he broke off the embrace to raise her from his sweat-slickened belly. For an instant, a lick of cool air tickled between their fire-kissed bodies, then he thrust upward.

"Ye gods, ye gods." A groan—definitely a groan—wrenched from deep within his chest as he sheathed himself to the hilt in her tingling warmth.

Heat surged through her. Gasping at the ebb and flow of new sensations, Caro watched the wildly flickering shadows of their silhouettes dance across the wind-carved stone.

The two of them, their passions joined. She wanted to make the moment last forever.

This fullness, this friction, making her so intimately aware of her body, and his. Suddenly aware she could set the rhythm of their lovemaking, she rocked back, slowly at first, then faster, faster.

Alec responded with a ragged growl. His body quivered, his hands roved eagerly over her thighs. Then he delved between her legs, his touch found her peak, just above their joining, and all at once her cries were thrumming against the surrounding stone. Waves of pleasure rose in her as he filled her again and again. She slid her fingers through his hair, twining with the salt-damp silky strands.

A primal joy clenched within her.

Alec.

She tightened her legs around his hips, riding him hard. His gaze swirled with smoke and lightning flashes of gold and sapphire. His face, so beautiful in the sputtering light, mirrored her own wondrous joy.

Rising to match her need, he quickened his strokes. The tension coiling within her was becoming unbearable.

"Caro." He called her name, his voice ragged with need. Beneath her, his hips bucked, and as she arched back the fierce pounding of her heart overwhelmed the fury of the drumming rain.

Dark and light—shadows and flames spun together in a whirling dervish dance of desire. The fire sparked and crack-led, and in the next instant she came undone.

The first pale rays of dawn crept into the cave, softening the deep shadows. A damp chill misted the early morning air, but as Caro came slowly awake, the first thing she felt was the steady pulse of Alec's warmth resonating along the length of her body.

She shifted slightly, smiling at the new sensation of her limbs entangled with his.

"Hmm." Alec stirred with a lazy yawn and propped him-self up on one elbow. "Awake, are you?"

"Yes." She snuggled closer. "But I'm thinking of falling back into a slumber. For a week, or maybe a month."

"A pleasant idea," he drawled. "Assuming our bed were made of something softer than stone." He gave a mock groan. "I think I am getting too old for roughing it in the wild." A kiss feathered against the nape of her neck. "Besides, the next time I make love to you, I promise it will be in more elegant surroundings."

"I don't care about the surroundings." Turning, she pressed her palm to his chest. "I care only about you."

Alec gave a grimace as he rubbed at his bristled jaw. "Even though I look like a wild Highland savage?"

"I thought the savage Scots painted their faces blue." She leaned in closer and brushed her lips to his cheek. "And unless I am much mistaken, yours is a glorious shade of sun-kissed bronze."

"I would demand a more detailed explanation of that hue from you," he said. "However, if I don't coax the fire to life, I fear my skin shall indeed turn a rather hideous shade of azure."

Untangling from the blankets, Alex began adding sticks to the bed of coals. Naked, he was a breathtaking sight, his rippling muscles radiating an animal grace. Watching him, she felt her breath quicken.

He caught her gaze and lifted a brow. "Have I sprouted horns, or broken out in purple spots?"

"Are you fishing for compliments?" Caro let her eyes slide down his chest and follow the wispy trail of golden hair leading lower and lower.

A breathtaking sight, indeed. He was a rampantly masculine man, all lithe muscle and sleek sinew.

"I would rather fish for breakfast," replied Alec dryly. "But the nearest lake is some distance away, so we will have to content ourselves with a spot of tea until we return to the inn." He fetched the rain-filled pot from outside the entrance. "I'm famished. What about you?"

"Actually, I'm quite content feasting my eyes on your magnificent body," she answered.

His grin made her insides lurch. "I am trying to remind myself that I am a gentleman, not a wolf. It is exceedingly hard, for my beastly urges are to devour you, morsel by lovely morsel."

Her skin began to tingle all over.

"But I shall restrain myself." The wood began to blaze, the flames catching the clench of concern on his face. "You've been through a hellish ordeal. You need sustenance, a hot bath, warm clothes."

"I—"

"No arguments." He passed her a mug of steaming tea. "Drink this, then we will be off. The sooner I get you back to the inn, the better."

"Are you always this tyrannical in the morning?" The hot liquid did, however, taste ambrosial. She took another long, grateful gulp and exhaled a contented sigh.

He waggled a brow. "My tyranny seems to be going down rather smoothly."

She passed him the cup to finish. "I daresay there are some rough edges, but we shall work on chipping them off later." She smiled. "I seem to have lost my hammer and chisel."

Alec's eyes lit with laughter. "I've warned you that Scottish flint has a great many sharp edges. You may have your work cut out for you."

"I'll take my chances."

"Brave girl." Alec pulled her close and held her for a long moment. "How are you bearing up? It makes my blood run cold to think of you with that monster."

"I am fine. Truly." Caro expelled a rueful sigh. "I have been yearning for years to experience an Exceedingly Exciting Adventure. And now it seems I have finally gotten my wish."

"And?"

"And . . ." For an instant, her breath caught in her throat as a glimmer of light played through the red-gold strands of his tangled hair. "I hope I shall have lots more. However, just like the heroine in Anna's novels, I shall find it very nice to always have a swashbuckling storybook hero to rescue me if I stray into trouble."

"I shall be happy to play my part," replied Alec. "But for now, let us pen 'the end' to this adventure." A smile curled at the corners of his mouth. "And tomorrow we will turn the page and start a new one."

The End . . . The Beginning.

"I have a feeling that Life will be endlessly exciting," she murmured. "Especially with you by my side."

"Always," he murmured. "Always."

Forever and ever. It had a lovely ring to it.

Caro wrapped her arms around Alec and let out a fluttery sigh. "That's worthy of an ode."

He laughed. "I was rather thinking it was worthy of a kiss."

She looked up and their eyes met. "That too," she murmured as his lips touched hers. "For at the moment, I'm not thinking of fancy words or rhyming meter."

A burst of fire-bright sparks lit in her heart.

"I'm just thinking of you."

Alec framed her face between his palms and held her with his gaze for a long moment. When he spoke, his voice was edged with humor, and yet a smoldering heat seemed to glitter beneath his lashes. A possessive look that said You. Are. Mine.

"I shall do my best to keep your attention."

A thrilling little shiver slid down her spine. "Always," she said. And knew it was true.

* * *

A short while later, with Caro wrapped in the blankets and settled safely in his arms, Alec guided the big bay down through the mist-shrouded hills and back to the inn.

The proprietor and his wife, desperate to avoid any trouble with the authorities, scurried to minister to their needs— a generous breakfast, steaming baths, a change of clothing while their own muddied garments were being laundered.

With Caro tucked away out of sight upstairs, Alec arranged to meet with the local magistrate. It took more than a little embroidering on the truth, but he managed to stitch together a story explaining the dead body on the moor and the miscreant held captive in the cellar. It was, thought Alec wryly, a tale worthy of a Sir Sharpe Quill novel, involving a stolen antiquity, quarreling thieves, and his own fortuitous arrival at the out-of-the-way inn, where he had immediately recognized the suspects. In trying to apprehend them, a wild chase through the storm-lashed hills had ensued, which resulted in Thayer coming to his demise while trying to evade capture.

The magistrate had raised a skeptical eyebrow at several points during the long-winded narrative. But he had heard of the theft in Bath, and that combined with Alec's rank had apparently convinced him to accept the story without further question.

And Dudley, when dragged up from the depths of the inn, had corroborated the account. Alec had met with him earlier and convinced him that confessing to theft would lead to a far lesser sentence than if he were charged with kidnapping a lady.

As for the part that Dudley had played in the traitorous betrayals...

Alec was quite certain that his fellow members of the Scottish independence movement would eventually mete out their own form of justice for the crime.

With that onerous task taken care of, he turned his attention to the most important task at hand. Calling for pen and paper, he retreated into a private parlor.

"This," he murmured to himself, "will be the true test of my creative skills."

Caro retied the sash of the oversized wrapper and edged in a little closer to peer over Alec's shoulder. She blinked—and then let out a chortle.

"As you see, I can plot convolutedly complex intrigue as well as Anna," he announced with a grin, after a last little flourish of his pen.

"I confess, I'm impressed."

"With a bit of luck and a little fancy footwork, we should be able to keep the tattlemongers quiet," he added.

Caro nodded. "So far, so good. Though from now on, things do turn a trifle complicated."

"I'm sure my aunt and Isobel will hasten to do as I request."

The letter he had just penned would be sent off with the next mail coach. By morning, the plan should begin to start falling in place. "Thank God that Aunt Adelaide was offered the use of Lady Webster's country house for the coming fortnight. If she and my sister move quickly to take up residence by tomorrow, we can avoid scandal by going there directly. Once we're all together, with every propriety in place, no one will think to parse over the exact timing, especially as the country interlude will be used to announce our engagement. Even the snippiest of the tabbies will have trouble stirring up gossip when there's no real scandal to come from it."

"Very clever," conceded Caro.

"I have my moments."

"More than a few."

Alec slipped his arm around her waist. "It's a *very* long journey back to the outskirts of Bath. I don't dare speculate on exactly how many moments that comes to. But I am sure it is quite a lot."

Caro took up the pen and teased the feathered tip against his chin. "Plenty of time to compose a sonnet to your silvery tongue."

"Among other activities." He curled a wicked smile—a new expression that invited all sorts of interesting ideas to take shape in her head. "I've ordered Thayer's carriage to be brought around in an hour."

Chapter Twenty-Four

The trip south proved a good deal more enjoyable than the trip north. Still, Caro couldn't wait to step out of the dark, dreary carriage for the last time. The creaking woodwork, the threadbare seats—the ghost of Thayer's presence seemed to taint everything, even the air, despite the shared laughter with Alec.

As if sensing her mood, he reached over to brush a caress to her cheek.

"We are almost there," he murmured, as the hired driver guided the horses past a stone gatehouse and began the climb up a long, winding drive lined with stately oaks. He shifted and slanted a look out the window as the vehicle rounded the first turn.

"Hmmph." A frown furrowed between his brows.

"What?" asked Caro, his expression stirring a frisson of alarm.

"Aunt Adelaide wouldn't be so bacon-brained as to invite any acquaintances to visit. And yet..." He let out another grunt. "Perhaps the barouche belongs to Andover."

"Andy doesn't own a barouche." Pressing her nose to the window glass, Caro squinted into the sun. The light must be playing tricks with her eyes, for the glint off the distinctive brass trim on the door panels looked horribly familiar...

"No, it couldn't be," she whispered.

"Is something wrong?" asked Alec.

She pursed her lips. "I must be mistaken."

But as the carriage rolled closer to the manor house, the crest on the paneled door was all too clear.

"Oh, dear."

Alec edged forward on the seat and angled his head for a better look. "Perhaps Andover borrowed—"

"It's not Andover," intoned Caro. "That is Wrexham's traveling coach."

Not that she wasn't delighted that Olivia and her husband had returned to England. But seeing them at this precise moment...

"Then I take it the dark-haired, willowy young lady descending the portico stairs is your eldest sister." A pause. "I need not ask the identity of the petite blond who has just joined her."

Anna? Anna was here as well?

"I thought Anna and Davenport were in Russia," mused Alec.

"So did I." Caro expelled a sigh. "That will teach me to write a letter late at night when my emotions are aroused. I thought I was being exceedingly clever, but apparently I was simply being exceeding dramatic."

His brows tilted upward in question. "Dare I ask?"

"I'd rather you didn't."

I have enough explaining to do.

Crunch, crunch. The wheels rolled over the gravel. Resigning herself to the inevitable, Caro tried to smooth the worst of the wrinkles from her much-abused gown, then abandoned the effort in favor of snagging an errant curl and refastening her hairpins.

Alec was watching her in bemusement. "They are your sisters, not the Royal Princesses."

"You don't understand." *Tug, tug.* "Men may take courage from a bottle of brandy, but ladies take heart from feeling they don't look like something the cat dragged in."

"Ah."

Her eldest sister uttered the same brief syllable some moments later as the carriage steps were let down and Caro climbed out from the shadows. Olivia was clearly making an effort to keep a myriad of questions in check. But her face, always very expressive, betrayed not only affection but also a quirk of appraising amusement as she caught sight of Alec.

"You must be Lord Strathcona. I have heard quite a lot about you, but look forward to forming my own impression..." Olivia paused to envelop Caro in a fierce hug. "Once I've had a lengthy chat with my sister."

"Indeed, you and McClellan will have much to talk about—other than this little adventure." Anna hurried down the portico steps to stand by her elder sister. "But as you say, politics can wait for a bit."

"I—I can explain—" Caro untangled herself from Olivia's embrace, only to find the air squeezed from her lungs by the middle Sloane sibling.

"I am looking forward to the story," drawled Anna. "It promises to be more entertaining than any horrid novel."

"So am I." Anna's husband, Lord Davenport—better known as the Devil Davenport—sauntered up to the carriage. "I thought you a sensible man, Strathcona. Didn't the experiences at Dunbar Castle teach you a lesson about the dangers of getting involved with the most impetuous member of the high-spirited Hellions of High Street?"

Caro huffed.

"If you wished for a quiet existence in your wild Highland hills," went on Davenport, "you have made a very grave mistake."

"Only a paltry, lily-livered fribble of a fellow would prefer peace and quiet to having his life turned upside down," replied Alec.

Davenport chuckled. "In that case, welcome to the family."

"Adventure seems to run in the family." The Earl of Wrexham, Olivia's spouse, chose that moment to join them. He eyed Alec for a long moment. "You *are* joining the family, aren't you? Otherwise my mother-in-law might demand that I call you out."

"Wait, wait, everyone!" Caro felt things slipping out of control—not an unusual occurrence when the sisters were together. But Alec was not yet used to the experience of having all three Hellions of High Street together, so she wished to give him a moment to catch his breath. "Before you all begin to rake Alec over the coals, please allow us to wash off the travel dust and partake of some refreshments." She hugged both her sisters again. "One needs to be well fortified to face our family."

"It's not only Alec who is going to feel his skin get a bit scorched," murmured Anna. "Your letter lit the direst of fears. Devlin and I commandeered a naval dispatch sloop to rush to your rescue. And naturally I alerted Olivia that trouble might be brewing. So we decided to rally the forces, as it were, and come to Bath to rescue our little sister from the perils of her passionate nature."

"How—" began Caro.

"Never mind that now," said Olivia. "We'll have a comfortable coze shortly—about a great many things—but first, let us take you in to tea."

"Yes, you must be famished." Isobel had been waiting for the sisters to finish their greeting before releasing her hold on Alec and coming to offer her own embrace. "I am *so* relieved to see you." She glanced back at her brother. "Both of you. Thank God you are safe."

"Alec was a true hero—" began Caro.

"Hero?" interrupted Anna, a mischievous gleam lighting in her eyes. "Oh, don't say anything more about heroes until I can fetch my journal and jot down some notes. I am always looking for fresh inspiration."

Isobel smiled uncertainly.

Caro patted her arm. "In case you haven't yet learned it, both my sisters have a very peculiar sense of humor."

"That is rather the pot calling the kettle black," observed Olivia.

"Indeed," chimed in Anna. "That's another thing we will discuss at greater length as soon as you have had some refreshments."

"Aunt Adelaide and I have a lovely repast waiting," said Isobel brightly. "Shall we go inside?"

"Of course we will talk," said Caro softly, as her sisters each took an arm. "But surely it can wait until evening. I can't abandon Alec—"

"Oh, don't worry about Alec," said Anna with an evil chortle. "Davenport and Wrexham will keep him occupied."

* * *

As the maids cleared the remains of the bountiful tea and pastries, Alec watched Caro's sisters hustle her away to one of the upstairs bedchambers. It would be quite a while before she reappeared, he reflected, given how much had happened in the last half year.

A few short months. The sun and the moon revolving through their usual cycles. And yet his universe had utterly changed. An inexorable force, a powerful magnetism, had realigned all the stars in the heavens, and suddenly his inner compass had no trouble navigating through the vast stretch of darkness and the countless points of winking light.

Love. Strange how the word suddenly felt so right on his tongue. Watching the sway of her shapely hips disappear through the archway, he was tempted to shout it aloud for all to hear.

"You look like a hound bewitched, who is about to begin baying at the full moon," drawled Davenport. "I have a feeling you would welcome something stronger than tea. Allow me to pour you a brandy."

"Pour one for me as well," said Wrexham.

"The Perfect Hero drinking while it's still daylight?" Davenport waggled a brow. "Marriage must be softening your steel."

The earl responded with a very un-Wrexhamlike grin. "My steel has suffered no ill effects from wedlock."

The retort earned a mirthful snort from his brother-in-law.

"But we are not here to discuss *my* matrimonial state," went on the earl. "Rather that of Lord Strathcona." He fixed Alec with an inquiring look. "Please assure me it won't be pistols at dawn. Not only is it cursedly uncomfortable to rise at such an early hour, but I am accorded to be a deadly shot, and you appear to be a decent fellow." A pause. "Aside from having seduced my wife's baby sister."

Davenport let out a bark of laughter. "Perhaps it would be wise not to open Pandora's Box on who in this room might be guilty of anticipating the marriage vows."

Wrexham allowed a hint of a smile. "Perhaps you are right."

"I, too, am accorded to be an excellent shot, Lord Wrexham," replied Alec calmly, once the banter had ceased.

"Having seen him in action on the Scottish moors, I can confirm that," offered Davenport helpfully. "What a pity you are both so skilled," he added with a theatrical sigh. "The sight of blood upsets my delicate sensibilities."

"However," went on Alec, ignoring the Devil's barbed teasing, "I trust that any test of marksmanship will be confined to a more pleasant use of bullets and powder—like shooting apples off the top of Davenport's head. Because, I assure you, my—"

Andover, who had tactfully kept himself removed from the reunion until now, chose this moment to poke his head into the room. "Is this a private family gathering, or might I offer my greetings to Alec?"

"From observing you with Strathcona's sister, it appears you are *almost* family," quipped Davenport.

Andover coughed and colored slightly.

"So by all means, join us."

Alec wasn't unhappy at having the chance to divert the attention from him, at least for the moment. "Oh? Is there a development I ought to be aware of?"

"Nothing formal," replied Andover in a strangled voice. "I was, er, waiting for you to return to speak, um..."

"First things first, Andy," interrupted Wrexham. "Before we discuss your matrimonial prospects—congratulations, by the by—I think we ought to settle the matter of Strathcona's intentions."

"Which are, of course, completely honorable," answered Alec. "I have proposed, and Caro has seen fit to accept."

"God only knows why," murmured Davenport.

Wrexham moved to the sideboard. Ignoring the decanters, he opened the cabinet door and brought out a silver urn containing a bottle of champagne nestled in shaved ice.

"I was hoping you would say that. It would have been a pity to have to return such a fine vintage to the cellar." He popped the cork and filled four glasses. "Shall we drink a toast, gentlemen?" he said, passing them to the others.

"To the Hellions of High Street," said Davenport. He winked at Andover. "And their soon-to-be sister in the Black Magic art of bewitching their men."

Crystal clinked, punctuating the low rumble of male laughter.

"To the Hellions!"

"So, shall we draw straws to see which one of us recounts her story first?" Settling smoothly into the role of eldest sister, Olivia took a seat in one of the upholstered chairs by the bedchamber hearth, while Anna assumed an elegant sprawl on the settee. "Though I must say, mine will be the shortest and least interesting."

"Oh, that doesn't matter," said Caro hastily. "The men will likely want to take a leisurely interlude to trade masculine jokes over port and cigars, won't they? So you should take precedence."

"The men might well be taking the leisurely interlude to

trade masculine punches," said Anna. "Wrexham was very concerned that you had been placed in a very awkward situation."

Caro had just taken a perch on the edge of the bed, but shot up in a flash. "Oh, you don't think—"

"No, I don't," replied Olivia firmly. "They won't come to blows...assuming John decides Lord Strathcona is worthy of your hand."

"And assuming Strathcona asked for it, and not just some other part of Caro's anatomy," added Anna dryly.

Caro felt a heated blush rise to the very roots of her hair. "Just jesting."

"I—I should hope so." She lifted her chin. "Alec is a man of stalwart honor and unimpeachable integrity."

Olivia slanted a look at Anna. On receiving a confirming nod, she relaxed her shoulders a little. "Not that I truly feared the worst, but some gentlemen can be very charming rascals, and..."

"And with my passionate nature, you worried that I might be swept off my feet by a few poetic phrases."

"Well, since you put it that way."

All three sisters began to laugh.

Oh, it was beyond marvelous, thought Caro, to have them here teasing her. And sharing her joyful news. If anyone could understand how she felt about the wonders of love it was Olivia and Anna.

Brushing away a tear, Caro quirked a watery smile. "I've missed you both so very much."

"And we you," answered Anna. "But don't think you'll wiggle out of explanations by sweetening us up. Forget about how we came to be here. It's simple enough—by a serendipitous twist of luck, your letter happened to reach me just as Davenport received a note from the Foreign Office asking him to return early from our visit. So a fast naval sloop was waiting to whisk us back to England."

"And Wrexham and I had just arrived back at Wrexham Manor when Anna's warning arrived by special courier," chimed in Olivia. "Naturally, we set out immediately to meet up in Bath."

"So now it's your turn," said Anna. "Isobel has told us some of the details of what has been going on, but we expect a full recount." She grinned. "I know a good story when I hear it."

"Oh, very well," conceded Caro. "I'm not nearly as skilled at this as Sir Sharpe Quill, but I shall do my best." She slid back onto the coverlet and drew her knees up to her chest. "It was a dark and stormy night—really, it was!" she added quickly, seeing Anna roll her eyes. "Isobel and I were attacked on a country lane just outside of Bath, and that is how the whole adventure started."

"A dramatic beginning," mused Anna. "I couldn't have written it any better myself."

"*Shhhh.* Stop interrupting, or we'll never get to the end," warned Olivia.

"Sorry."

"Do go on, Caro."

And so she did, with a bit of stumbling at times, and with a bit of glossing over the exact details of the intimate interludes. Both her sisters exercised considerable restraint, though there were several occasions where they couldn't refrain from pressing for clarifications.

Crafting a narrative was devilishly difficult, she realized, her admiration for Anna growing even greater. At last, however, she managed to bring her account to an end.

"My, my." Olivia leaned back in her chair and let out a bemused sigh. "You've certainly had an eventful few weeks."

"What she means is, we've known for years that you've been yearning to have your own adventure." Anna tapped her fingertips together. "And now you have."

"And now I have," agreed Caro.

"Was it all that you hoped it would be?"

Even if she had wished to, it would have been impossible to hold back a smile. "It was all that I hoped for—and more."

"Yes, well, the 'more' part does tend to happen when a handsome, stalwart, honorable man is involved," quipped Olivia.

"You forgot sexy," pointed out Anna. "Speaking of which..."

Ummm. Caro considered pleading sudden fatigue and crawling under the covers.

"Now that we've settled a number of questions, I have just a last burning one left to ask." Anna glanced at Olivia and flashed a mischievous wink. "Knowing our impetuous sister all too well, I can't help but wonder—do you think she did or didn't?"

Deciding three could play the teasing game—after all, she was no longer the baby sister—she retorted, "Ha—don't look so smug, you two. Are you trying to say you were perfect paragons of propriety?"

Her sisters exchanged guilty grins, and then began laughing.

"We are, after all, the Hellions of High Street," said Olivia. "What fun is it to have a slightly shady reputation if you can't be a little naughty."

"Despite all the trials and tribulations, we *have* had fun, haven't we?" mused Caro.

Silence settled over the room for a long moment, the bond of sisterhood wrapping them in unspoken love.

"And it promises to get even better," said Anna. "I'm sure our extended family will keep us on our toes."

At the mention of family, Caro climbed down from the bed. "I'd like to invite Isobel to join us. You will like her very much."

"We already do," assured Olivia.

"Andy has found the perfect match," added Anna fondly. "It's delightful to have him join the clan—he will make a wonderful brother."

Isobel was a little shy about joining in, but Caro and her sisters quickly drew her into the spirit of things. A lengthy interlude ensued as the conversation danced through a number of topics—most of them having to do with men and their foibles.

"Oh, my. You all seem so knowledgeable about these things, while I..." Isobel blew out a sigh. "I confess, I—I have several questions to ask about...love."

Caro put her arm around her sister-to-be and gave her a hug. "I'm not sure there are any easy answers, but we shall be happy to share our thoughts."

"Indeed," said Olivia. "But as that will likely take quite some time, I suggest we wait until later. It's almost supper-time, so we ought to go down and join the others." A rumble of male laughter suddenly made its way up from the drawing room. "It sounds like the celebration in progress will put us in just the right mood for talk of Cupid and his arrows."

The festivities soon turned even merrier. Champagne corks popped, punctuating friendly jests and flowery toasts to the impending nuptials. Wrexham was just finishing his speech when a thumping and bustling in the entrance hall drew everyone's attention.

"Who could that be?" wondered Caro.

"I expect it will be Mama," explained Olivia. "When Alec's note arrived here, I sent word that she ought to hurry and join us if she didn't want to miss a momentous announcement. After all she has been through with three headstrong daughters, it seemed only right that she be here to savor the fruits of her labor."

The drawing room door flew open with a thump, and the baroness marched in. "What is this about an engagement?"

Caro opened her mouth to speak, but Anna and Olivia were even quicker to elaborate on the happy event.

"Hmmph." Lady Trumbull pursed her mouth and huffed a few rapidfire breaths as she mulled over the news. "I must say—"

Olivia intervened before she could go on. "Mama, surely this is cause for great celebration. Just think—your travails are over. You will soon have all three daughters married."

The baroness sighed, as Wrexham hastened to present her with a glass of champagne. And then, to Caro's great surprise, she broke into a broad smile.

"I will, won't I?" She took a moment to survey her children, then slowly moved her eyes around the circle. "A marquess...an earl...and a baron."

Her gaze lingered on Alec. "I was hoping for..."

"Yes, yes, I know—a prince," said Caro. "Princes may sound oh-so grand in fairy tales, Mama. But my sisters and I have found something infinitely more wonderful than paper and ink royals." She leaned against Alec's shoulder and curled her fingers around his big, warm hand. "We have found flesh-and-blood heroes."

For a moment there was silence as the baroness signaled to Wrexham for more champagne. She then cleared her throat.

"So you have, my dears." With that, Lady Trumbull raised her glass and drained it in one gulp, much to the hilarity of all.

"So we have," chorused Caro and her sisters. Their three glasses came together in a flutter of cut-crystal sunlight and a resounding clink.

"To heroes!"

"Well, I, for one, am quite content to let our eloquent ladies have the last word," murmured Alec.

As Wrexham and Davenport laughed, he caught Caro's eye and smiled. "With their passions and their pens, they have shown that they have an unerring knack for creating a happily ever after."

"Actually, that was only the second-to-last word—I have one more toast to make," announced Caro, lifting her glass yet again.

The pale gold wine seemed to shimmer and sparkle with an inner fire.

"To love. Which is, at heart, the only word that really matters."

Young firebrand Olivia Sloane shocks all of London with her fiery political essays. But when she attracts the attention of the rugged Earl of Wrexham, Olivia discovers that scandal—and seduction—may be just what she needs...

Please see the next page for an excerpt from

Scandalously Yours.

Chapter One

$\mathcal{A}$ soft flutter of air stirred the emerald-dark leaves, releasing the faint scent of oranges. Drawing a deep breath, the Earl of Wrexham slid back a step deeper into the shadows of the large potted trees. He closed his eyes for an instant, pretending he was back in the steamy plains of Portugal rather than the gilded confines of a Mayfair ballroom. The caress of sticky-warm humidity against his cheeks was much the same, though here it was due to the blaze of dancing couples in their peacock finery, not the bright rays of the Mediterranean sun...

"Ah, there you are, John." The leaves rustled again, loud as cannon fire to his ear, and the earl felt a glass of chilled champagne thrust into his hand. "Your sister sent me to inquire why the devil you are cowering in the bushes when you should be dancing with one of the dazzling array of eligible young beauties." His brother-in-law gave an apologetic grimace. "Those are her words, by the by, not mine."

"Tell her I've a pebble in my shoe," muttered John after quaffing a long swallow of the wine. Its effervescence did little to wash the slightly sour taste from his mouth. "And that I'm simply making a strategic retreat to one of the side salons to remove the offending nuisance."

Speaking of removal, he thought to himself, *perhaps there is a side door leading out to the gardens close by, through which I can escape from the overloud music, the overbrittle laughter, the overzealous Mamas with marriageable daughters.*

"Pebble," repeated his brother-in-law. "In the shoe. Right-ho. Quite impossible to dance under those conditions." Henry cocked a small salute with his glass. "If you turn right at the end of the corridor," he added in a lower voice, "you'll find a small study filled with exotic board games from the Orient. Our host keeps a large humidor there, filled with a lovely selection of cheroots and cigars from the Ottoman Empire." A sigh. "I'd join you, but I had better remain here and try to keep Cecilia distracted."

"Thank you." John gave a tiny tug to the faultlessly tied knot of his cravat, feeling its hangman's hold on his neck loosen ever so slightly. "For that I owe you a box of the best Spanish *cigarras* from Robert Lewis's shop."

"Trust me, I shall earn it," replied Henry, darting a baleful glance through the ornamental trees at his wife. "Your sister means well, but when she gets the bit between her teeth—"

"She is harder to stop than a charging cavalry regiment of French Grenadier Guards," finished John. He handed Henry his now-empty glass. "Yes, I know."

In truth, he was exceedingly fond of his older sister. She was wise, funny, and compassionate and usually served as a trusted confidant—though in retrospect it might have been a tactical mistake to mention to her that he was thinking of remarrying.

My skills at soldiering have apparently turned a trifle dull since I resigned from the army and returned to England, he thought wryly. Bold strategy, careful planning, fearless attack—his reputation for calm, confident command under enemy fire had earned him a chestful of medals.

The Perfect Hero. Some damnable newspaper had coined the phrase, and somehow it had stuck.

So why do I feel like a perfect fool?

It should be a simple mission to choose a wife, but here in London he felt paralyzed. Uncertain. Indecisive. In contrast to his firm resolve and fearless initiative on the field of battle. He tightened his jaw. It made no sense—when countless lives were at stake, everything seemed so clear. And yet, faced with what should be an easy task, he was acting like a craven coward.

Henry seemed to read his thoughts. "It has been nearly two years since Meredith passed away, John. You can't grieve forever," he murmured. "Both you and Prescott need a lady's presence to, er, soften the shadows of Wrexham Manor."

"I take it those are also my sister's words, not yours," replied the earl tightly, finding that the mention of his young son only served to exacerbate his prickly mood.

His brother-in-law had the grace to flush.

"I appreciate your concern," John added. "And hers. However, I would ask both of you to remember that I am a seasoned military officer, a veteran of the Peninsular War, and as such, I prefer to wage my own campaign to woo a new wife."

He paused deliberately, once again sweeping a baleful gaze over the glittering crush of silks and satins. A giggle punctuated the music as one of the dancing couples spun by and a flaring skirt snagged for an instant in the greenery.

Ye gods, was every eligible young lady in the room a silly, simpering featherhead?

"Assuming I decide to do so," he growled.

Why was it, he wondered, that Society did not encourage them to think for themselves? His wartime experiences had taught him that imagination was important. And yet, they were schooled to be anything but original...

John felt a small frown pinch at his mouth. His military duties might be over, but he had no intention of living the leisurely life of a rich aristocrat. He wished to be useful, and politics, with all the intellectual challenges of governance, appealed to his sense of responsibility. As a battlefield leader, he had fought for noble principles in defending his country's liberties. He felt he had made a difference in the lives of his fellow citizens, so he intended to take his duties in the House of Lords just as seriously... which was why the idea that the only talk at the breakfast table might be naught but an endless chattering about fashion or the latest Town gossip made his stomach a little queasy.

"Point taken," replied Henry. "I—" His gaze suddenly narrowed. "I suggest you decamp without delay. It seems that Lady Houghton has spotted us, and I can't say that I like the martial gleam in her eye."

Taking John's arm, he spun him in a half-turn. "She has not one but two daughters on the Marriage Mart. Twins."

"Bloody hell," swore the earl under his breath, as he cut a quick retreat between two of the decorative urns.

Civilized London was proving to be filled with far more rapacious predators than the wolf-infested mountains of northern Spain.

* * *

"Bloody hell," swore Olivia Sloane, as she eased the door shut behind her. "If I had to endure another moment of that mindless cacophony, that superficial chatter, I might...I might..."

Do something shocking? Like climb atop one of the flower pedestals and dance one of the shimmying, swaying tribal rituals that her father had described in his scholarly papers for the Royal Society?

Olivia considered the thought for a moment, and then dismissed it with a sardonic smile. *No, probably not.* She was already considered an outspoken, opinionated hellion by Society. And with no beauty and no dowry to her name, it was best not to draw *too* much attention to her eccentricities. Not that she would ever blend into the woodwork. However, there were her two younger sisters and their future prospects to think about.

"Still, it would be fun to shock the look of smug complacency off all those overfed faces," she murmured softly. But she quickly reminded herself that she was doing that already in more meaningful ways.

Looking around, Olivia saw that the room in which she had taken refuge was a small study decorated in an exotic Indian motif of slubbed silks, dark wood, and burnished brass. As her eyes adjusted to the low light, she realized that it was a distinctly masculine retreat, a refuge designed to keep bored gentlemen amused. The flame of the single wall sconce showed a large painted cork bull's-eye bristling with feathered darts hung on one wall. In the opposite corner, grouped to one side of the hearth, were several brass and teakwood game tables. *Cards, dice, an intricately inlaid board with stone markers that she recognized as a backgammon set...*

And chess.

A sudden pang of longing squeezed the breath from her lungs. Her father had taught her to play when she was a child, and over the years they had engaged in countless matches.

Chess sharpens your mind, poppet—it teaches you to be logical, to be daring, to attack a problem from unexpected angles.

Skirting around a pair of leather armchairs, Olivia made her way into the shadowed recess and took a seat behind the double row of ivory figures, which stood waiting to march into battle against the opposing ebony force. *Black and white.* And yet, like life, the game was not quite so simple. One had to make subtle feints and oblique moves, one had to be clever at deception. And most of all one had to be willing to make sacrifices to achieve the ultimate goal.

No wonder I'm very good at it, thought Olivia, as she fingered the polished king...

"Oh!" It shifted slightly under her touch, and a flicker of moonlight from the narrow leaded glass window illuminated the ornate carving. Olivia leaned down for a closer look. "Interesting."

Like the rest of the room's decorations, the chess set had an exotic Eastern flair. Instead of the traditional European figures, the pieces were far more fanciful. The Knights were mounted on snarling tigers, the Castles were carried by tusked elephants, and all the human figures, including the Kings and Queens, were... stark naked.

Not only that, observed Olivia. The men were, to put it mildly, all highly aroused.

"Interesting," she repeated. The sight of a penis wasn't at all shocking. She had seen plenty of them before—though mostly in drawings or statues such as these, not in the flesh. Her father, a noted scholar of primitive cultures, had written extensively on tribal rituals for the Royal Society. His notebooks had been filled with graphic sketches, and he had not hesitated to explain his research to his three daughters. Men, he had lectured, held an unfair advantage by keeping women ignorant of the ways of the world. So he was determined that his girls learn about Life.

Much to the chagrin of his far more conventional wife. Who had nearly had a fit of apoplexy when, several years ago, Olivia had enthusiastically agreed to accompany her father to Crete for a season and serve as his expedition secretary.

Thank you for such a priceless gift, Papa...though leaving us with a few more material assets would have made our current situation a trifle less worrisome.

But for the moment, Olivia decided to put her practical anxieties aside. She nudged the naked pawn—whose monstrous erection looked more like a battle sword than a fleshly appendage—forward two squares, then reached for the opposing ebony pieces. Playing a solitary game against herself was always an intriguing challenge and would help pass the tedious minutes until it was time to take leave of the ball.

A second nudge moved the black pawn over the checkered tiles.

The game had begun.

Lost in thought, Olivia was not aware that someone else had entered the study until she heard a sudden whooshing exhale, followed by a satisfied sigh.

"A room free of simpering ladies. Thank God."

She froze as a pale puff of scented smoke swirled in the shadows. Flint scraped against steel, and a candle flame flared to life.

"*Lord Almighty*," intoned the same deep masculine voice, though this time he didn't sound quite so pleased with the Heavenly Being.

Slowly releasing her hold on the ivory Queen's voluptuous breasts, Olivia looked up and squinted into the silvery vapor. For an instant there was naught but an amorphous blur. Then, as the gentleman took another step closer, the flickering light brought his features into sharper focus.

For an instant, she couldn't blink. She couldn't breathe. Sharp lines, chiseled angles—an aura of strength seemed to pulse from every pore of his face, holding her in thrall.

But then, willing herself to break the strange spell, Olivia quickly regained control of her wits.

"Have you never seen chess played before, sir?" she asked calmly, ignoring his gimlet gaze. Honestly, one would think that a man would not look so shocked at seeing a graphic depiction of the male sex organ. Granted there were rather a lot of them, but still . . .

"Actually, I am very familiar with the game." As he lifted his gaze from the checkered board, the undulating flame lit a momentary spark in his dark eyes. They were, noted Olivia, an unusual shade of toffee-flecked brown.

A powerfully mesmerizing mix of gold-flecked sparks and burnt sugar swirls that seemed to draw her in to a deep, deep vortex of shadowed spice . . .

She made herself look away.

"However," he went on, "I have always been under the impression that it is not an activity that appeals to ladies."

"Then you think wrong." Olivia moved the ebony knight, putting both the ivory bishop—who in this set was depicted as a wild-eyed whirling dervish—and a pawn in danger.

The gentleman didn't answer. Drawing in another mouthful of smoke from his glowing cheroot, he studied the arrangement of the remaining pieces for several long moments.

His reaction was a little unnerving, as was his aura of calm concentration. Olivia wasn't quite sure why, but her fingertips began to tingle.

"Which one will you save?" he asked gruffly.

"The pawn, of course," she replied.

A look of surprise shaded his face. Looking up through her lashes, Olivia watched as the low, licking light accentuated the chiseled cheekbones, the long nose, the sun-bronzed skin. It was an interesting face, made even more intriguing by his oddly expressive mouth.

Sensuous. That was the word that popped to mind.

And like the sinuous coiling of a serpent, her ribs suddenly contracted, squeezing the air from her lungs.

With an inward frown, she shook off the unwelcome sensation and quickly shifted the pawn out of danger. "It's easy to see why if you look three moves ahead."

"Strategy," murmured the gentleman. "You seem to have"—a tiny cough—"a good grasp of the game's strategy," he went on as she picked up the whirling dervish bishop by its phallus and placed it aside.

"Do you think that ladies are incapable of conceiving a plan of attack that requires thinking three or four steps ahead?" She knew the answer of course. Most men were predictable in their prejudices, assuming the fairer sex had naught but feathers for brains.

Which made his reply all the more unexpected.

"I have a sister," he said slowly. "So I am acutely aware of how sharp the female mind can be." A rumbled chuckle softened his solemn expression for just an instant. "Indeed, their skill at riding roughshod over an enemy's defenses put the efficiency of many of my fellow officers to the blush."

He is a military man?

That explained the ramrod straightness of his spine, the hint of muscled hardness beneath the finely tailored evening clothes, the tiny scar on the cleft of his chin.

The unmistakable impression of steely strength.

She made herself shift her gaze from the intriguing little nick. "So, you are a soldier, sir?"

"A former soldier," he corrected. "Duties here at home made it imperative for me to resign my commission in Wellington's forces and come back to England from the Peninsula."

Olivia returned her attention to the chessboard, but not before muttering under her breath, "There are plenty of important battles to be fought on our own soil."

"I beg your pardon?"

She repeated what she had said in a louder voice.

His eyes narrowed—in censure, no doubt.

That was hardly a surprise, thought Olivia bitterly. Ladies weren't supposed to have opinions about anything meaningful. Especially if they were one of the three poor-as-a-churchmouse Sloane sisters.

Of course that did not stop her from saying what she thought. It didn't matter that Society dismissed her as a rag-mannered hellion, tolerated only because of the beauty and charm of her younger sister. She could take a measure of inward satisfaction in knowing there were far more effective ways of being heard...

Clearing her throat with an exaggerated cough, she added, "If you must blow a cloud, sir, might you do it on the other side of the room?" She had come here for the express reason of avoiding the other guests. With any luck, he would take the hint and go away.

"I beg your pardon," he repeated, quickly stubbing out the offending cheroot. "Had I known there was a lady present, I would not have been so ill-mannered as to indulge in a smoke."

Olivia gave a brusque wave without looking up. "Apology accepted, sir." Hoping that silence would help to encourage a quick retreat, she propped her elbows on the table and continued to study the position of the remaining chess pieces.

The gentleman didn't budge.

Repressing a huff of impatience, Olivia pushed the last ivory pawn forward with a touch more force than was necessary. It slid over the smooth marble tiles and collided head-on with its ebony counterpart. With a soft *snick*, the two erections hit up against each other.

A glint of emotion seemed to hang for an instant on the fire-sparked tips of his dark lashes. But surely she must be mistaken—it was only a quirk of the candlelight that made it appear to be amusement.

In her experience, military officers were not wont to display any sense of humor.

"Madam," he murmured, after another moment of regarding the board with a hooded stare.

"Miss," she corrected.

A frown flitted across his face, but after a tiny hesitation he continued, "I concede that you seem conversant in the concept of chess. But this evening, perhaps, er, playing cards would be a more appropriate choice of entertainment."

"I loathe cards," said Olivia. "They require such little mental effort. Chess is far more cerebral."

"Indeed. However, in this particular case, it is the, er, *physical* aspect of the game that is cause for concern—"

"Why?" she interrupted. "Seeing as chess is considered by many to be a metaphor for war, it seems singularly appropriate that male figures display their swords." A pause. "Sword is a euphemism that you gentlemen use to refer to your sex organ, is it not?"

His bronzed face seemed to turn distinctly redder in the uncertain candlelight.

Good—I've truly shocked him.

Now perhaps he would go away, thought Olivia, quickly moving one of her pawns to another square. She had been deliberately outrageous in hopes of scaring him off. His presence—that tall, quiet pillar of unflinching steel—was having a strangely unsettling effect on her concentration.

"You might want to reconsider that particular strategy." To her dismay, the gentleman slid into the seat across from her and took charge of the ebony army.

The faint scent of his spicy cologne floated across the narrow space between them, and as he leaned forward for a closer survey of the board, the candle flame flickered, its red-gold fire catching for an instant on the tips of his dark lashes.

Breathe, she told herself. It was the exotic smoke that was making her a little woozy.

"If I move here," he pointed out, "you are in danger."

His words stirred a prickling sensation at the nape of her neck, as if daggerpoints were teasing against her flesh.

In and out, in and out. Olivia forced her lungs to obey her silent order as she studied the positions of the pieces. The blood was thrumming in her ears, and for one, mad, mercurial moment, she feared she might swoon.

No—only feather-brained gooseberries swooned. And of all the derogatory comments she had heard whispered behind her back, nobody had ever called her an idiot.

"True," she replied to him.

The sudden scuffling of approaching footsteps in the corridor prevented him from making a reply.

Damnation. Fisting her skirts, Olivia shot up from the table, belatedly realizing that she had put herself on the razor's edge of ruin.

Damn, damn, damn.

The rules of Society strictly forbade an unmarried lady from being alone in a room with a gentleman. Her name would be blackened, her reputation would be ripped beyond repair.

Ye gods, if I am to be sunk in scandal, at least let it be for the right reason, she thought, quickly whirling around and moving for the narrow connecting portal set in the recessed alcove.

Clicking open the latch, she darted into the welcoming darkness of the adjoining room.

John watched as the lady flitted away in a swirling of shadows, smoke, and indigo silk.

Who the devil is she?

It had been too dark, too hazy for him to make out more than a vague impression of her face. *Arched brows. Slanted cheekbones. A full mouth.* And an errant curl of unruly hair—it looked dark as a raven-wing, but he couldn't be sure of the exact color—teasing against the curve of her jaw.

The lady's voice had been the only distinctive feature. Slightly husky, slightly rough, the sound of it had rubbed against his skin with a heat-sparked friction.

He frowned, feeling a lick of fire skate down his spine and spiral toward his...sword.

Good Lord, had the lady really uttered such an utterly outrageous observation? He wasn't sure whether he felt indignant or intrigued by her outspoken candor.

"No, no, definitely not intrigued," muttered John aloud. He shifted in his seat, willing his body to unclench.

Everyone—including himself—knew that the Earl of Wrexham was, if not a perfect hero, a perfect gentleman. He respected rules and regulations. There were good reasons for them—they provided the basis for order and stability within Polite Society.

Don't think. Don't wonder. Don't speculate.

No matter that the blaze of fierce intelligence in her eyes had lit his curiosity.

Granted, she might be clever, he conceded. But a lady who flouted convention was his exact opposite. And like oil and water, opposites never mixed well.

"John? John?"

It was his sister calling. The muted echo of his name was followed by a tentative rapping on the study's oak-paneled door. "Are you in there?"

Women.

At the moment, he would rather be pursued by Attila the Hun and his savage horde of warriors.

The latch clicked.

Deciding that he had had enough uncomfortable encounters with the opposite sex for one night, the earl hesitated, and then, like the mysterious Mistress of the Exotic Chessboard, he spun around and made a hasty retreat.

Fall in Love with Forever Romance

PASSIONATELY YOURS
by Cara Elliott

Secret passions are wont to lead a lady into trouble... The third rebellious Sloane sister gets her chance at true love in the next Hellions of High Street Regency romance from best-selling author Cara Elliott.

THIEF OF SHADOWS
by Elizabeth Hoyt

Only $5.00 for a limited time! A masked avenger dressed in a harlequin's motley protects the innocents of St. Giles at night. When a rescue mission leaves him wounded, the kind soul who comes to his rescue is the one woman he'd never have expected...

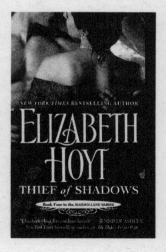

Fall in Love with Forever Romance

RESCUING THE BAD BOY
by Jessica Lemmon

Donovan Pate is coming back to Evergreen Cove a changed man...well, except for the fact that he still can't seem to keep his eyes—or hands—off the mind-blowingly gorgeous Sofie Martin. Sofie swore she was over bad boy Donovan Pate. But when he rolls back into town as gorgeous as ever and still making her traitorous heart skip a beat, she knows history is seriously in danger of repeating itself.

NO BETTER MAN
by Sara Richardson

In the *New York Times* bestselling tradition of Kristan Higgins and Jill Shalvis comes the first book in Sara Richardson's contemporary romance Heart of the Rockies series set in breathtaking Aspen, Colorado.

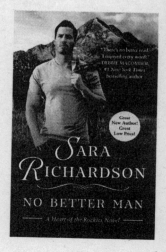

Fall in Love with Forever Romance

WEDDING BELLS IN CHRISTMAS
by Debbie Mason

Former lovers Vivian and Chance are back in Christmas, Colorado, for a wedding. To survive the week and the town's meddling matchmakers, they decide to play the part of an adoring couple—an irresistible charade that may give them a second chance at the real thing...

CHERRY LANE
by Rochelle Alers

When attorney Devon Gilmore finds herself with a surprise baby on the way, she knows she needs to begin a new life. Devon needs a place to settle down—a place like Cavanaugh Island, where the pace is slow, the weather is fine, and the men are even finer. But will David Sullivan, the most eligible bachelor in town, be ready for an instant family?

Fall in Love with Forever Romance

SANCTUARY COVE
by Rochelle Alers

Only $5.00 for a limited time! Still reeling from her husband's untimely death, Deborah Robinson returns to her grandmother's ancestral home on Cavanaugh Island. As friendship with gorgeous Dr. Asa Monroe blossoms into romance, Deborah and Asa discover they may have a second chance at love.

ANGELS LANDING
by Rochelle Alers

Only $5.00 for a limited time! When Kara Newell shockingly inherits a large estate on an island off the South Carolina coast, the charming town of Angels Landing awaits her...along with ex-marine Jeffrey Hamilton. As Kara and Jeffrey confront the town gossips together, they'll learn to forgive their pasts in order to find a future filled with happiness.